ORDINARY

POWERS BOOK ONE

STARR Z. DAVIES

PANGEA
BOOKS

Starr @ Pangea Books
PangeaBooks.online
www.starrzdavies.com

Publisher's Note: This is a work of fiction. Names, characters, places, and incidents are a product of the author's imagination. Locales and public names are sometimes used for atmospheric purposes. Any resemblance to actual people, living or dead, or to businesses, companies, events, institutions, or locales is completely coincidental.

Book Layout ©2020 Pangea Books

Cover Design by Fay Lane Graphics

Ordinary / Starr Z. Davies. -- 2nd ed.

1] Survival Fiction 2] Superheroes 3] Post-apocolyptic 4] Coming of Age

ISBN 978-0-578-54098-6

For Tazz and Brynden, whose random conversations helped create this story.

ORDINARY | noun | or·din·ary | ˈȯr-də-ˌner-ē : of standard quality or rank, something regular or commonplace; of a person with no unique or distinctive features.

Part One

"THE CONSUMPTION TAX HAS BEEN A STRAIN ON the people, and the Directorate understands that. However, with regression looming over our heads, preservation of our way of life must be the top priority. Elpis is all that remains in this broken world. If the city falls, humanity will go extinct."

~ Dr. Joyce Cass
2 Months Ago

1

I CONSIDER MYSELF AN HONEST PERSON. I TRY TO keep my promises. Try to do the right thing whenever possible. But sometimes something happens that pushes all of us to the edge, that challenges our beliefs and how we see the world.

For me, it's the desire to be ordinary.

2

THREE DAYS DEFINE WHO A PERSON WILL BE FOR THE rest of their life. The day they are born. Testing Day, where their abilities are determined. And, of course, Career Day, where social status, wealth, and future prospects are decided for them by an exhibition hall of employers.

I passed my birth with great pains. According to stories Mom told me, my labor gave her particular difficulty. After arriving too soon, too weak to survive on my own, I lived in an incubator for the first six weeks of my life in a struggle to survive. It's why she sometimes—annoyingly—calls me, "tough guy."

Up until Testing Day, everyone—from my teachers to my neighbors—called me a late bloomer and constantly reassured my parents that eventually I would fall into one of the Four Branches of Powers. They said it as if doing so was something I would just stumble over on the sidewalk one day and say, "Oh look, there's my Power!"

Testing Day came early in my ninth year of schooling, alongside everyone else in my class. Those who had already developed their ability were divided into groups based on their Branch of Power: Somatic for Powers relating to the body; Naturalist for those with organic Powers; Psionic for the Power of the mind; and Divinic for those with Powers outside our world. Mostly, this division left me and three other kids—Mo, Dave, and Leo—uncategorized. By the end of the day, only I remained unclassified. Testing Day was a bitter disappointment for everyone in my family—including me.

Ordinary people have Powers and prospects. I have neither.

Now I face Career Day, where I get to parade around a convention center with all the other doe-eyed, eleventh-year students and try to convince businesses why my Power is worth employment. Except I still don't have one, and probably never will.

I've dreaded this day for years. Now, there's no escaping it.

Miraculously, my parents haven't given up on me. They still hold on to the hope that everything is about to change.

For all our sakes, I hope they are right.

3

"UGENE, YOU'RE GONNA MISS THE TRAM!" MOM hollers up the stairs.

I rush down, my feet hardly touching one step before I'm moving to the next. I grip the railing and sling myself around the landing at the bottom toward the kitchen.

Dad stands at the polished granite counter, barely registering my presence. His uniform is perfectly pressed, and medals attached to his jacket chime as he closes his metal lunchbox. His broad shoulders often overwhelm me—a polar opposite of my very average build—but I suppose they are ideal for a high-ranking military man with Enhanced Strength. I never bothered to ask exactly what he does, but I know he works in the Department of Military Affairs.

Mom sits at the table with a steaming cup of coffee cradled between her hands. The bright white mug peeks through her dark-skinned fingers as she raises it to her lips. A knowing smile sparkles in her dark eyes and I can't help but wonder if she's Reading me or Dad with her Telepathic Power.

"Love you, Mom," I say, grabbing an apple from the bowl on the countertop. Before I can say the same to dad, he has already left the room.

"Good luck, Tough Guy. Knock 'em dead." She laughs as I brush a kiss across her cheek and bolt through the back door.

"Where's your jacket?" Mom calls after me, but it's too late to turn back now.

The tram roars down its line, coming in flashes between the

houses at the end of the block. The stop is down a nearby alley. Crap, it's gonna be close.

A Somatic frowns at me as he rushes by at a sprint several times quicker than I could ever manage, his stocky form giving away his Power before I spot the Somatic mark on his arm. Sometimes, things move too fast for my taste.

Cursing under my breath, I tuck the apple into the pocket of my dark blue dress pants and pump my legs as hard as I can to catch up. The tram stops at the corner of the block just as I break out of the alley's mouth. A slender leg—one I'd recognize anywhere—just disappears through the open tram door.

"Bianca!" I call out. "Hold the tram!"

Bianca sticks her head out, then leans through the open door, gripping the handle inside. Her black hair cascades around her shoulders.

But the tram is already moving.

"You're late again, Ugene!" she shouts, holding a hand toward me.

I reach, just missing her fingers.

Bianca leans farther, her foot hooked on the edge of the doorway—an easy feat for her and her Somatic muscles. "Jump!"

Without hesitation, I throw myself at her and the moving tram.

Bianca's hand clamps down on my arm and yanks me into the tram as if I weigh the same as a gym bag.

I thump awkwardly against the front of the self-driving tram and stumble to the floor, dirtying my pressed dress pants. No one on the tram moves to help me up.

Bianca easily swings her body inside and smooths her red blouse over her toned stomach. "What would you do without me?"

Probably die? I chuckle, causing Bianca to scrunch her nose. "Catch the next tram, I suppose," I say, examining the blood slowly seeping from a fresh scratch on my elbow. "You could try a gentler landing."

"And you could try being on time for once," Bianca says, offering a hand to help me up.

I take it, stand, and brush myself off, then notice that everyone else on the tram is staring at me, shying away like I have a catchable illness. Everyone here knows me somehow—through school or just the commute or my neighborhood. I have a reputation as that Powerless kid. Regression from Powers is a real danger to Elpis, which makes me look like Undesirable Number One. Heat rushes to my cheeks, and I'm thankful for my darker skin.

Bianca makes her way to a seat. I sit nearby.

For the remainder of the ride to school, I admire Bianca when she isn't looking. I can't help it, really. The perfect shape of her long, muscular legs revealed beneath a tan skirt. Her wavy black hair, which shines even when the light isn't hitting it. The way her smile lifts the corner of her eyes when she shifts over for an older woman who boarded the tram.

I would have missed the stop for school if she hadn't been going to the same place. Shaking out of my stupor, I step off, remembering the lump in my pocket.

I reach into my pocket and my fingertips brush against the wet skin of the apple. Upon examination of the apple's skin, I spot a large bruise where it must have hit the tram floor along with me. Sighing, I bite into it anyway and enter the tall, arching doorway proclaiming Memorial High School in all its glory engraved in the stone.

Everything about Memorial High School screams upper-class from the gleaming windows to the pristinely polished tiled floors. The students all bear the same *I'm better than you* body language. The clothes reflect high fashion. Salas borough schools are for the well-off. The eighty-plus percenters. All the parents rank high on the Cass Scale—a scientific algorithm that determines the strength of each person's individual power based on rigorous Testing Day exams. In another day, I will be cast out of this society and thrust into the lower classes, where the Consumption Tax will inevitably land me in prison within months.

The Tax was introduced when I was ten to balance the scales. Everyone's Power creates an output into society—whether it be growing food or offering services to help others, basically anything to help society run smoothly and efficiently—but for those who consume more than they produce, their Taxes are raised. Basically, the more your powers contribute to society, the lower your taxes because you give more than you take. The inverse is true as well. The less your powers contribute, the higher your taxes. When you can't pay, you end up in prison until the debt is paid. My contribution is at zero. I'm in serious trouble.

Tomorrow, once Career Day has had a chance to dole out job offers to the students, my class will graduate. I may not feel great about my prospects, but at least I will be out of this place. I doubt even the wasteland beyond Elpis could be worse than high school. And I may have no choice but to find out.

Lowerclassmen rush off to class. The graduating class gathers in the gymnasium on bleachers, waiting to be bussed off to Career Day.

Bianca rushes over to her friends.

I stand near the bleachers watching when someone bumps my shoulder, nearly knocking me to the ground.

"Watch it, Pew-gene," says Jimmy, probably one of the dumbest, but most talented, Naturalists in our class. He tested into the 85th percentile for his Naturalist power on Testing Day—particularly in Hematology—and ever since his arrogance inflated to cosmic levels.

"Your wit is astounding, as always," I grumble, rubbing my shoulder.

He smirks. Then the air thins and the room tilts slightly to the left. I stumble, catching my balance on the nearest bleacher before easing my unusually heavy weight onto the bench. Jimmy's laughter reaches my ears as my blood thumps hard.

"Mr. Richmond, you've been warned about using your abilities on another student," a stern male voice says.

I blink as the air rushes back and the world rights itself. Mr. Springer, the Natural Biology teacher, stands between Jimmy and me with his arms crossed.

Jimmy rolls his eyes and joins Bianca and her friends, sliding his arms around her waist. Watching it makes my stomach revolt.

Mr. Springer turns to me. "Are you okay, Ugene?"

"Peachy," I mumble, rubbing my aching temple. That twat gave me a headache.

"Well, okay then. Get to your seat."

Mr. Springer removes himself from the situation, allowing me to recover with some modicum of dignity.

Unlike most of the teachers at school, who gave up on teaching me anything useful when no Power emerged, Mr. Springer taught me genetic biology, power mutation, and the potential indications for latent Power triggers. At first, I think he still believed he could help me discover my Power. But my affinity for understanding the science behind Powers—along with my hunger for the knowledge—encouraged him to continue. Together, we examined my DNA in relation to his to see what made me different, or if any hope remained.

"There's nothing exciting about being ordinary," he used to say. "But you don't need Powers to have brains." Easy to say when you have both.

About ten minutes into the school day, everyone is loaded onto buses and carted off to the convention center downtown. In the overcrowded bus, I sit alone and watch the buildings grow as we approach, until they loom high over our heads. The tallest is Paragon Tower, home of biomedical research and pharmaceutical giant Paragon Diagnostics. The four corners of the building twist clockwise into the sky like a massive helix, coming to a point at the 200th floor. On cloudy days, the top stories disappear.

We pass a construction site for a new skyscraper. Two workers hoist a steel beam, barehanded, from a truck and walk it toward the skeleton of the building. They lift it above their heads, and the beam floats out of their hands, rising toward the highest point of the building, where another team of men works to guide the beam into place using Telekinesis.

Some of the strongest Somatics and Psionics work in construction, lifting building materials with muscles and Telekinesis. The stronger your Powers, the more you're paid.

The bus pulls up to the largest of the three squat towers outside the convention center, and everyone pours out. Crowds are gathered beneath the overhang that covers the convention center's sidewalk.

I hang back at the end of the line, not at all eager to haul my unspectacular backside into the exhibition hall. As I inch toward the front of the bus, I examine the signs reading "Powers are Powers no matter what" and "Abolish the Cass Scale."

While some signs are more creative than others, they all convey the same feeling—that people shouldn't be discriminated against based on the strength of their Power; that they shouldn't be imprisoned because they can't pay the Tax. It's irrelevant to me either way.

I don't have a Power.

As we make our way to the doors of the convention center, protesters sneak flyers into the hands of everyone unfortunate enough to make eye contact with them. A woman with blonde hair pulled back into a severe braid shoves a blue page into my hand. I don't know what to say—not that there is time to say anything—so I read the flyer as I follow the others toward the exhibition hall.

Fight Prop 8.5! jumps out in large, bold letters across the top of the page. It goes on to invite those opposed to Proposition 8.5 to join the fight. Unsure exactly what this proposition is or what difference I can really make, I stuff it into the pocket of my dress pants to throw out later.

4

STUDENTS FILTER THROUGH THE OPEN DOORS OF THE exhibition hall where the cacophony of noise filters out. As we enter the hall, each student gives their name and is handed a glass tablet illuminating their selections. I peer over Mo's shoulder as he turns his unit on and the holographic results display on the tablet, showing his rank on the Cass Scale, 19, and his potential job prospects: 52. He heads deeper into the hall.

"Name?" the woman at the door asks.

"Uh, Ugene Powers."

She looks bored as she enters my name and a code into the tablet, then hands it to me, revealing her Naturalist brand—the encircled Oak Tree—on the left hand.

I step through the open doors into the noise of the exhibition hall. Employers are divided primarily by the Branches of Power— though some of them have jobs in multiple branches. Banners hang from the ceiling advertising the different Branches: Somatic in red with the logo of flexed muscles, Naturalist in green with the logo of an oak tree, Divinic in blue with the logo of the Milky Way, and Psionic in yellow with the logo of a brain. In each section, rows upon rows of employer booths stretch across the massive floor.

I stumble forward as an excited student rushes past, shaking me out of my shocked stupor. I activate my tablet and look down at my results. The bright blue lettering and zeros mock me.

Cass Scale Rank: 0.0001

Employment Booth Listings: 3

The option to see the listings or bring up the exhibition hall map rises from the tablet. I chew my lip and tap the choice to bring up the location of my three potential employers on the exhibition hall map. As the hologram changes, I glance over in time to see Jimmy showing off his results to his posse.

Employment Booth Listings: 1,298

Great. Jimmy the Idiot has so many listings he will have to filter them to choose what he wants. Mine would fit on the top quarter of the tablet's surface. There's no justice in this world.

I head toward the nearest location dot on the 3D map, keeping my head down. I also have no desire to see all the opportunities that I am literally passing by.

A friendly, broad-shouldered man with skin even darker than mine hands out samples of food to the students who stop at his booth. It creates quite a crowd of hungry teens.

"You on my list?" he asks a young man across the table from him, his voice deep and booming.

"No," the boy laughs as if it were the most insane idea out there.

The man shrugs, revealing his nametag. *Harvey Worthington, Owner.* Harvey hands the boy a square of a sandwich anyway.

"Nothing nobler than filling a man's stomach," Harvey says.

I nudge my way forward inch by inch as students take a sample, engage briefly in conversation with Harvey or his assistant, Joan, before moving on. The banner on the wall of the booth reads "Lettuce Eat: Where our meals are about more than just food."

"You look like you could use a whole plate," Harvey says, eyeing me up and down as I nudge my way to the front of the crowd.

Subconsciously, I glance at my shirt and dress pants. There's no denying that I'm like a pencil, lanky.

"You look lost." Harvey laughs, and the sound booms over the noise around us. "You on my list?"

"Y-yes."

Harvey reaches a colossal hand out toward me, and I extend my own to shake, but he takes my hand and pulls me behind the table where two chairs face each other. Joan closes the space he previously occupied, engaging with the students in his absence.

"So, tell me a little about yourself," Harvey says, settling back comfortably in the chair across from mine. I can't help but notice how dwarfed the Somatic brand is on his bicep, barely peeking out from his shirt sleeve.

"Don't you want to look at my rank?" I ask, shifting my own tablet across my lap, turned off.

"Does it matter?"

I then realize Harvey doesn't have a tablet. I glance around the booth and see it on the floor inside one of the boxes of supplies he brought along.

"I guess… not?" I bite my lip again and try to gather some sense of confidence. "My name is Ugene Powers. I go to Memorial High, but I don't know what I want to do with my life yet." Well, that was a lie. I'm forming a habit of lying today.

For a second, I think I might have said the wrong thing, but Harvey smiles at me. "I don't think anyone ever knows what they want to do with their life," he says. "We all just move from one thing to the next, searching." That seems interesting to me. "What's your core focus at Memorial High?"

That's the dreaded question. Harvey hasn't looked at my rank yet, or he would know I'm Powerless.

"Sciences, mostly," I answer. "And writing."

"What sciences are most interesting to you?"

"Biological, mostly," I say. "I'm interested in how the body works." Truth. There must be some reason I am the way I am. The answer is somewhere in science. Unfortunately, only Divinics—like Bianca's older brother, Forrest—and Naturalists land those jobs. I'm severely unqualified.

"So, you're a Divinic?" asks Harvey, brows lifting. Is he impressed? Well, time to let him down gently. "No."

"Naturalist?" he guesses, and I shake my head. Harvey sits forward, massive forearms resting on gigantic thighs. The chair creaks a little under his weight. "You aren't a Somatic." His calculating look makes me uncomfortable. I hate when people look me over and just assume I can't possibly be a Somatic just because I'm not stocky enough. Not strong enough. "So, you're a Psionic. Well, that could make for a good dishwasher or busboy, I suppose. What's your specialty?"

The words come out slowly. "I don't have one."

Harvey just stares at me like I grew an extra head. The silence is awkward and painfully long. Suddenly, he bursts into laughter.

"Oh, now that's a clever joke!" The depth of his voice vibrates against my chest. "I like you! I never would have thought to answer with that."

Harvey wipes tears from the edges of his eyes. Not exactly the reaction I was expecting. The amusement dies with slow, awkward chuckles as he notices my deadpan expression. Then, the silence becomes very real. The calm before the storm. Harvey and I just watch each other.

Finally, he cocks his head. "You're serious."

I nod again.

Harvey sits up straighter, smoothing his pants with those enormous hands. "So," he pauses to clear his throat, "you have no Powers? At all. You're Regressed?" He rubs at his brow and sighs heavily, adjusting in his seat. The news has made him anxious. "Well, Ugene, I—"

The clock is ticking, and I know any moment he will dismiss me politely. This is my last chance to sway him.

"Mr. Worthington," I say. "I know I'm not your typical dishwasher or whatever, and I can't keep the plates from hitting the floor with Psionic Powers, but it doesn't mean I can't do the job." Am I really so desperate that I'm struggling to hold on to a dishwasher job?

"Ugene," Harvey sighs so heavily his whole body appears to

deflate. There's something in his eyes I can't identify. "It isn't that. It's just… with the current climate around Proposition 8.5, it puts my business in a tricky place. If I hire you, it could come back to my restaurant. I could lose business."

The implication is clear enough. Harvey shifts and I can tell he is about to get up. I hate it but realize that if I don't succeed here, I only have two more prospects.

I jump to my feet. "Please. Just give me a week to show you I can do this. One week. You don't even have to pay me for that week."

The students at the table watch us now. I try not to look, not to let them know I notice.

But Harvey notices and hesitates.

Fear! That's what it is. The look in his eyes is fear. People fear what they can't understand, and apparently, Proposition 8.5 has some significance I don't understand. I understand fear of regression, but this is something else. Something deeper.

One week of free labor must be enticing. If I can just get that one week to show him I can do the job, it could make all the difference.

The slope of his shoulders gives Harvey away.

"Ugene, I'm sorry," Harvey says, and I can tell that he really is by the way his brows pull together. His hand falls on my shoulder like a weight. "I wish you all the best, but I won't lie. It's gonna be tough. You might want to learn a little more about what's going on out there. But stop by any time for a meal, on the house."

Harvey's expression suddenly changes back to the jovial, smiling man he was earlier as he approaches the table again. The weight of his hand shifting off my shoulder feels like a mountain sliding into place.

I want to stand on the table and scream that there is nothing wrong with me. But it won't do any good. People already fear the danger of Power regression, and whatever this Proposition is, that fear seems to be growing. With a sigh, I pull up the second employer on the map. It takes about five minutes to make my way through the crowded aisles of the exhibition hall to the right booth.

No tables or chairs occupy the second booth, nor are there

pamphlets or digital sharing links for the tablets, allowing me to scan a code for more information. Two men in plain grey uniforms talk to one another, one of them holding a tablet and both ignoring me standing there. The sign that hangs behind them on the booth wall is plain, displaying a white trash can logo with thick arrows circling each other. *City Waste Management* stands out against the green banner in white letters.

"Look at this one," one of the men says, huddled over a tablet with the other.

"Even Gus' rank is higher than that, and he's worthless," the other says.

"Excuse me."

Both stop and look at me blankly. After a moment, the one holding the tablet says, "Name?"

"Ugene Powers."

He taps the screen, and his brows shoot up his forehead as he passes the tablet off to his partner without comment.

"Is this for real?" the partner whispers back, his disbelief evident across his wrinkled brow.

The first guy squares his shoulders, making his shirt shift enough to reveal the Somatic brand on his arm. "We don't got an opening for you, Powerless."

I lick my lips and prepare for protest, but the way their brows draw down and their jaws set in contempt forces me to take a step back, then a couple more until my back bumps into a student from another school.

"Watch it," she says, brushing her hands over her peach dress.

I turn to her and apologize, then move up the aisle quickly to the first corner and bolt out of the crowded walkway. I have to twist sideways to get by a group blocking the path.

The next listing is in the Somatic area as well, but I'm in no rush to get there. Instead, I move toward the back wall of the exhibition hall, shifting and twisting to make my way through the crowd. The voices sound louder, and, for some reason, my heart is racing. I press a hand to my chest as my back finally rests against the cool brick wall.

A chill bleeds through the cloth of my dress shirt, relieving some of the tension.

"Ugene?" Bianca approaches, the heels of her red dress shoes making her muscular calves stand out. She wasn't wearing those on the tram. "What's going on? Why are you over here?"

"I'm fine," I lie. "Just some jerks reminding me I'm Powerless is all."

"Don't let them get to you," she says. "Jerks will always be jerks, but you're smarter than anyone I know."

"Anyone?" A smirk tilts the corner of her mouth.

"Well… maybe not smarter than Forrest," she admits, referring to her older brother. For a moment, her face takes on a haunted expression, but it quickly passes.

Forrest has the job I dreamed of one day attaining at Paragon Diagnostics. But without a Power to give me an in, there was no way it would ever happen. "Glad you're okay. I gotta run. I have, like, a few hundred booths to make my way through and so little time. Good luck."

Right. A few hundred. And she probably narrowed her list based on her own interests. Bianca Pond: Somatic Muscle Memory 68th Percentile. She could pack more punch in one finger than I could with my whole body.

With a mutter of disgust, I turn my attention to my tablet and tap the dot for the last prospect while making my way back into the flow of the aisle.

The name pops up from the 3D display and pulls me up short.

Paragon Diagnostics.

I blink, my breath catching, and my feet become rooted to the floor. There must be some mistake. I tap the screen to bring up the booth's location on the exhibition hall map. Swallowing hard, excitement and hope pumping through me for the first time in years, my feet carry me swiftly along the crowded aisles from one end of the hall to the other.

5

PARAGON DIAGNOSTICS' BOOTHS CONSUME MORE than half of the long aisle. So many, in fact, that my contact is specifically marked out among their booths. Three booths line either side, and each of them could fit just one of the standard-sized booths within it. I have to pass five of them to get to the pulsing dot on my map, and along the way it's impossible to resist my curiosity, pausing at each booth to learn a little more.

Four of the booths are set up basically the same, with a massive silken banner in each color bearing the logo for the Power represented. The banners stretch the full length of the booth.

First is the Psionic section, with its long yellow banner and Psionic brain logo and the recruitment slogan: "Become a Psion of knowledge. Join Paragon's Psionic Department." The back-to-back PD logo fills the lower half of the banner. Students have crowded around as a Paragon employee stands at each of the four tables with two students, their hands calmly resting on the yellow cloth-covered high-top pedestal table.

One cluster of students watches a candidate on a simulation platform—similar to what they used on us in testing—as she focuses on the sim around her. Objects fly at her, and she easily knocks them aside with her Telekinetic Power as she hoists massive pieces of equipment and moves them across the sim station. Some of the students cheer her on. But she performs pretty basic Telekinetics—even if they are heavy objects.

My attention turns across the aisle, where the Naturalist section spreads out. The setup is much the same, but this banner is Naturalist green with their tree logo and the slogan: "The Power to affect change begins with nature. Join Paragon's Naturalist Department." I glance at the tables, with three students crowded around each of the four, green cloth-covered high-tops with an employee of Paragon. The crowd around the simulation platform is so thick on this side that I have to stand on my toes to see who is using it. As I bounce up for a better view, the crowd collectively releases a gasp of awe followed by thunderous applause.

Jimmy the Idiot stands on the simulation platform in front of a sim-table containing vials of various liquids. Some are clear, others milky or blue or green. One of the stands includes a host of empty vials with traces of what appears to be blood. Jimmy chews his lower lip as he leans closer to something on the table. I can't quite see through the crowd. A moment later the applause sounds again, and Jimmy beams in that arrogant way he has mastered, raising his arms victoriously above his head as the simulation disappears.

Disgusted by Jimmy's antics, I move on. These people are all sheep, too stupid to understand that knowledge is more potent than Powers.

The Divinic booth is much the same, but in blue colors with the slogan: "Without Divine Power, we are but heathens," followed by the same recruitment line. At one of the tables, Forrest talks to a couple of recruits. Their conversation is lost in the cacophony of cheers as students watch the sim tests. A boy on the Divinic simulation platform reads the history of items by touching them and predicting their potential future. I would guess that his Cass Scale rank is around the 40th percentile based on the accuracy of his predictions—marked on a display where he can't see them.

I turn to the Somatic booth in its bold, bright red to find another crowd gathered. It's hard to see what's going on over the other heads, but I recognize the movement of silky black hair on the simulation platform. Bianca. Hopeful to see more, I nudge my way through the crowd, but most of the students crowded around are also Somatics, which means their bodies are broader and more muscular than mine by far. It makes me look like a twig among branches.

Still, I manage to nudge forward just enough to see flashes of her movement between heads. A simulated instructor shows moves in quick, fluid motions, and Bianca has no trouble keeping up. Her Muscle Memory allows her to watch actions, register how each muscle acts during those moves, then mimic them perfectly. I've never watched her copy so fast before. The simulation finishes and a holographic graph of her results appears in the air above the simulation platform.

Speed: 92
Accuracy: 89
Power: 75
Balance: 81

I can't see her face from here, but those results send a bolt of awe through me. Her rank is in the 60's, and she just scored an 84. How is that even possible?

The Paragon employee running the simulation directs Bianca to one of the tables and the next student steps on the platform. I glance up at the slogan: "The mind cannot exist without the body. Join Paragon's Somatic Division."

Excitement pumps through my veins as I approach the next Paragon booth. Unlike the others, this booth represents all four of the Branches of Powers. A holographic recording plays on repeat, touting the importance of the research at Paragon, and how it wouldn't be possible without the bravery and selflessness of the medical test subjects who volunteer their time to the betterment of mankind.

A soothing, prerecorded voice beckons me as I approach the booth. "Why be ordinary when you can be extraordinary?"

A simple table covered in light blue cloth and a stack of fanned-out brochures stands to the corner of the booth near me. I grab one of the brochures as the Paragon employees talk to a few other students. Before reading it, I consult my map.

A lump of saliva forms in my throat. This is where I'm supposed to be. Helping with research, just like I always wanted. But when did they expand out into a fifth division, and what does it do? Excited, I glance up the aisle at the other booths crowded by students—unlike this one. Eagerness makes my limbs heavy. *Just go and talk to them.*

But what if it's a mistake? Three matches are far more than I ever could have hoped for. What if this one was a glitch in the system? And why are there so few students at this booth?

"Ugene Powers," says a young man in a red collared shirt embroidered on the left side of his chest with the PD logo.

"Um, yes."

He thrusts out a hand, a broad smile on his face. "I'm Devon, and I'm so thrilled to meet you."

I take his hand, getting a waft of sarsaparilla from his clothes as we shake. The smell reminds me of home. His handshake is firm.

"Me?"

"Of course! Your name is at the top of our list." He taps his tablet and shows me the list, and sure enough, there is my name right at the top, along with my abysmal rank.

I only have a few seconds to scan the names beneath mine, more interested in their ranks. All of them are low. Mo's name catches my interest, but Devon pulls the tablet back to his side before I can see anything more.

"So, what is it about me that interests you?" I ask.

"Your potential," Devon says. His pleasant demeanor doesn't slip once. "Our research is the fuel for the future of everyone with Powers, and you have the potential to help us find the answers."

"What exactly do you do?"

"Genetic and non-genetic linking mechanism differential anomalies for the creation of non-regressive solutions." Devon shifts to a casual stance, leaning on the high-top table beside him with an elbow. "That's a lot to take in. Sorry."

"No. I get it." At least I think I do.

Devon's brows arch in surprise. "Cool. So, all our subjects receive a generous compensation package and benefits. You won't have to worry about anything for the rest of your life."

Subjects. The word strikes against my chest.

They don't want me to do research. Idiot. Of course not. All the excitement and hope that bubbled up from the moment I saw the name of the company on my list bursts in one shot. My shoulders slump and the weight of Harvey's words press heavier on my back.

Devon continues his sales pitch, but my mind is already elsewhere.

I look up at the holographic slogan, surprised that the edges of my vision blur. *Why be ordinary?*

It's all I ever wanted. To be ordinary. To have a Power. To belong. Why be ordinary? Because only those who've never been could possibly understand how wonderful it really is.

"So, what do you think?" Devon asks, clearly excited, assuming I'm interested. "We can get you started right away."

"Ugene." Mr. Springer appears beside me, eyeing Devon suspiciously. "A moment?"

"I'm… I'm sort of busy." Is this a good idea? Should I really offer myself as a test subject?

Devon smiles so warmly that I want to stay. It can't be bad, right? Someone has to do it, and I don't have much else to offer the world. Maybe this is how I make a difference.

"We will only be a few minutes," Devon says.

"It really can't wait, Ugene," Mr. Springer says, taking my upper arm and encouraging me gently to come with him. "It's urgent."

Helpless and confused, I flounder over words and let Mr. Springer guide me away from the booth, stammering apologies to Devon. He just offered me a hard sell, with the potential to be set for life. I can't decide if this is a good thing or not, and Mr. Springer isn't really giving me a chance to think it through.

We pass the last Paragon Diagnostics booth, featuring displays, testers, and equipment on the cutting edge of what they have to offer.

"What's going on?" I ask as I'm dragged along with him.

The only response he offers is, "Just trust me."

We pass booths for churches, palm readers, medical facilities, grief counselors. The best of Divinic Powers are out on display for everyone to peruse.

Mr. Springer enters the main aisle running through the center of the massive hall and lets go of my arm, but doesn't let me slow the pace. We rush past aisle after aisle of Psionic businesses offering employment in sales, counseling, social services, detective agencies. Finally, we break free from the booths in the food court, surrounded by tables occupied by students gossiping excitedly amongst each other and teachers looking bored. Fresh pizza smells waft up my nose and make my mouth water.

"Where's the fire?" I ask, dropping into one of the plastic Naturalist-made chairs. My stomach growls.

Mr. Springer glances around, then pulls up a chair closer to me and leans in. The urgency in his posture makes me nervous.

"You can't go there, Ugene."

"Where?"

"Paragon."

I open my mouth to ask why, but the ferocity of that look in his dark eyes freezes any further protest in my throat. Tension seeps into my shoulders, and I sit up straighter.

Mr. Springer glances around, then gives me a level gaze. "Go home."

"I can't yet. I still need—"

"Ugene, I'm not asking. What's this?" He takes the brochure and grimaces as he gazes at the front, then tosses it on the table.

I stare at the discarded brochure, brows pulling together. "What's going on?"

"It's complicated, but I need you to trust me. Have I ever steered you wrong before?" He pauses to wait for my head shake. I oblige. "Then go home. I'll tell them you got sick. Paragon wants you, Ugene."

"Good. I want to go to Paragon."

"No—it—" Mr. Springer growls low and runs a hand through his chestnut hair, greying at the temples. "I can't tell you more here."

The cryptic way he's acting, the hard sales pitch Devon threw at me about non-regressive solutions, the way the garbage men looked at me with so much disgust and called me Powerless. Something strikes me as wrong about all of this, and Mr. Springer has answers.

Curious if my hunch is correct, I pull out the flyer in my pocket, smoothing it out on the tabletop. "Does it have anything to do with this?"

He snatches the flyer before I can let go, crumbling it again and tossing it aside. "Yes." After a glance toward the booths, Mr. Springer shoots to his feet and yanks me to mine, then nudges me toward the exit. "This isn't what your parents want. Stay away from Paragon. Go home."

I stumble a step, confused. Questions tumble through my head in a jumbled mess as I start toward the exit. How does he know what my parents want?

As I reach the door, I look back in time to see Devon approaching Mr. Springer, who moved back toward the booths. At Devon's side, a handful of broad-shouldered men and women in black, form-fitting Paragon security uniforms stand alert, their hands on their utility belts. No weapons would be allowed in here, would they? Their stance certainly appears menacing.

Security. Who did Mr. Springer tick off to bring security out? The guards scan the room with their eyes. What are they looking for? Mr. Springer's urgency has my stomach in knots. It couldn't be me, could it? Devon knew my face. I'm at the top of their list. But would they really come for me like this? It doesn't make sense.

Fear grips my chest and I dart between two groups of students standing in the food court. The din of conversation and the scent of pizza and boiled meats overwhelm my senses, making me dizzy. What am I so afraid of?

When I reach the door, the cool tablet presses into my sweaty palm, reminding me of its presence. Afraid it may be able to track me, unsure what exactly it is I'm so scared of or why Paragon would search for me with security, I drop it on a nearby ledge like it bit me and slip out.

Everything has turned upside down, and there's only one place I can go to clear my thoughts... my lab.

6

THE NOISE OF THE CITY IS TOO MUCH. THE ENCOUNTER at Career Day is too much. Together, they make my heartbeat hasten. My own mind is at war with itself— one part wants to rush home and hide, and the other part wants to find out exactly what just happened.

As I slink away from the convention center, it's impossible to shake the feeling that someone is following me. Every time I glance back, all I can see are the crowded city streets.

Downtown Elpis is compressed. Buildings butt up against each other, narrow and tall. Various shops—cafes, diners, pawn shops, music stores, specialty stores—occupy the first level of each building. Awnings loom over doorways and sidewalk cafes. Traffic is particularly heavy along the narrow street. Anyone who wanted to follow me would have any number of places to hide whenever I look back.

I head away from the gleaming spires of big business towering over the cramped buildings, stretching their necks proudly toward the clouds. Years ago, a great war between humans with and without Powers began. NonPowered feared those with them. During the Purge, when NonPowered people attempted to exterminate those with Powers, a young man we now call Atmos lost control of his Power. He created the perfect storm to trigger the apocalypse. Only a few thousand people with Powers survived the fallout.

Elpis began rebuilding the ruined city. It once spread across miles of land around several lakes, with the downtown as a hub for businesses and the university. Now, downtown is the hub of life as we know it, with Paragon Tower in the center of it all where the main campus of the university used to be. Sunlight reflects on the glass walls, making them sparkle in the early evening light. It's several blocks away, but the height of the monolith makes it feel too close.

Glancing back again, I cross the street to where a florist tends to her plants with delicate touches. Each time her fingers brush a flower, it perks up, standing straighter and renewed as if it had just bloomed. The scent of roses, orchids, and lilies mingle pleasantly as I pass. The myriad of colors is breathtaking, and for just a moment I just watch her work until something else catches my attention. A movement from the corner of my eyes. Startled, I turn quickly, only to be greeted by a holographic news display.

"Proposition 8.5 isn't the end of our basic human rights," the hologram of a pleasant looking woman says. Her calm demeanor is almost contagious. "It's the final step toward the end of regression and the dawn of hope for us all. Together, we can step into the future stronger."

Holographic news displays like this one are on every other corner, showcasing propaganda about city improvements, faith in the Directorate, and anything else the Directorate wants to brainwash us with. I stand in front of this one waiting for the holographic woman to expand on this, but instead, she changes to the improvements under way downtown and increased security along the borders of Elpis. I turn away and stuff my hands into my pockets.

The wail of a siren makes my back stiffen, and I step behind a post as a police vehicle whizzes past. *I'm being ridiculous.* Why am I hiding—afraid of some sirens? Why am I fearful in the first place? Because of Mr. Springer's cryptic behavior and a few security guards? It's irrational, and I know it, but I can't help the tension in my shoulders and stiffness in each step.

I stop on a busy corner, waiting for the light to change so I can cross, and debate which direction to go from here. West, toward home, or east. In all my life living in Elpis, not once have I visited the east boroughs, Pax and Clement. My parents never visited anyone on that side of the city. Sometimes I wonder what it's like on the east side. It's where the lower-ranked citizens live, and I've heard my dad complain about the high crime rate in Pax and Clement. It gives the Department of Military Affairs quite a hard time. I suppose I'll find out about life on the east side soon enough. I won't be able to afford living anywhere else.

There's another couple of hours or so until the sun starts to set. It won't be safe for me then, so taking a trip east isn't advisable today. Not if any Somatic thugs are out wandering with their Telepathic buddies, looking for someone weak enough to mug. A good Psionic Telepath will read me like a book, know I'm an easy target for mugging and sick their Somatic friends on me.

It's a lesson I learned all too quickly in school.

Feeling eyes on me, I glance over my shoulder, afraid of seeing Paragon security. A skinny guy with narrow eyes and dirty clothes is watching me from a gap between buildings. Psionic. Most likely a Telepath. Now that he knows I've spotted him, he will either move in or abort. I turn the corner, hoping for the latter. As a distraction, I pat down my pockets and remind myself that they are shamefully empty.

The sound of their steps, heavy against the ground from one and light from the other, continues to follow me toward the metro entrance. *I can't believe they're gonna mug me*, I think. *What are they gonna take? My shirt?*

As I start down the stairs into the cool, but crowded, underground metro station, the sound of their footsteps disappears in the hum of the metro crowd. I glance back, thinking maybe the din of the crowd has masked the sound, but they're gone. A sigh pushes out of my lungs, and I fumble in my pocket for the metro card.

Home. This is the moment of truth. Going inside means facing my dad. More than once he reminded me that this day was critical to my future. I had to wrangle job prospects, or I would become a basement-dwelling weight. Slowly, I grip the handle with a sweaty hand and press the other against the edge of the door to soften the sound. I slip in as quietly as I can and ease the door shut.

I pause inside the door. The stairs to my lab are just on the other side of the room, and I know the floorboards like a maestro knows a piano. My pulse beats against my eardrums. I peek around the doorway into the living room. Dad is on the sofa, pulling a needle out of his arm. What is he doing? Curiosity gets the better of me, and I step into the living room.

"What's that?" I ask.

Dad jumps, pushing the needle down and out of sight. Too late, though.

"What's that?" I ask again, nodding toward whatever he is hiding on the sofa cushion.

"You're home early," he says. "I assume that means you blew it today." His eyes are hard.

A lump forms in my throat. "I only had three prospects because I have no skills to qualify me."

"Oh, give me a break."

The words are like a gut punch. "I tried, Dad. I really did. The first guy said he couldn't because it would hurt his business. The second didn't even want to consider me."

"I can't do this anymore," Dad says like he's talking to one of his military lackeys. I flinch. "You had so much promise."

Used to have. And now I'm good for little more than a test subject, and worth even less to him. All the anger I've held inside for the past two years erupts. "Do you have any idea what it's like being me, Dad? Have you ever bothered to think past your ignorant perception of the world?"

His eyes flash dangerously. "Excuse me—"

"Other kids use me for target practice!" My blood is boiling, heart pounding, pulse racing. "I've been tortured every day at school since I was thirteen."

"We all got problems, that's no excuse for being lazy."

"Lazy?" Some part of me knows I'm going too far, but my anger propels me forward. I can't stop raging. The words pour out, molten hot. "I'm not lazy, Dad. I'm just not qualified. And now because of this new Proposition, I can't even get hired as a busboy or garbage hauler."

For a moment he hesitates, but it passes so quickly I may have imagined it. He continues glaring, my words like gnats buzzing around him.

I raise my hands in defeat.

His face turns red beneath his darker skin. The heat of our argument dims the sound of chimes of the in-home special alerts, used to automatically keep everyone updated on critical changes. But I push on, unable to stop myself.

"But you're right. As always, Dad, you're right. I'm worthless, and I enjoy being that way. I love the fact that girls won't look at me because I have no prospects. I love the fact that I disgust you and everyone else because I have no Powers. It's *exactly* what I wanted out of life!"

"Don't you dare talk to me like that!"

"Or what?" I hiss. "What can you possibly do to me that's worse than what you already said or what I've already been through?"

Dad grits his teeth and clenches his fists. The veins in his arms pop out like they do when he's pulsing with his Enhanced Strength ability. His military training should scare me—he could take me down in a second—but the anger burning through me creates a feeling of invincibility.

"Stop," Mom calls, rushing into the living room and staring at the holotv.

Dad gives me one last glare before turning his attention to the TV as well. I cross my arms and join them, standing on the other side of the living room Dad.

On TV, Dr. Joyce Cass, CEO of Paragon Diagnostics, sits upright and pristine in a white chair. Across from her is Elpida Theus, the top reporter in Elpis. Dr. Cass' blue dress suit stands out against her pale white skin and cropped blond hair.

"We are facing dangerous times," Dr. Cass says calmly, long, pale fingers folded delicately in her lap. "Nearly twenty-nine percent of the population live with Powers at lower than thirty percent of what we know as the median for maximum potential. And that's a fifty-eight percent increase over the last five years. If this trend continues, we face forty-five percent of the population on Testing Day having a significant decrease below the citywide average in the next five years. And in as little as twenty years, we could face a complete regression from Powers.

"The foundation of our society is built on our ability to use these Powers to survive, which begs the question, what will we do if this regression completes? Life as we know it faces total collapse. The world beyond Elpis will not be habitable in time, and our Powers are the only reason we still survive. That is why I, and my fellow board members at Paragon Diagnostics, fully support the Directorate's proposition to institute mandatory re-testing on any who show signs of regression. It could help us pave the path to a brighter future."

Mandatory re-testing. So, this is what Proposition 8.5 is about? Forcing people with weaker Powers to undergo further testing? The tests are already so brutal. I passed mine by thinking outside the box, but not well enough to show any sign of Powers. And what will these tests mean? My arms drop to my sides.

"This was recorded earlier today and edited," Mom says.

"How can you tell?" Dad asks, sinking down onto the sofa, shifting the black bag beside him.

"Look at the background. It's later than that."

I squint at the image and see what she's talking about. The windows of the building are tinted to protect from too much sunlight, but it's clear the sun was higher in the sky. But what does that mean to us?

"Does this mean I have to test again?" I ask, unable to shake the chill gripping my spine.

Mom says, "no" at the same time Dad says, "yes."

Before I can ask further, a pounding on the front door silences all three of us. Dad moves to the window, pulling back the heavy drapes to peek out. He looks at Mom and shakes his head.

"Okay." Mom reaches over and takes my hand. "Ugene, go to your room."

Her hand trembles in mine.

"What's going on?"

"Go. Don't come out until I call you."

"But—"

"Go," Dad says. The dangerous edge to his voice matches the look in his eyes.

What is going on? I've never seen my parents so unsettled.

7

AT THE TOP OF THE STAIRS, I ROUND THE LANDING and crouch down in the corner behind the hallway bureau Mom uses to store extra towels. The lemony scent of furniture polish drifts up my nose as I press a hand against the side of the wood. It's as smooth as glass. For a moment all is absolute deafening silence. I hold my breath, waiting for something to happen, though I'm not sure what. I know it's my imagination, but it feels like my sense of hearing has heightened. Probably just from the adrenaline pumping through me.

The familiar sound of creaking floorboards echoes up the stairs as my parents move in the entryway below.

Dad breaks the silence, his voice so low I barely hear what he says. "I thought we made ourselves clear."

"Just open it, Gavin," Mom says. Her voice sounds almost breathless, anxious. It doesn't help my already pounding heart.

The hinges on the front door creak as it opens.

"I don't suppose it's a coincidence you're here today," Dad says in a tone I know too well. He's ready for a fight, and if there's one thing I know about my dad, it's this—no one should want to ever try to pick a fight with him.

Heels click on the hardwood floor near the door, and a familiar female voice says, "I'm merely here to follow up."

"You're wasting your precious time," Dad says. I can't see downstairs from my hiding place, but I can picture my dad, arms crossed over his chest, which is puffed out stubbornly.

"Far from it." The moment she speaks, I realize who it is. *Dr. Joyce Cass.* And somehow my parents know her.

"We told you before, he won't be coming to Paragon," Mom says. The strength in her voice surprises me.

"I don't think that's up to you anymore," Dr. Cass says. Her heels click on the floor again.

I edge tighter against the white rail, hoping my shadow isn't casting on the wall.

"I'm not sure you fully understand just what your son has to offer—and I'm not just talking about our research. I'm talking about our society."

"We won't let you torture our son in your tests," Mom says.

"Torture?" Dr. Cass laughs out the word. "Do you really think so little about the pursuit of knowledge and science? I hear he has an aptitude for our research. Perhaps if he helps us find a cure, we will be able to find a place for him in R&D."

My breath catches, and not with fear. But something unfamiliar—hope. Could there really be a solution to my problem?

"You would be generously compensated, of course," Dr. Cass goes on. "Your illness is progressing rapidly, Gavin. We could help. Paragon is on the brink of a breakthrough in curing illnesses like yours. You will be first in line."

Illness… No one said anything to me about Dad having an illness.

"I'm already getting treatment."

"Ineffective treatment," Dr. Cass says. "You know the injections will only slow the illness. Paragon could reverse it."

"*If* you get to experiment on our son," Dad says flatly.

"You can't force Ugene to go with you or undergo more testing," Mom says. "You don't have the authority."

"Yet."

The word hangs in the air, and the implication is clear enough. Even for me. My heart drums so loud I'm afraid it will give me away, and I close my eyes to try and calm it.

Dad's voice lowers into a threatening growl. "You have some

nerve—"

"You knew this day was coming, Gavin," Dr. Cass cuts him off. "It's time. Give this to him. He can call me any time, day or night. I'm happy to answer his questions. But don't wait too long." Heels click again, and the door opens. "Ugene has the potential to save us all. Don't let him waste that."

The door slams shut, and for a moment all is dead silence again. I can't move a muscle, frozen in place. After everything that's happened today, my mind is spinning. I can't quite figure out how the pieces go together yet, but, if I really do have that much potential, Dr. Cass would be the one to know.

"What do you think?" Dad asks.

Mom sighs. "I don't know, Gavin. She's hiding something. I can't read her. It's like she's mastered her mind and I can't penetrate the barrier. But something is off."

Mom's Psionic Telepathy ranks strong—89th percentile—and she works as a desk clerk in the Department of Social Welfare.

"I don't need Telepathy to know that," Dad says. "But she will be back."

Mastery of the Mind is hard to accomplish, and usually, only Psionics can do it. Dr. Cass is a Naturalist, so if she has a barrier to block my mom, it wasn't put there by her.

I ease out of my hiding place and move to the top of the stairs.

Mom leans against Dad, her head against his shoulder and his arms around her.

Despite all the confusion in my mind, only one question comes out. "What illness was she talking about?"

Both of my parents jump and turn their attention to me.

"What…what dear?" Mom asks.

"What illness? What treatments? Is that what you were doing when I came in?"

Dad has always been a rock in my life. Unyielding sometimes, but that wasn't always a bad thing. I chalked it up to him being a General. Despite the problems the two of us are having, I love him. He's my dad. Even unyielding and harsh as he might seem, he cares about me—on some deeply buried level.

"It's nothing for you to worry about," Mom says, moving toward the bottom of the stairs.

"But it is. I'm part of this family still, right?"

"Of course you are, sweetheart."

"Then tell me."

"Ugene, you can't listen to that woman," Dad says. "She can't be trusted."

"But you need treatments," I say. "Is Dr. Cass right? That you can't get them without their help?"

"No!" Dad's hand falls on the railing, and it rattles under his grip. "You listen to me, Ugene. For once in your damn life, listen to me!"

Mom places a hand on Dad's other arm in an attempt at reassurance. "Gavin—"

Dad barrels over Mom's protest. "That woman is sneaky and slippery and conniving, and she won't stop until she gets her way, no matter what."

"I am listening, Dad," I say, taking a step toward the edge of the stairs. My hands clench into fists at my sides. "I'm listening to the fact that her offer has an expiration. And if the Proposition passes, I won't have a choice, and you won't be on that list."

"I don't want to be on any list she has!"

"Why are you so stubborn?"

Dad says, eyes wide. "Go to your room."

"Typical. Can't win, so you send me away. Fine. But Dr. Cass is right. This isn't your choice."

I storm away to my room and slam the door.

In middle school, I went from being the bright kid to the late bloomer to that Powerless kid. By the time I reached high school, most of my friends had moved on.

Dad assumed the same as everyone else. One day my Power would manifest. I just hadn't discovered one yet. He recognized my interest in the sciences, though, and for my fourteenth birthday, he bought me a secondhand microscope and slides set. He believed I'd develop a Power that would allow me to get a prestigious science job. Over the next four years, I collected odds and ends—glassware, tongs, and clamps, a chemistry set, measuring scales, slides—until the assembly grew so large I had to move it to the basement. Tonight, after my parents go to bed, I sneak down the stairs to my basement laboratory.

The basement smells of an odd mixture of mildew and bleach. I do my best to keep my area sterile.

I cross the barren floor to my metal desk littered with a dozen lab notebooks. Each contains information about my experiments with the different Branches of Power. So far, the only thing I have been able to discern about myself clearly is that my cells lack the linking mechanism Dr. Cass became so famous for discovering. Somewhere in these notebooks, there has to be some clue I've missed, some answer to what gives me so much of the potential Dr. Cass sees.

Of the four Branches of Power, each has its own unique linking mechanism; its own way of bringing the cells together to create just the right Power. One of my notebooks is filled with notes about Somatics. I begin digging for answers.

Somatic cells bind together when abilities are activated. Not all the cells in their body, but only the ones connected to the physical ability. For instance, someone with Enhanced Touch would have cells that bind in a chain from the point of origin—say the fingertips—through the nerves that send the signals to the brain, enhancing the sensation. No matter how many times I've tested myself under a microscope, I haven't been able to make it happen. The cells repel instead of bind.

Through the course of my research, I've learned that Somatics have a cellular structure that responds differently to particular acidic chemicals. Because their bodies are more physically adaptable, they are more attuned to response than the other three Branches, which causes their cells to react. It wasn't my breakthrough. Paragon published it years ago. In a few rare cases, the type of response generated can indicate the type of Somatic Power one has.

When I learned this three years ago, I ran out and bought a chemistry set. I scraped off my cells and started testing them in every acidic chemical I could legally get. After months of testing and retesting, it was evident Somatic could be checked off the list. I would never develop a physical Power. Today's review of the notes doesn't reveal anything new. My scribbled comments, diagrams, and formulas all reach roughly the same conclusive results. I reach for the next journal.

Naturalists are the most uniquely diverse Branch. The linking mechanism for them is fascinating. The Power to tune into nature and shape, mold, or heal it is directly connected to how the cells respond to the environment. For instance, someone with Natural Mutation—the ability to mutate energy or objects into something of similar natural energy—would have cells that bind with the energy or object itself during manipulation. It doesn't change their body. It merely allows them to transform it into something else.

When putting my cells against those from natural energy, nothing happens. I have two notebooks of various experiments to prove it, and today the notes lack just as much revelation as they did when I wrote them. No dots connect. I scrub through the next two journals looking for something, anything.

Divinics and Psionics are somewhat similar in their recordable activation. Both are best tested by watching brainwave patterns to see which areas light up, and how brightly they do so. Of course, this makes them the hardest to prove at home because I don't have access to the equipment necessary. Mr. Springer and I worked on a couple experiments, hooking up electrodes to record responses while doing various tasks. For instance, we recorded my brainwaves while testing cells—hoping for some hint at any of the Healing Hands abilities within the Divinic Branch. While he was impressed with how my brain lit up for certain parts of the test, none of them were even close to textbook indicative of Divinic ability. We also tested my brainwaves while I attempted to read his mind, testing for Psionic Telepathy. That came out to be a complete dud. Turns out I'm very creative, though.

After years of research, I'm no closer to an answer than I was at the start. If anything, I'm farther away. This reality is nagging at me as I pour over the notebooks, hoping for something, anything, to rocket me on to answers. There must be some reason I'm so different.

Frustrated, I thrust the notebooks away and sit back in the chair, fingers dragging down my face. I lace them together behind my head as my gaze falls on the diagrams of the Branches of Power stuck on the wall above my desk. Each diagram shows a complicated web of each Branch and the Powers within it. All of them have an X over them as I eliminated options.

But I do have one option left.

The only option, really.

I sweep my journals off the desktop into a neat pile and peek under the metal desk for my messenger bag. It's tucked back in the corner near the wall. I dig it out and stuff the notebooks inside, then head upstairs, tiptoeing all the way.

8

DAD'S SNORING REACHES ALL THE WAY DOWN TO THE kitchen, where I'm digging through the stack of mail on the table. The number of medical bills gives me pause, but that's not what I'm after. I'm not even sure what it is I'm looking for. Dr. Cass gave my parents something, and my only assumption would be a business card.

Nothing on the table is suspect, so I move on to the counter, searching everything on any surface as quickly and quietly as I can. A creak upstairs freezes me in place, and I hold my breath, listening, but the only sound to return is Dad's snoring.

I can't find it. Everything is sickeningly normal. I brush my fingers against my fuzzy black hair and turn. Think. Think, Ugene. It must be somewhere. What would happen if I just walked into Paragon and asked for Dr. Cass? Would the people at reception know me like Devon did?

Something in the trash reflects as I drop my hands, and I rush over. The red PD logo shimmers on the business card. But it's only a logo. Frowning, I turn it over. Dr. Cass's phone number is hand-written on the other side. Glancing over my shoulder, I pocket the card and drop the note I wrote for my parents on the table. Hopefully, they will understand I'm doing this for them.

At the back door, I give the warm kitchen—with its modern wooden cabinets and granite countertop—another look, then turn off the light and slip out into the darkness.

The scent of sarsaparilla reaches for me like a familiar caress as I make my way around the house. The Salas borough of Elpis is far enough from the heart of the city for the house to resemble houses and not compressed brick buildings. Regent Road is always quiet at this time of night, not quite midnight but still dark. Some of the neighbors' windows are still lit.

The houses on my street are in fair condition—all sided in different natural colors and trimmed in bold white. The smell of the gardens in a few of the sprawling front lawns has a calming effect on my nerves—jasmine, lavender, and spiderwort. The gray sided house beside ours has a freshly mulched bed of Sessile Bellwort, the bloom of the flower hanging its head as if in sympathy for my fate. Sarsaparilla cowers in tree beds on one side of the road, hidden by taller plants. But the smell is familiar. Like home.

I turn right and start up the street. Trams don't run as frequently at this time of night so far from downtown, so I'll have to walk. Not that it matters too much. Once I'm far enough from home, I'll make the call.

"Ugene?" Bianca's voice draws my attention toward her front porch. Even at night, the pink staghorn sumac is bright with color, weaving over the latticework that covers the porch crawlspace.

Bianca glances back at her house before she stands from the steps and jogs down to me. Her eyes shift over the messenger bag strapped across my chest.

I pause, captured by the way the moonlight casts luminous highlights and shadows over the contours of her heart-shaped face. "Hey."

"What brings you out so late?" she asks, smiling in a way that makes my heart race.

The smile reminds me of the time when we were seven. Bianca had a thing about playing in puddles in the rain, but our parents wouldn't let us out during the storm. As soon as it ended, Bianca was at my door in her rain boots, smiling like the sun. I remember the way rain clung to her clothes, and how her boots were coated with a layer of mud and water. She made sure to hit every puddle between her front door and mine on the way over, so by the time she arrived she was already half soaked. We spent the better part of the afternoon under cloudy skies, playing in the puddles and making mud castles. It wasn't until Forrest pulled her home that the fun ended.

"I'm just... hoping that a late-night stroll will give me some answers."

"To what?"

Awkward silence settles. It's apparent that the boy who splashed in puddles and was the knight to her mud castle kingdom was forgotten. Now, I'm nothing more than the Powerless boy across the street.

"How did Career Day go for you?" I ask, trying to break past the uncomfortable feeling between us.

"Great. A lot of prospects, I think. I'm looking forward to graduation tomorrow." She glances at the house again, then pulls her hair over her shoulder and absently braids it. An old habit. "How about you?"

"Um, I got a lead, so we'll see I guess."

"Cool."

"Anyway." I shift and glance up the road.

"Right. Sorry. Enjoy your walk." She moves back toward her porch, and I start back up the road. "I hope to see you tomorrow, Ugene."

I don't for a second believe Bianca thinks she will actually see me tomorrow. We both know it isn't true.

Salas is peaceful. The only sounds are the night birds on the hunt, crickets, and the occasional hum of a vehicle as it passes down the road. Each time I hear the engine, I glance over my shoulder, praying it isn't my dad. The houses are all quiet as the residents slumber, oblivious to my own inner turmoil.

This has to be done. For my dad's sake. For all of us. Maybe they won't tell me what's wrong, but it doesn't mean I can't help. Earlier today, I hesitated, unsure if volunteering for Paragon's program was a good move. But if it really can help Dad, what choice do I have?

The park at the edge of the Salas borough is simple. Swings, a slide, and a climbing wall for little kids. Bianca and I used to climb that wall. She was always better at it than me.

I settle on a bench.

For a few minutes, I just sit, leaning forward with the card in one hand and my phone in the other. Suddenly I understand what Dad meant when he told Dr. Cass it couldn't be a coincidence. Paragon wants me. The convention center. The hard sell. The security. And when that failed, Dr. Cass showed up personally. The profound lack of trust my parents have toward her isn't lost on me, and, as it all comes together, I wonder if I'm really doing the right thing. But something Dr. Cass said lingers.

"Your injections will only slow the illness. Paragon could reverse it."

Swallowing the anxiety knotted in my chest, I punch the numbers into the phone, and before I can change my mind, it rings.

9

A HALF AN HOUR AFTER MAKING THE CALL, A BLACK car with darkened windows pulls up to the park, and a woman with auburn hair and skin as pale as the moon beckons me to get in.

"I apologize for the delay," she says, sliding over for me. Her apology sounds civil enough.

I can't help wondering what her Power is. With those thin, shapely legs jetting out of her black pencil skirt and her slender build, there's no way she's Somatic. "Dr. Cass is waiting, and she's a busy woman, so let's not delay."

It's still hard to believe I'm going to meet Dr. Joyce Cass, my role model. By the age of twenty, she had discovered the linking mechanism that distinguishes specific Powers within each Branch. It's work others had started and could never complete.

And if I'm meeting Dr. Cass, then the woman beside me is most likely her assistant, Hilde Long. How many holonews reports have I seen these two women in? And how did I not recognize Hilde immediately?

The ride is silent. Hilde sits rigidly, legs crossed and hands in her lap, staring out the opposite window. Clearly, she has no interest in talking to me.

The corners of Paragon Diagnostics twist up and disappear in the night sky when we step out of the vehicle. This building promises hope. Curing Power-related diseases. Improving the lives of those with weaker Powers. The swell of hope I felt at the upstairs railing at home earlier returns.

The massive glass doors slide apart, granting entry into the large lobby of the building as Hilde and I step up to them. The ceiling rises through the center of the building five stories up, lined with glass panel railings at each level. Pristine whites and deep blacks make the slashes of red, blue, yellow, and green stand out in striking contrast on walls and fixtures. It's beautiful and clean and everything I remember it to be.

Employee pass-stations block off the far end of the lobby where another foyer and a bay of elevators waits. Hilde swipes her arm over the station, and we pass through easily.

In the elevator, she smiles at me. I realize I'm staring and avert my gaze to the red and black elevator doors as they close in front of us, then up at the increasing number on the digital display. My ears pop as the pressure changes. The elevator doesn't stop until the number reaches 200.

"This way, Mr. Powers," says Hilde as she steps out.

This lobby is different from the other. The coordination of red and white still contrasts, but there is no black at all, and it's redder.

Hilde leads the way to a large office with glass panel walls. Dr. Cass sits on the other side, her blond hair in waves down to her shoulders. Her skirt and suit jacket are blue, the same outfit she wore on the broadcast earlier in the evening. Through the glass wall, she looks up and sees the two of us approaching.

Everything inside me freezes.

I'm about to enter the office of the woman I have idolized since the age of eight. And all I want to do is run.

Hilde is holding the door open for me: "After you, Mr. Powers."

Each step is heavy as I swallow the lump in my throat and proceed into the office.

Dr. Cass's office is like the rest of the floor. Red and white without a single trace of black. An expansive desk of glass guards one end of the room, but there's nothing on the surface. No computer or phone or lamp. No files. It's just a polished glass surface.

"Ugene Powers." Dr. Cass stands, and the way she moves is

smooth. Like gliding. I can't look away as she rounds the desk and sits on the edge, facing me. Her long fingers curl around the edges of the glass. She holds out her hand to me. "Joyce Cass, CEO—"

"—Of Paragon Diagnostics," I say along with her. "I...I know who you are. I've read all your reports on the Power classification linking mechanisms. It's... It's just brilliant."

"Really." She cocks her head to the side and clicks her tongue. "So, you have an interest in genetic science then. I suppose that makes sense, all things considered."

All things considered? I struggle to hold back the wince trying to leap out.

"Well, Ugene—I can call you Ugene, yes?"

I nod, but she goes on as if it's already assumed.

"I won't bore you with typical interview questions. You don't have to tell me about yourself. I already know everything I need."

Dr. Cass turns and touches the desk a couple of times, then swipes her hand over the surface. A holographic image rises out of the glass. I know already that she's a Naturalist with Transmutation Power—changing one organic object into a different organic object. And a strong one, at that. She's one of the few who ranks above the 95th percentile. But what she is doing with her desk goes beyond computer programming and well beyond my level of understanding.

Then I notice the image is of me. A report about my birth, childhood, pictures with my family. The exposure should creep me out, but instead, I'm fascinated.

"I don't think there's any question about whether or not there is a place for you here," Dr. Cass says as she flips her hand through the air, causing the images to whir by until it stops on one. My Testing Day results. "The work you would be helping us with could benefit the future of our entire society. *You* could be the key to unlocking the genes that trigger Powers, the key to helping us stop regression for good. It's a once-in-a-lifetime opportunity for Paragon Diagnostics to study the genetics of someone without a Power. You could help us identify exactly which gene determines Powers and how those powers can be boosted by comparing yours with others. This discovery could help us cure Power-related illness, regression, and so much more. The only question is, are you interested in helping the future of humanity?"

I stare at the image of the blood test results, trying to decipher the meaning. A sigh slips out, and I look at her, my hands folded in my lap to keep from fidgeting. "Maybe. But… what exactly would I be doing in this research testing?"

"A great question," Dr. Cass says. "You would be paired with one of our more promising researchers. Together, you would test against each of the Branches of Power while your muscular, skeletal, and chemical reactions would be monitored for discernable changes. Those results will be compared with subjects with Powers in the hopes of discovering the key to the Powers mutation. A standard compare and contrast methodology." Dr. Cass pauses. "I haven't lost you, have I? I assume since you read my research you know what I'm talking about."

I nod.

"Good." Dr. Cass glances at the test results on display. "We would also be taking blood and other genetic samples. Nothing to be alarmed at. All perfectly safe and painless. You would live here, in a dormitory space we provide, along with other volunteers so we can be sure your diet and environmental exposure are optimal."

"You mentioned compensation and health care earlier," I say, feeling my cheeks heat and hoping my darker skin covers it well enough.

Dr. Cass gifts me with a soft, matronly smile. "Of course. Everything comes at a price." She swipes her hand against the air again, and images whir by until she finds what she seeks. A medical bill with the name Gavin Powers.

The number clenches my throat and makes my stomach twist in knots. My dad makes a lot of money, but these bills… There's no way he could ever pay this off, even with his significant military salary. It's absurd.

"Here is my offer, Ugene. We will pay off your father's current and future medical bills, give your family a generous stipend to alleviate cost of living pressures, create a trust in your name to help you move into the future, provide you with a private dormitory, and seek options for full-time employment for you once the study concludes."

Each item she ticks off makes me dizzier. This isn't real. It *can't* be real. Why are they willing to offer so much to me?

"I can tell you are hesitant," Dr. Cass says, after a glance over my shoulder. "This is all too good to be true, right? I promise you it isn't." Her hand pushes the image down into the desk, and it disappears, then she slips into the red chair beside me. "You're special, Ugene. I get the feeling that no one else sees you that way. You don't think you deserve all of this, but I assure you, if your genetics can do what we are hoping they can do, you deserve far more than I could ever offer you."

"You… you are guaranteeing to help my father?" I point at the now blank desktop, unsure what 'that' even is.

"With his treatments? Of course. His treatments and anything else that might arise out of his disease. Effective immediately."

My eyes snap to attention. Disease? I gathered he was sick, but a disease?

"You don't know, do you?" Dr. Cass's face falls, and she reaches over a cool hand, giving mine a reassuring squeeze. "Ugene, your dad has Muscular Degeneration."

My stomach twists. I should have guessed. A Power-related illness. Thousands of thoughts tumble through my mind, and I can't grasp any of them long enough to make sense of any of it. One thing is abundantly clear. Degeneration of any sort kills.

"Hilde, get him some water." Dr. Cass's voice is like a distant bell. I'm aware it's there, but it's so far away like I'm drifting away from the world.

I wipe my sweating palms over my legs and stand. The room spins and I close my eyes to regain control.

"Are you okay?"

"I'm fine." The lie comes out of me in a croak.

"Ugene," Dr. Cass's hand falls on my forearm. "I know this is hard. And I'm sorry to break the news to you. I honestly thought your parents would have told you about this by now. He's been sick for nearly a year. Please. Take a few minutes to digest all of this."

My legs give out, and I drop back into the chair.

Dr. Cass hands me the glass of water Hilde retrieved.

Acceptance of the glass is automatic. I don't realize, but now it's in my hand, the cold glass contrasting starkly against the heat of my sweating palm.

"His disease doesn't have to be the end, Ugene," Dr. Cass says. "Some of the best Divinics of our age are finding ways to heal even the worst diseases. They are only months away from a cure for cancer. A real, viable cure. There's every chance your dad's treatment can cure him. Your participation in our study will improve those odds."

I want to believe her, to hope she is right, but her conversation with my parents rings in my memory.

"The sooner you can get him on our health plan, the better his chances are," Dr. Cass says, pulling me back to reality. "What do you think, Ugene? Will you help us unlock the mystery of how these Powers work?"

The sooner, the better. I gulp down the water, coating my empty stomach and insides with the icy liquid.

"How long?" I manage to ask.

"Well, that all depends on how your future test results come out," Dr. Cass says. There is a shine in her eyes that reminds me of an eager child, curious and desperate to know more. "It could be a few months. But it could also be years. We won't know for sure until we get started."

This feels like a mistake, but Muscular Degeneration will kill my dad. If he's already had it for a year, he probably only has another year left—maybe less. The very thought makes me feel sick. And I can't help but think of Mr. Springer's warning, too.

She raises a brow, then glances at my messenger bag. "Can I count you in?"

"Yes." The acceptance is more of a croak than a real word.

"Excellent." Dr. Cass slides the glass out of my hand and passes it to Hilde. "Do you need a ride home to collect your things?"

"No." The word jumps out, and my gaze locks on hers. "No, I've got what I need." Going home would mean facing my parents. It's better this way.

Dr. Cass's face lights up, making her ice-blue eyes shine in the artificial office light. "Then there's no need to delay further."

Hilde steps forward with a glass surface in hand and holds it toward me. The holographic black letters of the contract rise off the surface of the tablet as if beaconing me.

"Just sign at the bottom of that first section there," Dr. Cass says, pulling my attention away from the contract in front of me. "The time and date will be automatically stamped on the document."

My eyes skim over the legal jargon, trying to make sense of what I'm supposed to sign.

"It's really quite standard, Ugene," Dr. Cass says. "You agree to cooperate with our tests and offer the appropriate samples determined by your assigned researcher, agree to stay until all tests are complete, any samples we take are our property, and you do not have right to remove them. The basics of any research contract we offer, apart from the benefits terms we discussed."

My mouth goes dry. *She can't be trusted.* Dad seemed so vehement about that—as did Mr. Springer—that it makes me hesitate, makes my chest compress.

"I-is there a pen or something?" I ask, buying a moment longer to think. The research belongs to Paragon, which is understandable. In fact, the more I rush through what she said in my mind, the harder it is to find a flaw in what she says. Maybe Dad is wrong.

"Not necessary," Dr. Cass says. "We use bio-signatures. Just press your finger to the box. Any finger will do."

As I raise my finger over the document, I chew at the inside of my cheek. I'm stuck here once I sign this. At least my dad will have his medical benefits, however long the research takes.

I press my finger at the bottom of the document.

Dr. Cass quickly slides the tablet out of my hand and waves toward Hilde. "Hilde will take you to processing, then to your new living space." A smile splits Dr. Cass's face, flashing teeth so white they make her light skin seem dark. "You have just saved us all, Ugene. You're already a hero."

The words don't quite ring true in my head. I push myself to my feet, shaking a little, and follow Hilde back out of the office. Before we slip out the door, I glance one more time over my shoulder at Dr. Cass. She is perched behind her desk, long fingers running over the surface. All the pleasantness that dominated her demeanor a moment ago is gone, replaced by excitement and pure concentration. And it makes me wonder.

What have I done?

Part Two

"SUCCESS IS SIMPLE. PERSISTENCE. PERSEVERANCE. Knowledge. Education never stops. The most successful people continue to learn, continue to innovate, and continue to question what they have to offer and how they can provide it. Wisdom is a moral duty. If we stop learning, progress stops as well."

~ Dr. Joyce Cass
3 Years Ago

10

PROCESSING.

That sign above the door runs chills down my spine. Hilde holds open the door to a sterile room with institutional white walls and cold metal tables and chairs. Industrial-strength cleaner permeates every surface of the space, invading my senses as I step over the threshold. I've never been in a room that felt so … *clean*.

On the table, a set of plain gray scrubs is folded in a neat pile. Beside it is a pair of matching loafers.

"We will give you a moment to change," Hilde says.

I turn, but Hilde is already gone, and the door clicks softly shut. Chewing my lips, I move toward the clothes, inspecting them, picking at the surprisingly soft fibers of the top. *They just need to make sure I'm not bringing contaminants on my clothes, I suppose.* It makes sense, though why they wouldn't make me relinquish my messenger bag doesn't fit the logic.

Oh well. This is what I signed up for.

I set the messenger bag on the table, then strip down and slide into the scrubs. The material is smoother than I expect. Possibly enhanced for sensitive skin by Naturalists. I slip my feet into the loafers and find the insides have a nice cushioned comfort my sneakers didn't provide—like walking on a cloud.

Soon after I finish, two men in white coats and rubber hair caps enter. Both wear goggles and blue rubber gloves. One of them motions toward a chair. I ease into it, hoping they can't see me shaking. The other collects my clothes and discards them in a bag marked with my name. He reaches for my messenger bag.

"No!" I rush over, putting a hand on the bag. "I need the stuff in there." All my research—the last pieces of my life—are in that bag.

"It will be returned to you once it's gone through processing," he says, sliding the bag away.

I wrap the strap around my hand and yank back. "No. It isn't like the bag will contaminate me, and if you send it through processing, it could ruin some of the contents. You can't have the bag."

Something jabs in my neck and my limbs weaken. I stumble back a step, caught by the second lab tech who eases me back into the chair. The metal is so cold it instantly soaks through my clothes. It's hard to tell if the shivering in my bones is from the chill or the uncertainty gripping me. The bag slips from my weak grip.

"It's easier if you cooperate," the second tech says.

I try to protest, but my tongue feels too heavy to talk. I make one last, feeble attempt at getting up but hardly do more than slip awkward hands over the chair's armrests.

The room sways, forcing me to sit back in the seat. The rattle of the metal cart's wheels over the smooth floor echoes loudly in the room. I blink slowly, and my head lolls to the side as the tech wipes my arm with something cold. He slides a device shaped like a giant tube over my right hand. It reaches almost all the way to my elbow. Blue UV light emits from inside the tube, warming my skin.

Sharp pain radiates along the inside of my forearm, burning hot. A scream rises up my throat and comes out as more of a guttural choking than a scream.

What's going on? But the words don't come from my mouth. They only echo in my head.

Something burns red hot through my blood and into my brain, then a shock hits me. My eyes shoot wide, and I grip the chair with my free hand, then my entire body tenses. A moment later it passes, but the heat of the pain remains. Still, I can't keep my eyes open. I blink. Struggle to stay alert. But darkness descends.

§

Whippoorwills croon and the smell of sarsaparilla subtly fills the room as my eyes drift open. Everything is blurry for a moment as I blink to get my bearings. It was all a bad dream. I'm at home, listening to the birds outside my window and smelling the plants that line the street. A warm comfort fills me.

As I sit up on the bed, my feet hit a cold floor. I frown, looking down and wiggling my toes. My room at home has carpet, not tiles.

I smooth my hands over my thighs and raise them, blinking at the lingering smooth, soft sensation on my palms. Grogginess begins to clear as reality sets in.

This isn't home.

These aren't my clothes.

It was all real.

I'm on my feet, turning to take in the room around me. It's boxy with simple furniture—a twin bed and nightstand, desk and chair, and tall narrow bookshelf. My messenger bag is neatly hooked over the back of the chair, and the notebooks are stacked precisely on the bookshelf. The walls of the room… They look like the walls of my bedroom. Tan paint, but barren without any of the traces of my personal touch.

Remembering the pain in my arm earlier, I lift it in front of me, running my left hand over smooth, untouched skin. Not even a trace of a needle mark lingers.

"What happened?" I mutter to myself. And how long was I out?

A chime from the desk makes me jump, and I spin around as the wall behind the desk changes from tan to white. Dr. Cass's hologram appears, visible from the waist up. There's no background, so I can't tell where she is.

"Ugene," she says, her voice coming from above. "Thank you for your patience. We understand that processing can be difficult for some and appreciate your cooperation."

Is that what she calls sticking me with a needle to make me limp as a noodle?

"We pair new subjects with mentors, selected from among our more experienced subjects, to help ease the transition into this new life. Your mentor will arrive soon to show you to the cafeteria, showers, and other facilities available to you. For the integrity of the research, I ask that you stay on your floor and follow the rules your mentor will lay out for you. Your personal researcher will monitor your brain waves, muscular changes, and genes at all times using the nanomonitors injected during processing."

Nanomonitors. So, that's what happened during processing. I knew it had to be something, but I didn't fully understand.

"When necessary, he will escort you to a lab for samples. All your personal belongings have been returned, with the exception of your cellular phone. The signals can interfere with studies some of our other participants are working on, particularly the Naturalists."

That's convenient. Without my phone, I don't have a way to contact my parents. I'm cut off from the rest of the world.

"Testing will begin tomorrow. I hope you are comfortable in your new living space and thank you for joining Paragon Diagnostics."

Dr. Cass disappears, and the wall reverts to its previous tan painted color.

So, I have to stay on this floor, and my only known means of communication with the outside world is gone. I glance around the room, which feels much smaller now.

An alarm resonates loudly overhead, and the door to the room opens, revealing a brightly-lit hallway. Eager to see more, I slip on the provided loafers.

Before I step into the hallway, a guy in identical gray scrubs to my own steps into the doorway, blocking me in. Shaggy blond hair hangs around his face. His gray-blue eyes appear bored as he looks me over critically.

"Ugene?" he asks.

"Yes," I say, taking a step back. "And you are?"

"Miller, your mentor," he grumbles, rubbing his eyes. "And I'm tired, so let's get this over with."

For some reason, it takes that statement for me to notice the dark rings around his eyes. His face is drawn, and his lids are heavy. In fact, he looks almost like my dad when he's hung over. I offer my best smile, but he only grimaces. My stomach twists in knots. I hate feeling like an intruder.

"Come on. I'll show you around." Without waiting for me, Miller heads along the hallway. I rush to catch up, glancing back at the open door of my room and making a note of the number.

The floor is a maze of hallways. Others roughly our age pass along the halls with intent destinations. Everyone wears the same gray scrubs and loafers. I fail to keep track of where we're heading, forget exactly where we turned left or right, but Miller seems to know exactly where he's going. Part of me can't help wondering if he's messing with me, walking in circles to try and confuse me or something, so I start watching the room numbers.

"How many people are on this floor?" I ask as we pass room 1177.

"Don't know." Clearly, Miller isn't much for conversation. "Testing doesn't exactly allow for much socializing. I only know about fifteen or twenty others. But there are more." He points at a door as we pass it. "Bathroom. Showers are in there."

I grimace. What an excellent guide he's turning out to be. Like I'll ever *find* the bathroom when I need it.

We turn another corner and Miller waves absently at a large room with glass-panel walls, revealing rows of round white tables with matching chairs. The cafeteria. Before I know it, he's taken me full circle back to my room.

"Welcome home." He waves into the room. "Looks like you get the night off. Have a nice life."

Night? I thought it was morning. No windows along the tour revealed the truth.

Miller steps away to leave.

"Wait a minute!" I grab his arm before he can slip away, then immediately realize my mistake as his eyes flash narrowly at me. I quickly let go. "I just—You're supposed to be my mentor, teach me the rules and stuff. And is there anyone else on the floor you can introduce me to?"

Miller laughs. Not a funny, ha-ha sort of laugh, but more like you're-an-idiot sort of laugh. What have I done to him?

"Look, kid."

Kid! He can't be more than two or three years older than me! My best guess is twenty.

Miller crosses his arms. "You wanna know the rules? Here they are. Participating in tests is compulsory. Be in your room by testing time and nightly lockdown. No fighting with other test subjects. Obey the commands from Overwatch." He points at the ceiling. "And finally," Miller steps closer, "and this is the most important rule, so remember it. Everyone likes their privacy. No one is looking for friends. We all have a job to do, and we do it. That's it."

"But we are all in this together. Why—?"

"Privacy. If a door is closed, don't knock. If a door's open, don't knock. Just... don't knock."

Miller turns and starts up the hallway.

"Hey, is there a key for my room or something?" I call.

"Why would you need a key?" He laughs before disappearing around the corner.

The response bothers me. Experience tells me that people with Powers—like all the other test subjects in here—like to pick on guys like me. And I can't even lock them out.

Anxious, I inspect my door for a lock and find the thick rods inside the door, but there isn't a knob or anything on the door to engage the bolts into the frame. Experimentally, I close the door and tell it to lock, but nothing happens.

No key, and no way to lock the door. How can anyone expect to have privacy at all?

11

MY STOMACH GRUMBLES. WHEN WAS THE LAST TIME I ate anything? I don't even know how long they knocked me out. I do a quick scan of the room, but there's no clock. No window either.

"How do I know the time?" I ask, not expecting an answer.

"The time is seventeen forty-seven." The female voice comes from overhead. I spin, looking up, but can't spot the speaker. Above me is nothing but a featureless tan space.

My stomach protests again, and I acquiesce, wandering the maze of halls in search of the cafeteria. Again, I pass dozens of rooms just like mine. The same steel door, furniture, and tiles. Some have walls that portray gardens or city streets. Projections just like the tan walls of my own room. Some rooms are occupied. A few still have doors closed. I pass a handful with views out into the city—real views. Obviously, these rooms are on the exterior of the building.

The scent of the food gives away the cafeteria before I stumble into the room. The floor is stark gray tiles, but the walls aren't walls. They project a forest on all but one wall. Birds chirp happily, but it's canned noise meant to be calming, most likely.

One wall reveals the outside world, by my best guess. City lights, skyscrapers, and squat buildings below. The noise doesn't reach us here. Either distance or soundproof walls block out sound from the rest of the city. Is that to protect us or the city?

Close to two dozen round white pedestal tables fill the large, open space. Only a few have occupants in gray shell-backed stacking chairs. None of the people look at me.

On the far side of the room, a series of vending machines. A Drinkables. A Snackables. A Hot-Serve. Everything automated. No chef on this level at all. Not even regular catering service and the trash goes into a shoot that likely takes it to another floor. I inspect the menu options for dinner on Hot-Serve. Chicken wrap, chicken panini, chicken quesadilla, chicken... It's all chicken.

I press the chicken wrap button and the display flashes at me.

IDENTITY UNCONFIRMED.

What does that mean?

I press a finger to the display, but nothing happens.

Glancing over my shoulder covertly, I watch a young woman with cropped brown hair at the Snackables machine hold her wrist in front of the display. A moment later her food comes out. Injected bio-identification? I try the same. The Hot-Serve beeps confirmation and I move on to Drinkables as the machine hums to life.

Hot-Serve machines don't always serve hot food. They were invented before I was born as an alternative to a full kitchen. The idea was to use them in offices so employees could have healthy foods. Except it's all processed. Chemical compounds of proteins, carbs, and vitamins. After selecting, the machine creates the food out of the compounds.

And yet, somehow, people still starve in the streets.

I punch an apple juice button and scan my wrist. A cup drops out and starts filling up. By the time it finishes, the Hot-Serve dings. A cardboard boat waits in the dispenser, cradling a chicken wrap with lettuce, tomato, onion, and sauce. It smells incredible and makes my hunger kick me in the stomach. After taking my prize, I turn and scan the room.

Miller sits alone at a corner table, picking lettuce out of his chicken burger and watching everyone. I wave, but he just blinks, looking right through me.

"He doesn't make friends," the brown-haired girl says, sitting at a table beside where I stand. "I've only ever seen him with one person before, and the guy tested out of the program a couple months back."

"Tested out?" I sit across from her at a table by the windows. Having a view is nice.

She nods. "It's what happens when you complete the program. Paragon kicks you out."

"Then what?"

"Who knows." She picks at her snack absently, keen eyes on me, then holds out a hand. "Jade."

"Ugene," I say, shaking her hand. "He said people don't like making friends."

Jade falls silent, paying too much attention to her oat bar as she plucks out the raisins. I wait for her to say more, but she doesn't. Instead, awkward silence descends over us. I just accept that she doesn't have much more to say and focus on my food. The flavor of chicken explodes against my taste buds as the juice saturates my tongue. Lettuce and tomato accentuate the flavor. Maybe it's just the hunger, but this tastes better than any chicken wrap I've ever had.

Jade has fallen into sullen silence, so I attempt making eye contact with any of the other ten people in the room. These people are here for the same reason as I am, right? So, why not try to make friends. It can't be that bad. But everyone looks at me only when I'm not directly looking at them. I can feel it in the way my skin crawls every time I hear a shift in movement. From the blond guy at the table behind me, or the other three sitting two tables to my right, as they move their heads in another direction the moment mine turns toward them. I want to strike up a conversation, but old habits are hard to break. Instead, I bite my lip and focus on my food. The uneasy feeling rolls up and down my spine. This feels like a prison.

I watch them as I eat. The red-haired girl across the cafeteria sits alone, hunched over her meal and poking at it like she has no desire to eat... or live. The three to my right talk to each other, but their voices are so low it barely sounds like more than a hum. Each of them is making a visible effort not to look in my direction. Two of them—a large Somatic and the other so pale I wonder when he last saw the sun—seem to defer to the third even though he's the smallest of them. With his black hair and the way he perches on his chair, he reminds me of a raven.

I nod toward their table, not really looking at them. "Who are they?" I ask Jade.

Her gaze flits briefly to the trio, and I watch her swallow hard. "Trouble," she says so softly I almost don't hear. "Particularly for you."

"Why me?" The space between my shoulder blades itches as I fight off the urge to look at them.

"He doesn't like you."

They guy doesn't even know me. What could he know about me? And how could Jade know this? Unless… "You're a Telepath."

Jade's eyes meet mine. "Be careful, Ugene." She collects her trash from the table. "You are grossly unprepared for what's coming."

Before I can ask what she means, Jade is marching across the room, giving the trio wide berth.

I turn my attention back to them as she disappears into the hallway.

I don't understand any of what's going on here. Everyone looks like they are an inch from death. A few look like they would even welcome death. And for no apparent reason, I already have an enemy.

My appetite is gone. I get up and head back to my room for one of my journals and a pen. My loafers squeak on the polished gray tiled floor with each step. I need a firm handle on my surroundings. And that starts by mapping out my new home.

The adventure begins by looking for a map on the wall, or something to give me a general lay of the land. Even just arrows on the walls pointing room numbers one way or the other, or guidance toward emergency exits. But there's nothing. The walls are stark white, ordinary.

The floor is a maze, but I do my best to navigate the halls and draw a map of them as I go. Recognizable doors I mark on the map. Bathroom. Rec room (a few chairs and sofas; a holotv that only plays one channel). Library (occupied only by books, a couple of padded armchairs, and small round tables).

In the middle of the floor, a large, dome-shaped room with only two doors on opposite sides. The place is unoccupied, plain, just like everything else. I set down my notebook and brush my hand on the wall. It's as smooth as glass.

"Curious," I mutter.

The alarm chimes once, followed by a soothing female voice from overhead. Overwatch, Miller called her. "Evening lockdown in ten minutes. Please, return to your rooms."

Frowning, I step back from the wall and pick up my notebook, then head out to finish mapping. I still have a few minutes.

Only one bank of elevators is on the entire floor. Three main stairwells lead off the floor, but the doors have no handles and no window into the stairs. What would happen if a fire broke out on the floor? How would we open the doors? Or maybe they would open on their own.

Except for the rooms. Some of them, anyway. The ones on the exterior of the building offering views of Elpis. We are in Paragon Tower, in the heart of the city.

I pause a moment outside the elevator and slowly turn around, looking again for a map of the floor or some directional signal. Nothing. Just white walls and gray tiles. The elevator doors are stainless steel like the room doors.

After a moment of biting my lip, I push the button for the elevator. I'm not supposed to leave the floor, but what will happen if I do? The elevator doesn't respond. A light comes on, but no sound of movement comes from the elevator shaft. I push again.

"What're you doin'?"

I jump at the sound of Miller behind me, spinning to face him, journal clutched tight against my chest. The soft hum of the elevator resounds from behind the closed door.

Miller snorts. "You aren't the brightest, are you?"

The question makes me frown.

"Five minutes until evening lockdown," Overwatch says.

"Go back to your room, kid. You don't wanna get caught in the hallway after lockdown."

"But—"

"Go. Now." The edge in his tone makes me confident he means business.

I clutch my notebook to my chest and slip past him.

After turning the corner into the next hall, I can hear Miller's muffled voice. The words are indistinct, but he clearly is arguing with someone else. Part of me wants to go back and investigate. Part of me is afraid.

Sadly, fear wins out.

12

SLEEP IS FITFUL. I DREAM OF MOM TRYING TO CONVINCE me to come home. Dad telling me how much of a disappointment I am and how I can never listen. Jade tells me the raven perched on a cafeteria table wants to peck out my eyes. As it attacks, Miller stands over me with his arms crossed, telling me he warned me, but I'm too thick to obey. I wake up screaming, sweat beading on my forehead.

"Good morning Ugene," Overwatch says as the lights come on, revealing tan walls like home again. "Your scheduled testing will commence in thirty minutes. Please proceed to the cafeteria for breakfast, then return to your room. Participation in testing is compulsory."

The lock on the door slides and the door swings open. I grab my shirt and pull it on, then slip into the loafers and obediently head toward the cafeteria with the other test subjects.

The cafeteria is crowded this morning. Close to fifty other test subjects shuffle along the line to get food, then move to a table. With so many, there's no choice but to sit with someone else.

I hold my food and glance around the room. Miller is alone, and I notice no one else makes a move to sit with him. Jade is at another table, but all the seats are taken. The Trouble Trio she warned me about are near Miller, but I don't dare sit in the open chair at their table. With little choice, I set my things on Miller's table and sit. He doesn't even glance up at me.

"Do you need something?" he asks.

"Just a chair," I say, shifting to see out the window. "We don't have to talk, but I do need to sit."

Miller's lips thin as he pokes at his eggs with a disposable fork.

As I eat, I gaze out the window. It's hard to tell exactly how high up we are—my guess would be floor 100 or 101 based on the room numbers—but it's high enough that I can see beyond the limits of Elpis to what remains of the world.

Broken and crumbling homes, highways, factories. Dead trees. Brown grass. The War between those with Powers and those without destroyed everything. When Atmos lost control of his Atmokinesis Power, nuclear power plants lost control all around the world. Billions died when they blew up or leaked, creating full-scale nuclear destruction of cities, towns, and life as it was known.

Elpis rose from the ashes of ruin, the last bastion of hope for our world. At the foundation of the city, Powered people worked together to heal the ruined soil and rebuild a safe zone. For the first few years, people trickled in from the world beyond the city. Eventually, it stopped. Only those with Powers remained; the survivors of our race.

No one knows what happened to the rest of the world. No one outside Elpis ever made contact once refugees stopped coming, so it's hard to say if anything else even exists. I find it hard to accept that we are all that is left of humanity.

Miller breaks through my pensive silence. "Where's the fire?"

"What?"

He waves an empty fork at me. "You're thinking hard about something."

"Well… just the War."

Miller harrumphs, gazing out the window. "It's the excuse they use for Proposition 8.5."

My gaze snaps back to him. "You know about it?"

"You don't?"

"I… a little, I guess." Maybe he can enlighten me. "Just that people with weak Powers will have to be retested."

Miller snorts. "Most of the people here would fall under the purview of the law." He takes a drink of juice, then tosses the empty cup onto his plate. "The powers that be believe that we are going backward, and if we lose our Powers we won't survive. No more fixing the soil or building up new structures for growth. No more moving forward. They're using fear of regression and complete societal failure as an excuse to force people into this testing so they can get answers." He waves around the room. "And if you aren't useful, you're worthless."

"What's wrong with the testing here?"

Miller gives me a flat stare, then gathers his trash and stands. "Better finish up and get to your room on time for testing."

I watch Miller leave, then look out at the land beyond again. What if everyone else is right, though? What if society can't survive without Powers to save us? What if I'm both the problem and the cure?

My room feels oddly comforting. I sit on the edge of my bed, staring at the hallway, thinking about what Miller said. The door suddenly swings shut, and the bolt clangs into place.

"Please stand on the simulation platform. Testing shall commence in ten seconds," Overwatch says. "Participation is compulsory."

A group of tiles in a five-by-five square turn red, pulsing with light.

Chest pounding, I shuffle forward onto the red light.

The walls of the room are no longer there. Everything that was my room blinks out of existence, replaced by a doorway carved into a glass-panel wall.

"Step through the doorway, Ugene, and I will guide you through the test," a male voice commands from overhead, and something familiar about it itches at my mind.

I step through, trembling.

The room is a white dome. Two other test subjects in their gray scrubs are the only color in the room. They both stare at me, eyes wide with fear. One—a short girl with long black hair—cradles her arms over her chest, shaking. The other—a young man with a chubby face and sunken eyes—holds his hands in fat fists at his sides. No one moves.

Forrest Pond, Bianca's older brother, appears between us and the other two take a cowering step back.

Forrest has worked at Paragon for four years now, to my knowledge. It makes sense that Dr. Cass would pair me with him. Not only is Forrest brilliant, but he's familiar. I never heard what his official Divinic rank was, but my guess would be pretty high to score this job so young.

"Use the materials given and your Powers to create this," Forrest says, holding up his palm. A holographic image of a dense rainforest appears. "The rainforest must reach at least seventy-five percent viability to complete the test. Testing will not end until the task is completed. Some materials have limited availability, so use your resources wisely. Again, testing will not end until you successfully complete the task, no matter how long it takes. Participation is compulsory. Begin."

Forrest disappears. The room transforms into the dead remains of a rainforest in the blink of my eyes. Trees with dead bark and no leaves. Brittle brush dry as tumbleweeds. Spotty patches of water. The smell of something like rotting fish fills the air. The girl gags, losing part of her breakfast on the dry ground.

Create a rainforest out of this? What is the goal here? I have no idea what Paragon is after, and I have no Powers. I can't do this alone. I can't do this at all. But there's no way I'm just supposed to sit back and wait for the other two to do all the work—nor would I feel good about it.

The other two are wandering in opposite directions, setting to work. Their Powers aren't terribly effective. I can't be sure what either can do, but as every time one revitalizes a section, the dead space around it closes in and destroys their work. I'm not the only one who can't do this alone. It's evident to me that their Powers aren't going to be sufficient on their own.

Unsure what else to do, I take some time wandering the space between them, examining what could be useful as resources. Forrest said there's something. Maybe one of these two can identify those resources.

Deciding that I need to know who I'm working with, I approach the boy first. He takes several quick and ill-placed steps backward, tripping over a dead tree root and tumbling to his back.

"It's okay," I say, holding out a hand to help him up. "I'm Ugene."

His eyes narrow as he considers whether to take my hand, but resignation takes over. He slips a hand in mine, and I help haul him to his feet.

He brushes the dirt off his scrubs and says, "Boyd. Wh-what's your-your…"

"Power? I don't have one."

Boyd's sunken eyes suddenly come to life as they widen in shock. "None?"

I shake my head. "You?"

"Tran-transmutation. E-energy."

Useful. Boyd can transform matter into related energy.

"You don't have to be afraid of me," I reassure him. "Maybe we can work together on this."

"Together?" Boyd shakes his head. "No. We aren't supposed to…"

"Why?"

"I…" Boyd suddenly appears uncertain. "I don't kn-know."

"Well there's no way Forrest honestly thinks I can do anything in here," I say, motioning to the dead landscape around us. "Which could only mean one thing."

Boyd appears thoughtful, then nods.

I turn to the girl, who is pressing a hand to the trunk of one of the trees. "What about you?" I call over. "What's your Power?"

She flashes me a dangerous look, then disappears around a tree. I squint through the bramble and see her in flashes as she moves from one tree to the next.

"What's her problem?" I mutter.

"E-enid doesn't like people," Boyd says.

"Why?"

"Everyone ha-has their rea-reasons," Boyd says it so matter-of-factly that I can't help but agree.

"So what can she do?"

"Env-environmental Cre-cre-creation." Boyd struggles with each word, and I wonder how long he's had the stutter. And why no one has helped him overcome it.

"Enid!" I call out, jogging in her direction as her form darts between trees. Boyd's loafers scuff the ground as he tries to keep up. "Wait, we can work together."

"Leave me alone!" she calls from behind a tree.

A loud pop shakes the floor, followed by the crackling of breaking tree branches and bramble. I look up just in time to see the tree falling directly toward Boyd and me. With a yelp, I throw my weight against Boyd, and the two of us roll across the ground, twigs, and rocks cutting our skin. Before we have a chance to recover, another falls right beside it.

"Move," I say, grabbing the back of Boyd's shirt as our loafers scramble away. They were too close to be a coincidence. "Enid, stop!"

"Leave me alone," she says again.

What is her problem?

"But if we—"

The roots shoot up out of the ground around us, forming a cage over Boyd and me. The roots are old and brittle, but too thick for me to break no matter how hard I tug. Why is she doing this?

Enid steps around the fallen trees and prowls closer. "Stay out of my way, and we won't have a problem."

"Enid, we need each other to finish this test," I plead, but she doesn't care. She's no longer cowering and shaking. Enid stands straight—though a bit short—her palms turned outward toward the cage.

"I don't need anyone." Desperation clings to her voice. "This is my test. I will finish it alone."

"Enid, please!"

But she's already walking away.

"Resources are limited," I call after her. "That's what Forrest said. You're using up resources you need. Boyd can help you restore the rainforest."

"I don't need anyone!" Her small voice echoes off the dead trees.

The ground rattles and little by little green color returns to the ground as Enid pumps her Power into the earth. But the earth fights back, refusing to accept her renewal. She can't do this by herself. None of us can.

The cage around us grows from the ground, the roots of the trees around us. It isn't terribly significant. Just big enough to give us space to stretch out our legs in front of us but not enough to lay or stand. The bars are not evenly spaced. I shift toward one of the larger gaps and try to squeeze my slim body through, but it's just barely too narrow. A quick scan of the ground doesn't reveal anything useful to break the bars, and I can't reach far enough out to grab anything of use. It's an efficient cage, and I'm powerless to escape.

I turn to Boyd.

"You okay?" I ask, seeing him cradling his left arm.

"I think it bro-broke."

"Okay."

I kneel beside him and gingerly press my fingers to his forearm for a distinct break. Tears roll down Boyd's cheeks, but he doesn't make a sound. His arm is swelling, but I can't feel any noticeable breaks. "I'm not sure if it's broke. It might just be sprained. Here."

I dig at the bark on the branch closest to us until a long strip comes free, then place his arm against the smooth inside of the bark. Without any vines around, the only thing we have to create a sling is our clothes. I pull off my shirt, rip the fabric to make it longer, and form a sling to cradle Boyd's arm against his chest.

"Sm-sm-smart," Boyd mumbles.

"You don't need Powers to have brains," I say, helping him to his feet. We have to hunch over in the cage. It won't be long before our muscles cramp up in this space. We need out. "Can you do anything about these roots? Even just one or two so we can slip out."

He shakes his head.

"What about their energy? Do the roots have enough energy for you to manipulate and break them?"

Boyd doesn't respond. He stands, hunched, holding his sling, staring at the branches as tears wet his cheeks and sweat beads his forehead.

"I do-don't," he gasps.

A high-pitched scream shatters the air and all the green that had crept across the forest floor retreats. Gone.

Enid.

"We need to get out of here." I kneel in front of Boyd, hoping he can sense the urgency. "Can you do anything at all about these roots?"

"I don't think so."

What kind of testing was this?

"Boyd, listen to me. Something is happening to her. The testing won't end until we complete the assignment, and we need her to do it. You have to get us out."

Boyd nods reluctantly, then returns his attention to the bars of the wooden cage. If the branches weren't so thick, I would just break them, but at nearly six inches around, there's no way I could get through without a knife or ax.

Sweat rolls down Boyd's forehead as he pours his Power into his task. I hold my breath, hoping beyond hope that he will succeed. A branch cracks. I grin and throw my weight against it. It takes a couple of attempts, but eventually the root snaps like a twig. I offer Boyd a hand to help him out of the narrow space. I slip through easily enough, but it's a tighter fit for him.

"Enid!" I call out, headed in the direction she disappeared. She couldn't have gone too far.

I run, and even though my feet occasionally slip on the ground, Boyd has a hard time keeping up.

Some of the trees have thorns that look more like twisted horns, and more than a few lean half-out of the ground. I try to give these the widest berth, with no desire to impale myself on one of them in my haste.

Enid's cries guide me as I draw closer until a clearing opens among the trees. Enid is pinned down on one knee, her calf pierced by one of the thorny trees that fell. Unlike the others, this one is green beneath the thorns.

"Leave me!" Enid cries, pushing me away with one hand feebly as I move around her to inspect the damage.

"Be still, Enid." I can't grab the tree to and hoist it up without sticking myself and doing so would risk further damage to her calf. Right now, it only looks like two of the thorns found a way into her leg. A couple more scraped her skin. "We have to move the tree."

"No." She breathes out the word. Tears stream down her cheeks. She searches the sky above and calls out. "I failed the test. Let me out."

"Fine, just relax." I search for a branch thick enough to wedge under the trunk.

"I can't do it! Please!" she calls out to the sky—to Overwatch. Is Forrest watching all of this?

A branch pokes out of dried up brush. It isn't as thick as I would like, but it's long enough and will have to do. As I carefully wedge it under the tree close to her leg, Enid cries and pleads for me to stop, for someone to come get her, for the end of the test. I wrap both arms around the branch and pull, but it barely moves. Boyd moves to help, but I wave him back.

"When I pull it clear you need to help her slip out quick," I tell him. "I won't be able to hold it long."

Muscles. Something I never really had, but now really wish I did. I wrap my arms around the branch again and hug it close this time, hanging my weight from it and dangling above the ground.

Enid screams as the thorns pull out of her calf, and Boyd awkwardly uses one hand to pull her out. The whole trunk shifts. The branch snaps. My back hits the unforgiving ground, knocking the air out of my lungs. My head hits the ground hard enough to make my vision momentarily go black.

I roll on my side, rubbing all the sore spots. Enid and Boyd both lay on the ground, staring at the sky. Both injured. Why would Paragon let something like this happen?

13

AFTER TEARING OFF THE LEG OF ENID'S PANTS AT THE knee and inspecting the wound, I wrap it in the cloth, then the three of us lean against the trunk of a massive tree, staring at the dead land around us. Mist falls on us, making our clothes stick to our skin. The scent of wet dirt fills the air. Mist... I sit up and look toward the ceiling—it is a ceiling after all—and realize we are supposed to revive this rainforest. If water is already here, we just have to convert the energy to bring it back to life.

"You didn't leave me," Enid says in a small voice, staring straight ahead.

"Why would I?"

"Everyone does." She looks over at Boyd, who has his eyes closed, though I know he isn't sleeping. "You helped us both. Why?"

I don't understand the question. Helping is just what people do. It's what my mother taught me, and my dad instilled in me. "I don't really understand what's going on here, but I do know one thing. This test requires both of you." I pick up what looks like an orange almond shell and chuck it at one of the loathsome spiked trees. "I'm the one who doesn't have anything to offer. Why am I here?"

What good does my presence do in a test like this? Maybe Forrest is hoping a Power will just spontaneously pop out. Good luck with that.

"What can you do?" Enid asks, brushing tears from her cheeks. Or is that mist? I can't tell.

"Nothing."

For the first time, she looks at me—just like everyone else, examining, weighing.

"My rank is a fraction of a decimal," I explain. "And I'm pretty sure that fraction is only there because I used my brain quite a bit to problem solve out of Testing Day. I barely survived."

Enid shifts her leg and winces. "My Testing Day was horrific. And I only ranked at 28."

Not nearly enough to fix this forest alone. Silence falls, and I can hear the chirping of birds somewhere in the distance.

"Maybe that's your job," Enid says. At my questioning look, she pokes at my head. "Brains."

I chuckle. "Maybe." But somehow, I doubt Paragon brought me here to test my intelligence. They want something else from me, something that will save everyone, according to Dr. Cass.

An alarm sounds once. I frown up into the mist. "What was that?"

"We missed lunch," Boyd mumbles.

How? We haven't been here that long.

"Time passes differently in the tests," Enid explains at seeing my confused expression. "I don't get how, but it does. If we don't finish soon, we'll miss dinner, too."

"What happens if we don't finish by lockdown?" I ask, hefting another orange almond shell in my hand.

Enid shivers and rubs her arms. I stare at her, waiting for an answer, but she won't look at me.

Finally, Boyd sighs and shifts into a straighter position. "We won't be let out until morning, even if we finish."

Stuck in this all night? "What's the longest you've been in a test?"

"Four days." The answer is a whisper from Enid.

I grimace at the shell in my hand, turning it over. The orange color is more vivid, alive, as the mist coats it. I scramble to my feet, holding the shell toward them.

"This is it."

Boyd's thick brows pull together. Enid rolls her eyes.

"Enid, what do you need to create an environment?" I ask, thrusting the shell toward her, because it isn't a shell, as I'd thought initially. It's a nut.

"Similar energy," she says, shifting so she can stand. The motion is obviously painful, and she leans against the tree for support, but she clearly understands where I'm going. A nut would contain similar matter to the tree it fell from.

"And Boyd, you need matter that can convert into similar energy." I pinch the nut between thumb and middle finger, holding it toward him. "What could be more similar than a living nut from the same trees in the forest? You can use the matter from this nut to create energy that Enid can use to revive the rainforest."

Boyd stands, taking the nut from my hand. After a moment, he smiles brightly at me. "Yes! I can feel it!"

The plan quickly comes together. It's a simple one, but it will take a fair amount of time with their weak Powers. Plant the seed, convert the energy, revive the forest.

Once the first seed is planted and the energy dispersed, Boyd and I stand by and watch Enid struggle to bring it to life. The mist wets the soil, bringing up a rich scent the longer Enid focuses her Power on the seed. It isn't until the colors spread outward from that spot, giving all the plants within two feet new life that I realize I'm holding my breath. Boyd and I both let out a whoop of victory. Then, we move on to the next seed.

I gather as many different nuts as I can find, then use a stick to dig a hole and plant them in the ground. Boyd converts the matter from the nut into energy. Then Enid uses that energy to transform the environment one seed at a time. The entire process takes quite a long time. Digging, planting, energizing, reviving. Over and over in a two-foot square grid.

Sweat and mist mingle on my forehead, and I swipe it away before it can reach my eyes. The motion leaves a trail of dirt on my skin, but it doesn't matter. We need to finish this. Hunger begins to gnaw at my stomach, and I gaze back at Boyd as he works his Energy Transmutation Power on the last seed I planted. His face is drawn, and sunken eyes are ringed with circles of exhaustion. A glance at Enid reveals the same. This work is draining them faster than it is me.

I sit back on my heels and look around the forest. The work is nearly done, but for the first time, I wonder if the two of them have the Power to finish the job. Enid is no longer hopping from one seed to the next but dragging the injured leg along and daring to put her weight on it a little. Boyd's arm is turning black and blue from the swelling and injury, and I'm worried about necrosis, nerve damage, or blood clots causing him severe and long-term trouble. He needs proper healing.

Not for the first time today, I wonder why Paragon lets this happen. What do they really stand to gain by allowing the participants to deal with injuries like this? It's all a simulation. What if the injuries aren't real? I run a finger over the scratches on my elbow from where I fell earlier in the day. They certainly feel real.

Boyd collapses on the ground. I spring to my feet and rush to his side, checking his pulse like Mr. Springer taught me. Is it just my imagination, or is his pulse slow? I don't know how to tell.

Enid shuffles over, and I notice she is supporting her weight on a large branch she uses as a crutch. "We need to wake him. We have to finish."

I shake my head. "He needs rest. The injury and the use of his Powers are draining him. There's only one way to recharge."

Enid yelps as she lowers herself down on her good knee and slaps Boyd's cheek.

"What are you doing!" I push her arm away.

Boyd's eyes flutter.

"We're running out of time," she says, and the exhaustion is clear in her tone. "I'm tired, too, but if we don't finish soon, we won't get out on time."

"You both need rest."

"She's right," Boyd mumbles.

"No, she's not."

Boyd pushes himself up slowly, cautiously, despite my protests.

What's wrong with these two? We can eat here if we need to—there must be something we can forage—but they can't do this to themselves. What if we end up here overnight? What's the worst that could happen?

I move to stop Boyd, but Enid grabs my wrist tight in her hand.

"You don't understand, Ugene." There's a madness in her eyes. "We have to finish before lockdown." No. Not madness. Desperation. "We have to."

I open my mouth to protest, not understanding the urgency, but there's no point in arguing. Both of them are already at work again, and if I refuse to plant more seeds until they rest, they will just do it themselves. It isn't like they really need me to finish this. Grumbling my complaints to myself, I return to the task, planting the last few seeds and keeping a careful eye on my companions.

When Boyd completes the last seed, he drops to the ground and leans his head against a tree, closing his eyes. Not long after, Enid finishes. The rainforest looks like it did in the hologram Forrest showed us, or at least near enough.

I sit beside Enid, who is checking her bandages, her eyes giving away the exhaustion she stubbornly attempts hiding. Boyd hasn't moved since he sat, but his breathing is even, so I'm not too worried.

I roll my head against the tree trunk toward Enid. "When this is over, you can find me—"

The rainforest disappears. As do both my companions.

"Testing complete," Overwatch's voice announces as the lights come on.

Instead of sitting on the forest floor, I'm on the floor of my room with my back pressed against the side of the desk. The only remnants of the test are the dirt on my pants, loafers, and hands. The lock on the door grinds, and the door swings open.

"Forrest," I call, wondering if he is listening right now. "I have a few questions for you."

Overwatch responds overhead, "I am here to assist you in any way I can. What questions do you have?"

Why is Overwatch the one responding? I frown and push myself to my feet. "Where are my companions from the test?"

"Unknown."

"Their names are Boyd and Enid. Both Naturalists. Both test subjects. What rooms are they in?"

"Unknown."

I don't for a second buy that Overwatch doesn't know. She controls the whole floor. "I need to speak with Forrest Pond."

"Dr. Pond is unavailable at this time, but I will notify him of your request. Are you in immediate danger?"

"No." I clench my hands into fists. "Just tell him I wanna talk." Unavailable. That's convenient.

"Message sent."

"How long until lockdown?"

"There are two hours and sixteen minutes remaining until nightly lockdown."

Enough time to shower, change, eat, and find them myself.

14

THE HOT SHOWER FEELS SO GOOD AGAINST MY SKIN. I scrub away the layers of dirt and sweat before toweling off and grabbing a fresh set of scrubs from the neatly organized stacks in the bathroom. Unsure what else to do with them, I toss the dirty clothes into a bin containing other laundry, hoping that will take care of it. Once I scrub the dirt from my loafers, I slide them on and head to the cafeteria for food. The sound of my growling stomach echoes in the hallway. Or maybe that's just my imagination.

Some of the doors are closed. How many are stuck in tests? Why were Boyd and Enid so determined to exhaust themselves versus staying in the rainforest overnight?

As I step into the cafeteria, I do a quick scan for the other two. Surely they will be here getting food, too. But they aren't.

Miller, however, is sitting in his usual corner table by the windows. As soon as I enter, he sits up straighter and quickly looks away. I bite the inside of my lip to keep from smirking. No matter what he says, he cares.

I make my selections and sit at an empty table next to his, giving him his distance but remaining close enough to feel some form of companionship. After that test, I need it.

"Survived your first day, I see," Miller says casually, picking at his grapes as he watches the night sky out the window.

"Was it really in question?" I tease. I rest my elbows on the table and wince as pain shoots through my forearm. I move my arm and see the scratches inflicted during the test. Everything ached during the shower, so I didn't really notice them in my haste to get clean. But it's apparent to me now. The entire test was run under simulation, but the injuries incurred during testing are real.

Silence.

I wolf down the food, starving after missing lunch. It doesn't even matter what I'm eating. I eat it too fast to taste anything.

I glance again at the door, wondering if either of the other two will walk through. No one does. Were they real? What if my test was really just to find a way to complete the simulation, and Boyd and Enid were fake proxies created for the construct just like the mist or the trees? Maybe their warnings about being there overnight were just pressures to get me to complete the test faster, lies created by the simulation to push me on.

"You ever do a test with someone else?" I ask Miller.

"Sometimes."

"Ever with anyone you know, though?"

Did his pallor just change? Miller chews a grape thoughtfully as he watches me. "Sometimes."

"What happens if you're in a test overnight?"

Miller grabs his grapes and stands, patting me on the shoulder as he passes. "Good to see you made it through day one. Good luck tomorrow."

Well, that wasn't helpful. I finish the last of my food and head to my room to collect my notebook. If I want to know what's going on in Paragon, I need to break a few of Miller's house rules.

Everything is quiet, which is pretty ordinary no matter what time of day it is. There's never a lot of conversation going on around these halls, nor a lot of foot traffic. I need names and abilities to go with the faces—and I need to find Boyd and Enid, to verify they are real. Nearly a hundred rooms are on this floor, and I have this sinking feeling a lot of them are occupied. The question is, by whom?

I start with the open doors. A few people just close the door in my face. One girl introduces herself as Madison, but she won't say more. For some reason, no one seems eager to talk to me. And after covering an entire hallway with about twenty doors, I still haven't found Boyd or Enid.

The next door I try slides open at my knock and the Raven—who glares at me in the cafeteria regularly—sneers. His gaze sweeps over me like I'm a caveman who just climbed out of the underground. "Powerless prick. Get lost."

My jaw twitches. I'm the prick?

Then his expression darkens, focus on me intensifying.

I instinctively step back. *Psionic Telepath.*

He doesn't need to say it. I've seen that look enough to know better. He reminds me so much of one of the Telepathic bullies at school.

The corner of the Raven's mouth curls up in a cruel smirk, and another guy steps up and towers over his shoulder. The pale Somatic who sits in the cafeteria with the Raven—and the brand on his bulging arm confirms his Branch. I don't need to ask. He's most likely got Enhanced Strength, a Strongarm. It's a common pairing I've seen before. Telepaths and Strongarms. The hunter and his weapon.

And I know enough about the pairing to realize it's time to go.

"Sorry," I mutter, then move away from the door.

As I disappear safely around the corner into another hallway, I can hear the Somatic speak in his deep voice.

"He gonna be trouble, Terry? I can deal with it now before it happens."

"No," Terry says. "We have bigger problems."

I make a note on the map of his room. *Terry: Telepath.* I know better than to knock there again.

I move on to another room.

"I'm just trying to get to know my neighbors," I tell the guy with a square jaw after he asks why I care who he is or what his ability is.

The door closes in my face, but not before I catch a glimpse of the Naturalist brand on his hand.

This happens several times. A few people I can easily classify as Somatic just by their build, though I don't know what their particular specialty is. Some are more conversational than others, but still not terribly forthcoming. A few know who I am but won't tell me anything about themselves.

Despite the secretive nature of most of the subjects, I'm collecting data. One thing is already abundantly clear: only four Divinics—identified by their brands—are being subjected to testing. Why? And where are Boyd and Enid?

"What are you doing, kid?" Miller asks, strolling up the hallway.

"Getting to know the neighborhood." Let him call me out for it. I don't care.

Miller laughs. "How's that going?"

"Not well, but I have a few written—"

Miller takes the map out of my hands and scans it, shaking his head. "You never learn. Just looking for trouble." He glances up and down the hallway, then leans closer. "Be careful whose door you knock on, kid. The rules exist to protect you."

"I'm sure they do," I mutter.

But I don't think the rules truly exist to protect me from the other test subjects. Paragon created the rules, which means for some reason they want us to avoid each other. It doesn't make sense.

I snatch the notebook back from Miller's hands. "'Night."

Miller gives a sharp salute and strolls away.

Frustration sets in, and I am considering putting the project aside for the night when a set of eyes through the crack in a nearby door stalls my steps. I turn to see a thin young woman with unkempt, black hair peering out at me. I recognize her face from another time when I was wandering this hallway when she sneaks to the bathroom or cafeteria.

There's something about the way this girl watches the hallway, sharp and anxious, that piques my curiosity. She tips her head out for just a second before ducking back in.

"Sorry if I interrupted your sleep," I say.

"Not sleeping," she mumbles. "Perching. Watching stars."

I am more than a little surprised when she opens her door.

"Come witness." Her green eyes are dull and sunken and sleep-deprived like everyone else.

This girl is the first person to invite me into her room, and I'm ashamed to admit it makes me hesitate. How do I know I can trust her? I've hardly seen her. Against my better judgment, I nod and step past her through the narrow opening, closing the door behind me.

It's dark in her room. The only illumination comes from thousands of lights on buildings across the city, shining in through the window-wall. It's still easy to tell this is a standard room. Her bed is against a different wall, and the bookcase is stuffed in the corner beside the bed. Her desk is against the wall opposite the bed. This arrangement makes way for a clear footpath along the window. And the room is spotless. All the books on her shelf are organized by size, and a few bins are stuffed in with labels on them. Odds and Ends. These and Those. The desk is immaculate. The bed made. And the smell. Clean, like fresh lemon cleaner. It reminds me of my mother, of home.

"Powerless participant," she says in a quiet voice as if afraid someone will overhear. Maybe she's right. Overwatch seems to hear everything.

I only nod, taking in the view.

"Bearing flesh of the night," she says.

Her cold, dry hand slips into mine, and she looks at me, her green eyes now shining bright. It's like something unknown is pumping life back into her. "Witness." She pulls me toward the massive glass window wall.

The city is alive, and I have almost forgotten how beautiful it is. Everything twinkles with light. I place my other hand against the window and lean toward it, looking down. So far down. Life goes on. Car headlights and taillights crawl along the streets. Herds of people go about their evening, a congealed mass of shadowy forms and dark colors from this distance, completely unaware of what is happening high above them in this skyscraper.

I was one of them once. One of the herd who walked past this building, looking at it with hope because I believed the research was for the benefit of all of mankind. The reality may not be what I imagined.

My breath collects on the glass, forming small rings with each exhale. If I had a view like this in my room, I might not be so terrified of the confinement.

"The stars are beauty in the sky," she says. "They ebb and shift but never change."

My gaze turns upward, but the lights from the city are too bright for the stars to shine through. Not a single star reveals itself. "I can't see them."

Her free hand touches my temple. It's warmer than the one in my hand. Something about her is different. As if our touch creates a connection.

"Witness."

I turn my gaze to the sky. The lights of the city become dull compared to the brilliance of the stars shining. A breath of awe slips from my mouth. I can't remember ever seeing anything so majestic. And it isn't just the stars. It's the colors. Various shades of blues and purples and blacks swirl around the stars, propelled away from them with motion so hypnotizing I can't look elsewhere. No words exist for such beauty.

This girl is a Divinic—amazingly, powerfully, beautifully Divinic. Only a Divinic could do this.

The two of us stand in silence, watching the stars and swirling sky. The hand she placed in mine grows warmer the longer we stand there. Her head rests against my shoulder. Like an embrace. Time seems to fade, and it's just her and I and the sky.

I could stay here forever, but the shaking of her tiny frame brushes against mine, breaking the trance. I blink and look at her.

Vibrant green eyes stare at my expression, but her skin has grown paler, ghost-like. It's me. Whatever she's doing by touching my temple, it's hurting her.

I gently take her hand away from my temple and lower it.

"Don't hurt yourself for me," I say.

"Celeste."

"What?"

She puts a hand to her chest, and I can just see the edge of the Divinic brand over her heart peeking out of the V-neck cut of the scrubs top as it shifts. "Celeste."

The irony of her name pulls out a small chuckle. "Does the world always look like that to you? So…"

"Wondrous?" Celeste smiles weakly, then looks out again. "The sky. An ebb and shift of color, but never changing."

"You're Divinic." I'm an idiot for stating the obvious.

"The walls whisper your name in esteem."

Walls whisper. Does that mean she hears people speak highly of me? Why?

"You don't know me," I tease back, looking at the now drab lights of the city. The night sky's brilliance is gone, and without it, the city is flat. "I'm bad news."

Celeste cocks her head in a bird-like manner and peers through squinted eyes—dull again—then shakes her head. "No. I see what others can't in depth, and yours is like a light."

"My name is Ugene." I glance at the window again, seeking distraction.

"Irony is for those who lack imagination," Celeste says from a couple of feet behind me.

I have to turn to see her face. In the dark, only the highlights of her pale features are evident through the mess of black hair.

She crosses her legs on the bed and rests her hands gently in her lap. "People are not defined by Power, but by how they rise and inspire."

"Inspire." I snort. "I wouldn't call myself an inspiration."

"Time is in constant flux."

"You can read auras." I stuff my hands into my pockets, uncertain what else to do with them.

She nods as if she knew the question before I even asked it.

"When did you come here?"

She cocks her head as if she doesn't understand the question.

"How long have you been at Paragon?"

Celeste glances around her room, holding a finger to her lips, then looks back at the stars I can no longer see. "Mysteries. There were parents. An accident. Sixth grade. I don't... don't remember the mysteries. The night... They died under stars. I bore witness before."

"So, you can foretell." I pick up a snow globe from the desk and shake it.

She shakes her head. "I bear witness to all at all times. Not futures or pasts. All. The flash of red and blue in tandem. Faces with light and without. Here." Her hand waves around the room.

Sixth grade and they snatched her up? There's still a dull, youthful glow about her. She's younger than me.

"The sun has courted the moon three times. The moon has shown anger at the sun four, but they danced thirty-seven other times." She turns her gaze toward the sky. "The moon will be angry again soon."

A riddle. I'm starting to notice most of what she says comes out in riddles. I like puzzles, and immediately start doing the math. If Celeste is referring to the sun courting the moon, she may mean a total solar eclipse, which happens about every eighteen months. And the anger of the moon makes me think of the red moon, a total lunar eclipse. There have been four in my recollection in the last three years. If she was twelve when she first came in, that makes her, Christ, only fifteen, possibly sixteen.

"What do you do in the tests?" I ask.

"Nothing." The answer is so innocent it makes my head spin a little. "The nice man with white teeth comes with gloves each cycle. He brings me candy."

I see the jar of hard candies in the glass container on the bookshelf. "May I?"

Celeste nods, and I walk over, taking one from the jar and popping it in my mouth. The caramel flavor melts against my tongue. The tension slowly eases from my shoulders.

"Why don't you come out of the room more often?" I ask, stuffing the candy into my cheek with my tongue.

Celeste leans toward me and whispers, "Their eyes are globes. They see only death."

I frown. What does that mean? I try to puzzle it out, but exhaustion must be kicking in. It's hard to grasp my thoughts for more than a second before they drift off.

I stay in the room with her until my eyelids get heavy and Overwatch announces the approach of nightly lockdown. Neither of us speaks. We just sit together and enjoy the view, as if it were the most natural thing in the world to be together.

Celeste is by far the most fascinating person I've met since arriving at Paragon, and for the first time in years, I feel ordinary.

15

I FALL ASLEEP THE MOMENT MY HEAD HITS THE PILLOW, even before my door locks down for the night. The dreams come in swirls of color similar to the sky Celeste showed me. Boyd and Enid, their bodies indistinct, swirling together, turning to vapor when I try to touch them. Mom crying in the kitchen, thinking I've died. Dad withering away. Forrest reminding me that time is running out as a chasm opens in front of me, the edges always shifting, never the same, continually flowing or rippling like a flag in the wind—except there is no wind. Just me, the endless shifting chasm, and the nagging feeling that I will never escape.

A chime startles me awake, and I sit up, swinging my legs over the edge of my bed. My head immediately begins pounding furiously, forcing me to lean my elbows on my knees and press against my pulsing temples.

"Good morning, Ugene," Overwatch says as the lights come on, revealing tan walls. "You are scheduled for testing to commence in 30 minutes. Please proceed to the cafeteria for breakfast, then return to your room for testing. Participation is compulsory."

The lock on the door grinds out of place, and the door swings open. But I can't move. The headache is too much. What would happen if I just lay down and went back to sleep? Temptation pulls at me. The test must have had a stronger effect than I realized.

Grumbling and moving slowly, I pull my shirt on and slip into the loafers. Maybe food will help.

The churning threatening my stomach makes me second-guess

the decision as soon as I enter the cafeteria. Bacon, eggs, pancakes, and oats bombard my senses. I swallow down the revulsion and tuck my head, squinting against the bright lights.

"You look like shit," Miller announces behind me as I gather my toast and oats from the dispenser.

I grimace and rue the motion as even the scrunching of my eyes hurts. "You're always sunshine," I grumble, regretting the sarcasm only a little.

Miller huffs and heads to his usual table. I shuffle along behind him. Neither of us speaks as we eat. For once, I'm grateful for his silence. By the time I finish my breakfast, the pounding has reduced to a dull ache. Miller has already disappeared to his room, so I follow suit as Overwatch kindly reminds everyone only two minutes remain until testing begins.

It takes nearly that much time to make my way back to my room. Two men and a woman in Paragon security uniforms usher test subjects into their rooms. I watch as one subject—a mousy-looking girl my age—whimpers and resists. She turns to run up the hallway, but security pulls a gun and shoots. I jump. Did they just...?

She drops to the floor convulsing, and one of the guards drags her into her room. Another guard turns to me, and the grim set of his jaw make me dodge into my room without further protest, heart pounding. What the hell was that?

What have I gotten myself into? What's going on here?

Before I have time to think it through, the door swings shut and locks in my face. My room disappears, replaced by another room even more institutional—gray walls and smooth grey floor. I brush a hand against the wall and can feel the texture of soundproofing. Is that really necessary in a simulation?

"Please be seated," Forrest says, his voice coming from above.

My hand slides off the wall as I turn, and breakfast rises up my throat.

A medical chair greets me. The sort of chair you see in a dentist office or in an awful old horror film right before something terrible happens. I can't help but think back to the previous test. What will happen if I sit in the chair?

"Can we talk?" I ask, scanning the ceiling for a camera. "I'm not really comfortable with this, and I have questions about yesterday's test."

"Please sit, Ugene," Forrest repeats. "Participation is compulsory. The test will not complete until the task is finished."

And what if I don't comply? I plant my feet firmly and cross my arms. He isn't here. What can he do?

Forrest sighs. "Ugene, we just need to take a few samples. This is very simple."

"What happened to Boyd and Enid?"

"Please, sit."

Two security guards appear at either side of me. Before they can grab my arms and drag me to the chair, I straighten my back and walk myself over. Resistance is futile. My strength is nothing compared to theirs. As soon as I settle back into the medical chair, straps appear, pinning my arms to the armrests and my legs to the foot of the chair.

Panic rises in my throat. "Why am I restrained?"

"It's a simple test, Ugene, and I need you to comply."

"If it's so simple, come do it yourself," I snarl, tugging at the straps. There's no point. Without a Power I don't stand a chance of escape, and even if I did where would I go? It's a simulation. There is no escape.

Dad. I'm doing this for Dad. And for myself—for the hope that maybe these tests will help Paragon find a way to give me a Power. At this point, I'll take anything.

A door in the previously smooth wall swings open Forrest enters. Well, there goes that threat. Two others enter the room. Only one is clearly a test subject as well.

"The purpose of this test is to take samples," Forrest says.

Meanwhile, the non-test subjects begin setting up their tools, but I can't quite see what they are. "It is simple and straightforward, but we need complete compliance. Testing will not complete until all samples are taken. Let's begin."

I open my mouth to protest, but no sound escapes me. No matter how hard I try, I can't say a word. My gaze sweeps over the three of them. The boy with the square jaw has a Naturalist brand on his hand. The boy wouldn't talk to me yesterday, and I'm starting to understand why as Forrest and the female Paragon employee approach.

Beside the bed, a surgical table appears with a small stack of empty bags, a tube, a tourniquet strap, and a needle. Blood. They're going to draw blood. That's not so bad, right? Those are standard-size bags.

The woman cleans the spot where the needle will go into my arm, then ties on the rubber tourniquet. The needle is steady in her experienced hand.

"It's just a little blood," she says softly like she thinks it will reassure me.

I clench my hands into fists and tense my body but stay rigid. The needle doesn't hurt going in. She has a surprisingly gentle touch like she barely touches my skin at all. As soon as the needle is in place, thick red blood pumps out of my veins, down the hose and into the bag.

The woman licks her fat lips and turns away to another table that has appeared.

"Michael," Forrest calls.

The square-jawed boy takes uncertain steps toward my chair on the side where they aren't taking my blood. What is his job here?

"Make sure you get a good sample," Forrest commands.

Michael nods, making a lock of dark hair fall across his forehead. He rubs his hands together, anxiety knitting his features tight. My own chest tightens. What sample is he supposed to get? His cold hands wrap around my free forearm, and for a moment he just holds them there, but I can see the sweat beading his brow and the way his eyes widen.

Nothing changes for me. No tingles on the skin or pulls at my biological DNA.

He feels something, though.

Michael snaps his hands back, and his whole body is shaking as he stares at his hands. Suddenly, his body convulses like he's having a seizure and he collapses to the floor. The woman snaps on a fresh pair of blue rubber gloves.

"Hurry, Cinthia," Forrest says with excited urgency. "You're wasting precious time."

I try to ask what's going on, but there's no point. No sound comes out.

Cinthia grabs a scalpel from her tools and rushes over to Michael. I tug at the restraints fruitlessly and watch in horror as she grabs Michael's hands and carefully removes the top layers of skin from each. Michael chokes on his scream. Blood drips on the floor and Cinthia's gloves as she places the pieces of skin on slides Forrest offers.

What are they doing? They need to help Michael!

I pull at the straps again, but the pinch of the needle in my arm makes me stop. Tears roll hot down my cheeks, and I can't wipe them away. The agony presses against my chest and forces me to look elsewhere as I blink back tears.

Is this why they restrained me? Did Forrest know I would try to intervene? The thought sickens me.

When I dare a glance toward Michael, a new test subject—the girl with mousy hair—tends to Michael's hands. The skin Cinthia sliced off grows back as I watch. The moment it's done, the girl disappears as if she were never there.

But the damage to Michael is done.

Michael stops convulsing on the floor and rolls over into a fetal position, hands cradled against his chest. His entire body quivers.

Forrest moves to the now full bag of blood and deftly replaces it with a new one. Less than a minute, and he has more blood pumping out of my veins. He takes the first bag to the lab table where Cinthia works. She carefully puts some blood in each vial. Hematology. She must be using Hematology. Forrest is now reading something on his tablet.

I turn my attention back to Michael, and my head swims a little as I lift it off the cushioned chair.

But Michael is gone.

A quick glance around reveals he isn't with us anymore. Did he finish his testing?

Cinthia mutters something, but with the pounding of my heart in my eardrums, I can't hear her.

It all happens so quickly. Forrest glances up from his tablet after a few minutes and rushes to my side as the next bag is filled. I blink, watching as he removes it, then hooks on another. I shake my head, which makes the aching worse. I can't lose any more. Four pints— then death. Desperation grips my chest, but I'm restrained.

Silenced.

Too weak to do anything. Too powerless.

Grogginess overcomes me, and I struggle to stay alert, to see what's going on, to hear anything but the beating of my heart, but the loss of blood is getting to me. I don't have the strength to resist as Cinthia carefully scrapes away a small square from the top layer of skin on my free arm. It hurts, but the pain is distant, and my cries of agony are more like garbled mumblings of a madman.

I watch as the third bag fills, fighting off the sleep threatening to overcome me. Tears heat my cheeks. But it's too much. The last thing I remember is fearing just how much blood they plan on taking from me as I lose the fight to sleep.

My eyes drift open, greeted only by dim light. Pain aches in my head, arms, and back. The sensation of being violated clenches my throat and I close my eyes, willing back the tears as I roll onto my side. I don't know where I am or what time it is. I don't care. I just want this to be over. If I sleep long enough, it will all be over.

Tears still escape despite my closed eyes, soaking my cheek and the cloth pressed against it. Hugging my arms tight against my chest, cradling the places on my arms that sting, I let sleep consume me.

At some point during the night, I wake from nightmares that disappear as soon as my eyes open and am back in my room again. My heart pounds, and I brush hands over my arms, seeking signs of the test, or something else. Though I'm not sure what. I find nothing.

Michael. That agony on his face. It was part of my nightmares. I'm sure of it, even though I can't remember.

The only thing I'm certain of offers only little reassurance. Michael is real. Boyd and Enid may still be in question, but Michael is real. So is the mousy girl. I shuffle to my desk and open the map in my notebook, searching for the room I marked yesterday.

Room 1157 – Michael: Naturalist

Exhausted, I rub my eyes and lay back down. I hope Mom and Dad are doing okay.

Sleep captures me without protest.

The morning chime wakes me, and a sense of dread fills my stomach as I lay in bed.

"Good morning, Ugene," Overwatch says as the lights come on. "You are scheduled for testing to commence in 30 minutes. Please proceed to the cafeteria for breakfast, then return to your room for testing. Participation is compulsory."

The lock on the door grinds out of place and the door swings open. Yesterday I wondered what would happen if I went back to sleep. Today, I intend to find out. The last thing I want is to get thrust into another horrific test. I close my eyes and let sleep take me.

A hand on my shoulder makes me cringe, and I edge away from it until my back hits the cold wall. I blink away sleep, gazing at Miller perched on the edge of my bed.

"What happened?" Miller asks.

I sit up straighter, pulling my blanket up to my chin and looking toward the hall.

"Nothing."

Judging by the way Miller's lips thin, I can tell he doesn't believe me.

"You didn't turn up for dinner last night," he says. "I assumed your test went over time. But this morning you weren't there for breakfast." Miller shoves a cranberry muffin and a juice pouch at me. "You need to eat, or you won't get through today. There's only about five more minutes until it starts."

"I can't."

"You don't have a choice. Eat."

Maybe Miller is right. Maybe I don't have a choice. Maybe the testing would start whether I wanted to participate or not. I take a drink of the orange juice. The cold rush of liquid coats my insides as the sweet and sour taste coats my tongue.

Overwatch breaks the silence. "Five minutes until testing begins. Please return to your rooms."

Miller stands and throws a fresh shirt at me. "Gotta go. Don't skip meals, Ugene. It never ends well."

I set the food down and replace my sweat-soaked shirt with the fresh one. How much worse could it possibly get?

16

I HAVE NO IDEA WHERE THE CENTRAL DOME IS. THE change of location has me curious.

As I search, Overwatch announces one minute. I come across the doorway into the room I found during my initial investigation of the floor. Nothing marks the room out as different, but instinct tells me it's the right place, so I step inside with seconds to spare.

The door swings shut and the lock slides into place.

Two others appear in the room, and I instantly recognize them both. Why did I have to ask myself how much worse it could get?

The first is Forrest, who stands near the edge of the room with a tablet and a contemplative look on his face as he reads something on it.

The second is Bianca, who doesn't appear nearly as surprised to see me as I am to see her. Instead, she stands about as far apart from Forrest as she can, her arms crossed over her chest.

I freeze near the door, staring at Bianca in her Paragon security uniform. My heart leaps, and I'm back to being that infatuated schoolboy. She can't be part of this. Does she have any idea what's going on here? As I debate what to do or say, a sparring mat appears in the middle of the room.

"Let's get started," Forrest says as if I don't have layers of tension leaking through every part of me. "Step onto the mat."

Bianca's looking me over as she moves toward the mat, and her alarm is in response to what she sees. Not me. But the condition I'm in. I have no doubt my face gives away my exhaustion, and perhaps even the fear hammering away at me. Heat flushes my cheeks, and I can't bear to meet her gaze a second longer. I haven't seen her in a few days, not since that night on our street.

Then Forrest's words sink in. I have to spar with Bianca? This hardly seems fair. She's a Somatic. Not an exceptional one, but well above average. I step hesitantly toward the sparring circle.

Bianca offers a kind smile and pulls her black hair back into a ponytail, but something else hides behind her eyes as she looks at me. "I'm sorry," she mouths, glancing furtively at her brother.

"This is the Muscle Memory test," says Forrest, as if I couldn't guess it myself. "Bianca will teach you the basics; then you will spar and try to mimic her in preparation for the next phase of the test."

"I… can't fight her." The words come out meeker than I'd intended.

"Because I'm a girl?" Bianca teases.

"No. Because you're Somatic. And I'm so not. It's hardly a fair fight."

Bianca strips off the security guard belt and collared shirt, leaving her in just a black tank top, skin-tight leggings, and boots. "I'm sparring with you, Ugene, not fighting."

Warmth spreads through my whole body and the hairs on my arms and neck rise. My gaze fixes for a moment on the newly exposed cleavage. It's one thing to have to spar, but it's something else entirely to have to fight with the only girl I've ever had such strong feelings for. Forrest just motions me onward.

The training is exhausting. Bianca walks me through each move only once—though in fairness, she does so in great detail—then moves on to the next. Each time she instructs me to mimic what she does, shifting my stance or controlling my motions by placing her hands on my arms or torso. Each time she touches me, a flare of excitement shoots through my body, and my cheeks heat all over again. Everything she does is precise and professional, but I find it hard to focus on any of this. Instead, I become more aware of her closeness, the scent of citrus soap on her skin.

That feeling of comfort quickly dissolves when she tells me it's time to spar. I hesitate to move toward her, well aware that I will look like a weakling.

She calls out the moves—one at a time—with the name she taught me. It starts slow, and I have to think a second before responding. After a round, she starts calling the names faster: knife hand, high block, uppercut, knife hand block, reverse punch, hammer fist, and on and on.

Faster.

Each time she calls out a block, she throws the punch at me so fast I rarely make it in time to block.

Faster.

She mixes them up, trying to confuse me. One small mercy is that she pulls each of her swings to lessen the impact. But each strike still staggers my stance.

Even amid all this chaos, she looks glorious. Sweat makes her skin glisten in the bright lights of the room. Her soap mingling with her sweat. I struggle to keep up with her, enveloped in every little motion and scent and sound of her. The intensity of her gaze penetrates to my soul. It's distracting me from where my focus should be.

And despite the sweat on her brow, Bianca isn't tired. In fact, she looks invigorated. It has a rejuvenating power over me. I'm stronger in her presence, feeding off her energy. Drinking her in. She hasn't given me this much attention in years. Not since we were kids too young to understand the class difference between Powers.

Bianca calls the spar to a halt. I hadn't been aware of how exhausted and weak I am until we stop. Her soft hand falls gently on my back as I double over, gasping for breath, nearly collapsing to the mat. Every part of my body feels like pins and needles. My muscles threaten to give out. I try to ask how I did, but I can't form the words between ragged breaths. She rubs my sweaty back a little as if that helps at all. The action only serves to speed my already racing heart. My stomach twists in a frenzy.

Forrest sits to the side, taking notes and reviewing the tablet as it receives reports from my nanomonitors. A stylus flicks between his fingers.

"You okay, Ugene?" Bianca asks, bent over to see me better.

All I can do in response is give a half-hearted thumbs up.

Bianca's gaze turns away from me toward Forrest. "What is it?" she asks. Her interest grabs my attention, and I watch her, hands on my knees, as she walks to her brother.

"I don't know." Forrest is making notes furiously on his tablet. "Do it again."

I stand, pressing my thumbs into the small of my back. My breath is slowly coming back to me, but I still can't make my legs move. "What?"

"Do it again," Forrest says.

I heard him the first time. Just wish I hadn't. Bianca drags her feet toward the sparring circle again, helping me along.

"I can't do it again," I say. My throat is raw.

After a glance at a distracted Forrest, she leans closer. "I'm gonna hit you. Stay down."

Right. Just let her hit me. Like it won't hurt. But it can't be any worse than the fire running through my skin right now.

The two of us take up position again, but this time my stance is frail. Hardly worth standing. Sweat rolls down into my eyes, and I try to blink and wipe it out. I manage a few swings and blocks, but there's no way Forrest would believe any of it is real. Searing pain lances across my skull, knocking me to the floor with a pounding headache.

"Bianca!" Forrest's voice is distant.

I blink, pushing against the mat. If I can stand, I can keep her out of trouble. But my arms quiver and give out. Their voices are muffled, but I can't focus on what they are talking about.

I close my eyes, and when they open, everything is clearer. Hands help me upright on the mat. Blinking, I work my jaw, then realize I'm no longer sweating.

"Good to have you back," Forrest says. "You did great, Ugene. We're nearly done."

This confuses me. What exactly did I do right? I was *more* distracted today than any of the previous tests. In the end, I'm pretty sure Bianca knocked me out.

Bianca.

I rub my aching temple and seek her out. But she's gone. And in her place stands the giant Somatic who glared at me from Terry the Telepath's door. What was his name? Derrek.

Nearly done. Forrest's words sink in, and the horrifying realization comes to me.

I have to fight Derrek. Just remember, this is for Dad's treatment. For my cure.

I shake my head and take a step back, but ropes appear around the ring. I could climb over them, but there's really no escape, is there? Where will I go? Bianca was just the warm-up. Or maybe an instructor to prepare me for this. Except I'm not prepared. Not in the slightest. Derrek is twice my size with Enhanced Strength. As he stalks toward me, fists up like a boxer, I know that I don't stand a chance.

My insides writhe as I watch Derrek stalk toward me, towering over me, his muscles straining the short sleeves of his scrubs. And he smiles. I gag and can't help but wonder if it would make his stop if I just vomited on his feet. With Forrest here, probably not.

Forrest isn't watching us at all. He's staring at his tablet in deep concentration. The corners of his mouth are turned down like he's disappointed.

Derrek's feet hammer against the mat, drawing my attention back to him and raising my elbows defensively like Bianca just taught me. I won't last long.

"I've been waiting for this," Derrek says, and that smirk on his face is no longer teasing. It's menacing, like a predator stalking its prey.

Unsure what else to do, I kick out, but he grabs my leg, throws a punch into my ribs hard enough to knock all the air from my lungs, then sweeps me down onto the mat. My back smacks the floor, and I gasp for breath, scrambling backward to gain the space I need to stand. Just don't let him kick or punch me in the head.

I barely have time to put up my arms in defense before Derrek swings again. Pain lances through my arm as I block, and I'm distinctly aware that another hit like that from him will break my arm. Sweat and tears sting my eyes, but I don't dare move my arms to wipe it away.

"Crying already, Powerless prick?" Derrek taunts. "I knew this would be easy, but you could at least try."

I swing an upper cut, but he knocks my arm away effortlessly and drives his fist into my ribs again. Something cracks. I cry out and lower my arm to my side for protection. A fatal mistake. I don't even see Derrek's fist, but the crack against my jaw momentarily blackens my vision. Ringing sounds in my ears. I stumble to the side, but it's too late. I lose balance long enough that even a chance at escape is gone. I still try, stumbling into the ropes and catching them before I can tumble to the mat.

Derrek doesn't give me a chance to breathe. His hand closes around my arm and yanks me back, then his foot connects with my chest. I have no hope. Never did. My back hits the mat again, and no matter how hard I will myself to get up, I can't. My ribs throb in pain, my arm aches, and I can't breathe. A fist grabs my shirt and pulls me up until Derrek's eyes are close, locked on mine. He stands over me, gloating.

"This wasn't even a fight."

My arms ignore my commands. My lungs refuse to listen. But my legs, despite being shaky, still have strength. On knee shoots up, connecting between Derrek's legs, and the other leg kicks out at his chest.

Derrek lets go and stumbles back.

I roll over on all four trembling limbs and spit blood on the mat. The metallic tang fills my mouth and nose. My breaths come hard, and as I stand the room spins. I blink away the stinging sweat and tears in my eyes as I see Derrek attempting to recover. He's stronger and faster. I don't have time.

How does this end? What is Forrest looking for? The thoughts drift like a rowboat lost in the sea. I blink again, and Derrek is in front of me. I manage to get a punch into his chest just as pain lances through my cheekbone beside my eye. Blood and blackness cloud my vision.

My knees give out, and the mat feels like ice against my burning face. A muffled voice announces the end of the test just moments before I hear my arm snap. The pain knocks me out.

The world seeps through the darkness in a haze. Muffled voices. Clicks of a machine. Patches of blurry light appear and slip back into shadow. Can't think. Can't breathe. I gasp, scream, pull and tug. Something bites into my wrists and ankles, immobilizing me. Muffled shouts. Warmth seeps across my skin. Then everything slips away.

17

I OPEN MY EYES AND BLINK AT THE WHITE CEILING. MY hands are leaden. My legs don't want to move. Everything weighs me down. I can't remember what happened or where I am. Just me and the white ceiling.

"Ugene…"

Bianca's voice brings everything rushing back. The sparring. The test. The pain… I roll my head to the side. Desk. Shelves. Journals. This is my room. How did I get here? And Bianca.

"What…?" My throat hurts. It's hard to swallow.

"They brought you in like this," Bianca says, sitting on the edge of the bed, her hands fidgeting in her lap, then her warm hand slides overtop mine. The simple touch tightens my chest even though it's a friendly gesture. "Forrest said the second part of your test didn't go well. No one would tell me anything more. So I looked for you. And when they brought you back to your room, I asked if I could keep watch."

"How long?" I croak.

"A day," Bianca says. "But they just brought you in a couple hours ago. What happened?"

My stomach growls. I force myself to sit up, leaning against the wall behind the bed for support. The words start tumbling out. The fight against Derrek after she left. Her brother ignoring the beatdown Derrek gave me. Everything I remember. Overwatch is listening. I know it, but I can't help telling her the truth.

As Bianca listens, her eyes narrow, her grip tightening over my hand. By the end, she is shaking her head.

"No." Her hand pulls out of mine, leaving me cold. "But Forrest…" But she hesitates, looking away as if she doesn't want to admit something to me.

A knock comes at the door. My muscles tense, then ache. Why does everything hurt?

Bianca slides off the bed and glides to the door, her boots registering no sound as she moves across the tiled floor. When she pulls it open, she yanks Miller in and slams him against the wall, her forearm against his throat.

"It's okay," I tell her, relaxing back against the wall again. "It's just Miller. He's harmless."

Bianca doesn't look at me. She glares at Miller and holds him like she expects him to fight back. "I know who he is, and he's anything but harmless. What do you want?" Bianca growls at Miller.

A groan slips out as I push myself off the bed. Pain lances through my back, feeling stretched thin, and for a moment the room spins. There's no aching in my ribs or arm, where I know Derrek at least fractured something, if not breaking it completely.

Healing. They had to heal me after the test.

"I heard about what happened and came to check on Ugene," Miller replies.

I shuffle toward them and rest a hand on Bianca's upper arm, giving her a small nudge back.

"He won't hurt me." I manage to draw Bianca's gaze.

She hesitates, then gives a slight nod, taking a small step back.

Miller rubs at his throat, watching her as he steps further into the room. "How are you, kid?"

"I'm okay, I guess," I say. "There was a Strongarm test and… it didn't go well."

"How's your shoulder, lovely?" Miller asks Bianca.

"Healed," Bianca snaps.

The terse response pulls me back into the moment. I rub my temples. "Okay, clearly you two have a history—"

"She didn't like getting beaten by a Naturalist." Miller is so smug even I am irritated by it.

"You are *not* a Naturalist!"

"It's Matter Mutation," says Miller, looking at me now. "You know, manipulation."

I nod. It never occurred to me to ask about his ability, though I have spotted the Naturalist brand on his hand—the Oak Tree—and I wondered what his Power was. He never said, won't tell me much, to be honest. I've never met anyone who hoarded so many secrets. But Matter Mutation. That I understand.

Bianca turns to me, fury burning in her stunning copper gaze.

I tense.

"He pulled my arm out of socket using what he calls Matter Mutation. A bolt of lightning went from my shoulder to a nearby one-ton weight. Nearly ripped my arm off."

The physics of what she claims is impossible, and despite my better judgment, I only have one reaction. "Cool."

Bianca's eyes flare wildly.

I cup my elbow with one hand and tap my lips with the other, trying to piece it together. Miller didn't just zap Bianca like his ability should do. He nearly ripped her arm off. That's only possible with Reversed Divinic Regrowth. So, if a Naturalist can create lightning from a metal anchor, and a Divinic can manipulate a person's cells, what did that make Miller?

"The strength it would take to pull that much energy from something." I'm muttering, pacing back and forth, just a few steps in the confined space. "No one has that much strength in *any* Power. It would take… superhuman strength. Unless…" I stop and spin on my heels, hands rubbing together, facing Miller.

Miller crosses his arms as if he knows what's coming.

"You have two Powers. Two Branches." The words rush out. "That's why Paragon wants you."

Miller shuffles his feet, lips pulling in a taut line. "Technically, it's just borderline duality."

"Brilliant!" I skip a few steps closer, excitement balling my chest.

"Do they have any idea?"

"Of course they do," he says, scoffing. "That's why they brought me on."

"Right. Of course." I shake my head.

Miller clearly doesn't get it. He isn't just special. To create lightning that came *out* of a person instead of going in would take far more Divinic Power than borderline. Someone at Paragon must know this. I wonder what his rank on the Cass Scale is.

"Have you always been borderline?" Feeling dizzy—either from the healing or excitement—I sit on my bed, the cotton sheets pressing into the tips of my fingers as I grip the edge. Bianca comes to my side to check on me, but my mind is reeling, trying to process the new information. I only notice her joining me by the proximity of her warmth and the citrus smell.

"No." Miller rubs a hand over his face and glances toward the open door as if considering an exit. "There was an accident." Lines of pain cross his face, and he looks anywhere but in our direction. There's silence. Whatever the accident was, he doesn't want to talk about it.

"And you've been able to do this since?"

"Yeah. Some freak event. Paragon tried to recruit me a couple years ago on Career Day. I refused." Miller licks his lips, then teeth. "The new Power went out of control at work a few weeks later. Nearly killed someone. I knew I needed help, so I reached out to Paragon. Been here ever since."

I stare at Miller with newfound respect.

"At first, I was here to try and find a way to keep from killing anyone on accident." Miller swallowed so hard I could see the large lump in his throat. "They helped me figure out how to control it, to some degree. But it's still… unpredictable. They promised to find a way to control it or get rid of it. Maybe use it to help others. Eventually, they decided to keep me to enhance their research. Imagine being able to give others a second Power. That sort of knowledge…"

I open my mouth to finish the sentence for him, but Miller presses a finger to his lips and looks around the room. Overwatch.

Silence settles over the room. Bianca shifts beside me and the warmth of her proximity is only slightly distracting. Do either of them understand? Miller can not only show Paragon how each identifying marker for Powers works, but how they work together. They can learn to control who has what Power with that kind of knowledge. Or how to give that Power to someone else—like me. And all it takes is the right mind to unlock Miller's genetic code.

Dr. Joyce Cass.

Something Dr. Cass said during our meeting comes back, and I chew my lip in excitement.

You could be the key to unlocking the genes that trigger abilities.

If I'm the key, the lock is standing right in front of me. Miller is my solution, my cure.

Bianca stands and moves toward the door. The bed feels colder. For a moment she pauses in the doorway, giving me a curious glance, then disappears into the hall. What's she thinking?

"She's an odd one to fancy," Miller says.

My thoughts distract me too much to respond. "Miller, don't…" I glance around the room, then stand too fast to go to him. The world dims, and I grab the cool wall to keep from falling over, sliding along it toward him. My voice is as low as I can whisper while making sure he hears me. I'm not certain why, but I don't want Paragon to follow my thinking just yet. "Don't skimp on your tests."

"Why?" Miller whispers.

"Just… trust me. Please."

Miller nods, but his expression is uncertain.

"And hey!" I call out as he steps into the hall. "If you need to talk about what happened, either the accident or whatever, I'm here."

Miller hesitates, looking pensive. He runs his hands through his shaggy blond hair, taps at the metal frame of the door with his palm, mumbles something to himself, and is gone.

If I'm right, and Miller and I are the keys, all the test subjects play into this somehow. But I need more time to find the answers.

18

REST HAS BECOME ELUSIVE. I CAN'T STOP THINKING about the conversation with Miller and Bianca—about what Paragon could be doing here. There's still nearly an hour until lockdown, so I opt for a shower.

For a while, I just stand there and let hot water roll down tense, sore muscles in my back. The hot water feels incredible, easing away all the aches and pains, rinsing off the foamy lather of musk-scented shampoo. Then, the water unexpectedly grows warmer.

Before it's too late.

The voice is familiar, echoing off the tile walls. My slick fingers linger on the knob. No. Not off the tiles. It's in my head. And it isn't mine.

The stalls are enclosed on all sides, with a bleached white curtain to close the space off, yet I don't feel alone. Nakedness and the voice fill me with twisting vulnerability.

My hand slips off the knob, and I inch toward the curtain. It flutters. I jerk back.

I have to— A girl's voice.

A shower turns on across the narrow passage. Is she in the bathroom? A door thumps closed.

I wipe the excess water off my face. It's all my imagination. I'm being ridiculous.

Using practiced, measured breaths, the tension melts from my shoulders. I turn off the water and reach through the curtain to grab my towel.

It's gone.

I peek out. The towel and my clothes are on the floor a couple of feet from the bench—the cloth is wet. The only sound in the room is that of the other shower. I peer up the aisle between stalls, making sure I'm alone before stepping out and grabbing my clothes. What other choice do I have? I don the garments without toweling off, slip on my flip-flops, and take my shower caddy from the stall. The experience leaves me uneasy, craving the false security of my room.

As I pass the cafeteria, water dripping in my wake, I get the same feeling someone is watching me. No one is, but I can't shake it. My jaw twitches.

Irrational. I'm being irrational.

All the same, my pace quickens back to my room. The click of the door closing behind me offers little reassurance.

Once I reach the false security of my room, I slip into my jeans and flannel shirt for dinner.

Before I open the door to my room, a scream rips through my head.

No. No! No no no!

My stomach lurches. The scream breaks the silence, echoing up the hallway.

A real scream.

I throw open the door and head in the direction it came from, away from the cafeteria. At the end of the hall, I wait to hear something more. Heavy breaths heave my chest, making my ribs ache. My pulse quickens the longer I stand there. Another test subject passes me, giving me a funny look as she heads toward the cafeteria.

"Did you hear that?" I ask her.

Her brows pull together, and she shakes her head and continues.

Closed doors, empty halls—everything appears normal.

Silence.

It's nothing, right? Maybe it was just in my head again. Maybe all this Somatic testing has loosened a bolt or two. Or maybe Derrek hit me too hard in the head. It's nothing...

Yet, I'm compelled onward until I'm standing in front of room 1126. Jade's room. The door is shut.

I raise my fist to knock but hesitate. Miller warned me not to knock, and I've been superb at ignoring his advice. But something tells me this is different. That I should actually listen to him. Instead of knocking, I rest my palms against the door and press my ear flat to the metal.

Nothing.

I'm going crazy. That's the only explanation. I step back, a breath rushing through my lips.

Just open the door.

The knob turns without challenge, and I creep the door open slowly. Silence.

The first thing I notice is the blankets on the floor. The desk is shoved haphazardly into the middle of the room. The mattress is askew, the corner hanging precariously off the frame.

"What the hell?" I mutter, stepping in. "Hello? Jade?"

Nothing.

A few more steps reveal more signs of a struggle. Books strewn about the floor. A clay pot fragmented everywhere.

But no Jade.

The silence makes my pulse race. Did another test subject attack her? That was her voice I heard in my head. It had to be. And if it was, she knew this was coming.

I rush back out into the hallway, hoping for clues to help the poor girl.

But there's nothing.

Like an idiot, I can't help hoping. So, I follow the hallway in the opposite direction from which I came. At a fork in the hall, I glance in both directions, then choose left and jog to the next intersection, the muscles in my calves burning in protest. There's only one way to go from here. Even as I turn up the next hallway, I hear the elevator doors slide shut.

In moments I'm standing there, watching every direction and

finding nothing.

What happened to Jade?

Turning this way and that through the halls, I seek answers and find nothing except a busy cafeteria.

And still no Jade.

No more voices. No screaming.

Everything is just...ordinary.

19

THE DAYS START BLURRING TOGETHER. ONE TEST after another, all pushing me to my limits physically and mentally. It's far more exhausting than I expect. Lift this. Change that. Read those. None of it bears any fruit, but Forrest hasn't lost interest in the work, nor does he have any interest in striking up a conversation with me. Any time I try, the simulation cuts off, and he's gone. It doesn't take long for me to realize why all the other test subjects appear so exhausted all the time.

I'm going stir crazy.

The security doesn't help. I've stumbled across Paragon guards ushering test subjects toward their rooms when they have not complied with compulsory participation—and always less than gently. One girl tried to resist, but the guard grabbed her arm and thrust her through her doorway. Her door clanged shut as she screamed. The memory haunts my sleep.

Every morning is the same. The alarm sounds once, startling me awake. Overwatch announces the same thing she does every day. Then the doors unbolt and swing open, and test subjects shamble like a blind herd toward the cafeteria. Testing begins. By evening, those who completed their test shuffle to the cafeteria again for dinner before lockdown. I've avoided Terry and Derrek since that first week. Whatever Jade thought was a danger to me, I have no intention of finding out.

Once a week, Forrest takes me into a special room on our floor to collect necessary samples. It's never pleasant. Needles and skin samples. Blood, plasma, and sometimes bone marrow. Every time it reminds me of that test with Michael.

I just have to remind myself why I'm here. Every day gives Dad another day of medical attention he needs. Occasionally, I do consider whether or not Dr. Cass is holding up her end of the deal, but lingering on these thoughts will drive me mad. I just have to trust her.

The tension in the cafeteria gets thicker every day—and sometimes it feels like it's directed at me. It's the way they look at me. Especially Terry. Like he's trying to read me. It's the way some of them *don't* look at me. The way they whisper to each other. The edges of their whispers brush my ears every day, but I can never grasp what they're saying. Sometimes they sound like my name, but I could just be going a little crazy. It probably wouldn't be such a stretch to believe I'm imagining things.

Despite the tension, my group of companions grows slowly. There's Sho—a boy with dark spikey-hair, Divinic Psychic Navigation, and eyes that tilt toward the bridge of his nose—who participated on a maze test with me. His mapping ability is minimal, but it helped us find our way out of the dangerous maze. The morning after our test, we saw each other at breakfast and struck up a conversation. He's nineteen and has been in Paragon for three years and doesn't think he will ever get out. Even Michael has taken to sitting at our table during breakfast, though he never speaks or looks at any of us and always stays as far from me as possible.

Tonight, the cafeteria's lights are overly bright, forcing me to squint as I make my selections for dinner. Meatloaf with roasted potatoes and steamed vegetables from the Hot-Serve machine, milk from the Drinkables. Once I have a tray full of food, I seek out a seat in the corner. I sit with my dinner and my notebook alone, watching.

Everyone is hushed again, as usual. A few of the other test subjects occupy the round tables. Some are in Paragon-issued scrubs. Others are in street clothes. I have yet to find out why some get away with street clothes. I have mine back, but the scrubs seem to be a requirement for testing. Maybe street clothes are for days off.

I've started taking notes on who comes and goes from the cafeteria. Not just trying to see who is talking to whom or if I can hear anything—though I am—I'm looking for little ticks. How long does any one person stare at the wall without doing anything? Has anyone been behaving differently? I'm not really sure what exactly I'm looking for, but Dr. Cass said it herself. Wisdom is a moral duty, and something about what's going on at Paragon has started feeling off. Inhumane. Immoral. The answers are in front of me. I know it. I just can't see it.

While I write notes and chew juicy, savory meatloaf, a hush falls over the room. I look up in time to see Vicki dragging her feet as she follows Forrest along the hallway, past the cafeteria. Vicki and I made fast friends in our Psionic Telekinesis test, but she doesn't sit with me. She never sits with anyone.

All eyes in the room are downcast at the tables. Not one person dares to look up like I do. I stand, palms pressed to the tabletop, but have no idea what to say or do. I don't understand what just happened. A moment after Forrest and Vicki are gone, everyone resumes their dinner and whispered conversations. Forrest is collecting Vicki for some purpose. I should follow. Maybe it will lead me to Jade as well. I'm still not sure what happened to her.

Decided, I take a step around my chair, focused on the doorway.

A tray slides onto the table across from me, stopping me before I've taken more than a step. A familiar girl sits in the empty chair across from me. Her long, dark hair cascades around her face, momentarily blocking it from sight.

I peer closer, and my breath catches.

"Enid." She's real! Relief sags my shoulders.

"You're a hard guy to find," Enid says under her breath. Her eyes dart around the room, peering through strands of black hair.

"Likewise." Does this mean Boyd is real, too? I can only hope. But where is he? "But…can you wait a bit? I just need to do something."

Enid follows my gaze to the door and shakes her head. "Don't follow them. People who leave with Dr. Pond don't come back."

Her words seize my heart. Vicki…

"What do you mean?"

"Testing out, I think." But Enid doesn't appear convinced. She waves at my chair with her fork. "Just sit and eat, Ugene."

But I want to follow, find out where they are going. Could Vicki really be tested out? That still doesn't explain what happened to Jade. Against my better judgment, I sink into the empty chair.

Enid leans over her meatloaf, poking at it and keeping her voice to a whisper. "Did you hear the news?"

I shake my head. I've been too absorbed in my own studies to know what she's talking about.

"It passed."

"What?"

Enid shoves a hunk of meat into her mouth and chews it like she hasn't eaten in days. Maybe she hasn't.

"Proposition 8.5," she says through a mouthful of meat. "With an overwhelming majority."

I've been too distracted. With everything going on in here, I completely forgot about the world outside these walls. And about Proposition 8.5. Now the Directorate has the right to force people in the bottom third of ranking to go through testing again. I hated testing, but it wasn't as bad as what we suffer through here. My back stiffens.

"It's for the best, right?" I ask. It's what I thought when I first heard about it, but do I still feel the same? Could additional testing really help stop regression? I thought I was the key Dr. Cass needed. Maybe I'm failing.

Enid gives me a flat stare, pausing with her fork of potatoes halfway to her mouth. "Look around you," she hisses. "It's already started."

I close my notebook and look around the cafeteria. So many test subjects are on this floor that I rarely see many of them at once, and I don't know all of their faces. Just the few that I see regularly. Typically, about four or five tables are occupied during dinner. But then I notice it. Ten. Ten tables are nearly full. I flip through my notes and see that I've been taking note of more people each night for the past week, but the reason never occurred to me. People who fall under the purview of Proposition 8.5 aren't just being tested again.

Paragon is forcing them through this testing against their will.

"Why are you telling me this?" I ask.

"Because you helped me." Enid nods at my notebook. "So, I'm helping you. Brains. Remember?"

My Power, according to Enid. I open my mouth, but Enid just shakes her head and glances at the ceiling. At the invisible ears of Overwatch. Something Celeste said makes so much sense. The walls are always listening.

Enid slides a piece of paper to me, and I unfold it. I read her name with a room number, along with Boyd's. It's all too much, the frenzy of questions indecipherable, making my head spin.

Time. I need time to process all of this. Time and a clear space to think. And I know just the place.

20

WHEN I KNOCK ON CELESTE'S DOOR, SHE DOESN'T open right away. I wring my hands, wondering what time it is. Maybe she's asleep. Just as I'm about to give up, the door opens a crack. It's all she ever gives me. I slip inside and push it closed until I hear it butt against the doorframe.

Celeste's room is dark, as it always is at night. She prefers the light from the world outside over the lamp. The sheets on the bed are in disarray, and she sits atop them in her black cotton matching pajama top and pants. The buttons on the top are one-off, leaving the lapel resting at an odd angle. Celeste doesn't seem to notice. Her gaze is on the night sky.

"You walk in darkness today," she says as if it's the most ordinary statement in the world.

Moving closer to the windows, I rub the heel of my palm into my eyes. "Been a long day."

"Life takes us on a current that rages and flows. Fight the course and find yourself in darkness."

I sigh, searching the night sky for the moon while stuffing my hands in the pockets of my scrubs. Absently, I lean a shoulder against the window. Fight the course of the raging current… If only she knew. Or maybe she does. My gaze draws back to her. The lights from the city illuminate her pale skin. Skyscrapers and flashing billboards making the colors on her face shift from blue hues to red, purple. Something about this place affects Celeste. From where she's perched on the bed, her eyes are dull, and her hair wild.

"What do you see out there tonight, Celeste?" I ask, looking back out the window.

Bare feet pad against the swirling mosaic rug on her floor. Then she stands beside me, one hand pressed to the glass, gazing up at stars I can't see. When she stands close to the window like this, the color slowly returns to her skin. Her eyes become a vibrant shade of green. Even though her hair is unkempt, it shines brighter the longer she stands close to the window—like the cosmos breathes life into her.

"Cassiopeia will fall from her throne." Celeste traces a finger across the glass. "Andromeda's chains are breaking. The sea will part, and the hero and the stag will ride in for liberation." Her finger slides down the window, leaving a smudge, and I can see the creases at the edge of her mouth. "He's still so far away…"

A rare few Divinics have the Power to read the stars. But Celeste seems more in tune with the cosmos than any other I've met. So far, I've discerned that Celeste can read auras and the cosmos. What else can she do? Somehow, I can tell she is capable of amazing things, but her isolation prevents her from genuinely showcasing her Powers.

The more time I spend with Celeste, the more I connect with her. Like a sister. I yearn to set her free.

"Paternal bonds always tie. The day will come soon," Celeste says. "They will shelter you from the storm."

I pull my gaze away from the city to find Celeste's eyes locked on me. Well, not really on me, but around me. She's reading me again. At first, I found it unnerving, as if I couldn't have any secrets from her. Now, I don't care. It's comforting to be able to talk to someone without fear of being judged.

A weak smile curls the corner of my lips, but it fades when I see the way her face scrunches up as she looks around me. The way she bites her lip and how her chest heaves as she shudders a breath.

"I'm sorry, Ugene," she says in that soft voice. "All things are conditional. Even when the light breaks through the darkness, the darkness fights back." Everything inside of me presses together as fear strikes. "Choices must be made."

"A choice? What sort of—?"

Celeste shakes her head and returns to her bed, pulling blankets up to her chest and leaning back against the wall.

Whether she won't tell me or can't, her statement makes her dissolve into a ball of anxiety. I try to press for more, but no words will come out. I can't even begin to fathom what sort of choice I will have to make. Or is it even my choice? All is consumed by that now-familiar sickening twist in my gut.

We fall silent, looking out the window at the stars. I can't see them as Celeste can. All I can think of is a choice, one that won't be on my terms. Then, something from a previous test bubbles up to the surface.

"Celeste," I turn to her, arms crossed over my chest. Beside the bed, the jar of candies catches my eye, and a sudden craving for them hits. "During my Aurology test a few days ago, they were talking about my aura as if it were a blinding light."

Celeste cocks her head to the side like a bird. She nods.

"What does it mean?"

Her lack of response quickens my breath. The cold of the window seeps through my shirt and into my shoulder.

I push off and step toward her. "Please, anything you can offer would help."

"Aurology is an unpredictable river," Celeste finally says, looking over my shoulder, reading my aura. Her knees are drawn up toward her chest under the blanket. "Understanding meanings doesn't mean understanding."

My head spins. "What?"

"Your bed is calling you," Celeste says, still looking over my shoulder. Is she reading me or looking at the sky?

I'm not ready to go, but when I open my mouth to protest, a yawn rolls out. Asking her more about it now is pointless.

Celeste's focus isn't on me anymore, but on the stars beyond her window.

Lockdown warning sounds overhead.

I stifle another yawn with the back of my hand, then trudge over to the door, bidding Celeste goodnight. I can't take any more riddles tonight.

"Copper is like a penny. Pick it up and keep good luck," she says as I open the door. "Your fates dance together like the sun and moon."

This pauses me halfway through the door, but, after biting my lip, I slip out and close the door behind me.

The hour is late, and lockdown is only minutes away, which doesn't give me much time to get back to my room. Some of the doors are already closed tight. Everything is silent, which makes the sudden sound of someone else's shoes against the tiled floor sound even louder. I pull up short, holding my breath afraid that security will strongarm me back to my room for lockdown, then turn and prepare for the worst.

But it's Miller. He stands five feet away, hands in his pockets, scowling at me.

"What?" I ask, trying to catch my breath, hand against my pounding heart.

"Don't ask questions."

"But I didn't…" The rest of the sentence just falls off when I see the scowl on his face.

"Follow the rules, kid," Miller says.

"What happens if I don't?"

"You don't want to find out."

I half turn, wondering if I should follow him. Preservation gets the better of me, and I stick to my initial course of action.

After lockdown, I sit back in my chair and run my fingers through my hair, lacing them together behind my head as I stare at the pages spread out before me. A map of people and their Power, but I have no idea how strong any of those Powers are. The answer is itching at the edge of my mind, but I can't seem to grasp it. Maybe if I understand precisely why I'm here, I can glean some sort of answer.

Dr. Cass called me the key to unlocking the secrets of the genes that trigger Powers. If that's part of my purpose, what role do the other test subjects serve? Were they told the same as me? And what about Miller?

I need more clues. The answers are here, and I'm an idiot for not recognizing them. I'm almost there, so close the frustration makes it hard to sleep as my mind races.

For the next few days, I have dinner in the cafeteria and take the same notes, observing changes in others to see if there could be any other potential disappearances. Then I go back to my room and compare the new notes to all my previous ones.

Occasionally, Forrest will enter and take a test subject with him. Every time he comes, the room falls silent as if everyone hopes not to be noticed.

I flip back through my notes and review them as Forrest and the test subject walk off, comparing all the notes again. Vicki hasn't returned, nor has the girl who left with Forrest just two days ago. The other two girls who sat with her are abnormally quiet. What are they hiding? I have a sickening feeling that nothing good happens to those who leave with Forrest.

Others are quieter as well, staring at nothing for long periods, flinching when anyone comes too close. Those who once sat with a friend or two now come early and disappear. As if they're ashamed or exiled.

I understand how they feel.

Sleep pulls at me, and I gather my things and head back to my room. I used to love going to bed. It was my favorite part of the day, laying my head on my cool pillow and drifting off. Now I approach the end of the night with a sense of dread. Nightmares plague my sleep, along with the knowledge that when my eyes open, I will have to comply with yet another test. But sleep is natural, and even if I wanted to fight it, I can't. It claims us all.

I fight it off, trying to rub the sleep from my eyes while rounding a corner. The small group gathered outside my door pulls me up short. For a moment, I think it's exhaustion making me see things, but after a moment it's clear. I know every last one of them—and not from this place.

"Ugene." Mo's face lights up, and he smacks Leo on the shoulder. "I told you it was him."

Leo's bushy brows drop down over his eyes as he winces and rubs his arm.

Three of my former classmates and one girl a year ahead of us cluster together, staring at me. I open my mouth to ask what they're all doing here, but I already know the answer. Proposition 8.5.

Mo's rank was below the thirty percent mark. Leo and Dave barely came out the other side of Testing Day, so it's probably safe to assume their ranks were just as low. And the girl. I can't recall anything more than her heart-shaped face and big nose, but if she's with them, it's probably for the same reason.

Mo takes a few steps closer. "I told Leo I saw you come out of this room a couple times, but none of them believed me. But it only makes sense, right? I mean, if we're forced to be here, you would be, too."

Time to tell the truth, I suppose. I close the distance between us, clutching my notebook to my chest. "I, um, I volunteered, actually."

The girl's eyes widen unnaturally. "Why?"

"Well, I was told my participation would help people like you guys," I say. "You know, stop the regression."

"And?" Dave looks hopeful.

I hate to dash his hope, but I shake my head.

His shoulders slump.

"Can we talk?" Mo asks, stepping toward my doorway.

I jump in his path, blocking the door with one arm, and shake my head. "Not in there."

To my knowledge, Overwatch doesn't listen in the hallways, though I have no doubt Paragon can see everything in the halls. The cafeteria is good for conversation when it's full and noisy, but not this late at night. There's only one place on the floor I suspect Overwatch doesn't have eyes and ears—at least I hope not. I nod down the hall for them to follow and we head toward the bathroom.

Bright lights blink on overhead as I step through the door. The girl—who I learn is named Trina—stops in the doorway, but I reassure her it's okay. We're just talking.

"What's going on out there?" I ask as soon as the door is closed. "I heard the Proposition was passed, and there's been a surge of test subjects since then."

"It's horrible." Leo pales as he speaks. "The cops came to my house to bring me in for testing. My parents refused, tried to fight them off while I ran, but they caught me in the alley." He wrings his hands anxiously. "I don't know what happened to them."

"Same type of thing for everyone," Mo says. "The cops are rounding up people with regressed Powers, citing Proposition 8.5, and forcing us into rooms here to do this testing."

"The tests are horrible," Trina interrupts, her lips curling up to show her disgust. "How did *you* survive them so long?" The "you" is like a stab of disgust.

"They need me," I shrug. "But it hasn't been easy, either."

"They're starting with kids our age," Mo continues. "And a group of protesters has been acting out against the Directorate in response, but the media is sweeping all the accusations under the rug, excusing them away. Anyone not affected by the Proposition won't believe us."

I let out a breath as I listen to them. If I'm really the key to stopping this, I need to make sure Dr. Cass locks that door—soon. I don't want anyone else to have to suffer through these tests. Paragon is using the Directorate to get what they want—the answers to regression. And something else. Something more that I still can't quite wrap my head around. I chew my lip as I mull it over.

"What are you thinking?" Dave asks. "I've seen you scrunch up your face like that right before you spout off one of your brilliant ideas."

Really? I look up at Dave with those hopeful brown eyes. He really thinks I'll come up with an answer.

"I mean, if we could get out of here—" I start to say.

"Let's do that!" Leo pipes in eagerly.

I shake my head. "It's not that easy. Everything here is set up to lock us in."

All four of them deflate, then Dave waves us off and heads to the door. "Never mind. He's no good to us."

Leo hesitates, half turned toward me, then follows Dave out. Mo stares at me like he's willing me to say something different. Instead, he just looks disappointed as he says, "I hoped you might know something to help us." Then, he follows the other two out.

Trina lingers a moment in front of me, and her cold hand touches my shoulder. "I have faith in you. They told me how smart you are. If we don't have Powers to get out of this mess, we need brains." She squeezes my shoulder and leaves me alone as Overwatch warns that lockdown is coming.

What do they think I can do?

21

CHAOS IN THE CAFETERIA.

After Overwatch woke me this morning, I noticed she didn't warn me about testing times. Thinking I had the day off, I headed to the cafeteria for breakfast, then planned on returning to my room for much-needed sleep.

But what greets me makes me rethink my whole strategy.

I stand just inside the cafeteria doorway before a room crowded with test subjects. Dozens of them. Maybe edging near a hundred. Certainly, more than I've ever encountered at once.

Everyone is dressed for the day—some in street clothes and some in scrubs—and all the veteran subjects have some sort of backpack slung over their shoulders. They shove at each other, a mass of elbows and shoulders like people trying to escape a crisis. Except no crisis exists. Many of the weaker subjects are pushed away from the commotion while the newer recruits—like myself—hang back near the doorway or along the walls.

Near the Snackables machine, Terry watches with his arms crossed over his chest. His gaze meets mine, and something about the look on his face is satisfied as if he's been waiting for this moment and now knows a dark secret.

A fight breaks out between two Somatics over an overstuffed backpack. The bag spills out on the floor in the scuffle. Protein bars, bread rolls, dried meats, packaged water pouches. The taller one kicks the other down, then stomps his stomach. And a sinking fear hits my gut.

They all know what's coming.

And I don't.

I catch a glimpse of the tables through the mass, just for a moment. Just long enough to see the mad wrestling for food and water.

"Ugene." Miller rushes toward me. Another test subject grabs the strap of his bag and yanks, but Miller elbows the boy in the face. The boy stumbles back, holding his nose. "Grab everything you can."

"Why?" Panic clenches my throat.

"Just trust me. When it starts, head east and find me at the building with the bird wall."

Before I can ask what he's talking about, Miller jogs out of the cafeteria with his bag and disappears around the corner in the hallway.

I step forward when a hand clamps around my arm and pulls me back. I jump, jerking back, then immediately feel ashamed as I realize it's Trina.

"Ugene, what's going on?" The fear in her eyes is genuine.

I shake my head, unsure what to say. Are we leaving Paragon?

"Tell the others to grab what they can," I say, unsure what else to do. I then tell her the same thing Miller told me. Hopefully we can all find each other, wherever we are headed. Without another word, I rush back to my room for my messenger bag.

Other test subjects are running through the halls, clinging to their bags or their rations with desperation etched on their faces. I spot Enid disappearing around a corner toward her room and am tempted to follow, but I need rations if anything remains. I can't follow her.

By the time I return to the cafeteria, the veterans have disappeared. I elbow my way into the chaos. More than thirty other subjects uncertainly tug at what remains, which isn't much. Not nearly enough for all of us. Each of us reaches for something before it's gone. Judging by the looks on their faces, they are just as uncertain as me as to the reasons we need these supplies in the first place. I grab some water and protein at the very least before fading back. My bag is far from stocked, but something is better than nothing.

I return to my room with my bounty and sit on the edge of my bed, waiting, though I don't know for what. Miller's urgency made my stomach clench. It hits me that I didn't get any food from the machines. Why? As I stand to head back to the cafeteria, I realize that no one did. Not even the veteran subjects.

I freeze, steady my breathing, and look around the room. By instinct, I grab my notebooks and stuff them into the bag strapped across my chest along with the meager supply of food. Without thinking, I strip the bed of sheets and pack those, too.

"Five minutes until lockdown."

Lockdown? Overwatch didn't say anything about it earlier. After a moment of hesitation chewing at my bottom lip, my feet carry me out of the room, my loafers pounding on the tiled floor as I run to the bathroom. I stuff an extra set of clothes from the bathroom into my bag, then set off for the cafeteria.

The chaos has ended. The room is abandoned. Only toppled tables and chairs show signs of what happened here today.

"Two minutes until lockdown."

I head to the Snackables machine and make a selection, then swipe my wrist. While the machine prepares it, I do the same at the Drinkables, sticking with water. As I wait, the seconds seem to drag on. I shuffle from one foot to the next, glancing over my shoulder occasionally to see if anyone else is coming.

The halls are so quiet. Eerily quiet. It makes my skin crawl.

"One minute until lockdown."

"Come on, come on," I mumble.

The snack and drink drop out and I snatch them up, stuffing them in my bag before pivoting and running back to my room, feet pounding on the tiles. The sound echoes off the walls. A glance at open doors along the hallway reveals anxious faces clutching at their prizes.

I slip through my door as it swings shut and locks. Everything in the room disappears, and a two-foot round, white table appears in the center. Three items sit on top. A small cup of water. A pill in a cup. And a gun.

My stomach drops. What is the gun for?

"Survival Testing will commence once all participants have taken the pill," Overwatch announces.

I pick up the cup with the pill and stare at it. The medicine is small—about the size of an allergy pill—and blue. The water is likely there to wash it down, but I doubt it's necessary. No markings are visible on the pill. What is it? I shake the cup like it will knock loose answers.

"What is the pill?" I ask Overwatch.

"Participation is compulsory. The pill assists in the administration of the test."

Not really an answer.

"What is the Survival Test?"

"All test subjects participate in a Survival Test to determine the effectiveness of the pill. Participation is compulsory. Test subjects are permitted one stun gun for protection. No other weapons are permitted. The testing will end when the simulation completes."

The gun sits on the table surface, mocking me as if it knows I could never actually pull the trigger. The image of subjects fighting over food makes me wonder how far some will go to survive this test.

"Survival Testing will commence once all participants have taken the pill."

The pill slides down my throat easily on its own, but I drink the water anyway, wondering how long this test will last. The supply of water in my bag is limited. I can't afford to waste this cup.

The gun still waits for me. Other subjects will have this weapon as well. I can't afford to be left defenseless. My lack of Power already puts me at a disadvantage. My hand wraps around the cool metal handle. The gun is surprisingly light. A quick examination reveals nothing unusual—no strange markings or indicators of any kind. It looks like an ordinary gun. I'm not comfortable with the unfamiliar weight, so I fold it into the spare clothes in my bag.

A click in front of me makes my head snap up from the buckle securing my bag shut. The table is gone, and I stand in an empty white box. The door is open, but far from inviting. What would happen if

I just waited out the test in this room? My supplies might run out, eventually forcing me out to find more, but I could last at least a day in here if I ration the protein and water. Unless someone comes for me. If anyone shows up at this box looking for extra supplies, there will be no escape.

Already, the sounds of guns firing and people shouting filter through the open door. I swallow and wonder if I will need the gun. I hope not. Even if it is just a stun gun, I'm not sure I'd be able to fire at another person.

Maybe I take too long thinking it over because the longer I stand there, the more apparent it is that the walls are closing in on me. Literally. The size of the box has shrunk at least half the size it was. At first, it was the size of my room. Now, it's more the size of a bathroom.

Staying isn't an option. Paragon wants us out there, facing off against each other and whatever simulation it has created.

A hot breeze blows through the open doorway. Where are we? Anxiety creeps into my chest, but I edge toward the door and lean against the frame to peek out into the hallway.

But it isn't a hallway anymore.

My loafers crunch the brittle, brown ground as I step out, taking in the barren wasteland. It looks just like the world beyond the borders of Elpis. Crumbling remains of long-abandoned buildings. Trees without leaves, their scraggly branches reaching desperately toward the hot sky. Street signs so rusted I can no longer read them. And somewhere beyond, hints of a crater apparent by the massive pocket of nothing in the skyline. A hole likely created during the War by explosive atomic Naturalkinesis.

Suddenly, the desperation from the veteran subjects to gather as much of the food and water as they could carry makes sense. Nothing could survive out here, which makes any hope of foraging for food moot and water doubtful.

A few other test subjects stand stiff, staring out at the landscape just like me. Newbies, most likely, just as I am. What are we supposed to do here? Just survive? That doesn't seem like a useful test, unless Paragon is hoping that the pill will help people use their Powers to survive. In which case, I'm screwed.

Standing in the open makes me a target, so I turn back to my box, but it's gone. Nothing but the wasteland surrounds me. The entire floor has been transformed into one massive simulation.

East. Miller told me to meet him somewhere east, and I relayed the message to others. Maybe he knows the lay of the land here. At the very least, he has a supply of water I don't have, and the sun is already making my skin hot. It won't be long before sweat dehydrates me. I only managed to get two pouches of water. One from the table and one from the machine. Those won't last long.

I shield my eyes and seek out the sun, which is rising in the distance. Shifting the strap of my bag into a more comfortable position, I head toward the burning heat of the sun.

At first, I just trek across the cracked earth, but after passing through a grove of dead trees, I climb through the broken remains of what was once a major highway. I eventually find myself standing at the edge of a dried-up riverbed. I hesitate, looking north and south for another way across, but none is in sight.

The sound of voices hastens my decision, and I step carefully along the edges of the riverbed and lean back as my feet slide down the side. Maybe they are friendly, but I don't intend to risk the alternative.

"—need water," a male says.

"There's a river up ahead," another says.

I hold my breath and press my back to the west wall of the riverbed, hoping they won't see me. Their loafers scuff at the ground, approaching, then recede north as the two express disappointment at the dry river. The water probably wouldn't be safe for consumption anyway. If this simulation is realistic at all, the water supply is likely contaminated either with chemicals or radiation from the Fallout. Contamination is a real danger in the world beyond Elpis. I imagine this simulation is no different. I don't intend to find out.

Once I'm sure they are gone, I make my move to the other side of the riverbed and begin the climb out. More than once the dirt gives out under a hand or foot, and I have to adjust my grip to avoid slipping backward. A hand closes around my forearm and pulls me up. I'm in no position to resist, so I push myself up as they pull until I flop on the east bank on my back and close my eyes against the sun. Dirt cakes my hands, and I'm sure it's sticking to the sweat on my face.

"We're glad we found you." The voice is familiar. "You breathe like a horse."

I open my eyes, shielding them from the sun, and see Leo and Dave stand over me. I let out a sigh of relief as Dave pulls me to my feet. Friends. That's a relief.

"Thanks," I say, brushing the dirt from my clothes as best I can.

Dave glances at the empty riverbed, expression unreadable.

Leo smiles though. "So, how do we finish this?"

I shift my bag and start east. Leo sticks to my side. Dave is slower to follow.

"I'm not sure," I say. "I would guess it has something to do with that blue pill."

Both fall silent. I glance over and see Dave's hands balled into fists, his thick jaw clenched tight. He looks every inch a Somatic like his brand proclaims, but I wonder what his Power is. How come I never asked when we were in high school?

Again, they are hoping I have answers.

Again, I have none.

Whatever that pill is supposed to do, doesn't seem to have any effect on me yet. I don't feel or think any different. I feel exactly the same. I can't help but wonder if the same is true for them.

"You don't have to come with me," I say.

"We want to," Leo says, but a glance at Dave makes me wonder if that's true.

Dave and I get along well enough, but it always seems like he would rather be anywhere else. Right now, he is watching everything around us as we make our way over dead and broken ground.

"I suppose now would be a good time to find out what you two can do," I point out, watching Dave.

"Atomic Sight," Leo says. "I thought you knew that."

Leo's Power lets him see the bonds between atoms.

"I knew it had something to do with vision," I admit as we climb over the remains of a broken building.

Dave remains silent.

"He's working," Leo says, winded as he reaches the other side and dusts off his hands. "Parabolic Hearing."

That explains the silence. Dave can focus on the sounds in a specific area and filter out any unwanted noise. For all I know, he can't even hear us right now—or at least has chosen not to. Still, having him around could be helpful. At least nothing will sneak up on us.

I take a sip from my water supply as I consider what to tell them. Dave's ability could help us find Miller faster, but then again, he wouldn't be able to listen for danger.

The road we travel is cracked open in some places and buckled upward in others. It makes the trek more of a challenge. Chunks of a few buildings at some point crumbled into the street, forcing me to climb over them to pass. The devastation and the obstacles slow me down significantly, often forcing me to find other ways around the ruins. It's a maze of destruction.

Miller said to meet him to the east, and I intend to do that.

At an intersection, I find a set of half-buried street signs on the ground and crouch to brush away several layers of dirt and rocks. The signs are rusted, but the raised letters are still evident. W. Wells St. and N. 29th St.

As we venture onward, keeping an eye out for Mo or Trina, Leo occasionally strikes up a conversation. About graduation and the careers they were given—he was placed in training as a phlebotomist—and how everyone speculated about what happened to me or why I disappeared on Career Day. Apparently, people just thought I couldn't hack it. Probably accurate.

But Bianca knew. Or at least, had some idea. Clearly, she never said anything to anyone else.

The day wears on, and the sun begins dropping in the west. The farther up the road we travel, the wider the gap in the skyline grows. Tall buildings in broken remains circle the opening. We haven't reached the crater yet, but I can guess we aren't far now. The closer we get, the harder it is to find ways around the rubble. More of the street is blocked. More of the passages are mounds of debris, forcing us to climb over.

My hands ache from abrasion against the metal and rock I've had to climb. Sweat makes my scrubs stick to my skin. Thirst overwhelms my thoughts, but I'm afraid of drinking too much water too quickly. My tongue sticks to the roof of my mouth. I cave in and take another careful sip.

Where is Miller? How far east do I need to travel?

Hunger seizes my stomach and I double over, slipping on a bent steel girder as I lose my footing. I grab hold before falling through a gap between the beam and the stones. Dave and Leo help pull me up, and we sit on the edge of the hole. I brush my aching, reddened hands on the scrubs and pull the protein out of the bag. There haven't been signs of food so far, so if I'm not careful, I could run out. Dave and Leo don't have much in their inventory, either. I eat a quarter of the protein bar and wrap the rest back up, packing it the bag and slinging it across my chest before carrying on.

Another couple of hours of hard travel leaves us all exhausted. My clothes stick to my skin and chafing has started in the sweatier places. We need to find a safe place out of the sun to stop and rest. Maybe I will discover Miller there.

Maybe I won't find him at all.

The thought is disheartening, but not nearly as much as the sight of the old bridge collapsed over a highway that blocks us from going further. A quick scout in either direction makes it clear we have only one choice: attempt to climb over it.

"Maybe we can head north to find a way across?" Leo offers, casting doubts about climbing over the remains of the bridge.

"Miller wants to meet me east," I say. "So, I'm headed east."

"Why do you trust him? For all we know, he could be leading us into a trap," Dave says, nudging a toe experimentally against one of the boulders we have to cross.

"He wouldn't do that to me," I say. Would he? I trust Miller—or at least, I have no reason not to trust him—but maybe my trust is misplaced. Can I trust these two? Can I trust anyone?

"I don't hear him," Dave says doubtfully. "I don't think he's this way."

"I say we go north," Leo repeats.

I won't be stopped. If they want to go north, they can. But Miller has answers I need. He knows what this is about.

I don't give them a chance to convince me otherwise. The boulders are all that remains of the bridge, collapsed in several places. Going down will make it too hard to climb back up. I need to try and stay at street level.

"Ugene!" Leo says, shifting. "It's not stable enough to cross."

"Someone's coming," Dave says.

I peek my head into a crevice between two of the boulders. It's dark enough and should provide cover from whoever is coming. "Here." I wave them toward me. "We can rest in here while they pass."

"It's that Telepath," Dave says, a quiver in his voice. What sort of encounter did he have with the Telepath? Is it Terry?

A chill rolls up my spine despite the heat. Terry will find us.

A scream echoes off the buildings, muffled by distance. I know that scream. I've heard it before.

Enid.

22

MY HEART STOPS, AND I HESITATE, UNABLE TO PINPOINT where the scream came from. The echo distorts the location.

"I'm not crossing," Leo says, panic in his tone.

"Where is she?" I ask Dave. Enid needs help.

Dave shakes his head but doesn't respond. I can tell he's hiding something. Not eager to waste another second, I rush to Dave, grabbing a fistful of his shirt. Dave flinches back.

"Where is she?" I ask, my throat tight.

Dave glances over his shoulder to the southwest.

Enid screams again, and I release Dave, rushing southwest. The sound vibrates off everything from every direction, into my bones. The boom of one of the stun guns follows the scream. Instead of freezing me, the sound quickens my pace.

Leo and Dave pound their feet against the ground behind me as they follow. She can't be that far. Not if I heard her so clearly.

We climb over and around rubble, racing through the broken city as sweat rolls down my back. None of us say a word.

Then I hear it. Voices.

Three male voices drift from a distance, but their words are unclear. I slip my narrow body through a crevice between slabs of broken cement. The concrete is cold against my hot skin. It's a relief, and I eagerly lay my back against it as I strain to listen. Leo and Dave soon join me, all three of us holding our breath.

"They're trying to decide what to do with her now that they have her supplies," Dave whispers. "Maybe pinning her between walls of one of the buildings."

My stomach churns. They would just stash her away like that?

I pull my bag close. The gun is inside. I hope I don't need it.

The sound of the stun gun firing is unmistakable. Anger surges through my veins, burning hot as I shift to step out and confront the three boys, not really sure what I will do once I have their attention. But Dave grabs my arm and yanks me back, shaking his head. I tug and try to tell him to let go, but the fierce look in his eyes makes me hesitate.

Dave doesn't let go until all falls silent again. The second he does, I dart through the narrow gap between buildings, ready to divert the assailant's attention away from Enid, but the three of them are gone.

Enid lays on the ground, unconscious. I crouch beside her and press fingers to her wrist. Her pulse is there. I roll her head toward me and tap lightly at her cheek.

"They're gone," Dave announces.

Leo kneels on the other side of Enid, eyes sweeping over her. "She's fine. Just stunned. And they dislocated her shoulder."

Anger. Pure, boiling hot anger burns in my veins. My jaw twitches. Part of me wants to rush after them, make them pay. Part of me wonders if it's really them I'm angry with, or Paragon for making this possible. Were guns really necessary?

Leo puts a hand on my arm, gentle and reassuring. "You can't go after them, Ugene. Even with a stun gun, you don't stand a chance against the Telepath."

Enid's gun peeks out from under the edge of a rock, where it must have slid. Did she fire the first shot?

"Someone's coming," Dave hisses, watching westward.

My jaw clenches so tight it hurts my head, and I grab Enid's gun, shaking as I raise it west and point.

"It's just me!" Sho calls, stepping around rubble with his arms up.

All the tension in my shoulders gives out, and I drop the gun to the ground. How easy it was to point. How angry I was. I can't do this. I can't be like them. I won't.

Sho taps his temple. "I found you but knew those three were trouble, so I led them away."

I understand well enough. That last shot was his. Sho's Psychic Navigation let him find me. He must have already been close because his range is short.

"Help me," I say, sliding my hands under Enid's arms. "We need to move away from here in case they come back." Safety first, then I will do something for her arm.

Leo grabs her legs, and the two of us follow Sho's lead as he makes his way through gaps between buildings. Dave grabs Enid's gun and brings up the rear, listening for signs of danger.

Eventually, we find ourselves back at the broken bridge. Leo and I carefully set Enid down just inside the doorway of a building, out of sight. The inside of the building is like everything else. Broken ruins. No lights or glass on the windows. Chunks of rock, drywall, and steel litter the floor. This building has been vacant since the attack on the city that caused the crater.

"Now what?" Sho asks.

If only I had an answer.

"You've done this before, right?" I ask. He had to have. Miller seemed to know what was going on, and Sho has been here a year longer. "So, what do you suggest? How do we finish?"

Sho scratches his cheek and stares out through the broken window toward the bridge. "Usually I just use my skills to stay away from troublemakers."

"How long are we stuck in here?" Leo asks. He sits with his back against one of the crumbling walls.

Sho just stares at him, and the silence makes my stomach twist. My rations won't last long enough, judging by his silence.

I scrub dirt from my hands, and the skin turns an angry red. "Do you know where the building with the birds on it is? Miller said east."

Sho nods. "It isn't far. A few blocks from here, but we can't get across the highway without difficulty."

A few blocks. For the first time since this started, relief pushes out of my chest. I heave a sigh. Finally, some good news. Crossing the bridge will be a challenge, but at least Miller's close by.

Beside me, Enid stirs. Her eyes drift open, and she blinks at me, pushing away before realizing who I am. A whimper cracks from her throat as she reaches for her arm.

"It's okay, Enid," I reassure her. "They're gone."

She shifts to her good side and pushes herself into a seated position, cradling her bad arm against her chest. "It hurts." The words come out breathlessly.

"Okay." I dig in my bag for the sheet. It isn't much, but I can use it to make a sling for her. "Let's have a look."

Using as gentle a touch as possible, I brush the tips of my fingers over her arm. Tears leave clean lines on Enid's cheeks, but she doesn't make a sound. Her eyes stay fixed on my face.

"We can pop it back into place," Leo says.

"What do you think, Enid?" I ask, keeping her eyes on me.

"Just do it."

I hold her steady as Leo shifts into position to pop the shoulder back in. "Just watch me," I say softly.

Enid swallows and blinks away tears, then clenches her jaw. Her good hand grips mine. Leo counts to three, then yanks Enid's arm back so sharply I wince. Enid sobs once, her hand holding mine in a death grip. She gulps down air and her breath hitches, but she doesn't complain. Her dark, watery eyes stare at mine.

"Have you done this test before?" I ask, trying to distract Enid as I tear off a strip of my sheet to make a sling. It's the best we can do for now.

"Once," Enid breathes, then hisses as I shift her arm into the sling. I mumble an apology as she continues. "It was a long time ago. And it lasted days."

"Three and a half," Sho says, pulling bread from his bag.

Leo watches Sho with ravenous eyes.

"Where can we find food and water?" I ask. "We don't have enough to survive that long."

Sho just shakes his head.

"Enid, can you use something we have to create a food environment?" I check the sling to make sure it's secure.

She shakes her head, clenching her jaw tight. "There's a place," she finally says through clenched teeth. "An old grocery. But we won't reach it in the dark."

I glance toward a nearby window facing the street. The light is dying outside.

And Dave is aiming Enid's gun out the window at something.

"What are you doing?" I rasp, rushing to his side.

"Getting us across the bridge," Dave says.

A short, chubby figure stands near the edge of the bridge as the pieces stitch back together. Boyd!

"Don't!" I shove the gun down.

It accidentally fires off a shot that hits the ground outside the window, releasing a blue flash of light.

Boyd jumps, spins toward the shot and stands frozen like a terrified animal. The sound will surely attract attention.

I yank the gun from Dave's hand. "He's a friend," I snap, then duck through the window and rush to Boyd.

"U-Ugene." Boyd's sunken eyes widen, looking at the gun. "You-you shot at me."

"No, it was an accident." I turn my gaze to the half-finished bridge. "Can you finish patching the rest?"

Boyd swallows, watching the gun uncertainly, and nods. "M-my Power is str-str-stronger."

The others approach us in a clump, Leo standing close to Enid like he's afraid she will fall over. Her face is ashen in the growing moonlight.

Together, we form a plan for finishing the bridge, finding the building with the birds for the night, then in the morning we will scavenge for the food Enid says isn't far away. All of us are hungry, and I share what little I have with those who have nothing—Leo, Dave, and Enid. It leaves me with only part of the snack I got from the machine—a package of pretzels that make me thirsty—but if we find food and water tomorrow, maybe it will be okay.

Or maybe we will find Miller tonight.

As Boyd finishes the bridge—using existing materials to stitch together a path across—we all agree that should for some reason we get separated, we will meet at the building with the birds.

The sun has set, and soon it will be entirely dark. It doesn't leave much time to get the two blocks to the building.

A voice calls out behind us. "There he is!"

We all glance back, and Sho grips his gun in one hand.

"No." I wave at the others. "Go. Cross the bridge."

"It isn't done!" Boyd's protests fall on deaf ears as the others rush across his newly created bridge.

Terry, Derrek, and a third boy with a hooked nose I've seen with them but don't know, burst out from a group of buildings toward us. The third guy has his gun raised.

"Run!" I scream and raise my gun to take aim. My stomach twists in knots. I have no idea how to aim. No idea how to shoot…or even if I can.

"Ugene!" Enid screams at me from the other side of the bridge. "Come on!"

Hooked-Nose smirks and fires.

I duck.

The shot fires wide and hits the bridge.

Then the gun in my hands begins to melt. His Power must be Naturalkinesis, turning a solid into a liquid. Instinctively, I let go and back up as the three of them rush toward me. Hooked-Nose fires again, this time hitting the ground where I just stood. I turn on my heels and take off across the bridge.

Dense fog rolls through the buildings, and for a moment I fear it may be an acidic remnant from the war. But the fog parts around me and trundles toward them. The moisture in the air offers some relief to my hot skin.

When my foot falls on the unfinished edge of the bridge, there's no hesitation. I launch myself over the five-foot gap. My steps falter on the other side, slipping on the gravel and concrete. Dense fog covers the ground in each direction right up to the east edge. The three of them will have a hard time crossing the bridge.

"Come on," Enid waves me after her.

The others didn't bother waiting, which is fine. We will meet up as planned.

A scream rips into the air from inside the fog, then cuts off suddenly.

Terry's voice is muffled by the fog as he calls out to Troy.

The others in our group are out of sight now. I take Enid's good hand, shift my bag, and we break into a sprint. My body aches and resists the motion.

23

SHARDS OF GLASS FROM BROKEN AND CRUMBLING buildings on either side of the street leave me little choice but to run over them. Hopefully, my loafers have thick soles. The last thing I need is a shard of glass cutting into my feet right now.

The trio managed to cross the bridge—or at least what remains of the trio. They pursue Enid and me, but experience has taught me how to run faster than the people chasing me. My feet slip a couple times as I run over the debris, but Enid and I cling to each other for balance.

A few blocks ahead, a structure built over the road has suffered near-total collapse. Going through isn't an option and going over will slow me down. The red brick building to my right is open in the front where the bricks have fallen into the street. No birds on it either. We could try finding a place to hide in there, but the integrity of the building makes me question our safety, and I have no doubt they would discover us eventually. The building isn't that big.

I push on, glancing across the street at a sprawling building with broken windows on the upper levels and a long, collapsed entryway. That's a dead end. But on another wall…

Birds. Three of them. Could I be that lucky?   Could this be what Miller was talking about?

I skid to slow my step, then turn toward the entrance to the building along the wide, broken sidewalk. Enid is quick to follow.

The glass doors are broken, making it easy to slip through, ducking under the bars across them. Glass crunches under our shoes, but I see tracks. Someone else is here. Or at least has been. Hopefully one or more of the others. Or Miller. If not, we could be in a world of trouble.

My pursuers' voices grow more distant as I turn east inside the wide corridor. Parts of the ceiling have collapsed into the building, offering partial vision in the dying daylight. I push on the doors to an interior room and peer in. Empty. Just seats and a sky. It's a dead end, too. If I'm followed, I'll have nowhere to go.

Nothing else along the wide corridor offers any potential. Enid and I head west of the doors.

"There!" Outside, Terry and Derrek are gathered on the sidewalk. After spotting me, they rush toward the door.

I utter a curse under my breath and sprint due west on Enid's heels, only to meet another dead end. Broken escalators to our right offer the only means of escape as they close in. Where are the others?

Our only choice is up—into the darkness above. It's a risky move. The floors could be collapsed. Any number of items or debris could block our path. Perhaps, those windows I spotted outside offer some light. Peering into the darkness doesn't give me much hope. But there's movement.

Dave stands at the top of the escalator, waving me up. Enid is the first to go. I follow.

My legs resist, shaking. A shot shatters the quiet, and blue light casts just enough illumination up the stairs to help guide my way before it disappears. Terry and Derrek fired at me.

Finally, I reach the last step, hearing the two of them climbing up after us into the darkness.

Dave presses a finger to his lips and takes my hand, pulling me deeper into the darkness. I quickly grab Enid's good hand, so she isn't lost in the dark. My heart hammering against my ribs, I shuffle along beside Dave. My feet kick at something just as Enid pulls back. I squint.

A gorilla. It takes a moment for me to recognize it's stuffed. I touch the plaque beneath the display and can only make out one word: Samson.

"It's too dark," Terry whispers. "Can you see?"

Derrek's voice is hard. Angry. "No."

Relief. I hold my breath. Dave gives my hand a small tug away, and I don't protest. Glass on the floor gives us away, crunching. We freeze.

"Did you hear that?" Derrek asks.

"Shh!"

Silence. The only sound is my beating heart. Then their feet begin scraping the ground. Dave tugs again, and we turn away from the sound of their feet to go deeper into the building.

Soft light glows ahead, and I realize Dave is being guided along by Sho. I glance back, but there's no way Terry and Derrek can see it. The light is at an angle away from us. We head toward it, and I pray that whatever waits ahead won't be more dangerous than what follows behind.

The floor becomes more uneven. As we draw nearer to the light, I can see that the ground is stone. Cobblestone, maybe. It's a street! How can there be a street inside the building?

We round a corner and carefully edge along the street. The source of light is apparent now. Boyd created it. He stands just up the street, holding a thin line of light between his hands. It's risky, casting any sort of illumination in this dark space. It will draw Terry and Derrek to us.

I try not to sneeze as dust kicks up under our feet. Miller, I pray you're here.

"Light this way," Derrek calls. Feet scuff the floor back the way we came.

They will find us soon. We need to move faster. We need to get off this floor. Maybe we can escape back to the first floor.

The five of us hurry as fast as we dare along the street, catching glimpses into bizarre old shops with ancient paraphernalia. Someone stares at me from a window, and I stumble back, bumping into an unlit lamp post. It takes a moment to calm my pounding heart once I realize it's fake—not a real person. Sho is grinning at me.

Trying to calm my nerves, I close my eyes and take a deep breath, letting it out slowly. It's no different than sneaking into my parents' house and avoiding the creaks. I just need to be careful where I step. Someone else in the test can probably smell fear. I need to control it. But my hearing is more acute because of the fear.

The wall beside me is suddenly gone. Is it moving or did it just end?

We explore deeper through the odd maze. Just keep moving away from sounds. They're closer now. Terry can probably sense us with his telepathy.

Enid steps so close to me our bodies are almost pressed together. "Straight," she whispers into my ear. The heat from her body warms me. She motions straight across the room, then points at me. She then points at herself and back. I get what she's saying. We need to split up, make it harder for them to track us. But I can't leave her. And I certainly can't let her go toward them.

I shake my head. No. This is a terrible plan.

Enid scowls and pushes me away with her good hand. I stumble, but quickly catch my balance and move toward her again.

Except Dave won't let me. He grabs my arm and pulls me straight ahead. The ground beneath our feet begins to rumble, and as I watch over my shoulder, Enid raises a wall of stone across the street, blocking it off.

I don't want to lose her. I don't want to leave her, but Dave gives me no choice.

Boyd and Sho are already gone, and with them, the last of the light.

Dave and I shuffle along carefully. Since he seems to have a keener sense of direction with his Hearing, I move him forward to take the lead. My ears strain for signs of Enid, and I keep wondering where she is and what's happened to her. She hasn't made a sound, so I can only hope for the best.

Suddenly, the whole building shakes. I grab a display case to my right to catch my balance. Dave screams, the sound echoing downward. Just enough light shines from below to reveal a new hole in the floor. Dave pushes off his back from the depths, coughing and brushing debris and dust from his scrubs. I didn't even see him fall.

"I'll get you back up," I call down to him.

"Don't. Just go. I can see an exit."

I open my mouth to protest, but he's already moving.

Biting my lip, I edge cautiously around the hole and continue until all is darkness again.

"I feel his mind," Terry says from somewhere beyond the darkness.

It's time to move. I don't fear Terry. But I do fear another fight with Derrek.

Taking a few breaths to gather courage, I glare at the darkness ahead of me, one hand pressed to the wall, muscles taut.

Go. Just go.

They're closing in.

Move, Ugene!

Closer.

If I bolt and something is in my way, I'm screwed.

Closer.

God, the walls are closing in on me. Pain presses against my chest. My breaths shallow. I push off from the wall and run, praying nothing will jump out at me from the darkness. I keep running.

Move. Just keep moving.

Cool air rushes past. The toe of my shoe catches on something, and I pitch forward on my face, tasting metal and blood.

A scuffle breaks out somewhere behind me, grunts and sounds of impact. A fight. Maybe one of my friends. Maybe not. Maybe Derrek. There's no way for me to tell. Something shatters, then there's a clatter as Terry calls for help.

I reach out, my face and ribs and knees aching.

Grooved metal brushes my fingertips, cold and straight, then up at a right angle.

Stairs.

Scrambling to my feet, I wipe the blood from my nose and mouth. Sweat prickles across my forehead. Taking steps two at a time, hand securely on the cold, smooth rail, I pray no one else follows. When

I reach the top, I turn sharply and run into a wall that vibrates upon impact.

A flash of blue light emanates from the bottom of the stairs, accompanied by the boom of a gun, then shoes climbing the steps. Dave or Enid? But I can't dare to hope. It could be Terry or Derrek.

Heart in my throat, I reach desperately out in the dark ahead until my hand brushes across a smooth, glass-like surface. A door? I grasp around for a handle but when I pull it's locked. I'm trapped. Whoever follows me will be here soon. A shaky breath slips out.

A taste of metal. Blood still trickles out of my nose and from the corner of my mouth, mixing with the sweat on my brow as it drips down. I press the hem of my shirt against it, then head the other direction away from the stairs.

My toe hits the bottom of a display, and I pitch forward, skidding on my stomach across broken glass. It rips up my shirt, and I bite my lip to avoid screaming out. And there's something else. Stairs. More stairs up.

"I heard him!" Derrek calls. "He's on this floor."

Hopefully, they will search this floor before moving on. I ease myself as slowly and silently as possible off the floor. There's a chance Derrek will stumble across me before I escape, but it's better than giving away my intention of going up another level.

I tiptoe up the stairs, using the rail to help guide me along.

Something crunches under my foot as I near the top. I wince. Freeze. Hold my breath. Wait.

Silence.

I breathe out and take the next step.

Steps pound behind me.

Something grabs my ankle, and I pitch forward, cutting my forearms on the edge of a metal step.

"Got him!" Derrek calls.

I kick back, praying his head is near my foot. It connects with something, and Derrek releases his grip. I scramble up the last few steps but don't make it more than a couple feet before Derrek tackles me to the ground.

I wince, my hand scrambling across the floor for something, anything, to help me. It closes around something solid and I swing as hard as I can at what I hope is his head. He yelps and falls to my side.

Heart in my throat, I dart out, praying for escape. Before I take a few steps, he grabs my arm and throws me to the ground. The air punches from my lungs as I land on my back.

Derrek pins me down. Shards of the debris dig into my back. Derrek's face hovers inches above my own.

"Don't make a sound, Powerless Prick," Derrek hisses, the stink of body odor makes me gag. "Or we make it look like a suicide."

Even in the darkness, I can see his face clearly, leaning in close to mine. His breath reeks. Something about the way his eyes dig into mine makes every part of my body freeze—nose curled up in a snarl, the corners of his eyes creased to show a clear warning, teeth bared.

Terry joins us, his loafers crunching on shards, and crouches beside me, leaning closer.

"Your questions are starting to cause trouble, Powerless Prick," Terry says.

Questions. How does he know? What does he know? My pulse quickens.

"Derrek here can't allow that, and neither can I. Your questions could shut down this program. This place might be hell, but it's a roof and three meals a day."

I say nothing. Having a Somatic pushing you into shards of glass and other debris will do that.

"Here's what's gonna happen," Terry continues. "Starting right now, you stop asking questions. Stop knocking on doors. Stop looking for answers. No more secret conversations. No more hanging with friends. You go about your tests. We go about ours. Everything is fine."

"I don't know what you're—" I cut off with a sharp hiss as Derrek drives the debris deeper into my back.

Terry watches me, but I can't see his expression as clearly as Derrek's. "Don't play stupid with me."

Right. Telepath. He probably knows something already.

"You don't knock the questions off, we come back," Terry says. His low, growling voice paints a crystal-clear picture as to how our next meeting will go.

Derrek lacks his friend's knack for subtle threats. "See, next time we'll—"

"—make it look like suicide," I say without thinking.

Derrek shoves me down again, driving the shards of debris in deeper. A few are almost entirely flush with my back now.

Pain clenches my teeth. Warm blood soaks into my t-shirt, sticking to my back.

"A word of this to anyone else…" Derrek says.

"I get it," I say, trying not to cry.

Derrek shoves me one last time to dig the shards deeper still as he pushes off.

Blinding, brilliant white light fills the room, and I squeeze my eyes shut. It doesn't block the brightness.

I hear Derrek and Terry scream. For a moment, the air is filled with shouts, commands from Terry and negative responses from Derrek. I raise an arm to cover my eyes. Terry and Derrek's voices are suddenly swallowed by silence. Something tugs at me and pulls me across the floor on my back. Shards of debris cut into what's left of my skin. I scream. The weight of an anchor holds me down. Then the light disappears.

I roll into a sitting position slowly, wincing in pain, rubbing at my eyes to assist in adjusting to the light changes. Jagged edges of glass stick in my back. Touching one sends hot pain down my spine. I clench my jaw so tightly it hurts my teeth and pull. When I remove the glass, it bites into my palm, cutting as I try to pull it out. I drop the glass and examine the wound in my hand, a gaping slash across my palm and in the folds of my fingers. I can't take care of the injuries alone.

Adjusting to the sudden near-dark is complicated after such blinding light. No one is around, as far as I can tell. I shift to my knees and try to stand. The pain around each of the jagged edges of the glow-shade cause searing hot pain with even the smallest of motions, also making it hard to breathe. It makes my knees shake, and the muscles in my legs buckle. I yelp and stumble, grabbing at anything for support. Darkness and blurred lines edge my vision. I squeeze my eyes to clear it.

Light. A dim glow. It drifts toward me, illuminating the familiar form of Celeste. Was she the one who created that light? What did she do to Terry and Derrek?

"You bleat like a dying sheep," she says with her timid voice.

"I don't suppose you have healing hands, too, do you?" The attempt at humor falls flat through clenched teeth.

"Come."

Celeste takes my arm, helps me to my feet. Every movement and step are sharp reminders of the pieces in my back, digging deeper. Poor Celeste carries most of the burden of my weight. The world flashes bright, blindingly white, then fades to black like a slow strobe. I can't focus on anything, trusting her to guide us and putting all my attention into taking substantial steps, one foot at a time.

The soft light guides our way, faintly illuminating displays of arctic life, past an igloo. We are in a museum. That explains a lot. The hallway twists and bends back and forth, and the two of us struggle along. Where is she taking me?

Asia. Or at least what we were taught Asia once was before everything changed. Celeste helps me up the step into a fake home. A woman—a mannequin—watches me with haunting eyes as Celeste shifts her grip to ease me down.

"Lie on your stomach," she says.

Tears streak my vision as I lie down, happy to hide my face, trusting her to handle the rest.

The space smells of must and old age. I turn my head to the side and can just see the rock garden outside—or what is supposed to be outside. Everything is manufactured, fake.

Celeste pulls on a chunk of debris. Each one feels like a razor slicing my flesh. Celeste isn't terribly delicate, either. The cold bamboo floor presses against my stomach, making the cuts ache. Celeste grabs the back of my shirt by one of the tears and rips it open.

One by one, she pulls out the chunks of debris—glass and pieces of wood—and sets them on the floor right in front of my face. Each covered in blood, which oozes off and drips onto the floor. Sometimes it feels like her fingers are ripping into my flesh, digging for chunks of debris. Every yank is like they are being shoved in again, and each rips another strangled sound from deep in my throat.

"God Celeste! That hu—"

She pulls another one, and my voice cuts out.

A chorus of panicked voices call out my name from somewhere in the distance. Or maybe it isn't any distance at all. I can't tell through the pain burning my body. Nor can I call back.

The stink of blood mingles with a metallic taste in my mouth. I squeeze my eyes shut against the pain and sight of blood-covered glass.

A familiar voice drifts through the haze. "Christ, your back!"

Miller! His voice is muffled by the sound of my heart thumping in my ears, but it's him. "What the hell happened?" he asks.

"A couple guys… warned me," I say through gritted teeth as Celeste presses her hands against my back. The words are like sharp needles of pain all their own.

Miller crouches in front of me. "I warned you about this."

"Not helpful." My words choke away in a wheezy gasp as the air locks up in my lungs. I can't breathe. I try to speak, but nothing comes out. Not even a scream of pain. The room starts to spin faster and faster, then fades.

Miller's voice sounds muffled. Distant. "What are you doing to him?"

I try gasping for breath, but nothing happens. Miller becomes more of a shadowy form in the fading room, pointing at me and yelling at Celeste. But I can't hear anything. Just the slowing thumps of my heartbeat.

24

THE ROCK GARDEN SWIMS BACK INTO FOCUS. THE shards of glass are gone. The skin on my back feels stretched to the limit. Some spots feel like they're burning.

More muffled voices.

A female. I almost recognize it.

"Thank you, Rosie," Miller says.

"You're lucky I found you when I did," Rosie says. Who is Rosie?

Feet shuffle and scrape against the bamboo floor. Shadows dance on the wall.

I'm still too weak to move.

"What…" My voice sounds foreign. Raspy and dry.

Enid crouches on her haunches in front of me—her sling gone—brushing a hand over my face. It burns hot against my skin.

"Cold," I mumble.

Miller puts my arm over his shoulder and, with Dave's help, sits me upright. Blood stains the floor where I had lain. I'm freezing; my whole body is shaking like I've been submerged in an ice bath. Miller helps me settle against the artificial wall, then sits across from me, perching his arms over his chest. Rosie lingers near the doorway. Rosie, the mousy girl I've seen before. A Divinic Healer.

"He's doing okay," Rosie says to Miller. "I'm going."

I want her to stay, but I can't think of a reason to ask, so I let her walk off until she dissolves into the shadows up the fake street and disappears around the corner. I watch her go and notice that Miller, Dave, and Enid aren't the only ones around me.

Trina leans against a wall, her clothes ripped. Leo has an arm around her, offering quiet reassurances. Sho and Boyd huddle in the fake street, their heads together and speaking quietly to one another. Mo sits on the steps of the phony house we occupy, arms wrapped around his knees, rocking himself. Everyone is here.

Except for Celeste.

"What h-happened?" My teeth chatter. I try rubbing my upper arms to warm back up.

"You died." Miller's lips curl downward, and for a moment he scowls at the door. "I don't know what she thought she was doing, but it sure as hell wasn't healing."

Celeste. It was an accident. Had to be. She wouldn't do that to me on purpose.

"If Rosie hadn't shown up when she did," Enid says, the implication of the rest clear enough.

Despite the chill in my bones, I blush. Taking in everything, the blood on the floor—and so much of it. The smell of it turns my stomach.

"Celeste... What did she do? Where is she?" I reach shaking hands into my bag and pull out the sheet and crisp shirt. Enid steps forward to help me pull the shirt on after she removes the ripped, bloodied one. I wrap the sheet around me, but it offers little warmth.

"Some crazy trick I've never seen before," Miller says. "She disappeared when Rosie showed up. And good riddance."

The look on Miller's face reminds me of my dad's right before I'm about to land in trouble. Only this time, it isn't directed at me. I notice that the light isn't coming from Celeste's strange glowing light anymore. Streetlights line the fake street, and somehow two of them glow with soft light.

"What happened, kid?"

"Stop c-calling me that!"

"We just want to know," Enid huffs, moving out into the street and looking both directions.

I shake my head and say, "Terry and Derrek. Something about

me asking the wrong questions and rumors about me shutting the program down. They were pissy about it."

"God…" Miller is clearly biting his tongue, raking his hands through his shaggy blond hair and tugging, staring at the lamp instead of at me, tapping a fist against the doorframe. He's struggling to keep his opinions to himself. His jaw clenches. "I warned you."

"It's not a big deal," I say. "Just leave it alone."

"Whatever," Miller grumbles.

"Miller…"

But the stubborn set of Miller's expression makes it abundantly clear that arguing my point won't matter. Miller is as stubborn as my dad.

"Are they watching us?" I ask, pulling the blanket tighter. "Because I can't understand why Paragon would let stuff like this happen."

Miller looks up at the ceiling as if Overwatch is there. Maybe she is.

Silence descends over us.

The others gather in the doorway of the manufactured Asian-style home. Miller digs a protein bar and water out of his bag and starts eating, then after a moment, he grimaces and grudgingly offers us some of his supply.

As the rest of us eat, Miller begins scouting up and down the road.

Paragon is obviously going above and beyond with their research here, but to what end? I roll my neck, then pull out one of my notebooks, the smell of the paper soothing my headache. I sigh, sit back and stare down at the pages again. What are they doing and what do they stand to gain?

Maybe they *have* found the links that bind the Powers to our DNA and are now just lining up the pawns to test their theories. I've read Dr. Cass's article on Power classification linking mechanisms a thousand times. Paragon may have everything it needs to corner the market on selling more than one Branch of Power to people. And if they can find a way to bottle specific Powers within each Branch…

I shoot upright.

It should have occurred to me sooner.

The pill.

We all had to take it. The pill has had no effect on me as far as I can tell, but Boyd said his Power was stronger, and he isn't the only one over-performing in this test. Enid created a fog she never could have created before. Sho found his way around without difficulty, and Dave seemed to hear better than he should have. The pill must have amplified their Powers. But for how long?

This test suddenly makes much more sense—wrong, but still understandable. The only way to truly test the viability of something that enhances Powers is to throw people into a situation where they have to push past their reasonable limits. It also means we are stuck in here for however long the effects last. Paragon will want to know how long it takes for the pill to wear off. And if they can perfect this pill, maybe, just maybe…

I could potentially gain a Power. Any Power.

It's the only thing I ever wanted. But in exchange, everyone is subjected to more of this testing as Paragon perfects their pill. Is this what I want? It helps my dad, being in here, but how do I know Dr. Cass is holding up her end of the deal? And am I willing to let others face this level of torture just to get him a few more days?

I watch the others setting up defenses and finding places to get rest on the bamboo floor. Enid settles in beside me, lying with her head close to my legs. It doesn't take long for her to fall asleep. Everyone needs rest, but I can't. I understand now.

And it's time to make a choice, just as Celeste warned me.

I can stay here, hoping for a cure to my problem, for a Power, while also potentially getting my dad more of the treatment he needs. But doing that means subjecting these people—my friends—to more of this torturous testing. While I may not understand why Paragon goes to such lengths, I've no doubt that their methods are immoral. Choosing to stay and continue the testing means forcing everyone else to do the same. Or…

I can create a plan that gets everyone out of here, saving the other test subjects—all of them. But doing so means I will never get a Power, and my father could die. Celeste's words ring in my head. *Choices must be made.*

Did her warning mean I should choose my father? Should I follow her advice? And what about the test subjects who've disappeared? What happened to them? My heart refuses to accept the answer my mind is trying to shelter me from.

They were the first to be tested with these pills. Taken from our floor and never seen again. If the pills work, it's possible those subjects were released back into the world to assimilate back into ordinary life. Yet, doing so would risk exposing everything Paragon is working for. They can't afford that risk.

Choices must be made.

Even though the answer makes me sick to my stomach, makes me fight to keep from throwing up, I know what I must do.

My choice is made. We have to find a way out, even if I never get a Power. Even if it costs my dad his treatments. I can't let others suffer through this anymore. Not if I can stop it.

Everyone else is settled in for sleep. Except for Miller, who still patrols the street. I wave him over, and a minute later he's settling in close to my side.

Celeste said the walls are always listening, so there's no safe place to talk. Not even in a simulation.

I keep my voice to a whisper and explain everything. The pill. The missing test subjects. The purpose of the testing, my dad. Miller has to lean close to hear, and he remains silent as I talk, not once interrupting. His face gives him away, white skin paling even more, pain in his eyes.

"So, what are you trying to convince me of?" Miller asks, his face puzzled.

"So… If I know who has what Powers, maybe I can figure out how we can get out of here." I pull out my notebook and show Miller the map I've been working on since that first day.

"Okay." Miller scans my somewhat detailed map. "Then what? Prop 8.5 just means we'll land back in here."

"Except Mo said there's a group trying to help people evade capture," I say. "They don't agree with the proposition."

Miller falls silent, examining his hands. He tugs the hood of his sweatshirt up over his messy hair and pulls on the hood string. His shoulders tense, and a couple times I think he's about to tell me something, but nothing comes out.

I nudge him. "What is it?"

Miller bites his lip, then looks at me. His grey-blue eyes are haunted. "What do you think happens to people who test out, then?"

I smooth my fingers over the pages of the journal. I can only answer with a headshake. Sure, I could wager a guess—but the answer wouldn't be good.

Miller glances toward the street, body rigid. "I had a friend in here not that long ago. A mentor. Jaymes Murphy. He could do amazing things with Mutation."

"Another Naturalist Manipulator, like you?"

Miller nods. "But Paragon was pushing him. Real hard. He was ragged and getting sick and weak, losing weight." Miller swallows. "One morning, Murph was just gone. I still don't know what Paragon was trying to get from him, but they told me Murph tested out. As weak as he was, I'm not sure he would survive out in the real world on his own, and he didn't have anyone else."

I close the notebook and rub my eyebrows. "So, what do you think Paragon actually did to him?"

Miller tugs at his hood again and turns his head away, but not before I notice he is on the edge of tears. "I can't—"

Both of us fall silent. No sounds but Miller's sniffles and shaky breaths as he fights for control of his emotions. Heat rises in my skin. Jade told me Miller only ever had one friend. Maybe the loss of Murphy was too much. Maybe that's why he's always so distant.

Jade. Vicki. Both of them are gone, taken out of testing by Forrest. What happened to them? I close my eyes and picture the blue pill in the cup.

If I were Paragon, and willing to go to such lengths as this test, how far would I go to find out if my hypothesis were valid, and to protect them from discovery? Judging by what we've been through in this test so far, Paragon will do anything—try anything—to ensure their theories were correct, including taking test subjects and doing additional, and maybe even more extreme, experiments on them individually. The blue pill may only be the beginning. The very thought chases away the chills.

"Oh, God…" A sickening feeling hits my gut like a rock.

"What?"

Jade's room was trashed when they took her. Someone on the brink of freedom wouldn't react like that. Jade knew she wouldn't be coming back. There's no such thing as testing out. I don't know what Paragon does with people they take from the floor, but I'm sure it isn't testing out. That would risk exposing the truth behind their tests. Whatever they are doing to those people must be more… permanent.

I don't dare tell Miller that Murphy is probably dead. He likely already suspects as much. "Miller… we need to get out of here." My body is shaking. Neck stiff. Legs numb.

I want to do this for my dad, but at what cost? My dad will survive a little longer—maybe long enough for me to get him proper treatment somehow—but we won't. Not if we test out. I can't risk putting others through it.

I wave a hand to cool off my burning hot face. "I can only think of one way Paragon lets us out of here."

Miller places a surprisingly steady hand on my shoulder. "Okay. So, we need to get out of here. How?"

It takes several swallows before I can speak. "We need a telepath to help get the guards attention and open the stairwell doors, but the only one I knew is gone. None of the Telepaths will talk to me."

"They aren't so fond of me, either," Miller smirks, and despite the apparent redness of his eyes and wet cheeks, there's a mischievous bravado about him.

"We can't walk out," I say. "Security."

"Right. The doors. But your girlfriend—"

"She's not my girlfriend." I shake my head. "And if something is going on, having Bianca help will only endanger her."

"So, how then?"

I close my eyes to try and stop the room from spinning.

"Don't know, but maybe…" I snap my gaze to him. "Persistence. Perseverance. Knowledge." Miller arches a brow, and I smirk. "My superpower. Brains. Brains and a dream team."

"You're insane," Miller laughs. "You really believe you can think your way out of this?" He waves absently at the museum around us.

"Yes." Despite the churning in my stomach, I can't help but grin. "I did it on Testing Day. I'll make a list of what we need and who we need to get it. Just make sure your stuff is packed and ready to go."

Dad is a problem I will have to solve later, but I can't wait around here for Paragon to test me out—to test any of us out. I need information, and to get it, I need the right Powers.

The museum disappears, replaced by blinding white light and Overwatch's voice.

"Simulation complete."

25

THE DOOR DOESN'T IMMEDIATELY SWING IN LIKE IT does when testing completes. I shift, limbs stiff and aching, and roll to my knees using the wall for leverage as I stand. My muscles feel strained beyond their limits, stretched too thin. For a moment, my vision swims and darkens. I press my shoulder to the wall to keep from falling over. Rosie's healing—along with whatever Celeste did to me—took more from my body than I realized.

It takes longer than I care to admit before I finally reach the door. There's no handle, so I try to dig my fingers into the edge and pull. Either I'm too weak, or the door is locked because it doesn't budge.

I'm not sure how long I attempt to get the door open. Long enough that my muscles are stronger again, and the exhaustion is waning in favor of hunger and thirst. After several more failed attempts to open the door, along with pounding on it to see if someone will come by and push it open, I just accept that it's locked.

But why?

The simulation is over. They should let us out.

I give up and sit on the edge of my stripped bed, staring at the door. Maybe if I try hard enough, Telekinetic Power will spontaneously reveal itself, and the door will swing open? At least, that's how hard I focus on it, willing it to open.

The hunger hurts, gnawing at my stomach, making my hands shake. They wouldn't leave me in here to starve, would they? Paragon needs me for their research. Letting me starve to death wouldn't be of any help at all.

A chime sounds, followed by the grinding of the lock on the doorframe. The door swings open. Finally!

I move as quickly as my body can handle toward the cafeteria.

All evidence of the chaos that ensued in this room before the test began is gone, as if it never happened. The tables and chairs are as they should be, grey tile polished, the walls displaying the sun setting over Elpis's downtown spires. Does that mean it's dusk? Is it the same day or not? How many could have passed without our knowledge? Enid said that time passed differently in simulations, so we can't honestly know how long it's been. Can't have been more than two days, or the hunger would have had more severe effects on subjects.

I shift from one foot to the other, waiting impatiently for my food. As soon as it dispenses, I make another selection, and again, until the machine tells me I have reached my limit for the day. I then move on to the Snackables machine and repeat the process, all the while eating as I wait.

No one else enters.

No one else is here.

I'm alone, and the silence is deafening.

Once I finish the meals from the HotServe, I take my snacks and leave the cafeteria. After a couple minutes, I'm standing in front of Miller's closed door. I knock.

No answer.

I push on the door, it doesn't budge.

If the simulation is complete and my door has finally opened, shouldn't his be as well?

I pound on the door this time, though I know there isn't a point. His door is locked.

"Ugene!"

I spin around to see Trina rushing toward me. As she draws closer, I can see that she is shaking, and her face is a more ghostly pale than her natural alabaster complexion. Before I can ask what's wrong, her hands grip my arms, jarring an oat bar from my grip. It hits the floor and breaks.

"Is this real? Is it—is it…" Tears well in her eyes, filling my heart with nothing but sympathy. What did she endure before finding us in the museum? What did she endure after I left?

"Yes." At least, I think it's real, but her question makes me second-guess my assumption.

Trina's body crumples as her legs give out, and I barely grab her in time to hold her up. I want to ask her what happened, but also don't want to make her relive something so traumatic. Instead, I hold her against my chest and stroke her stringy, sandy-blond hair. She whimpers into my shirt.

This isn't right. Any of it. Paragon can't get away with this. How have they gotten away with this so far? Does the Directorate not realize what's going on? They signed the bill, allowing people to get forced into this testing. Did they know what they agreed to?

Did I?

I give Miller's closed door one last glance before leading Trina away. She needs rest. I need help to bring this whole thing to an end. And to do that I need Powers—other people's Powers.

It doesn't take long to locate Michael and Dave, and we convene in one of the bathrooms on the floor. By the time I have both of them gathered, Trina has calmed down and now lays on a bed of folded clean scrubs on the bathroom floor.

The first phase of my plan is simple enough—gathering information that will help us either escape or help stop this madness once we get out. To do that, I need the help of these three. I explain my idea—to use their Powers to get a hold of Forrest's tablet and access it. Dave, Michael, and I discuss how to go about it. Michael resists at first, terrified that DNA imprinting won't work, that Forrest will suspect it and Michael will be caught, that Paragon will choose to test him out. I manage to talk him down. I admit it puts a lot of risk on his shoulders, but without a telepath to read Forrest's mind, there isn't much choice.

Trina begins sitting up straighter, hope blooming in her eyes.

"But how do we get the tablet?" Dave asks. "Forrest never lets it out of his sight."

"Let me take care of that," Trina says. The confidence in her tone brings us all to silence.

With our plan in place, we say goodnight as some of the other male subjects enter the bathroom for showers, giving all four of us strange looks—particularly Trina.

Before I can head back to my room, I need to make one more stop.

Celeste's door is open just a touch. Enough for me to know it isn't locked like Miller's was. No light emits from inside, so I rap lightly and call to her before slipping inside and closing the door behind me. I just want to make sure she's okay.

A lump on the bed tells me that Celeste is here, and her steady breathing says she's asleep. Not wanting to disturb her, I wedge myself between the desk and the bookshelf and pull my knees to my chest. She needs to know I'm okay, that whatever she did to me, there's no cause for concern. For now, I close my eyes and just let my tense, aching muscles relax.

A stream of light comes over the horizon, waking me. I turn to the side and am greeted by a row of books. Then it comes back to me. A strange room. Celeste's room. I must have fallen asleep waiting for her to wake.

The sunlight reaches to the ceiling, illuminating everything with golden light. I blink and rub the sleep from my eyes. My head aches from using the side of the desk as a pillow all night, and my cramped knees scream when I stretch out my legs and arms. A massive yawn escapes me.

Celeste rolls over, emitting a squeak when she sees me in the corner.

"I'm sorry." I try—and fail—to stand. "I just wanted to make sure you're okay. Let you know that I'm okay, too, I guess. I must have fallen asleep waiting for you to wake up."

Celeste pulls the blankets up and presses her back against the wall at the head of the bed, cowering away from me.

I manage to stand, but she shrinks away when I move closer.

"It's okay. It's me, Celeste. Ugene."

Her guard lowers, and she meets my gaze entirely.

"I'm not sure how to ask this," I say, fumbling to find the right words, "but what happened?"

Even though she is looking at me, Celeste still holds the blankets between us like a shield. "The circle of life. What once was, comes around again."

I shake my weary head, unwilling and unable to wrap my mind around her latest riddle. "Why did you leave?"

"The chains have broken." She starts rocking, clutching the blanket in white knuckles. "He has risen. He comes."

"Celeste."

She shakes her head back and forth, rocking. "The chains have broken. He has risen. He comes."

What is she prattling on about? I scrub a hand through my hair and glance at the door. "I'll be back later," I say, accepting I won't get any real answers from her. Not with the state she's in.

She just keeps rocking. "The chains have broken. He has risen. He comes."

I step into the hall and pull the door shut. There's a commotion in the corridor.

Security. They're everywhere. Two guards stand sentry a few feet down the hall. Others trot around the corner and take up position next to them. My gut tells me there will be more on the way.

Stuffing my hands into my pockets, I head back toward my room. But I come up short at the corner.

Forrest is at Terry's door. My heart leaps into my throat, and I dart around the corner to hide, then lean against the wall and strain to listen.

"—but he isn't easy to read," Terry says.

"Then force it."

What are they looking for? Terry warned me that I was asking too many questions. What did he already know?

"Stay put and keep your door shut," Forrest says. "Your test begins soon."

The door clicks shut. Forrest's feet scrape the tiled floor in long strides. And he's headed in my direction.

Crap. My breaths quicken. I fumble back a couple of steps until my hand brushes a door. I give it a test push, and it opens. I quickly slip backward, facing the door and not caring whose room it is. With another gentle push, the door clicks shut.

"What are you doing here?" the occupant asks.

I spin around.

The drawn features and dark hair are instantly recognizable. Omar. From one of my tests—Aurology, I think. His room smells of jasmine incense, burning somewhere out of sight. While his room has typical furniture, from what I can see, he's added ethnic touches. A golden and burgundy rug, a finely woven comforter with intricate mandala design of green and yellow, a document box on the bedside table with hand-painted scenes.

I press a finger to my lips.

"Harbinger of Hope." Omar steps toward me, his hand reaching out.

Instinct makes me lean away, but with the door at my back, there's nowhere to go.

He doesn't touch me. His hand floats through the air to the side of my head, as if he's feeling something.

I glance to the side, shifting my head away from his hand just a little. Nothing is there. The whole thing gives me the creeps. Part of me wants to know what Omar means. But the more substantial part of me just wants to get the hell out. My hand fumbles against the door before I manage to pull it open a crack. Back to the door, I slide away from Omar and peek out.

No one's in the hall, so I hustle toward my room.

Forrest appears in the hallway that intersects mine. When I round the corner, he looks at me, his shoulders sag. "Where were you?"

"What are you, my mom?" I say. "I went to take a piss."

"You didn't report to your room at lockdown."

Forrest steps toward me and looks me over. He yanks my clean shirt up and inspects my torso without asking.

"What the hell, Forrest?" I swat him away. "I went to visit Celeste."

He drops the shirt and steps back, clutching his tablet—his tablet! "You were healed."

"Of course I was."

"Why were you sleeping in a girl's room, and why didn't you report for lockdown?"

Does he know? Is he fishing for answers? I shrug. "It isn't like that. I went to talk, see if she was okay after the test, but she was asleep, and I must have fallen asleep on the floor. We're friends."

Forrest waves over my shoulder. Two security guards turn and head away. Every muscle in my body tenses. What do they know?

"We have work to do," Forrest says. "Let's go." He starts up the hallway as if I will just follow obediently.

But I don't. I throw up my hands. "Forrest, I'm exhausted." My arms are leaden. My eyes burn from poor sleep.

He turns to me. The look he gives me makes it clear I have no say in the matter. "It can't wait. It has to be now. Either come with me, or I'll get security to bring you."

"Jeez." I shuffle along behind him. "So dramatic."

As we make our way down the hall, I notice Trina peeking out her door and watching us pass. I give a small shake of the head, but she just winks and closes her door. Forrest rubs his neck and stifles a yawn.

What did she just do?

26

SOMETHING ABOUT THIS NEXT TEST IS OFF. I CAN FEEL
it before we even walk through the door into the room. It makes my
skin crawl, and I can't say why.

Forrest strides forward with a purpose that makes my head spin.
I'm following him, and when he stops so suddenly in front of one of
the doors, I almost walk into him.

The voice on the other side of the closed door brings back
phantom pains from that attack in the museum. My palms start to
sweat.

Terry. The same one who chased me and threatened me in the
simulation. The same one who mocked me in the cafeteria. Before the
door even opens my heart is racing.

Forrest swipes his wrist and opens the door.

It's a simple simulation room. With one exception.

Terry stands on the far side of the room, glaring at me. Forest was
talking about Terry reading me. It's now clear.

"I'm not sure if you've met before," Forrest says as he closes the
door behind him.

Yes, he is!

"But this is Terry. He's going to assist you with your Telepathy
test."

I ease into the seat across from Terry.

Terry has a somewhat smug smirk on his face, but only when
Forrest isn't watching. "I've seen him around," Terry says. "But I don't
think we've actually had the pleasure of meeting."

So, that's how we are playing this game. "No. I don't think we've had the *pleasure*."

"Good then," Forrest says as he checks his tablet. "This will all be fresh." Does he know about what happened in the Survival Test, and Terry's threat? "I'll be on the other side of the wall to make sure there aren't any disruptive thoughts."

Without waiting for a response, Forrest leaves us alone. A second latch clicks, locking us in. The moment the door closes, the simulation begins. The blank room becomes an interrogation room, empty except for a metal table and two metal chairs. I sit in one. Terry sits on the other.

"Troy is gone," Terry says in a low voice. But his lips aren't moving. And when I respond, mine don't either. He's opened telepathic communication.

"I'm sorry, should I know who that is?" I cross my arms over my chest and sit back, jaw clenched. But I do know who Troy is. Did he fall off the bridge in the Survival Test? Did he die?

Terry's expression darkens. "You're a smug bastard. When we're done here, I'll deal with you."

"You mean Derrek will," I correct. "Because you're too much of a chicken to do anything yourself." Sharp pain throbs in my head. I press my hands to my temples, but it stops just as quickly as it started.

"You have no idea what you're talking about," Terry says. "You and Miller are up to something. Tell me what."

I laugh, but it's cut short by another sharp, pressing pain in my head.

"Tell me what you're up to!"

"Nothing." The pain twists at my temples. I try to fight it off, but it feels like my head is getting pinched in a vice. I grind my teeth and press my palms to my temples, to little effect.

"Everyone has a breaking point," Terry says.

The pain intensifies.

"I just have to find yours."

I squint to try and regain control of my senses, but they're starting to slip. Everything is distorted. The lights in the room are brighter. Sounds are duller.

Terry leans forward, resting his forearms on the table. But this isn't him. Forrest told him to do this, to dig for something. I remember what Terry told Forrest in the hallway, and I force out a laugh; it sounds more like a rumbling groan.

Terry's brows pull together. "What the hell is so funny?"

"You can't read me," I say, gritting my teeth. The pain is like he's digging around in my head, but for some reason I don't understand, he just can't read me.

"I can read anyone," Terry says, his tone more defensive.

"Then do it. What am I thinking right now?"

Everything goes silent. He doesn't speak to me. I don't speak to him. The pain in my head progressively grows—sharp, digging, stabbing pains. I grind my teeth to keep from screaming. My brain is about to tear apart like he's trying to unravel the mysterious barrier to get to the truth. It makes the back of my eyes hurt.

After a few excruciating minutes, something warm trickles from my ear. I reach a shaking hand up to touch it and pull away, gazing at the blood through the welling tears.

"Stop!" I cry aloud, weak and shaking, hardly able to shift the slightest without intense pressure on my head.

"Tell me," Terry says through his teeth. Sweat rolls down his temples and beads on his lip. His eyes squint at me.

Good. This is painful for him, too. It's a battle of wills.

My jaw twitches and my teeth grind so hard I hear the crunch. The room starts pulsing between bright and dark. Every part of my body weakens, and the pain in my head is worse than any headache. I barely focus long enough to see Terry gripping the edge of the table, white-knuckled. The room spins.

Tile cools my cheek. I blink against the bright ceiling lights. Forrest looms over my face. His warm fingers are against my neck.

Forrest speaks to someone outside my tunnel vision, his voice thick and distant. "Get him back to his bed. I'll send someone to him."

"What about him?" The other voice is far off and unrecognizable. All I can think about is sleep. I need to sleep.

"Send him to floor 189," Forrest says, standing. He's so tall. As if he were stretched too high and thin.

Hands grab my shoulders and legs, lifting me off the floor. Pain pulses anew in my head. Sleep pulls me down.

A voice drifts into my sleep, pulling me awake. Bianca. I open my eyes and turn my head, feeling completely drained of energy. She is at the door of my room talking to someone in a white coat. She closes the door and turns to me.

"You're awake." Bianca hurries to my side. "My brother sent me to keep an eye on you."

"Your…brother…"

"Yes," she sits on the edge of the bed. "Forrest. I know. He said the other test subject went overboard. He nearly killed you, Ugene."

"Nearly." I snort. Like that would have happened. Forrest watched the whole thing. "Your brother—" I try to push myself upright on shaking arms, but my body gives out.

"Stay put," she says, tucking the blanket tighter around me.

"Your brother…"

"Shh. Later," Bianca brushes her hand across my forehead. "For now, rest."

The comforting motion aids me back to sleep.

27

FOG FILLS THE ROOM, MASKING THE FACES OF THOSE around me. Is this a dream? I try to move my hand, touch the mist, curl my fingers around it, but nothing. My being is omnipresent as if watching through the fog with no body. Distantly familiar voices reach out to me, but the words are just as bodyless as I am.

...subject took to...injection...he's in recovery and soon will...We must prepare for a Power surge. Anything...

Is this real? Are they talking about me or someone else? I try to speak but have no voice. Only eyes and fog.

...hasn't woken since the procedure...successful extraction...adrenaline boost to speed...

The fog and voices vanish. Just a void of darkness followed by nightmares remain.

§

Sarsaparilla. Chirping birds. My senses awaken, and I stretch aching limbs. When I open my eyes, I expect to be surrounded by fog, but the warmth of my blankets and softness of the mattress offer comfort as the walls of my room—so much like my bedroom at home but so different—greet me. I expect to hear Overwatch announce the daily routine, but she does not. I sit up, put my bare feet against the cold tile floor, and notice the door is already slightly ajar. Did I oversleep?

Hunger seizes my stomach, and I make my way to the cafeteria in bare feet. No one pays me any attention as I shuffle along and eat eggs with bacon and toast. The other subjects all have their own problems. I don't recognize any of my friends in the dozen or so faces, so I head back to my room when I finish.

The moment I open the door, a voice says, "There you are."

I jump out of my skin, press a hand against my pounding heart.

Forrest is seated at my desk, his tablet resting on the clean surface.

"Just got back from breakfast," I say, walking over to make my bed. It's something to do to recover and avoid looking at him, or the tablet resting on the desktop. "I didn't hear anything about a test today."

"You are still in recovery," Forrest states simply. "I'm just here to check up on you."

"Feelin' peachy, Captain." I settle on the bed, and notice Forrest appears worn out, exhausted. "You look like you could use some recovery. Rough bender last night?"

Forrest rubs his temple, then his eyes. "I'm fine."

But he isn't. And it isn't exhaustion. Forrest's normally copper skin is pale. I watch as he props his chin on his fist and fights off sleep. His eyes close. His body slumps. Then his head slips off his fist and falls to the desk.

I jump to my feet to help him, but pause when I realize what happened.

"Don't touch him," Trina says, slipping into the room. "If I did this right, he should be out for about an hour."

"He's going to know," I say, taking a step away from Forrest.

"No, I manipulated his cells days ago so this would slowly creep up on him. He shouldn't suspect a thing if we act quick."

Michael shuffles into the room, giving me wide berth as he moves toward Forrest. His hand is shaking as he reaches out.

"Keep it gentle," Trina warns. "Or he could wake up."

Michael nods and licks his lips, then carefully places his shaking hand on Forrest's hand. I can't see Michael using his DNA Mimicking ability, but I have faith he isn't wasting time. What will happen to us if

Forrest wakes up too soon?

"Dave—" I say.

Trina puts her fingers to her lips and shakes her head. "He's down the hall listening for trouble."

I nod. This was the plan. Knock Forrest out in a safe space. Mimic his DNA so we can get access to his tablet while Dave keeps watch.

Michael lets go of Forrest after a few seconds, then picks up the tablet and uses his Power to gain access. After checking the DNA, it prompts for retinal scans. Michael's eyes widen, and I can see him shaking. Holding my breath—as if breathing on Forrest will wake him—I reach out and gently open one of his eyes. Michael holds up the tablet to scan. It flashes, then beeps.

We release a collective breath when it works. The screen lights up, revealing a list of files. Michael frowns and hands it to me, careful not to touch my skin. What did I do to him when he made contact with me during that test?

No time for that now. I make quick work of skimming through the files, and one catches my interest. IVD Veritax. I tap the files, and an image pops up. Red, bold letters practically pop off the page. But it's what they say that intrigues me: *IVD Veritax: Why be ordinary when you can be extraordinary?*

It looks like an advertisement.

My fingers wrap around the edge as I study the image on the screen.

"What do you think it means?" Trina asks.

"I- It's…" Extraordinary… A lump forms in my throat. "I think it's some kind of Power boost, maybe?" Curious, I tap the screen, going back to find Forrest's files.

The answers I want about myself, and what Paragon is actually doing, are in here, somewhere. The way the data is coded and organized doesn't make any sense to me.

Until I find a file named, "IVD Test Subject 1."

Curious, I tap it and scroll through, quickly forgetting Trina and Michael hovering around me. Everything in here is about my test results. The blood tests and lumbar punctures. Another file inside is titled "IVD Probabilities," but I can't open it without a password. My finger hovers over the most recent test. I want to tap it, but I hesitate, uncertain. Why are these IVD files all concerning my testing?

"That's not what we're looking for," Trina says, pulling me out of my thoughts. "We need information to use when we get out or something to help us get out. And this IVD thing, if it's just a booster that doesn't sound so bad."

I shrug, then spot a file marked Proposal. Biting my lip, I stab it. A box pops up, requesting a password. No luck there. We only have minutes. Not enough time to try hacking his password. We need someone else for that.

I proceed to another file. "IVD Trials." I tap the folder, and a series of names appear. One, in particular, catches my eye.

Jade.

My pulse quickens as I open it and read the first few lines:

Jade: Subject injected with IVD B21
Failure.
Recommendation: Disposal

The air suddenly feels too thin. I can't seem to draw a full breath. Attached is a video file. I play it and nearly drop the tablet as we watch in horror.

Jade is strapped to a metal table. Tears roll down her cheeks as she whimpers. Forrest steps into view holding a syringe, inserts it into her arm, and depresses the plunger. After wiping the injection site and bandaging it, Forrest steps out of sight again. Jade fills the frame. Her eyes lose focus, body convulsing on the table.

Tears well in my eyes as I watch, wanting to look away but unable to stop. I need to see this for myself. After a minute, her body falls still. I hold my breath, watching, waiting for something. And I notice that her chest isn't rising and falling. Jade isn't breathing anymore.

"Oh god," Trina whimpers, hands over her mouth.

My finger hovers for a moment, angry, terrified of what else I will find but unable to stop. I strike another file.

Vicki: Subject injected with IVD B30. Potential feasibility in serum interaction.
Subject Failure. Potential control agent.
Recommendation: Termination.

I punch open the video, and we watch the same test on Vicki. As her convulsions stop, I watch the slow rise and fall of her chest, relieved that she survived.

And then the screaming starts. We can't hear the sound, but the anguish in her open-mouthed expression, the way her back arches unnaturally off the table, make it clear enough. Whatever she suffered at that moment was horrific. Then her Telekinetic Power surges. Everything in the room with her that isn't strapped or bolted down lifts off the ground flies around in a maelstrom of equipment, leaving dents in the walls and bending the leg of a surgical table. Suddenly it stops. Vicki shakes, struggles for breath, then passes out. I watch the irregularity of her breathing as Forrest steps back into view, checks her pulse and his tablet, then says, "Potential temporary Power removal" to someone off-screen.

And pure anger burns through my veins. I grip the tablet so hard in my hands that it bites into my palms.

"Ugene," Trina whispers. "We are running out of time."

But there is one more name I recognize. And I can't put the tablet down without watching this one.

Terry: Subject injected with IVD B32.
Potential feasibility.
Recommendation: General population and observation.

I watch the video. Terry reacts much as Vicki did. But he doesn't cry like she did at first. He pleads. We can't hear his words, but the movement of his lips and the desperation on his face make it clear enough. His reaction is initially the same as Vicki—a Telepathic Power surge without the maelstrom of equipment—and when he settles back, his breathing is more regular than hers as he passes out. Forrest checks vitals and clicks something on his tablet before retreating. What did he see?

Others are on the list before Terry, even before Jade. Most of the names I don't recognize. But we don't have time to watch. I'm also afraid of how hot the anger burns in me. Another video and I'm likely to lose it.

I quickly exit the video and search for Terry's file.

Trina shifts anxiously. "Ugene, we're out of time."

"Just a few more seconds."

Terry's file appears in a list, and I open it, scrolling through the contents until I find what I was looking for. They did it. They boosted Terry's Power. Was this before or after the test with me?

"Ugene!" Trina hisses.

If they had one success, Forrest would want to replicate it. He will bring in other subjects to test. The injection may not work on everyone. Miller! Where has he been? I haven't seen him since the Survival Test.

And what was that blue pill they made us all take?

Trina snatches the tablet from my vice-like grip and flips through it. "Video feeds," she mutters. For a moment she chews her lip as she taps the screen. "Taken care of."

"What?" I growl the word.

"I just deleted the video feed to your room for the last hour. Time to go."

I need more information. "Wait!" I lunge for the tablet, but Trina turns it off and returns it to the desk as Forrest stirs.

"After dinner," she whispers.

Then she and Michael slip out. I'm unable to say anything. I was right. About all of it. Forrest and Paragon are experimenting on test subjects, and not all of the experiments end well. Jade... Such a sweet, if quiet, girl. She deserved better. And why was Vicki's file marked for termination? She survived the experiment but hasn't been back. *Did they...?* No. I can't believe Paragon would kill her. I can't.

It takes all the energy I have to focus on calming the pure rage burning through my veins before Forrest wakes. It's one thing to test and monitor people's abilities. It's another to force people into experimentation that could result in death.

Forrest pushes himself upright and rubs his temple. He glances at the tablet, then turns attention to me.

"What happened?" he groans.

"You need sleep," I manage to get out, barely masking my anger. "Passed out."

"You okay?" he asks, stretching his back and rolling his neck.

Like he cares!

"Just worried." Not a lie.

"Sorry." Forrest stands stiffly, then grabs his tablet. "Let's get to work."

Work. Every part of me wants to resist, refuse. But Forrest can't know that I know. Still, I can't keep from asking the question itching at my mind.

"Hey, I've been wondering," I say, trying to sound casual as I slip on my loafers. "There was a girl, a Telepath named Jade, who used to eat with me. I haven't seen her in a long time. Do you know where she went?"

Forrest scratches his neck as he stands and grabs his tablet. "Jade... Jade..." He tucks the tablet into the pocket of his white coat. "Oh, yes. She tested out of the program a little while back. I think she went home."

The lie slams against my chest, and I do my best to hide the newest surge of anger rising in me. Forrest can't know that I know. But he is covering for Paragon, and those who fail the experiment aren't sent home.

Now, more than ever, I need to help get everyone as far away from Paragon as possible. I have to lead them out of this place somehow.

28

MILLER IS IN THE CAFETERIA AT DINNERTIME, AND I can't help feeling overwhelmed with relief. I tell him about the meeting after dinner but refuse to say more. Not until we are in a safer location. Then, I prepare to meet Trina and the others in the bathroom so we can talk about what we learned.

As I round a corner near the bathroom, I nearly collide with Bianca. Her hands grasp my arms to steady me.

"In a rush?" she asks, offering that teasing smile.

Suddenly, I remember the overwhelming urge to tell her what her brother did to me in the test with Terry. But she won't believe me. Forrest may not have always gotten on with Bianca very well, but he has always been a protective older brother.

"Um, just headed to the bathroom."

"Right. Well, don't let me keep you, then." She tucks hair behind her ear.

As I step around her and continue, the urge to tell her the truth aches in my chest. Bianca is a good person. She can't really know what's going on here.

Can she?

An uneasy hush falls over the group after Trina, Michael, and I finish telling the others what we saw on Forrest's tablet. Sho, Leo, and Boyd stare at me blankly, huddled close together. Mo and Enid both study the floor, leaning against a wall. Enid had been standing close to me at the start of the meeting, but as we go on, she shifts further away as if I have something she could catch by proximity. I can't explain why, but it hurts.

Miller leans against a sink, arms crossed, jaw set tight. The anger burning in his eyes reflects the anger deep in my soul. For once it feels like we are entirely on the same page.

And then he asks the question I don't want to answer.

"What about Murphy?"

Everyone else glances around at each other, confused.

But Miller doesn't look away from me, and the pure rage in his eyes feels directed toward me. Murphy is the only person ever to have walked through this program that Miller cared about. But he disappeared.

"I—I didn't have time to search for his file," I admit, flinching as Miller shifts upright.

"Then we get the tablet again," Miller says. "Now."

"It's not that simple," Trina says, shrinking back at the glare Miller shoots in her direction. "Sorry. It's just…if we do this to Forrest again, he'll know."

"I don't think you understand." Miller stalks toward her, arms still over his chest, fire burning in his gaze. "If you want to get out of here alive, we need to get that tablet again. And for longer than we had it before."

To her credit, Trina stands her ground. "It's impossible."

"Nothing is impossible."

No one else dares to move or speak. But I know that Miller is right. If we want to get everyone out of Paragon safely, we need to know more about the security systems. Camera placements, locked doors, the best route for everyone out of the building. Getting that information from a tablet carried by a researcher is a stretch, but it's the best option we have right now.

"He's right," I say.

Trina turns to me, her eyes full of shock. "Who put you in charge?"

"That tablet has information. And we need it. It could have something to help us get out of here, and I don't see anyone else stepping forward."

"If we do this and Forrest figures it out, we are all in serious trouble," Trina protests. "We could be the next ones strapped to that table. Most of us already have weak Powers. What if we aren't strong enough to satisfy Paragon?"

"We are in trouble even if we don't try," Enid says. She moves to stand beside me again, and her presence is warm. "At some point, any one of us is likely to be strapped to that table."

Her dark eyes turn up at me, and the faith in me makes me hesitate. What if I lead her to that table?

"We don't even know how subjects are chosen for the experiments," Leo says. "What qualifies one for selection?"

"Expendability," Sho snorts. "And let's face it, most of us are. At least to Paragon. They probably choose us once they can't get any more of their precious data from our tests."

Anxiety suddenly fills the room, thick and palatable. No one could know how the selections are made, which means they are right. Anyone could be next. And if it fails like Jade or Vicki…

"I'll do whatever Ugene thinks is best," Enid says. "He stepped forward and helped me when anyone else would have abandoned me. Twice. I'm still standing here because of him."

Boyd nods, and the others slowly agree. Please don't let their faith in me be misplaced.

"But we need to try something different to get that information," Mo says. "Trina is right. We are in real trouble if this fails. And so is everyone else."

"I'm open to ideas," I say.

Silence. Everyone shuffles, uncertain.

Dave frowns and looks toward the doorway, drawing my attention that way as well.

Bianca steps around the edge of one of the stalls. "I'll do it."

In an instant, blue lightning streams from Miller's fingers, forming a cage around Bianca. She freezes, raising her hands in surrender.

"Is it true, Ugene?" Bianca asks.

"How long have you been listening?" Dave asks, and he appears personally affronted. Probably because his one job in our group is to listen for unexpected visitors.

"Long enough. Sorry. I just…" Bianca turns her attention to me. "I worry about you. In here. Around all this Power." Pain shimmers in her dark eyes—not from any Powers, but from what she overheard. "Did he really do that to participants?"

I walk toward the cage and stare into it, captivated by the way the lines of worry etch her forehead and the corners of her lips and eyes.

"You are treading dangerous ground," I say softly.

"Did he?" Her eyes plead for the truth.

"Miller, let her go."

"Nope." He stands at my shoulder like a watchdog.

"She won't do anything."

Bianca keeps her hands up, glancing from one of us to the other. "Do you remember that time I broke my arm at the creek?" She waits for my recognition before continuing. "Forrest blamed you. He told my parents that you pushed me, and I fell into the rock."

"But I did."

"That isn't what broke my arm." Bianca edges closer to the bars, and her black hair charges with static. "I hurt it, yes. And Forrest marched me home, leaving you behind. But it was him."

I recoil. "What?"

"The whole way home he was yelling at me, calling you names. I tried to fight back, to run because I was so angry with him. But he grabbed my arm as I ran. It twisted the wrong way. The pain was so intense he had to carry me home. Before I could say anything, he poured out this whole story about how you did it, and I couldn't get in a word. I tried to tell my parents the truth later, at the hospital, but by then it was too late. They wouldn't listen, said you always found trouble and I was better off without you." Tears well in her eyes. "They forbid me from hanging out with you and wouldn't hear your name anymore."

All these years, she let me think it was my fault. I blamed myself for hurting her and assumed that she just didn't want to have anything to do with me anymore because of what I did. She could have at least said something. "But you never told me."

"Because he was always watching." Bianca's words catch in her throat. "I tried a couple times, but Forrest always stopped me. By the time he graduated and moved out, you hardly spoke to me anymore. I figured the moment for truth had passed."

All this time…

"Don't you see? I know what my brother is capable of. How cold and calculating he can be. And I won't let him scare me into submission again."

"I don't trust her," Enid says, hovering at my shoulder, Miller at the other.

"Let her go," I say.

The cage disappears. Bianca reaches for me, but I walk away. Enid puts an arm around my shoulder and shoots Bianca a dirty look.

"What you are offering is dangerous," Miller says. I can't see his face, but I can almost hear the smug satisfaction in his tone.

"I understand the risks." Bianca's voice is tight. "And I know how to do it right."

"Then let's talk," Miller says.

Everyone is attentive as Bianca explains her plan to get security information from Paragon and help us get our hands on Forrest's tablet again. Enid stays close to me, and her presence is oddly comforting.

29

"UGENE, I SAID I'M SORRY," BIANCA SAYS, FOLLOWING me into my room.

I don't stop until I reach my bed. Even then, I can't bring myself to face her, so instead, I just stand there, staring at the tan wall, hands clenched into fists at my side.

Her warm hand rests on my shoulder.

I shrug it off and move to my shelf, grabbing the journals and stuffing them into my messenger bag. The notebook with the map of the floor is heavy in my hand.

"Ugene, please, talk to me," she says.

The desire to keep Bianca safe and out of trouble with Paragon disappears, replaced with a twisting pang of betrayal. All these years, she let me think it was all my fault. But it never was. Maybe I'm overreacting, but I can't help myself. I worshipped Bianca, and all this time, I thought she hated me or dismissed me from her life or something because I hurt her. Seems ridiculous now that I think about it. I thought she hated me, but she didn't. It was her brother and her parents that kept us apart.

"It doesn't matter anymore," I say, snatching the pen off the desk and kicking the bag under it.

"But clearly it does!" Bianca grabs my arm and forces me to turn and face her. "Because you can't even look me in the eye. It was stupid. I was a stupid girl."

"But you could have done something," I say, gripping the journal tight. "Slipped a note in my locker, caught up with me between classes. Something. But you didn't even try! I thought…" I heave a sigh. "I thought we were best friends, but if so, you would have done something to let me know the truth. And you didn't."

"What can I do to make this right? Ugene, I'll do anything."

"Get me off this floor," I whisper, glancing around for signs of Overwatch.

"To where? It's nearly lockdown, so late."

Something tickles my memory, like reality obscured by stained glass. Telepathic pain. Forrest's voice. Cold tiles. A number.

"Floor 189. Before the Survival test, they gave us all a blue pill. I think answers are on that floor."

Without waiting for her answer, I march out of the room with my notebook and pen in hand, ready to make notes and map out the mysterious floor. Bianca will take me. I need her to. I have to know what is happening on that floor. And it may have been a few years since we were close, but I know her. The guilt is eating away, and she will do anything right about now to make up for it—I hope. The sound of her boots jogging to catch up confirms it.

"This is a terrible idea," she hisses. "If everything you said earlier is true, they will know what we're doing."

We reach the elevators near the center of the floor.

"Then you have to make it look like you are doing your job," I say. "Forrest takes people to that floor. I know it." My gut instinct is telling me it must be where the experiments are performed. "So take me up there and make it look like he asked you to."

Bianca pushes the button and swipes her wrist. She doesn't ask questions, but the way she looks sideways at me makes it clear she has questions. A moment later the lift hums to life, and the doors open. I frown, stepping in with her.

Bianca stands behind me, watching me like some nature documentary, waiting to see what I'll do next.

After punching in number 189, I swipe my wrist. I already know what will happen, but I want her to see it herself. To confirm what the rest of us already suspect.

The access panel buzzes and flashes a red **DENIED** on the screen.

Miller warned me more than once to leave the elevators alone. I look up, heart thumping in my ears, seeking out a security camera. Bianca hesitates, clearly debating whether she should try swiping her own wrist. Her shoulders square and with a quick motion, she swipes her wrist.

"Let me do my job," she roars. For anyone listening, I assume.

DENIED.

Whatever is on that floor, even Bianca doesn't have access to it. Which means our plan is foiled… and Paragon must be hiding something there. The question is, how do we get there?

The elevator lurches into motion, and my heart leaps into my throat. If we didn't make the selection and start the lift, who did?

Legs leaden, heart pounding, I know what I have to do.

I give the best shove I can muster. Bianca's back hits the back wall of the elevator, but as I hoped would happen, her Muscle Memory kicks in almost instantly. Before I have a chance to process her move, Bianca grabs my arm and wrenches it behind my back, slamming me against the side wall, pressing tight and close. The proximity and heat from her body almost make me forget my next move, but the slack as she starts to let go snaps me back to attention.

"Don't let go," I mumble, cheek pressed to the wall. It needs to look like she is restraining me now, or she could be in bigger trouble.

Bianca's grip is so tight I couldn't break it if I wanted to. She pulls me back from the wall, holding my arms behind my back. "I'm sorry," she whispers in my ear.

A metallic taste hits my tongue. Blood drips in from the corner of my mouth. Not much, but it should make the whole thing more believable.

The elevator stops and both of us look up at the floor number on the digital display. The blood drains from my face, and everything goes cold.

We've gone beyond 189.

The doors slide open and Hilde Long—Joyce's assistant—waits

with her tablet perched on her arm, lips drawn together in a thin line making her narrow face seem more severe despite her young age. A security guard stands at each shoulder, hands on the holsters of their stun guns. My stomach twists in knots and my palms sweat. My breathing is more labored.

"Mr. Powers." Hilde sighs and waves at the guards to stand down. "What are you doing up and around this time of night?" The tension in her shoulders melts away as she turns to Bianca. "Miss Pond, correct? You can let go of him." Hilde turns away from the elevator and heads toward the glass office on the far side of the floor.

Bianca hesitates beside me inside the elevator.

Hilde pauses in her stride, glancing over her shoulder at us. "Come along. Dr. Cass wants to speak with you."

I scoop my journal off the elevator floor, clutching it to my chest with one hand as Bianca steps out. The elevator doors start to slide closed, and I slip out just in time.

In the artificial lights of the building, the reds and whites that color everything on this floor contrast against the darkness of the night beyond the far windows. Like standing in a bright dimension on the edge of darkness. Bianca and I follow Hilde. Behind the glass walls, Dr. Cass sits at her desk, reviewing electronic files on the reflective surface. It doesn't escape my notice that she hasn't lifted them off the desk for everyone to see like she did with me last time. Whatever she's looking at, she apparently doesn't feel like sharing. That doesn't help the anxiety twisting in my gut.

Behind me, Bianca softly huffs out irregular breaths. A sentiment of fear I can share.

Security holds the door open as Dr. Cass looks up. Bianca steps through first, and when I step forward to follow, a guard holds up a hand to my chest. No doubt he can feel my heart hammering hard.

"We'll just be a moment, Ugene," Dr. Cass reassures me. Can she see the fear on my face?

The glass door closes in front of me, leaving me in the hallway with the security guards. A lump rises in my throat, and I watch as

Bianca approaches the desk. Dr. Cass doesn't invite her to sit, and Bianca stands with her back to me, so I can't try to guess what's going on. The expression on Dr. Cass's face is cordial, friendly. Her lips move, and I strain to hear, but no sound escapes the room. Not even muffled voices. Right. A privacy barrier. I won't hear anything no matter how hard I try.

"You can take a seat," one of the guards says, motioning toward a vacant red chair in the waiting area.

It doesn't feel like a request.

Trying not to shake, I move to the chair and sit, watching the glass wall. It's just Bianca, Dr. Cass, and Hilde, who stands close to Dr. Cass's shoulder. Unlike Dr. Cass, Hilde's expression is more severe, but she doesn't say a word. She only watches with intense interest.

Bianca's hands clasp behind her back, and after a few statements from Dr. Cass, Bianca nods, possibly speaks, but Dr. Cass's reaction doesn't change. She's so hard to read.

After a few minutes of this, Bianca and Hilde walk to the door.

"Mr. Powers, Dr. Cass will speak to you now," Hilde says, holding the door open as Bianca walks out.

My legs are shaking as I stand and walk to the door. Bianca doesn't even look at me as she heads to the elevator, which makes my gut sink. But her face is pale, and the set of her jaw is familiar enough to me. She's fighting to contain her emotions. What just happened?

As I step through the door, my journal is still clutched in my sweaty hand. I try not to hold it too close. If she takes it from me and reads my notes, she'll know what I'm up to.

Dr. Cass is sitting on the other side of her desk now, reading an electronic file on the surface. I try to peek, but it's hard to make anything out.

30

"UGENE." DR. CASS SMILES BRIGHTLY AT ME AS SHE swipes a hand over her desk. The files disappear, and the desk is just a desk again. "I apologize for the distance I've been keeping from you," she says. "Though I am a little concerned about what has you off your floor tonight. Miss Pond said she was bringing you in for special testing, but I can find no record of special testing requests from anyone."

I just shrug, trying to act as clueless and casual as possible.

Dr. Cass clicks her tongue, studying me. "Well, no matter. I've meant to speak with you anyway. I wanted to wait until the initial beta testing was completed before reconnecting. I've been following your progress. Interesting, but sadly not quite what we were hoping for. Your claim to be Powerless appears to be true."

"Sorry I've disappointed you," I say with some sincerity, though a bit of sarcasm bleeds through.

"Not at all." Dr. Cass shakes her head and rests her forearms on the desk. "You are hardly a disappointment. Having you here makes a huge difference."

Huge difference. Is that why she is killing people?

"Please." She waves a hand at the vacant red chair across the desk. The last time I sat here, she told me the truth about my father. "Ugene, do you understand why we take your blood and plasma, and why we take spinal fluid?"

I nod, trying not to wince at the memory of the horrific lumbar punctures. But they have to analyze these parts of my system to get accurate readings and to compare against other subjects.

"Good. I suspected as much. We've checked the samples against each other based on what abilities you are testing. While we haven't seen the results we were hoping for, Dr. Pond has identified something quite interesting. Your blood is different on a cellular level each time."

The news perks me up a little. "How?"

"We are wondering the same thing." Dr. Cass taps her fingers a few times on the desk and swipes her hand up, showing a partial record. "Dr. Pond mentioned that you have expressed an interest in your files. Knowing that you have a curious mind for this sort of science, I thought I could oblige. This is the record from your Survival test."

My breaths come with short, conscious effort. She knows about the test. Of course, she knows, but how much? She had to know what happened in that Survival test. Was she just okay with it? I work at taking careful, even breaths as Dr. Cass flips her fingers across the file and it changes to EKG readings from the nanomonitors.

"You see this?" She points to the first section. "This is what most of the test looks like for your muscles and your heart rate. The readings are slightly spiked but regular. But this," She swipes her hand over the file, and a new reading pops up. "This is your synaptic reading. The spike is much different, dramatic and irregular. The first part of the testing is regular. But something triggers this irregularity."

"What?" I stare at the reading, fascinated. For the moment, I'm more interested in my test results than the fear that she might know something.

"We don't know yet." Dr. Cass taps the desk a couple of times and pulls up another file, then swipes it into the air and pulls it over until the two tests overlap. "These are the same results from an average Survival test."

I stand and lean into the charts to get a closer look, still holding the journal in one firm hand.

The difference is dramatic. While the normal subject has elevated synaptic levels, they are ordinary for the ability. Steady. Mine are off the charts by comparison. It's impossible to know at what point during the test this spike happened. Maybe during the search and rescue of Enid, or the battle on the bridge. It could be anything.

"You said you compared my blood against the different tests," I say. "What does that look like?"

Dr. Cass shakes her head. "Aside from spikes in endorphins, it looks about how we expected."

"And what does all of this mean?"

The corner of Dr. Cass's mouth curls. "It means we need to replicate the results. When it happens again, we'll understand more."

Again? The very idea of another Survival test—that everyone will be forced into because of me—both twists my stomach in knots and fuels my anger. The room lurches. Remembered screams, flashes of blue light, death… Anger rises in my chest, chasing away nausea. I sink deeper into the chair to keep from lunging at Dr. Cass and screaming about how wrong all of this is.

"Ugene," Dr. Cass says. "Why were you really in the elevator?"

There's no right answer to this question. Especially if she can tell which floor I was trying to get to, which I have to assume is correct. I swallow hard and shift in the chair, clutching the journal. The sense that someone is watching me presses down on my shoulders and I glance back, only to find Hilde looming nearby, gaze fixed on me.

"I—I just… wanted to see the records. I told Bianca that Forrest told me to ask her to take me to the floor. It was a hard sell—don't be angry with her, she really tried to resist. But I needed to know more about what's wrong with me. I have this thing for scientific research, so I thought that maybe if I got to it myself, I could just, you know, review the files." I bow my head over my chest to try and sell this fake shame.

"I'm sorry we haven't been terribly forthcoming," Dr. Cass says. Her gaze flicks past me.

Hilde.

What is her ability? Joyce is a Naturalist, but I never considered Hilde. And the way she watches me makes everything inside me wrinkle up into a ball. I remember what Mom said, about how she couldn't read Joyce. About how her mind was behind a wall, something only a Telepath could do.

I try to block out everything from my mind and quell my anxiety. If Hilde is a Telepath, Bianca and I are both screwed. All of us are.

"We wanted to know more about your testing before we shared anything," Dr. Cass continues. "We didn't want to raise your hopes until the tests were replicated." She cocks her head and watches me like a predator stalking its prey. "Next time, please be patient with us. I understand that this has all been very challenging, but the rules exist for a reason. I must insist that you follow them. We'll share our results with you when the time is right. But you can't take matters into your own hands. We're trying to protect you, Ugene. You're our most valuable asset now. I hope you understand that is why we have you under contract to stay here. It's for your protection."

I fidget with the edges of the journal, remembering why I started this in the first place. "How is my dad?" I ask. If I am about to do something that will make him lose these treatments, I would like to know if he's shown any progress.

Dr. Cass offers a reassuring smile. "He is undergoing the treatments regularly, but his condition is advanced. He's better, but I can't guarantee anything at the moment."

Better. Not really what I expected, but knowing he's doing at least a little better makes me feel worse about what I'm going to do. "Can I see them? My parents?"

Dr. Cass clicks her tongue, then shakes her head. "It's too soon, Ugene. There's a lot for you to do and finding the time for a family visit will be hard to fit into your schedule. I'll keep the request in mind, though."

Dr. Cass and Paragon Diagnostics have no intention of letting me out. I just have to remember why I'm here and stick to the plan. Get information. Get out. Make sure Dad is still covered.

I nod, struggling to keep my mind clear and not glance back at Hilde.

Dr. Cass leans back into her chair and says, "Good. Before you go, there's one more thing. I understand you've been meeting with another test subject. A girl named Celeste. I would caution you against visiting her. She has been known to be unpredictable. It isn't safe to be around her."

Celeste dangerous? No. I don't believe that.

"You don't seem convinced," she says. "Celeste seems innocent, but her Powers and temperament are unstable. And as I said, your safety is critical." Before I can speak, she says, "Now, Ugene, it's time to return to your room. You have work to do tomorrow."

Dr. Cass closes all the open files and turns her attention away from me. I am apparently dismissed, despite lingering questions. She will say nothing more.

With a muttered *thank you*, I take my leave, escorted to the glass door by Hilde.

None of that put my mind at ease. What I did learn is that Dr. Cass acts like someone who knows more than she lets on. And when I leave, Celeste will come with me.

31

THE MEETING WITH DR. CASS LEFT ME UNSETTLED AND, more than ever, wondering how long it would take to get everyone out of here. Bianca's plan requires patience, a chance for her to gather as much intel about security protocols and the best escape route without raising suspicion. But since the meeting with Dr. Cass, I have yet to see Bianca. Another Survival test is coming if what Dr. Cass said is any indication. We need to be ready for that—or preferably gone before it begins.

But without Bianca, we are blind.

No one else liked hearing that there would be another Survival test soon. Particularly because Paragon wants more data from me. But at least we have some warning. I told them to prepare, to gather as many snacks and water pouches as we could each day and stash them in bags in our rooms. That way, when test day came, no one would have to leave their room to get food or water, thus avoiding the chaos we all witnessed before.

Mo raised the question of whether there would be time to save up enough resources, and his concerns were supported by Dave and Sho. To alleviate the fears, Trina and I agreed we would go in the second the doors opened to gather resources—since our rooms are closest to the cafeteria. She would scoop up as many water packs as she could. I would do the same for protein snacks. Then we would both quickly retreat to our rooms.

Boyd suggested we buddy up in rooms, but Miller shot that idea down, and I had to agree. It would raise too much suspicion if we did, and it could delay the start of the test and call up security.

Three days later, no signs of Bianca reveal themselves. Her absence brings all of us together again to reassess our strategy.

"Look, I know you two are like childhood whatevers, but Bianca works for Paragon," Enid says as we again gather in the bathroom for a strategy session. "We can't trust her. For all we know, Bianca set us up to just sit around and wait patiently while she does nothing—or worse, brings all security down on our heads."

"She wouldn't," I say. I can't believe it. Bianca wouldn't do that to me. I'm actually more worried about what has happened to her. Disappearing after meeting Dr. Cass isn't a coincidence. What if she was fired?

Or worse.

"Either way, we can't sit around and wait for her any longer," Miller says. "It's time for a Plan B."

Together, the group comes up with a new plan to get a hold of the tablet again, and this time we intend to copy information from it to take with us.

Tomorrow is the day. If Bianca doesn't show up with some answers by then, we will try to get our hands on Forrest's tablet when he comes for my weekly samples.

The smell of garlic and spices overwhelms my senses as I approach the cafeteria, and it raises hunger so intense it actually makes me feel sick. The problem with Bianca is still on my mind—always on my mind—but starving won't solve anything.

As I enter the cafeteria for dinner, everything overwhelms me. Conversation. Clinking silverware. Slurping drinks. Everything.

All these test subjects are trapped here just like us. Every one of us is subject to Paragon's injections. I need to get everyone out, not just our group. I can't leave these people here to torture or worse.

Two girls lean in toward each other and whisper softly. A young man is sitting alone, lips slightly parted and eyes wide with each slow, deliberate bite of food.

I approach the HotServe machine.

My gaze never entirely leaves the room at large as I make my chicken curry selection from the machine. So many people. There must be nearly fifty in here right now. Some I recognize. Some I don't.

All of this needs to end.

The smell of cumin, garlic, and curry rises from my meal and fills my nose. My stomach grumbles. Exhaustion from today's Hematology test overwhelms me. I want to collapse into the chair.

Miller sits at his usual table in the corner. Our gazes lock. Miller is just stone-faced. I join him.

"Everyone heard about your meeting with Joyce Cass," Miller says under his breath, focused on his food.

I glance around and see that several other test subjects are staring at me. Is meeting Dr. Cass so unusual?

My gaze falls on another test subject.

Terry stares at me. Grinning. I hate when he grins at me. Derrek watches with a hunger that makes me wonder if I'm to be his dinner. Still no Troy. Somehow, I doubt we will ever see Troy again. Was he in another of those video files I didn't have time to watch or did he actually die when he fell off that bridge?

Trying to keep my shaking hands steady, I focus on the chicken curry.

It's crazy. No matter how feeble the other test subjects look, they're more terrifying with their sunken cheeks and black-circled eyes than any of the bullies in high school ever were. In high school, it was all about showing off. Here, it's different. These people seem to bear resentment toward the world. I don't want attention drawn to me like this.

Despite my hunger and the delicious smell of the food, it hits my stomach like sour milk. My anxiety is momentarily broken when Celeste walks in.

Seeing Celeste is like a bit of sunlight on my darkening mood. I grin, wave at her, getting a few odd looks, but she doesn't seem to notice.

Celeste approaches the HotServe line, and everyone in it almost casually steps toward the drink machine or snack machine instead. Not a single person looks at her, or goes within ten feet of where she stands the entire time she's in the room. It's like she's plagued with a dangerous contagion. They are all doing everything in their Power to avoid acknowledging she even exists. I never took the time to really pay attention to how everyone else treats Celeste, but I realize it isn't the first time people have given her plenty of personal space.

Celeste is unstable. Dr. Cass's warning seemed insane at the time, but everyone else is treating her like Dr. Cass spoke the truth. But it can't be true. I may not understand her past, but I know Celeste. She has a child-like innocence. She isn't dangerous.

Unlike everyone else, Celeste doesn't sit down. When her food is prepared, she gets herself a drink then walks out of the room, her bare feet pattering on the tiles as she goes.

And as soon as she's gone, all the tension in the room melts away. Conversations resume without whispers. Gaps in lines close. People mill around the room again.

What is wrong with everyone today?

As soon as I'm satisfied that I ate enough, I get up, dispose of my plate, then leave. Shoes scuff the floor behind me, following.

I refuse to move faster. My breathing is more focused as my door looms in front of me, and I enter my room with haste.

Once behind the safety of my door, I step back and watch the shadows moving in the light from the gap underneath. The tightness in my chest won't relent. The shadows pass without pause. I breathe out a sigh of relief, not even sure why I was so spooked in the first place. I slip off my loafers and climb into bed, lying with my head facing the door.

I fall asleep watching shadows dance beneath it.

Nightmares again. Flashes of Jade's agony, strapped to the table. Screams. Rays of blue light and the muffled thump of the shots.

Smoke and burning lungs. Derrek's laughter. Celeste curled up on her bed, rocking and repeating the same riddle over and over. *The chains have broken. He has risen. He comes.* Hilde's penetrating, knowing gaze. Bianca clawing her way out of a pit, covered in blood and dirt, cursing me for getting her into this mess. The hidden truth behind Dr. Cass's mocking smile. Miller on his knees, holding Forrest's tablet, pure anguish on his face. Dad on his death bed, blaming me for it all.

I wake, drenched in cold sweat, shaking despite the blankets pulled tight up to my chin. I curl up in a fetal position and stare at the shadows still milling about through the gap under the door until Overwatch rings the morning chimes and the door swings open.

Still, I huddle, unable to move.

"Ugene?" Miller peeks his head in.

I expect to see the anguish from my nightmare still there, but he looks happy. Smiling. A look I've never seen on his face before. A stark contrast to my nightmare. And somehow, I can't bear to see it.

"Rise and shine," Miller says.

I swallow down a wave of fear. It's time to steal information from Paragon and attempt our escape.

Miller winks in a way that reminds me. *Today is the day.*

32

LEO AND BOYD ARE ALREADY DEEP INTO BREAKFAST by the time I reach the cafeteria. They sit at a table in the corner, whispering to each other. I join them, but they don't look up at me.

Miller pauses by the table, glances around the cafeteria, then looks down at them. "Done?"

He isn't talking about breakfast, not that anyone else would know. Leo and Boyd spent most of last night working together to create a copying device for the data we glean off the tablet. Miller managed to get a hold of some really basic materials he could manipulate into a makeshift CopyDrive—copper, crystal, metal, plastic. But he didn't have the knowledge or skills to finish mutating everything into the right kind of energy to make it work. All he could do was manipulate the materials into the right shape.

So, with Leo's atomic sight to assist him, Boyd worked on the finishing touches. Apparently, one of the few things he is good at is manipulating the energy necessary to build simple electronic devices. Nothing big enough to be useful in the escape, but the drive is a great place to start.

Hopefully, the device works. I want to trust that Boyd and Leo know what they're doing, but how often have they really created something like this? If the drive doesn't work, our plan for the day could blow up in our faces. The device is so small, I almost didn't see it on the table between them.

No one talks about the plan this morning. Everything is normal conversation. Overwatch is still there, after all.

At the end of the meal, Boyd slips the drive to me with quick, cryptic instructions on how to use it. Where to attach it. How long it should be connected. How to copy information over. I nod, gripping it casually in one hand.

Back at my room, I take the extra food and water I collected and stuff it in my bag, then make sure everything I need is still in the messenger bag. Journals. About a week's worth of food and water—if appropriately rationed. My street clothes—jeans and a hooded flannel shirt. It's a regular morning ritual I've grown accustomed to since we decided preparedness was vital. Everything is as it should be.

That just leaves the drive. I contemplate sticking it in the top drawer of the desk, but if Forrest takes me from the room, I won't have time to retrieve it. My scrubs have a pocket on the chest, but I don't trust it to hold anything securely and won't risk the drive falling out. Instead, I settle for sliding it into my shoe, careful to put it at the top of my foot instead of the bottom, so it's not so likely to break. The lump from it isn't comfortable, like having a small rock lodged in my shoe, but it isn't anything I can't deal with.

I breathe out a sigh of relief and flop down on the bed. Nothing to do now but wait for Forrest to come for his samples.

I toy with the idea of visiting Celeste. My warning to prepare for the next Survival test, that it could be worse than the last, fell on deaf ears. She didn't seem to mind much. Now, I worry that she should know more about our plan to escape. She needs to be ready when the time comes. Why didn't I tell her before? Visiting now wouldn't be prudent, though. If I'm not in my room when Forrest shows up and the others are ready to move into action, they will be furious. So I stay, staring at the smooth ceiling.

Nerves begin writhing in my stomach as I wait. After a while, I can't help but wonder if I'm wrong. What if Forrest doesn't come today? What if no samples are collected and I'm left with a rock in my shoe and no means of escape? The minutes feel like hours, and I get more anxious, shifting on the bed, staring at the door, at the wall, at the floor, at the ceiling.

At last! A familiar, muffled voice in the hallway. Forrest is coming. All the anxiety becomes a pounding adrenaline in my ears. Please, let this work.

The moment Forrest rounds the doorway into my room, I bolt upright in bed. My palms are sweating, and I rub them on my pants.

"Good morning, Ugene," Forrest says. His dark eyes scan me, and his brows pull together.

He knows!

"Everyone alright?"

"Yeah, fine," I say, hoping he can't hear the tension in my voice. "Just not looking forward to the tests today."

Forrest makes a sound in his throat and stands near the doorway. Why is he standing in the doorway? He needs to come in and set the tablet down.

"I'm sort of not… not feeling so great today," I say, hoping his concern draws him into the room to check me.

Forrest's frown deepens, and he turns on the tablet. After a few taps, he scrolls through data. "Everything looks normal. Though your heart rate is elevated."

Yes! The heart. If I'm so valuable, they don't want anything to happen to me. "That's what I mean. I can't get it to slow down. I tried to lie back and meditate, and it didn't help."

Forrest sighs and turns off the tablet, then steps deeper into the room to set it on the desk and sits on the edge of the bed beside me. First, he checks my pulse, which I'm trying so hard to control. Next, he presses his fingers to my temples.

A surge of Power pushes through me, through my blood. Forrest is Divinic—that much I already knew—and I never really stopped to think or care about exactly his specific Power. Now it's clear that he has a blood-born Divinic Power. Healing Hands with a focus on cellular activation. Which means he could potentially control the speed of my cellular activity.

As if to confirm this theory, my heart slows to a steadier beat. The anxiety that moments ago poured through me disappears. Forrest lets go, and a glance in his direction reveals just how much that took out of him. The exhaustion shows through the way his eyes droop.

"That's odd," he mumbles, voice thick as if drugged.

The lights in the room flicker off. I hardly have time to catch Forrest before he falls back, his head nearly hitting the wall had I not managed to pull him to the side a moment before. Trina's blood trick works again.

The plan is in motion.

Instead of deleting video footage this time around, Miller insisted on killing the power in my room. Now, the only light entering filters through the open doorway. We are all aware that we won't be as lucky as we were last time. Now, moving quickly and cautiously is more critical.

Trina and Michael enter the room as I retrieve the drive from my shoe. Trina quickly moves to Forrest and puts her hands on his head.

"Be careful," I say, watching her work but not really seeing anything she is doing.

"Why do you care?" she asks, shooting an angry snarl in Forrest's direction. "He deserves so much more."

"That's not up to us to decide. If we play God with people, we are no better than they are."

Trina rolls her eyes, and the color begins draining from Forrest's face. His normally coppery tone—much like Bianca's—becomes ashen. I jump at Trina, pushing her off. She slips off the edge of the bed, grasping it just in time to keep from losing her balance.

"I said stop."

"Who put you in charge?" Trina asks, pushing herself to her feet and brushing her scrubs off.

"If we hurt him, what was the point in killing the video feed?" I say, angry that she can't see the obvious in front of us. "Besides, do you really think they wouldn't figure it out eventually if you did something more drastic to him? Paragon will know if we aren't extra careful."

"Stop," Michael says, his voice small compared to the heat

between Trina and I. "Someone get me the tablet." Michael's hand is on Forrest's neck, and sweat beads on Michael's forehead.

Trina is closer to the desk, so she snatches the tablet and thrusts the device at Michael. A moment later, we are in. Michael hands the tablet to me so that I can attach the drive.

"Remember, we only have about ten minutes this time before anyone wonders where you and Forrest are," Michael warns, stepping away from me.

Ten minutes. Not nearly as long as last time. Not even close to enough time to find everything we need. But it's our best assumption of how long it would take for Forrest to collect me and head to the lab for samples. Any longer and security will most likely be on us.

When I access the data, I grimace. The files are code locked. First, I try to access the video files from before, hoping to at least copy evidence of the experiments, but every file I click to open prompts for a coded password.

Minutes tick by faster than they should. My fingers fly over the surface, hoping to find something—anything; security information, test data, video feeds—but the more I scroll through the tablet, the less hope I have.

A shadow fills the doorway as I work, and all three of us look up to see who caught us in the act.

33

"HOW'S IT GOING, KID?"

Miller. Thank God.

"Everything is locked," I say. "I've skimmed through just about everything on here, and the files are all locked. We can't get to anything."

"Five more minutes," Michael says, shifting anxiously from one foot to the other.

Miller moves into the room, carelessly nudging past Trina to stand beside me. "It can't be everything," he says.

Without giving me a chance to say anything, Miller pulls the tablet from my hand and scrolls through the files himself. After a few of his own hits and misses, Miller's jaw clenches so tight I can hear his teeth rubbing together. A glance reveals what I should have suspected he would look for all along.

Subject 0514: Murphy, Jayme.

Miller pulls in a deep breath and lets it out slowly.

"Miller, don't." I put a hand on his arm.

"Three minutes." Michael's voice changes pitch. "Guys…"

Miller shrugs me off and taps the file. The same box pops up, prompting a password. Instead of growling in frustration or lashing out—like I would expect from Miller—he begins pounding out potential passwords. Does he have any idea what the actual password might be? Watching him desperately try over and over to get into the file, I'm torn between stopping him and waiting to see if he really does get lucky. Does Paragon know someone is trying to hack into the archives?

"Two minutes," Michael says. As if we need a reminder that we are out of time.

"This is pointless," Trina says. "You can't crack the password. Why even try? And for all we know, even if we get lucky with the first one, there could be a secondary password for further access. It isn't getting us anywhere." She reaches for the tablet.

Miller doesn't look up from the screen. He shoves Trina with one hand. Trina's back smacks the wall. She yelps, stumbles sideways, and falls to the floor. Michael rushes to her aid while I turn on Miller. This isn't part of the plan, and his actions are over the line.

"Miller, that's enough," I say, wrestling the tablet from his one-handed grip. I fall back onto the bed, half landing on Forrest's legs. "We failed. I managed to copy some of the encrypted files onto the drive. We will just have to work with that for now." I drag Murphy's file across the screen. "I copied it. We can't do anything else right now."

Michael glances toward the doorway. "One minute. Guys, we gotta go."

Miller paces a few steps across the floor, glances toward the door. Michael feebly stands between Miller and the rest of us, as if he could actually do anything to stop Miller.

Miller's next move is so fast I can't react. None of us can. Miller snatches the tablet, pulls off the drive, tosses the tablet back at me, and storms out.

"Wait!" Michael races after him but stops at the doorway. We all know there's no way he could get that drive from Miller even if he caught up to him.

"Just give him time. Maybe we can figure something out." I don't really believe it even as I say it though.

"Time's up." Michael's words sound ominous.

"Breach!" Dave's voice calls out from down the hall.

Forrest stirs under me. I turn the tablet off and toss it to Trina, who puts it back on the desk. Anger and indignation tense her shoulders.

Down the hall, Dave's second warning cuts off mid-sentence.

"Go!"

But I don't have to tell Trina and Michael. The two of them are already bolting for the door.

The power in my room blinks back to life. Screams echo in the hallway, coming from all directions. Shouts to get back to our rooms. The sound of stun gun pops followed by a flash of blue lights from elsewhere in the hall. Trina and Michael both hesitate to leave the room, likely afraid of what will happen if they step out the door.

"There's nowhere to go," Michael says, locking his hands under his armpits. Is he afraid of touching others?

Despite the chaos, my pulse remains calm. Steady. An aftereffect from whatever Forrest did?

Trina is staring at me, fear etching lines across her smooth, pale face. Then her eyes slip past me into the room and grow wide.

"Please return to your rooms," Overwatch says in her always kind voice.

"Forrest," Trina yelps, then bolts into the chaos of the hallway.

A strange thump echoes in my head, then blackness.

Pulsing pain erupts next to my temple, yanking me back into the light. Why does the side of my head hurt?

And why are my cheeks cold? Wait, no… that's tile. The floor.

The world tilts as I push myself to my knees.

Then, a cacophony of screams. Gunshots. Boots and bare feet slapping the tiles. I wince at the growing pain at my temple as I glance lazily around.

My room. I'm in my room.

As are other dark figures, moving about, tossing my belongings around.

Everything's fuzzy.

I try to shake away the fog in my mind, but it only causes the throbbing to worsen.

Shaking, I push myself to my knees and look up to see the barrel of a gun pointed right at my face.

More gunshots, and I flinch. More screams.

Perspiration beads on my forehead.

"Don't struggle," Forrest's voice comes from behind me.

I blink, glance around. Three security guards are tossing my room, looking for something. Michael is huddled on the floor in the hallway directly across from my door. His fingers are laced behind his head, and the fear as his eyes meet mine pierces my heart. A security guard holds a gun on him while another binds his wrists together.

No. No this can't be happening.

"Wha—?" I swallow hard as Forrest steps around me, careless of the chaos and pain of those around us.

"Did you really think you would get away with it a second time?" Forrest asks. "Where is the drive?"

Trina's animalistic growl erupts somewhere in the hallway, cut off abruptly by a gunshot. But not before the guard binding Michael's wrists together collapses to the floor, blood running from his eyes, ears, and nose. My breath catches.

Forrest carries on as if nothing happened. So cold. Calculating. He crouches in front of me, grabs my chin, and tilts it toward his face. The clatter of the guards searching my room continues.

"Focus, Ugene. The drive. Where is it?"

How could he know? Did one of the others tell him? Did he overhear a conversation? But we were so careful.

"Please return to your rooms," Overwatch repeats.

Despite everything going on around us, I'm calm inside.

"I don't have a drive."

Terry. It must have been Terry. He used his Telepathy on someone in the group. Stupid! I knew he was fishing for information. Someone was bound to give it away. It had to be him… right? How else would they know? Unless Forrest had something tracking the use of his tablet.

"He had this hidden under the desk," a guard says, holding my messenger bag to Forrest.

Without hesitating, Forrest upends the bag, dumping the contents on the floor and rifling through them carelessly. He pauses at the clothes and food supplies and looks at me.

"Going somewhere?" he asks.

"Survival test," I admit truthfully—or at least partly truthfully. "Don't want to be unprepared for the next one."

Forrest rummages through my notebooks, flipping the pages quickly until he finds the map of the floor.

"What's this?"

"A map," I say. "I've gotten lost more than once."

"But why do you need to know who is in each room? What are you planning, Ugene?"

"A party. Any other dumb questions?" Sarcasm won't help me now, but my anger won't let me hold back.

Forrest's lips compress, and he picks up all three journals, handing them to one of the guards. "Incinerate these. He won't be needing them anymore."

"No!" I jump for the notebooks, but the gun in my face cocks and I fall back on my heels. "I have years of research about my condition in those."

"Wait," Forrest grabs the guard. "Put them in my office."

Every experiment I've conducted on myself. Every secret I've uncovered since arriving at Paragon. Everything I know is in those notebooks. In *his* hands. Without them, all I have when we escape is the drive—assuming Miller still has it.

"Please return to your rooms," Overwatch repeats.

My gaze slips past Forrest. A security guard lumbers past the door, carrying the limp form of Trina over his shoulder. Another guard drags Michael to his feet and pulls him along, wrists bound together so he can't touch anything.

"What will happen to them?" I ask.

"Come on, Ugene. You're too smart to ask such a dumb question." Forrest tilts his head to block my view of the hallway. "Breach of contract is a serious offense."

I shake my head, anger bubbling up from deep inside, spreading through my veins. They will be removed from the program. Injected with whatever experimental concoction Forrest currently has on hand and tossed in the trash if it fails.

"Trina didn't sign a contract," I say. "She was forced into this because of that stupid proposition. Don't be coy with me, Forrest. I'm not dumb. I know what you do to test subjects. I've seen the footage."

As soon as the words slip out, I know I've overplayed my hand, but it's impossible to hold in the rage burning through me. Never have I hated anyone so much in my life. Not Terry and his threats. Not Jimmy the Idiot in high school. Not even myself. Forrest came from a good family. His parents are model citizens. His sister has such a good heart. The family is perfect. How could something so ugly come from something so pure?

"Assuming such a video even exists, what do you think you can do?" Forrest smirks and shakes his head. "Powerless, locked in a cage. Do you really think you have any other way out but through me?"

"Come on, Forrest." Venom bleeds out from my voice. "You're too smart to ask such a dumb question."

Forrest appears amused by my reaction. "You are important to the program, Ugene. Everything we have learned about you has helped improve those tests. You are the perfect baseline, and soon we will know everything we need to stop regression. But you. You will be the same miserable, Powerless brat you've always been." He stands upright. "Just remember. What happened here today, and what comes next, is your fault."

One of the guards moves toward Forrest. "All clear. No sign of a drive."

Instead of losing his cool, Forrest smooths out the wrinkles in his white lab coat and walks toward the door.

"Check the others. Then initiate lockdown," he says as he enters the hallway. "Protocol 10-98."

The guard nods as if he expected that response.

"Please return to your rooms," Overwatch repeats.

Running on pure adrenaline, knowing my chance at getting out of the room—at getting my hands on Forrest—is slipping away, I launch my whole body at Forrest.

A shot rings out. A punch in the shoulder knocks me off track and spreading pain like burning fire through my shoulder and arm. I try to get up, blinking at the small puncture wound in my arm. Not a standard stun gun burn, but something else—like an injection, a tranquilizer.

The world goes fuzzy. The guards pull me back into the room and step over my body. Every part of me resists movement. Paralyzed.

A chime rings out. An echoing chorus of doors slam shut. I fight off the effects of whatever they tried knocking me out with, but for just a moment everything goes dark.

Part Three

"PARAGON ALWAYS STRIVES TO EXPAND OUR understanding of Powers. Sometimes, that means pushing the limits of what we, as people, are capable of. The ultimate goal is to stop regression and allow us to prosper in this broken world."

~ Dr. Joyce Cass
3 Years Ago

34

ALARMS BLARE, WARNING EVERYONE OF THE IMPEND-
ing lockdown. The sound keeps me from slipping entirely under. My
body is prone on the floor, numb, but the darkness recedes almost
as quickly as it came on, leaving behind a groggy feeling. It takes a
moment to adjust. The contents of my messenger bag are scattered
on the floor around me. I roll over and press my back to the wall. The
rest of my room looks much as Jade's room looked before she disappeared. Everything has been strewn about, turned over, or discarded.

I will find a way to make Forrest pay for what happened today.

"Testing will commence in one minute." Overwatch brings me to
my senses.

Testing. What happened here today, and what comes next, is your fault.

I scramble for the messenger bag and try shoving everything back
into it before time is up. Clothes, food, water, blankets. The strap of
the bag is secured over my shoulder as I wrestle the sheet in. The final
chime.

Everything in the room disappears, leaving me alone in a plain
white room.

No stun gun.

No blue pill.

No water.

I suspected that the blue pill was a temporary booster. Something
to enhance Powers for a short period. The test was probably to find
out how long that booster would last under pressure. But without a
blue pill, we are all being thrust into the Survival test with no bonuses.

And without the gun, we have no protection.

And some of us barely made it last time.

Maybe I'm the only one who isn't getting a booster. It's a feeble hope, but I must hold on to it.

No door opens. The room doesn't get smaller like it did last time. Instead, the walls around me are just…gone. I stand on an arid desert plain that goes on as far as I can see into the distance. Panic grips my chest. This isn't the city. It's somewhere else. No one will know where to go.

I spin in place, but it's more of the same around me. Cracked arid dirt. Endless. The sun, bright and high on the eastern horizon, casting an orange light across the sky. I shield my eyes with my arm. Not another person in sight.

Unsure what else to do, I begin the trek east to the building with the birds on it. That building may not exist here, but at least the others might still head that way. It's the best I have to hope for.

The sun is hot, burning my skin. I pull out the blanket and wrap it around my body and head like a thawb tunic. It protects my body and neck from exposure, but I have to keep my face down as I walk.

And I walk.

Forever.

How did Forrest know about the drive? We were so careful about speaking only in whispers, not showing anything where a camera might see. Only a handful of us even knew about the drive. The most logical answer is that Terry managed to glean something telepathically off someone who knew, then reported it back to Forrest. After that conversation between Terry and Forrest I overheard in the hallway, I wouldn't put it past Terry to tell Forrest anything he learns. Forrest probably already suspected we were up to something. That was why he put me in that test with Terry. It had to be. Terry was pressing for information hard but couldn't get anything.

Which means Terry didn't read it from me. He couldn't do it before. Somehow, I resisted. But if it wasn't me, that only left three others—Boyd, Leo, and Miller. Trina and Michael didn't know until they showed up in my room, or at least they weren't supposed to. As far as they were concerned, we were just looking for information on how to get out of Paragon Tower. Terry could have read any of them.

Miller was probably the least likely suspect. He wants out just as much as me so he can find Murphy. If Terry had tried to read Miller, I suspect we would have figured it out before we set the plan in motion.

Boyd seemed like the most natural target.

Not that I can blame any of them if Terry did read them and report to Forrest. It isn't like they did it on purpose.

The sun rises high in the sky, and I swear I can hear it baking the ground beneath my feet. I cover my eyes again and look for something—anything. Somewhere ahead, the ground changes. I can't see what it is from here. Maybe it's my imagination. Heat causes ripples in my vision, distorting my view just enough that I can't get a clear look at what lay ahead. So, I carry on.

Something else Forrest said tickles at my mind, and it takes a while in the unbearable heat to pull it back. We wouldn't get away with it *again*. Again, like he knew what we did the first time, despite deleting the footage.

The mere fact that Forrest knew about it before means we weren't nearly as smart as we thought we were in our execution and deletion of the footage. What did we miss?

Backups.

Of course. Why wouldn't Paragon have automated backups of video surveillance? I would if I were in their place.

I lick my parched lips, feet dragging a little more along the dry ground. Forrest saw what we did before. He knew that we accessed the files and watched the videos. He knew that we knew. So why did he wait to act?

The horizon changes. First a sliver, then a gap. It grows in size as I approach, until—at last—my feet come close to the edge.

It's a chasm. A canyon carved into the ground. I'm standing on a plateau that connects to other plateaus in an endless maze as far as I can see into the distance. Canyons break up the flat terrain like troughs in every direction. Nothing else is around. No people. No animals. Even the green things that may have once grown here are dead or dying.

Leaning forward, I peer into the canyon below. It isn't too far down. A hundred feet. Maybe more. I could climb that. And the slope is gradual, so if I do slip, I might be able to just slide down the rocky surface. Maybe I'll suffer a few cuts and scrapes, but it shouldn't be so bad. And the canyon could protect me from the sun.

Afraid of tearing the cloth, I pull off the thawb blanket and fold it back into my bag, then strap the bag across my chest. Once I'm confident it's secure, I take deep breaths.

In. Out. In. Out.

I turn and lower myself down the rocky surface, facing the wall for places to hold on. One hand in this crevice. One foot in that crevice. Slowly. Cautiously. One hand. One foot. Lower. I chance a glance up. Not quite as far down as I hoped, but I'm making slow progress. Scrubs don't really have a lot of forgiveness in the necessary places, and it makes my descent more of a challenge.

One hand. One foot.

Loafers also don't make for good climbing shoes. More than once I have to pause and adjust my footing to make sure my shoes are just as secure as my foot. Rock bites into my palm and I have no doubt it's raw and bleeding, but I can't stop. Not now. I glance up. Nearly halfway down.

One hand. One foot.

My pulse pounds in my ears. Thirst makes my throat and eyes dry. Hunger. So much hunger. I haven't eaten since breakfast, and lunch has long since passed. Focus!

One hand. One foot.

My foot slips. My loafer slips off before I can stop it, tumbling, tumbling far below. The bare foot dangles in the air. My breath catches in my lungs. I grip tight to the rocks, but my left hand doesn't have a good enough hold, and it falls free of the rocks. The jerking motion causes my other foot to slip. Nothing stands between me and a fifty-foot drop except the grip my right hand precariously maintains.

And it's slipping.

Fifty feet. Minor slope. I can do this. I can slide if I just let go at the right…

My grip slips, and suddenly I'm sliding down along the rough rock wall. The force knocks the air from my lungs. I do my best to control the fall, leaning against the wall, keeping my hands and feet from catching on anything and sending me head over heels. The strap on my bag snaps, and it goes careening away from me. The last few feet I lose my precarious, awkward balance and tumble. My arm slams against the ground, sending a jolt of pain into my back. My body rolls a few times when I hit bottom.

Dirt fills my lungs. I cough to get it out, but everything is already so dry that coughing has little effect. Every part of my body aches, covered in cuts and scratches from the fall. I push my face off the packed, hot dirt and sit up, shaking, brushing the dirt off my clothes with raw hands. Why did I think this was a good idea?

A quick scan reveals my shoe and bag. I crawl to retrieve the shoe first, then the bag. My hands are raw, scratched, and caked with dirt. I turn my heel to see the bottom of my foot, and it doesn't appear much better off. If I don't at least try to clean the wounds out, the cuts will get infected.

Since my scrub shirt is useless, I pull it off and turn it inside out, then tear open a water pouch from my bag and pour it on the cloth. Slowly, I wash away as much of the dirt as I can from cuts on my foot, hands, arms, and face. It isn't perfect, but it's better than nothing. Walking on this injured foot will be far from fun.

After a short respite to get cleaned and changed, I lean back against the rocks with food and water. Now what? How far can I possibly be from everyone else?

What if no one else is here with me? There was no blue pill. No sign of any other life here. Just what is Protocol 10-98?

I close my eyes and take a moment to rest, then slip my shoe back on—wincing at the tenderness of the sole—and limp southeast, following the canyon where it guides me. At each fork, I venture a few paces before deciding which way to go. East. Southeast. Northeast. The canyon seems to go on forever. Day wears out. Night falls, making it hard to see which way I'm going. With no other viable options, I wrap myself in my blanket against the eastern wall of the valley and sleep on the hard, rocky floor.

I hope Dad is still getting treatment if Paragon suspects what we are up to.

An endless maze with no way out. The canyon once probably had water, a river, but the war would have dried it up. Every turn takes me down another canyon to another turn. And another. Too many choices. I've been wandering this maze of valleys for most of the day, and no end appears in sight. Is there an end? Maybe this is the test. Dropping me in here like a rat in a maze that has no end. Maybe this is my punishment.

No one else is here. I've nearly given up all hope I will see anyone else. Maybe that's for the best. I wouldn't wish this nightmare on anyone. It's been nearly two days since this test started, and I haven't seen so much as a snake. Not even my accomplices. No footsteps or traces of anyone or anything else living. Does Paragon see me as the ringleader?

Food and water are in short supply. Three more water pouches. Four more protein bars. I'll die of dehydration before hunger, though.

I shake my head. No. I won't die. Paragon won't let me die in here. But I am confident they will push me to within an inch of death before pulling me out.

Yes. This is my punishment.

But who else are they punishing? Hopefully no one. I will take this punishment if it spares everyone else.

Bianca. What happened to Bianca? She broke the rules. Took me into the elevator. Joyce spoke with her. Then…nothing.

She's dead.

Why? Why do I think that? Forrest wouldn't let them kill his sister—would he?

I stumble along the canyon floor, feet dragging, completely exhausted, wishing for water.

A high-pitched siren echoes off the canyon walls, bringing my steps to a halt. My gaze sweeps in all directions. No one. But the sound doesn't stop, and the longer I listen, the more it sounds… human. Less like a siren and more like a high-pitched scream. My pulse races. Who is that? What's going on?

I blink and try to rub the exhaustion from my eyes, then focus on the sound. It ends with a throaty growl that sounds a lot like my name. No. No, it can't be. I'm losing it in this maze.

But my mind plays further tricks on me. The canyon isn't in front of me. Instead, it's a soundproof grey room with a surgical bed. Bianca is strapped down, her body still.

No. It's not real. I'm still in the maze.

I fall to my knees and squeeze my eyes shut, pressing the heels of my palms to my ears. Her voice still rings in my head, and I can't escape the image of her lying dead on the table. Just like Jade and Vicki.

No.

I dare to look again and am met by the canyon walls and setting sun beyond. It wasn't real. She's not dead. She's alive!

I stagger to my feet using the rock wall for support and press on. I have to beat this. For Jade. For Vicki.

For all of us.

Dusk falls on day two. Still no one else. Nothing else. Why am I still moving? Why not just lie on the ground and wait it out, let Paragon take me from this nightmare whenever they are satisfied I've been punished enough?

I stumble into a rock wall and lean against it for support. Exhaustion is taking control. Or dehydration. I'm not sure which. I'm not sure I care.

The ground calls to me for sleep, and I submit, sinking down, my back to the wall at the next intersection. I stare into the early twilight on the horizon. No stars yet. Still too early. But the wind blows across the open plains, caressing my skin.

Wind. Plains!

Excitement pulses through me as I stare through this new opening. Far ahead, another plateau appears small, distant. But all around it are wide open plains.

I've reached the other side!

Here. Just for a bit. I will rest. Up against the red rocks of the plateau, protected from the eastern sunrise, I pull out my blanket and eagerly devour a protein bar and half a pouch of water. My throat aches for more, but thankfully the exhaustion is stronger than the thirst. I dare to rest, hoping that maybe—just maybe—the nightmare is over.

Dreams of my dad begging at the doors of Paragon for his next treatment plague me, along with my friends wondering where I've gone, if I've abandoned them to Paragon.

35

BEFORE SETTING OFF IN THE MORNING, I WRAP THE thawb around my head and neck again, aware that the open plain means exposure. After a partial protein snack and sip of water, I head across the plain. Were it not for the aching in my foot, I would run. The open space calls to me, and I so desperately want to rush out to greet it.

But I can't run.

Hours. I cross the plain for what feels like hours, then turn to the horizon, watching for others. Some other sign of life in this dead place.

But there's nothing.

At last, I reach the plateau rising up out of the plain. I pause, debating which way to go. I can see the south side of the plateau and more open space. I am hardly eager to find myself locked in another canyon maze. Still, curiosity wins, and I walk toward the northern edge to peer around. If it's clear, I'll go that way. If it isn't, I will stick with the southern route.

"A road." I don't know who I'm talking to, but the voice that comes out of me doesn't sound like my own.

A long road winds around the northern face of the plateau into the distance, leading toward some sort of irregularly shaped rock formations. I take the road east, along the north face of the plateau. The concrete is broken, and now-dead shoots of grass and bramble rise from the cracks.

When I reach the other side of the plateau, rock formations come into sharper view. I pause to take in my surroundings. It's endless. More of the same over and over. Arid ground. Dead or dying brush. Three buttes in the distance, their forms dancing in the waves of heat. No one else in sight. Dehydration has me blinking away wavy lines and blurry vision.

You. The voice in my head is familiar, but not my own. Exhausted, I sag and spin slowly in place.

Something knocks the wind out of me as my back hits the concrete road. Terry kneels over me, his hands wrapped around my neck.

This is your fault! His voice screams in my head, making pain leach into my temples.

My hands claw at his wrists, trying to pull him off. I struggle for breath.

Terry's sunken, hate-filled eyes burn into me from his pale, dirt-caked face. His teeth bared in a feral snarl, made more menacing by the cracked and bleeding lips. I try to fight him off, tell him he's wrong, anything. But he has a death grip on my throat.

Unable to think clearly, I slam my knee as hard as I can between his legs. Terry lets go, falling forward on me and hitting my head in the process. Before he can grab me again, I shove him off and roll to the side, gasping for breath, scratching at the hard ground to gain purchase and stand.

Thankfully, I recover more quickly than him and stand over him, giving an extra kick to his ribs for good measure. The kick sends a jolt of throbbing pain across my wounded foot.

"You told him, jerk!" My voice isn't my own. It's hoarse, rabid. I cough, and it rips my throat painfully.

Terry tries to roll to his knees, but I give him another kick in the ribs. It offers some satisfaction.

"This is *your* fault," I say, rasping the words out.

Terry coughs, wipes the spittle from his mouth, and turns hate-filled eyes on me. "I didn't tell anyone jack!" His right arm grips his ribs over tattered scrubs. He has no pack, no supplies to help sustain him. How has he made it this far? "You and your friends did this."

My jaw twitches, teeth grinding together. I want to rip his throat out, gouge his hateful eyes and stuff them down his throat.

"Who did you read?" I ask, standing over him, ready for another well-placed kick. My hands are balled in fists at my sides. Bianca trained me to fight. I just have to remember her lessons.

Terry shifts to his knees and sneers. It's clear from his deep breaths and overall appearance that he's been through just as much as me. "You ask too many questions, Powerless Prick. I warned you. I told you to stop!"

My fist connects with his jaw in a right hook, just like Bianca taught me. Terry catches himself before falling, then snarls at me. Blood trickles from a fresh cut in the corner of his mouth.

"Not so tough without your muscle to protect you," I say.

"I don't need Derrek."

Sudden, overwhelming pain in my head brings me to my knees. Whatever Terry did to me in the last test, he is doing it again, pressing as hard as he can to get into my mind.

"Why can't I read you?" he asks, baring his teeth.

He can't read me, which means Terry didn't find out what our group was up to from me.

My entire head feels like it's being pressed together, squeezed as tight as it can be without mercy.

"No." The word is more of a growl coming from my aching throat than anything.

"It was her, you know," Terry says. "Your girlfriend, the security guard. She turned you in."

No. It can't be her. Bianca didn't know.

But she did. Maybe not our backup plan, but she was the one who organized the plan to get security information and plot our escape.

"No."

Terry's grip on my mind is blinding. It's hard to bring thoughts together clearly.

"Yes," he says. "Did you really think she wouldn't sing if it came down to you or her?"

She wouldn't. Bianca wouldn't betray me.

Breaths are harder to come by. My heart is pounding from the pressure in my skull.

"Stop," I say, the word more of a breath.

"Why should I?" Terry is shaking, resting more of his weight against the ground.

I press my hands to my head, but it doesn't help.

"I am stronger now," Terry says. "I suppose I have you to thank for that."

My vision blackens.

I can hear nothing but the beating of my heart pumping blood through my body.

Then suddenly the pressure is gone. Soft, smooth hands touch my face. I push them away, but whoever it is has more strength than I do. Arms pull me close in a hug. The scent of citrus soap washes over me. A familiar voice whispers in my ear, gentle and reassuring.

"It's okay. I'm here."

§

Bianca. It's really her here with me. It must be real. The smell of her soap. The feel of her soft, warm arm against my neck. That can't be simulated, can it? We sit with our backs to the plateau as I recover.

Terry lies sprawled on the ground a few feet away, blood oozing from his hairline. Bianca must have knocked him out. I'm overwhelmed with relief to see someone, a friend, but I can't shake what Terry said.

"Why are you here?" I ask as soon as the water and food she gave me have finally done their job. I'm about as recovered as I will ever be.

"To help you." Her thin brows scrunch together.

She turned you in. Terry's warning taunts me. But it can't be right. I can't believe she would do that to me.

"I thought you were dead." I can't meet her eyes, as much as I want to find the truth in them, I just can't bear to look at her.

"Why?"

"I've seen things, Bianca. I've seen them, and I can't unsee them, and you were escorted from Joyce's office, and I thought…" It's hard to breathe. I tip my head back and try to gulp in breaths. My throat hurts so much from Terry's hands.

"They are watching you, Ugene." Bianca leans forward, and I can't help but gaze into her bright eyes. "Even here."

"What did Dr. Cass say to you in the office that night?"

"Are you listening to me?"

I can't get Terry's voice out of my head. "Why aren't you answering me?"

"Forrest is obsessed with you," Bianca says, staring off into the distance. "He watches your videos and listens to your audio all the time. He's always reviewing test results and blood samples. Something isn't right."

Anger propels me to my feet, towering over Bianca. "What did she say, Bianca? What did *you* say?"

"Nothing! I didn't tell her anything. She just…" She swallows, meeting my gaze, tears brimming her eyes and making them shimmer. "She just knew things. About the tablet. The plan to escape. She *knew*, Ugene. I didn't tell her anything."

I shuffle a few feet back. Heat makes it hard to think clearly. "But you said something."

Bianca looks down, picking at her nails and chewing her lower lip. Tears roll down her cheeks unchecked.

I lower my voice dangerously. "What did you say?"

"Only that you supposed to go to floor 189, so I was taking you there." Her voice is strained with emotion. "But she knew something else was going on. She knew you were planning to escape Paragon, that you accessed restricted information and that you were acting de-lusional."

"Did you tell her?"

"I only said you were scared and wanted out. Nothing else. Ugene." Bianca reaches out, but I recoil. "I had to tell her something. She was threatening to question all of you with some sort of injection that makes you tell secrets or something."

Injection. A truth serum? Did she really have such a thing? And Bianca. In all my life she was the only person who never lied to me. At least, as far as I knew. Bianca was always there to defend me. Now Dr. Cass knows I'm trying to escape Paragon Tower. She probably knows I know about the experiments, and if she knows that, I will never be able to prove it. Dr. Cass will be one step ahead of me. She already is.

All we have is the drive, assuming it's still in Miller's possession.

"Ugene, please." Bianca shifts to her knees and reaches out for my hand, but I pull it away, glancing at the still unconscious Terry on the ground. "I came here to help you." Bianca doesn't pull her hand back.

My voice sounds empty as I speak. "You've done enough."

Despite the ache on the bottom of my foot, I turn and run east along the road, as fast as I can get away from her.

"Wait!" Bianca calls.

A glance over my shoulder shows that Bianca is following. I run as if my speed will save me—will save us all. I run as if it will help me escape this nightmare. Bianca doesn't pursue anymore.

More than anything, I desire the warm embrace of my mother.

But there's nothing but the howl of wind in my ears, throbbing pain in my foot, and a burn in my lungs.

The exhaustion in my legs makes my knees give out before I'm ready to stop. I trip, stumble forward, and land on aching hands and knees on the road, gasping for breaths. As I sit back on my haunches and tip my head back, a beep resounds nearby.

A semi-transparent and flat holographic screen appears in the air directly in front of me, roughly the size of a wall, revealing an image of Miller's head and shoulders against a white background. It could be anywhere.

Anywhere but here.

Everything remains the same around me—arid ground, concrete road, heat.

"I wanna know what happened to Murphy," Miller's image says to the camera. "I need to know, and I don't care what you do to me."

"It's not about what we will do to you," Dr. Cass' familiar voice says off screen. "It's about what you will do *for* us."

Miller scowls. "I'm not doing jack until you give me answers. Official word is he tested out, but you and I both know that doesn't happen. What did you do to him? Did he get one of those injections? Did you toss him on the rubbish pile with all the other bodies of your failed experiments?"

What is going on?

Dr. Cass makes a little trill. "For someone who acts like he knows so much, you know very little. Tell us what you and your friends are up to—exactly what they are up to—and I will tell you exactly what happened to your boyfriend."

Sweat rolls down Miller's temple, and he leans forward, rubbing his hands over his face. Has Joyce used that serum on Miller? Maybe he has no control over himself. Maybe he has to answer. After a moment he sits back, face calm and composed. It's hard to accept that someone so together is being forced into anything.

"I want everything," he says.

"I'll be sure you get it."

Miller. The first friend I had here. But were we ever really friends?

"It's Ugene's idea."

The words are like a knife twisting in my chest. "Wha—?" Is this in real-time? Miller was so insistent on not asking questions, on keeping things so quiet that no one would suspect. He was the one who suggested we get out.

"He is planning to use our collective Powers to break everyone out of Paragon Tower. Bianca is supposed to be gathering security information for us. Then we will hack into Forrest's tablet again to get information before we go."

What game is he playing at?

"I'm afraid I need more than that, Miller," Joyce says. "I need specific details."

"Fine." Miller looks away from the camera, his calm composure cracking. "But I need more than good faith. I gave you something. I expect something back before this goes further." He looks back, his expression hardened again. "Is Murphy alive?"

The video feed cuts out, slicing off a chunk of my heart as it goes and leaving me alone in the desert to bleed to death. Has Miller has been playing me? Was that even real? I don't want to believe it's true. I trust Miller. We want the same thing…

Don't we?

36

MY GUT SINKS AS A FAMILIAR FACE COMES INTO FOCUS
only a few feet away.

Miller. Dirty, tired, dehydrated Miller.

Breaths come quicker. My mouth goes dry, and I try to say
something, but nothing comes out.

Miller's voice cracks, and he takes a step forward, white knuckles
wrapped around the straps of his backpack.

"Ugene, I'm sorry."

The words punch me. It's true… He really sold us out.

Miller's face is contorted in agony, torture. Good. I hope he's
dying inside. The extra security on Forrest's tablet was his fault. Miller
told them what we were trying to do, so they locked everything down
tighter.

I hold out a hand. "Don't."

I won't fight him. I can't. Even though he turned us in, betrayed
us, I still can't bring myself to fight him. So instead, I walk away.

Jade had warned me that Miller didn't make friends, didn't seem
to care about anyone else. I assumed later that it was because of what
happened to Murphy. Now, it doesn't matter. Murphy is gone, and
Miller made his choice.

Maybe I don't know him at all.

Anger fuels me, crushing down the pain in my chest. Miller is the
reason Trina, Dave, and Michael were taken away. Are they lying on a
table right now, suffering the same fate as Jade?

My hand drops to my side. Miller takes another wary step toward me, closing the distance. What if they are dead because of him?

I swing out a hook like Bianca taught me. It connects with Miller's jaw with a *smack*. He stumbles back and works his jaw, reaching up to rub it.

"Maybe I deserved—"

I cut him off with another hook, unable to stop myself. This is his fault. He does deserve it. He blocks the hook with his forearm and shoves me backward, palms against my chest.

"I gave you a free shot," he says, rubbing the tips of his fingers against his palms. What is he doing? "That's all you get."

I flex my fingers out, then into fists. Is he my friend? He can't be. All he cares about is himself.

I launch forward again.

Miller's fingers suddenly stop their incessant motion, steepling toward each other. Bright blue-white lightning arcs between his fingertips, creating an energy field.

A shock hits me, and I bounce backward, landing on my back. Hot concrete burns through the fabric of my shirt. Breaths come in gasps. I slip off the strap of my bag and leave it on the ground.

"Stop," he says. "I don't wanna hurt you."

I growl and launch to my feet, ramming a shoulder into his gut, arms around his waist. He tosses his backpack on the ground. We barrel onto the plain. Lightning lances the earth around us, grazing my calf. Fiery hot pain burns my leg. A scream rips from my throat, but my fist still connects with Miller's gut.

He grunts, grabs my arm with one hand, and pulls. He shoves the opposite shoulder, bucking me off.

The burning pain won't subside. It screams at me, but adrenaline and anger push me forward.

"You betrayed us all," I say, pushing back on my good leg to launch again.

The air around us shifts from hot and dry to humid and moist. Rain begins to fall, but only from the cloud over us. It formed from nothing. Miller's doing, no doubt. The drops are cool against my hot skin.

"What should I have done instead?" he asks, standing and brushing himself off.

I narrow my focus on his hands. He's doing it again, rubbing the tips of his fingers against his palms. Charging up.

I hate this place! I hate Forrest for putting me in this position. I hate Joyce for luring me in. I hate Paragon for what they're doing to the test subjects. I hate Miller for betraying my trust. But most of all, I hate feeling powerless.

Miller looks upward for a moment, pointing his fingers at the sky. Mist falls in sheets around us, soaking through our clothes, relieving the heat. I push off.

"Stop!"

Miller's plea is too late. My foot slips on the slick concrete. I fall forward. A cage of lightning shoots down from the sky around me, catching the side of my forehead, jolting me backward. I hate myself for fighting one of the few friends I have in this forsaken place.

No. Not my friend. A friend wouldn't betray us like he did.

Groaning, I open my eyes, allowing them to adjust. Every part of my body aches. I rock on my back in agony. The cage is still up, blue bars made from the lightning he conjured. I touch the side of my head, coming away with blood. Everything spins as I ease myself upright. With every breath, my lungs burn, and my throat aches.

"Ugene." His voice is low. "You okay?"

I wipe mist and blood from my face. "Like you care."

"They had me cornered after the last Survival test, locked in my room until I talked," he says. His hand wraps around the lighting bars of my cage. Of course, it wouldn't faze him. "They just wanted information. In exchange, they gave me the materials I could manipulate to create the drive and give it to you. I tried to resist telling them, but…Ugene, Murphy is alive."

After pushing off the ground, I stalk toward the bars, careful not to touch them. Electricity buzzes in the air around them. "Good for him. Maybe *he* can trust you, but I sure as hell can't. I needed your help. I needed a friend."

Miller glances at the sky. "I don't do friendship. Friends disappear."

"Because you pull stupid stunts like this! Maybe that's why Murphy ditched you. Maybe he saw the truth."

Miller flinches. The lightning around me crackles, pulses, and grows as Miller's expression takes on a dangerous edge. "Who do you think you are, Ugene? You come to this place, act like the king of all—"

"What?"

"—and just expect that we'll be chummy because of a few conversations." The mist mats his blond hair against his head. I want to rip it from his skull. "I told you not to knock, not to ask questions. And you didn't give a crap about anything but what you wanted." Miller leans as close as he can to the bars. "Murphy is alive out there somewhere. Paragon lost him. He was taken to another floor for testing and just disappeared. No one knows what happened to him. I don't give a piece what you think of me, Ugene. But I need you to get out of this place and find him."

"I'm not a tool." It's impossible to resist the urge to reach through the bars, grab Miller's face, and smash it into my first. A snarl curls my lip upward and my hand darts forward, but the mixture of mist and electric energy stops me with a *bzzz*. I jump back, shaking out the jolt making the muscles in my arm contract.

"Get a grip," Miller says, backing up. "Nothing has changed. We still need to get out of here."

"Sure, but now they know how we planned to do it," I say.

"Then we change the game."

"Get bent." I turn my back to him and cross my arms. "I can't trust you won't lead us into another trap."

Miller sighs, and when he speaks again, he sounds defeated. "I'll let you out if you don't hit me again."

"Right." I laugh. I want to do more than just hit him.

"An act of good faith, then." The lighting bars disappear. "I need your help."

I half turn, debating if it's worth the effort to trust him or if I should try using fists again. But we are both stuck in here together, and time is running out. Our issues can resolve once we get out of here. "Do you love him?"

Miller rubs his hands together, and for a brief moment, before he looks away, I can see the pain in his eyes. Love will make you do crazy things. Stupid things.

"Miller."

"Yes! Okay? Yes." His shoulders slump, hands hanging limp at his sides. "And I will do anything you want to get out of here and find him." He snatches his backpack off the ground and slings it on his back again.

It's hard to accept what Miller did, regardless of the circumstances, but at least this I can understand. Love is the same excuse that put me in this place to begin with. All I wanted was to help my dad. Love is a construct that makes us do crazy, irrational things.

After another glance to the falling mist, I pull up my shirt and press it against the wound on my head. It hurts like hell when I touch it, and a hiss slips out through clenched teeth. These last couple of days have been hell. If Paragon knows what we were planning to do to escape, Miller is right. It's time to change the game. Surprise is all we have left.

"Does he love you?"

Miller shifts his bag straps on his shoulders, clearly uncomfortable. "Yes. And he wouldn't just leave me."

I examine the blood on my shirt to try and determine the depth of the wound. "You should have told me. We could have prepared for all this better if you had just been honest from the start. If you really still want the same thing as me, then keeping this all a secret was counterproductive to your goals as much as mine."

"You're right."

"I know that!" The blood on the hem of my shirt isn't so bad. Just a surface scratch, probably. "What happened to the drive?"

"I knew Forrest had people coming, so I took it," Miller said. "It's safe."

My teeth grind. "Again, a warning would have helped." A slow, deep breath steadies my nerves. "Hand it over."

"Not a chance. All of Murphy's information is on there."

I hold out my hand impatiently. "If you want me to even think about trusting you, I need that drive in my hand."

Miller shifts, clearly uncomfortable, but I don't relent. I still won't trust him. Not entirely, so there's no way I'm letting him keep that drive in his possession to betray all of us later. He must sense just how stubbornly I refuse to give up, because he holds out his arm to me, revealing an angry red cut.

"Go ahead. Take it out."

The drive is in there?

"Why?"

Miller shrugs. "It's the one place I knew it couldn't get lost, and if they searched my stuff, they wouldn't find it. I told you, it's safe."

As tempting as it is to cut open his arm and pull out the drive, I don't have the strength or the stomach for it.

"It looks infected." My words have more venom in them than I expect.

"I burned it shut. Let's find Rosie, and she can heal me."

Seeing little other choice, I pick up my bag, shift the strap across my chest, and start walking east. Miller doesn't say another word as he walks alongside.

No matter what Miller has done, I can't forget what's happened to other test subjects here. Jade. Vicki. Dave. Trina. Michael. They deserve justice, and I can't find it in here. That drive is my lightning rod to take Paragon down and deliver justice.

37

SILENCE SETTLES OVER EVERYTHING AS I SHUFFLE along, fighting off a limp from the pain burning in the sole of my foot. Miller's loafers scrape on the broken concrete a couple steps behind me. The tension between us is thick enough to make breathing stagnant—like trying to suck in deep breaths on a humid day.

My thoughts drift to Dad. How his treatments are going. Whether Joyce has already cut him off. What I might possibly do to help him once I get out of here. Something else must exist, another way to help him without needing Paragon's medication. Would he be proud of how I'm taking a stand against Paragon and what they're doing? I can't help but hope that—for once—I've done something right. How angry was he when I left home?

We round the eastern edge of the plateau.

"You found him!" Enid's cry of relief breaks through my thoughts as she launches her small body at me and throws her arms around my neck. "Thank God."

It's surprisingly comforting to have Enid hug me, filling me with warmth. For the first time since getting dropped in this nightmare, someone I trust is here with me. It helps ease some of the pain and fear.

"Yeah," Miller grumbles, lumbering past me.

My gaze follows his movements around the red rock wall of the plateau. Miller steps into an extended, shaded area and my breath catches.

Dozens of test subjects—near a hundred, even—sit on the cracked dirt ground, leaning against boulders. Others lay on the ground with their eyes closed. Every last one of them shows the telltale signs of exhaustion and dehydration—heavy or fluttering eyelids, dry lips, sometimes wild eyes. My hope that no one but me suffered the worst of this is dashed. Forrest put every last one of us in here.

Someone had organized a makeshift camp with sheeted tents here and there—though not enough of them for all the test subjects. Not nearly enough. Some of them wheeze for breath. Others cough so rough it sounds like their throats are raw.

I pry Enid's arms off my neck and step into the shade. "What is this?"

"We've been looking for you for days," Enid explains as we pick our way through camp, stepping around bodies of resting subjects. A weight of sadness presses against me that I don't know most of their names. "Some of these guys showed up on their own. Some of them we found while looking for you."

"You've been together… this whole time?"

"Well, not at first." Enid is clearly excited about what they've done here, but I can't share the sentiment. "Miller was the first to find me. He said this is it. End game. We needed to get everyone together and find you. So that's what we did. By the end of the first day, most of us were together. Miller and Sho went out to find you and kept coming back with others. Some of us were starting to lose hope that you were…" She cuts off, looks at the ground.

No need to finish the sentence. I wondered the same about some of them, if they were actually dead or taken.

Among the crowd, I spot Mo at the same moment he sees me.

"Ugene!" Mo rushes over and slaps me in a quick hug. "Glad we finally found you."

"How many are you?" I ask, taking in the sad state of all the test subjects.

"By our latest count, a hundred and thirty-nine," Mo says proudly.

What is there to be proud of? Everyone looks an inch from death. And so many. I didn't know we had so many on our floor.

As if reading my thoughts, Mo's expression slips. "There was no warning. Those of us who were preparing for this knew something was wrong when lockdown initiated, and we grabbed our packs, but no one else had a chance. There aren't enough supplies for everyone."

Paragon didn't supply anything this time. No food. No water. Some of these people were either starving or dying of thirst.

"We have to do something." I hardly notice the words as my own.

"We're doing everything we can," Enid says, resting a reassuring hand on my arm. "Boyd has been working almost nonstop to try and create food and water supplies for us, but there isn't much to work with in this place. Miller gave up most of his own supplies for Boyd to use."

Miller did that? For a moment, anger burns in my chest, but I let it go. Maybe he is trying.

"There's no way we can get all these people out of here if they don't have the strength to walk," I say, stopping to turn and take everything in. So many… I spin around to meet Enid's gaze. "I didn't get a blue pill. Did anyone else?"

Enid shakes her head. "Not as far as we know."

The situation is dire. Most of these people don't have what they need to survive, and few among us have more than a trickle of Power. How long have they gone without food and water already? And without the extra boost to their Powers, creating what we need will be much more difficult. But we have to try.

"Boyd needs help," I say to Enid and Mo. "Find him any Naturalist that can help create more supplies. If they have the strength to help, make it clear why they don't have a choice. All of our lives could depend on it. Where's Miller?"

"Probably there," Enid points at one of the tents. "Why?"

"Here." I hand my messenger bag over to Enid. "Use my supply, too. Not that there's much left." There's no time to answer. Time isn't our friend right now. Instead, I start toward the tent. "Get the other Naturalists to help Boyd."

We have the numbers. The question is, do we have the strength?

As I make my way to the tent, subjects sit up straighter or just plain stare at me. One guy with dark hair matted down by dirt and rips in his shirt, exposing his tawny skin, watches me as I pass. Omar, the Aurologist who called me the Harbinger of Hope. I feel more like the Harbinger of Doom. I do my best to stand straight and not limp from the pain searing in the sole of my foot. For some reason, they are all looking at me. I can't let them down, even if I feel like I've already failed them all.

I push into the tent and find Miller standing over a cowering Celeste. She hugs something against her chest, head down, avoiding Miller's gaze. Protective instincts kick in and I rush over, pushing Miller back and planting myself between them.

"What are you doing to her?" I can't help the rage puffing up my chest.

"Nothing!" Miller says defensively. "She's hugging that pack like a life preserver, and we want to know why, but she won't talk. She refuses to tell us what's in there."

"You're scaring her!" I say. "What do you expect her to do?"

"*I'm* scaring *her?*" Miller's eyes widen. "She's a killer, Ugene. Don't know you that? This girl is more dangerous than all of us combined."

"Shove off!" I step up in Miller's face.

Miller's voice suddenly takes on a calm edge. "Ugene, listen to me. I know you think you're friends, but I have seen what she does. And I know what happened to her parents. Everyone does." He waves a hand toward the camp beyond the tent, then pauses, waiting for me to back down. I won't. "She killed them, Ugene. With her own bare hands, she killed her parents."

I shake my head. Celeste isn't a killer. "I have very little reason to trust you right now, and every reason to trust her. Save your breath. Now get out and find Enid. We need water. You two can create it."

Miller flinches, glares at Celeste behind me, then storms out in a huff, muttering to himself, "As if we haven't tried that already."

It doesn't inspire hope, but I can only handle one problem at a time.

I crouch in front of Celeste and rest my hand on her shoulder. She recoils at my touch.

"It's okay. I won't let them hurt you or take your bag away."

Celeste's wild green eyes meet mine, shining brilliantly like emeralds caught in the sun—alive. "The chains are breaking. The sea is parting. The hero and the stag approach."

It takes my exhausted mind a moment to recall the riddle she once told me when I asked what she saw in the stars. Andromeda. And the fall of Cassiopeia. But who are the hero and the stag? What does it mean?

"I promise not to take your bag, but can you show me what's in it? It could help others."

Celeste licks her dry lips and stares at me with those wild eyes. With a shaking hand, she unzips the backpack and offers a peek inside. Caramel candies. The bag is filled with candies, and my mouth instantly waters at the sight of them. Behind the treats is a thick book. Despite the overwhelming curiosity about what that book could be, I promised Celeste I wouldn't take anything. I just nod, and she zips the pack shut again.

"We are leaving," I tell her. "As soon as we can figure out how. I want to take you with me."

She hugs her pack again and shakes her head. "The future is what we make, not what we take."

I frown and open my mouth to ask what that means, but someone enters the tent, cutting me off.

"It's Bianca! And she needs to speak to you." Leo disappears out of the tent as quickly as he appeared.

38

MILLER, ENID, LEO, SHO, AND MO ALL STAND LIKE A
wall between Bianca and the test subjects scattered on the ground
behind them. Some of the anger I felt toward Bianca earlier has
dissipated since learning what Miller did. Bianca's offense seems
much more insignificant now. Though I still can't forgive her entirely.
And I can't blame her entirely either. It's a terrible sort of limbo.

I nudge my way between Enid and Sho and step through their
wall.

"I'm sorry," Bianca says again before I have a chance to speak.

"What's she sorry about?" Enid crosses her arms beside me. "Is it
her fault the others were taken?"

A fleeting look of confusion crosses Bianca's face, but then her
gaze turns to me as she realizes I haven't told the others. Not that
there's been time. Or a reason.

"She did, didn't she?" Enid shifts to face me, and a stubbornness
sets in her composure. "She turned us in, and now she's here and we
are all screwed."

"No!" Bianca doesn't just deny Enid's accusation but turns on her
with full-blown anger burning in her eyes. "Will you please pipe down
and let the grownups talk?"

"Excuse me?" Enid's arms drop, hands curling into fists.

"It wasn't her," I say, stepping between them and putting a hand
on Enid's shoulder.

"I can't believe you believe *her*," Enid says. "*I* don't."

"I know for a fact it wasn't her, okay?" I put myself between her and Bianca, so Enid's glare has to be directed at me. "Do you trust me?"

"That's not—"

"Do you trust me?"

Enid heaves out a sigh that makes her shoulders sag. "Yes. Of course."

"It wasn't Bianca."

Enid grimaces, but nods. The hate still burns in her eyes as she watches Bianca's every move.

Miller clears his throat. "It was—"

"Terry," I interrupt. "It was Terry. He read someone, wouldn't say who, but it was him."

Miller's brows pull together as he stares at me, but he doesn't say anything. I don't know why I lied to them, why I felt the need to protect Miller. But at the moment, we have nothing to gain by turning on each other.

"Can I explain now?" Bianca asks, lowering her voice and looking around at the sky.

I find the action curious and nod. "This way." If anyone is watching, as she suggested before, maybe the tents will be a more secure place to talk.

The seven of us walk to the nearest tent and slip inside. A few test subjects are in there, working with Boyd on the meager supply of food to try and create more. They all look up at us as we enter, but quickly go back to work.

"First, I brought supplies," Bianca says, sliding a large hiking bag off her back. It hits the ground with a heavy thump and kicks up dirt. "It isn't much, probably not enough for everyone, but there's food and water in there. As much as I could fit."

Miller kneels beside the bag and unfastens the buckle, then loosens the drawstring. The bag is full all the way to the top with packaged food. She's right. It isn't much, but it should give everyone here something and fend off starvation just a little longer.

As Miller unzips the bulging front pouch of the bag, my gaze darts back up to Bianca. She doesn't appear proud or confident when her eyes meet mine. She's terrified.

Why?

I ask the question I know we are all thinking. "How did you get here?"

Bianca wipes sweat from her brow, streaking dirt across her bronze skin. "This test isn't like any of the others, Ugene. The place is crawling with security. There was a meeting a few days ago, security and personnel from PSECT were required to attend, but I didn't get invited. I only found out about the meeting because I overheard two other guys talking about it."

"What's PSECT?" I ask.

"Paragon Subject Experimental Conditioning Tests." She spits the words out so quickly it makes my head spin, then she carries on without missing a beat. "I work for the PSECT division, thanks to my brother, but I was purposely left out of the meeting, so I knew it had to be something Dr. Cass didn't want me to know about. After our encounter with her, she didn't trust me anymore. I had grown too close to the subjects and was temporarily removed from duty."

"What encounter?" Mo asks, confusing scrunching his face.

"Holy!" Miller stands abruptly, holding out a large silver tin to me. "She has the booster!"

Everyone crowds in to see for themselves. I snatch the tin from Miller and see sheets of the blue booster pill layered inside. Wide-eyed, I look at Bianca again.

"Where did she get all those?" Leo asks.

"I tried to tell you," she says, her gaze locked on mine.

I close the tin, holding it tight in my hand. "Start from the beginning."

"I'm trying!" Bianca huffs and lowers her voice. "Listen to me. They kicked me out, knowing this was coming and that I would try to help you. So I went to floor 189 since you were so curious about it before. I thought I would take a look around, and…" Bianca's voice trails off, her face paling. "I'm sorry Ugene. I should have listened.

Your friends…"

Trina. Dave. Michael.

My heart aches. I couldn't help them. I couldn't save them. Just like I can't save all of these people. Why does this fall on my shoulders? Why do the others look to me?

No words rise to the surface. Sickness twists my gut. I just give a small shake of my head. The rest of the group listens in horrified silence.

"But I found those pills, and I remembered you saying something about them before. I thought they might be important."

"That's convenient," Enid says, arms tight across her chest.

Bianca ignores her. "I knew I had to get the pills to you somehow. I packed everything I could in that bag and found Haily, one of the other PSECT security guards. She was always friendly to me. I got her talking, and she told me what was going on, that everyone was sent into this test without supplies and each security guard was given their own special way in and out to make sure the test subjects didn't congregate. Their job was to keep people apart and observe. I knocked Haily out and stole her access code to get in here."

"But they failed," I said. "I mean, most of us are here in this camp."

Bianca nodded stiffly. "Haily isn't the only guard I've had to fight."

The implication is clear enough, judging by the way Bianca's shoulders slump and her gaze averts. I notice for the first time the angry bruise near her ear, as well as the scratches and bruises on her bare arms. She did this—kept the guards away to buy us time. She probably stumbled across Terry and me as she patrolled to keep the camp safe.

"But I can't do it much longer," Bianca says, and the fatigue is clear in her voice. "By now, Forrest and Dr. Cass know I'm here. The other guards will descend on this camp and break it up."

Leo raises a hand to get our attention. "'Scuse me. Just wondering. If she has an in, that means she has an out. Doors open both ways."

Now everyone is at attention, staring at Bianca with renewed hope in their eyes.

"Yes."

Mo lets out a whoop of joy. Everyone starts talking at once as the excitement of the moment takes over. But it can't be that easy. Nothing about this is easy. Dr. Cass won't let us out just like that.

"We can't use the same exit," I say loud enough so everyone can hear me. My proclamation kills their enthusiasm.

"Why not?" Leo asks.

"It's obvious, isn't it?" I wait for someone else to catch on.

"They will be waiting at the exit," Miller says.

The corner of Bianca's mouth curls up slightly for the first time since entering the camp. "True," she says. "But they can't block them all. The location of the exits changes in the simulation, which is why each of the guards is given one of these." Bianca crouches beside her backpack. She unzips another front pouch and several flat, card-shaped pieces of tempered glass tumble out. "They can show us where the nearest exits are."

Our hope is immediately restored.

"What do we do now, then?" Mo asks, looking at me.

All of them are looking at me. Why? No one else speaks. They shift feet or scratch their chins waiting…for me.

"You are the brains of the operation," Miller agrees. "Just tell us what to do."

I swallow the lump in my throat. "We have to get everyone up and move," I say. "If PSECT is really going to come down on us, we need to keep moving toward an exit." They all nod, heads bobbing as if it makes perfect sense. I'm not sure it does, but I don't know what else to say. "Let's get everyone a ration of what we have here and start moving. Bianca and Sho can lead the way."

And just like that, they listen.

As the others scramble into action to break camp, I pull Bianca aside.

"How many guards are we talking about?" I ask, keeping my voice down so no one else interrupts. "What sort of Powers do they have?"

"Um, twenty. Maybe more depending on how many were called in for this," Bianca shifts anxiously. "As far as I know, everyone is either a Strongman—a Somatic of some sort—or Telekinetic."

That's some good news. Somatics can be beaten by our numbers, and Telekinetics can only do so much at once. It won't be easy, but it could be worse.

When I pull away to help break camp, Bianca takes my hand and pulls me back. I can hardly resist her superior strength, especially in my weakened state. Not that I want to.

For a moment she just stares at me, silent, terrified. And now I understand. Bianca risked everything to help us. She can't go back to Paragon. She can't go home. Bianca is in this with us to the end.

"Don't worry, we won't leave anyone behind," I say, pulling her into a hug. Bianca sags against me, her head resting on my shoulder. A wonderful mix of sweat and her citrus soap fills me, offering some comfort. She mumbles something, and we both pull back. "What?"

Bianca swallows a lump in her throat, then licks her dry lips. "There's something else you should know." She pauses, but I just wait for her to finish. "It's bigger than we imagined. There are more."

"Guards?"

"Subjects." Bianca glances around and steps closer, whispers to only me. "I found three other floors like yours, all full of test subjects. Paragon has been filling up ever since the Proposition passed."

My blood turns to ice despite the heat. "How many?" The words croak out.

"Including your floor, seven hundred, at least."

Seven hundred? The sheer magnitude of Paragon's experiments is overwhelming.

I shake my head. "Are they all here?"

The odds of all of them surviving these conditions without warning are—well "slim" would be an understatement. Getting sixty of us out of here seemed like a huge task, but seven hundred? Impossible.

"I don't know. I don't think so. Just your floor."

All I can respond with is a stiff nod. Better that way. For now, I can just focus on my floor. The rest will come later.

"Okay, well, we should… we should get to breaking camp," I stumble over the words.

Bianca nods, and together we walk out of the tent to set to work.

Everyone is moving with vigor and excitement, ready to break camp. Miller, Enid, and Mo dole out blue pills to give everyone a Power boost. Sho, Boyd, and a couple of Boyd's helpers distribute a meager offering of food and water to everyone. Bianca coaxes everyone to their feet, offering words of hope.

I go in search of Celeste.

"Time to go," I say, gingerly helping Celeste to her feet.

"A ray of hope. A final breath. A chance to cope. A kiss of death. And all the stars shall fall."

The words send shivers down my spine, but there's no time for riddles. If security is closing in, we have to move first, ask questions later. I slip an arm around Celeste's waist and escort her along with the others.

39

AFTER NEARLY A MILE OF HELPING CELESTE, NUDGING her along with us every time she begins pulling back, the ache in my arm and shoulder screams at me. I don't know if she senses it or not, because she finally pulls away and walks herself. I watch from the corner of my eye to make sure she sticks with us and doesn't try to fall back or run. Her loafers drag on the ground, scuffing the dirt and kicking up puffs in the air.

A glance around reveals that everyone in the group is doing the same. Dragging feet, slumped shoulders, lowered heads. Some people are coughing out the dirt we can't help but breathe in. Most of them don't have the energy to carry on much longer, not that we've made significant progress. It couldn't have been less than an hour since we broke camp. This pace will raise a red flag and bring security down on us anyway. There must be a better way to get all these people to the exit. Too bad teleportation isn't a thing.

Confident that Celeste will stick near the middle of the pack, I pick up the pace and join Bianca, Sho, and Leo at the front.

"How much farther?" I ask.

Leo rolls his eyes and grimaces, adjusting Bianca's pack on his shoulders. He must have offered to carry it a while back. "We don't even know exactly where the exit is yet."

"What?" How can they not know?

"We know it's in this direction," Sho says with more confidence than I expect. "It's just…we're not close enough for me to pinpoint where it is."

"Well this pace won't work," I say. "I don't know how long some of these people can keep up, and we're—"

Thunder rumbles in the distance, cutting off further objections. Everyone stops and looks at the sky, but no clouds mar the white-blue blinding light above. A chime echoes across the barren plain once, twice... over and over and over again. I lose count.

Then, silence.

Everyone holds their breath, but no one knows what we are waiting for. Seconds tick by excruciatingly slow. Dread fills my gut. We need to move.

"It's them," Bianca says, spinning in place to survey the land.

A shriek shatters the silence. Then another. And another. In a matter of seconds, the entire group of test subjects has descended into chaos, running in every direction, renewed with the instinct to survive.

"Don't run!" I call out, not confident that anyone heard me. "Stay together!"

Bursts of light flash from the group outward as some of the subjects launch Naturalist attacks north. The ground rumbles beneath our feet. In some places, the earth rolls outward in ripples.

"Celeste." The name comes out as a whisper, and a moment later my feet are carrying me through the chaos as Bianca screams out my name. But I can't stop.

I push, bump, elbow my way through the throng of subjects milling in every direction. I peer over shoulders and heads in search of wild black hair. Narrow rock formations suddenly appear amid the test subjects, lanky and thin and as tall as a human—maybe they are. I have no idea what's going on. All my focus is on finding Celeste.

"Ugene!" Miller's shout barely reaches through the screams of the other subjects. I spot the top of his blond head through the crowd as he throws lightning north. "Run! Security!"

My gaze follows one of his bolts to see dozens of security guards in their black uniforms approaching from the north, firing at the test subjects. They must have come over the ridge in the distance, a long line of them marching in time toward us.

Run. I do, continuing toward where I left Celeste, toward where Miller is fighting.

A glance to the right—at the line of security guards bearing down on us from the north—hastens my steps and provides the extra boost of adrenaline I need to ignore the throbbing pain in my foot. As I pass a girl in dirty scrubs, her face caked with dirt, she knocks backward off her feet, drawing my attention to my left.

"Oh, God." The words are little more than a breath.

Another line of guards—at least two dozen men and women clad in black uniforms—close in from the south as well. They're pinching us in, forcing us to break up, just like Bianca said they would.

Shots fire, ringing out from either side over the din. A boulder shaped like a rocket shoots out of the ground in my path, launching into the horizon toward the north. I stumble back into a sudden tornado of dust. It sweeps me from my feet and throws me off course. Pain lances across my temple as my head hits the hard ground. Boyd's hand wraps around my arm, and he pulls me to my feet.

"This w-way!" Boyd yells, pulling me east, away from Celeste.

I shove him off, calling out to Celeste, but my voice is swallowed by the cacophony of grinding earth, breaking rocks, gunshots, and screaming test subjects.

Bolts of lightning streak across the sky from all directions, moving toward each other, then striking outward and branching off toward the south and north. People in scrubs and loafers attempt to escape in any direction they find. A few make a stand, creating objects from rock and dirt to hurl at security. Others create winds or ripples of earth outward. Still, the guards are closing in, less than fifty feet from our writhing mass of bodies, maintaining a perfectly orderly line of march. A few gaps in their ranks is the only clue that they have lost a few of their own to our attacks.

A return volley begins. Rocks and boulders the test subjects hurled at the guards soar back toward us, launched by the Telekinetic guards as they continue firing, marching ever closer in perfect synchronization.

Subjects fall, some unmoving and some seizing on the spot. People scatter and run to avoid being crushed.

"Ugene!" Bianca's voice is distant, somewhere behind me.

And then I see Celeste.

In the middle of all the chaos, Celeste stands perfectly still, staring north. Test subjects jostle her in their haste to escape the debris, but she remains statue-still. The mere sight of her immobile form freezes me in my tracks.

My panic finally breaks, shattered by fear for Celeste's life. I break into a sprint. Too late.

Fiery hot pain slams into my spine, sending me sprawling on the ground. Booms shake the earth. I try getting up, then a shock in the back of my skull sends everything into darkness.

Ringing. Quivering earth. Muffled shouts. Everything hurts, but mostly my head and back feel like they've been ripped open. I try pushing away from the ground, standing, kneeling, anything, but my limbs are too weak and resist. My body collapses against the earth, and dirt coats my nostrils and throat. I cough, which induces intense, blinding pain from the back of my skull. Someone shouts beside me. I turn my head, unable to hear what's being said. Everything is fuzzy.

Enid kneels beside me, holding a hand in the air away from us. Tears streak down her cheeks, creating clear rivers in the dirt caked on her face. Cold hands press against my searing hot back, and the world snaps into sharp detail as the skin on my back stretches, tugs, pulls.

"Don't you dare die on me," Enid says with more affirmation than I've ever heard from her.

I try to speak, but all that escapes are coughs and rasps. And blood.

"Fix it!" Enid yells at someone beside her, sweat rolling in beads down her temple as she struggles to hold her hand up. I can't turn my head to see who she yells at.

"I'm trying!" the other girl snaps.

The ground rumbles and Enid growls, pushing her hand outward away from us. Her Power. She's using her Power for something.

"I can't hold it much longer," Enid tells the other girl.

"I just need another minute!"

My spine pops, and tears fill my eyes, but no sound escapes. Healing. The girl is healing me. Rosie?

Rock breaks somewhere on the other side of Enid and she bares her teeth and stands, rushing around to my other side with both hands in the air. Is that rock her doing?

"A tower!" Miller calls out from elsewhere, close enough to hear but too far away to see.

"Get everyone together again." Leo's voice is muted by a sudden thunderous rumble.

Enid unleashes a feral scream.

A body hits the ground beside me, and brown eyes stare blankly at me. It takes a moment before I realize who it is. Omar. Shame washes through me at the relief that it isn't me. Paragon is killing us. Nothing about this should offer relief.

"Up you go," Rosie says, hoisting me to my feet with her arm around my torso under my arm.

The pain vanishes, replaced now by a feeling like my body has stretched itself too thin. I stumble a step into Rosie, but she holds me steady. Enid releases a cry of relief to see me on my feet again, and the stone wall she created to protect us from attacks crumbles in a rocky heap as Rosie lets me go.

"Celeste," I say, blinking at the devastation around us.

Test subjects litter the ground. Those still on their feet fight back with their Powers. Rents dot the earth where the rock was ripped out as a weapon. But standing in the middle of it all with her wild black hair blowing in the breeze, utterly untouched by any of the chaos, is Celeste.

Miller runs toward me from his position at the rear of the group. I stretch a hand toward Celeste. Miller hooks his arm through mine as he runs past, jerking me away.

A hulking mass of man clad in a black uniform raises his stun gun at Celeste. No joy lives in his fixed gaze—nor hate, malice, or satisfaction. His expression is completely blank, devoid of emotion as he takes careful aim.

The arid plains offer no hiding places for us, no shelter from the assault. All around us, security forces close in, only twenty feet away now in perfect ranks, firing at test subjects. Some shots hit. Some miss. Bodies crumple to the ground, screaming in agony. A few subjects run toward the line, engaging their Strongarm muscles to throw punches or seize weapons, but the guards are stronger. Blood pounds in my eardrums, dulling all other noise.

Celeste slowly arcs a hand out in front of her. The guard squeezes the trigger.

"No!" I tug and jerk to escape Miller, but he's stronger than me.

Celeste's head kicks back, and her feet lift off the ground. I scream.

Sudden, brilliant bursts of light explode outward from Celeste. A blinding rainbow of colors. I cover my eyes and duck away with Miller, holding my breath as a wave of dust blows past. Before the dust settles, I shove Miller away and spin to find Celeste.

Her limp, huddled form lays on the ground face-down, and I've never run so fast in my life. I skid to my knees at her side, fearing the worst.

"Celeste." Grabbing her shoulder, I pull her over to look for wounds. "Wake up. Talk to me." Fear clenches my throat. Dirt mars her face, but no blood. I check her torso for an entry wound or signs of blood. Nothing. Did they miss? A bullet casing is lodged in the dirt beside her, spent but unbloodied. "Celeste?"

She blinks, dull green eyes gazing up at me. "Perception in moral character bleeds immoral hearts," she whispers in exhaustion.

I have no idea what she just said, and I don't care. Just the sound of her voice fills me to the brim with relief, and I lean over and kiss her forehead, deliriously laughing as if something inside broke under strain.

Test subjects—those not shot or fleeing—stand in clumps, appearing. Some lay unmoving, and I can't tell how many we lost. Paragon has resorted to killing, to seeing this carnage as an acceptable result of this test. *What comes next is your fault.* Forrest's accusation makes these deaths weigh heavy on my shoulders. Did they die because of me? It's not a burden I can afford to bear right now.

A brief glance tells me we are alone again. Security is gone, no traces of them remaining. Was that Paragon's doing, or the result of whatever Celeste just did?

"What did she do?" Miller stands over the two of us, looking in all directions.

"No idea."

40

EVERYONE IS CONFUSED AND DISORIENTED, TAKING
this opportunity to rest or deal with the dead. Fifteen confirmed
killed. Six mortally wounded. Nineteen with mobility injuries. Rosie
did her best to heal who she could, but she's too weak to do much.
Security has disappeared, but it's only a matter of time until they show
up again.

The landscape hasn't changed. Dry, arid plains with little more
than plateaus in the distance. And the newest development—a lone
shining tower twisting up into the too-bright sky, shimmering like a
mirage. Our small group of unlikely heroes stands in a misshapen
circle. Bianca on one side of me, Celeste on the other.

"We need to split up," Mo says. "It won't be easy to attack like that
if we're spread out."

"That's the dumbest idea I've ever heard," Enid says. She stands
near Mo, weight shifted to one leg and clearly bored with his idiocy.
"We are weaker separated."

"How many will they bring next time?" Mo asks. "You got a better
idea?"

"Stop." Miller stands at the edge of our small group, pinching the
bridge of his nose. He sighs. "Let's just go to the tower. It has to be
an exit."

"And so clearly a trap," Enid says. "Towers don't just appear out
of nowhere. That thing wasn't there before the attack, and now it is.
We would be walking right into their open arms."

Or worse, but I don't want to discourage them any more than they already are.

"Well, we don't have the strength to find another exit, and we don't have the time," Miller says, crossing his arms. "Either we go to the tower and take our chances, or we keep going and risk dehydration or worse."

Enid shoots her gaze at me like I'll butt in and disagree with him. Like I have some brilliant idea. But ideas fail me. I don't trust Miller, and Enid is right. It could be a trap, especially if Miller is the one saying we should do it. But Miller is right, too. Everyone was weak before that attack. Now… just getting some of these people on their feet has proven a monumental task. Rosie healed as many as she could, but she doesn't have the strength to treat them all, and no one else has come forward as a healer. The tower may be our only option.

Enid isn't the only one looking at me. They all are. All my friends. All the test subjects hovering near the group. But my ideas have led us to this—to fifteen dead. *Stop looking at me like I know what to do!*

I sigh. "I don't like it, but Miller's right. Most of these people won't make it to another exit. If we go to the tower, it's probably a trap. If we carry on and seek out another exit, PSECT will close in on us again. And splitting up isn't happening, either." I couldn't live with myself if I made it to the exit and any of them didn't. Living with fifteen dead is bad enough.

All fall into silence.

Bianca shifts beside me and takes my hand. "I'm with Ugene."

"Of course you are," Enid snaps. But she sighs and nods in agreement.

"There's an exit there, for sure," Leo says confidently, staring at the shimmering tower in the distance, one of the glass cards in his hand. The corners of the tower twist up into the sky like a helix. Like Paragon Tower. "Once we're inside, I can probably pinpoint where it is."

Something tells me the exit is in one of three places. Our floor. Floor 189. Or Joyce's office. None of them will be easy to get to over a hundred flights, at least, up in the sky.

One by one, everyone agrees.

"The tower it is," I say, exasperated. I'm tired of leading. But this is what they all want. "Do we have anyone in this group who can manipulate electronics? Because I have a feeling we will need a few."

"I can find out," Mo says. "But it will take time."

"Then that's your task while we make our way to the tower," I say. "Find as many as you can and send them to the front of the group. I want anyone strong enough to defend the group—Strongarms, Telekinetics, Naturalists—organized in ranks around us in case of another attack. We can't let the group scatter like that again. When we get to the tower, a group of Strongarms will clear the lobby, then we will figure out what step to take next."

With a pitiful plan of action, we begin moving the horde of test subjects toward the tower, and I can't help but wonder what kind of tests the building will have waiting for us.

41

JUST OVER A QUARTER MILE LEFT TO THE TOWER. IT looms high in the sky, the only bastion of safety in this dead world. But does it indeed offer safety? The wind picks up, making my clothes ripple and pull against my body. Sand and dirt kick up from the ground as the wind swells. In a matter of seconds, our path to the tower is obscured.

I raise an arm to block the blowing sand from my eyes, leaning into the wind to keep from falling over. A cry calls out to the left. I stumble toward it, helping a girl to her feet, pulling her along with me as we blindly make our way ever forward. No one else is visible in the dust storm. Nor is the tower. Are we headed in the right direction?

The sand stings as it hammers against my skin, like a bombardment of a thousand needles all at once. I would pull out my blanket and attempt to cover the assault—thought I doubt it would help much. Besides, I gave my bag to Boyd for supply replication. And if I stop, I'm afraid I'll lose my way. Maybe I already have.

Voices rise in the chaos, muffled by the howl of wind and sand. I squint into the dust storm but can't see anyone. Just the girl pushing through the storm with me. If anyone else is in danger or has lost their way, I would never know.

Just when I think I can't take another step, the storm in front of us breaks just feet from the doors into the tower. A group is amassing there. I look back to where we came from and suck in a breath.

The storm rises in front of us, climbing high into the sky, rolling up against an invisible barrier around the tower. Another simulation.

If Paragon can create such a storm in the simulations, why don't they use that to their advantage? They could separate us all…

Or maybe they already have. A quick count shows that our number is cut by a quarter. Where is everyone else? What will Paragon do to them?

Paragon Tower looms over our ragtag horde of frail miscreants. Last time I looked up at the shimmering windows of the tower, hope had filled me. Hope that I would make a difference, save my father, gain an ability, find out what's wrong with me. So much has changed since I walked through those doors. So much of that hope has died.

Staring at the glass windows rising high above, I realize I no longer care what happens to me—as long as these people can escape and find a new life outside these walls. That's my goal now. The only hope that remains, feeble as it may be.

Everyone files through the doors without an ounce of hesitation. The exhaustion from the journey here makes hesitation impossible for everyone—except me.

"It's not a real building, you know," Miller says beside me. "Let's get this over with."

"I know this is a trap," I say, meeting his gaze.

"Probably."

"You know it's a trap."

"Sure." Miller holds open a door. "But do we have another choice?" He waits for me to enter.

Every instinct is screaming at me, telling me not to walk through those doors, that this won't end well. There is always another choice, usually buried deep beneath the worst option. I shake my head.

Miller sighs. "Murphy is out there, and I'm going to find him. Whether you come with me or not. Ugene, I know you don't trust me, but we've come this far. I would rather finish with you than without you."

It would be easy for Miller to walk through those doors and leave all of us behind. He could find the exit and get himself out. We are this close. He doesn't need us anymore. "Why?"

"Because I…" Miller chews his bottom lip, looking through the open door. "I'm scared, okay? And we're, you know, friends."

I almost laugh. "You said you don't make friends."

"I'm also an idiot. Don't listen to me."

Friends. I can't accept his friendship, even though I want to. Not after what he did to Trina, Dave, and Mo. And if it meant getting to Murphy, he would do it to me. There's no doubt of that in my mind now.

But everyone else is inside. Enid stands in the lobby, watching Miller and me, waiting for us. For me. I have to get everyone out. No matter what. And for some reason, they are following my lead. I only hope I don't lead anyone else to their doom.

I look toward the dust storm, still rolling up the invisible barrier, hoping others will step through. But none do.

"Ugene," Miller says behind me.

Shoulders slumped, I turn my back to the storm and step past Miller into Paragon Tower—or the simulated version of the tower.

Cold air hits me, offering relief from the heat outside. Some of the subjects are sitting on the floor in clumps. Three subjects—those Mo found with potential Electromancy capabilities—walk along the walls, their hands brushing the seamless surface. Celeste stands in the dead center of the lobby, staring into open space that rises five floors up. I do a quick scan. Maybe a hundred of us remain. That means we lost nearly a fourth of our comrades in that storm. So many still out there, wandering or worse in the torrent.

The lobby is empty, with no tables or chairs anywhere. The building appears completely vacant. Only the long, built-in reception desk, currently unoccupied, and the bay of elevators on the far side of the lobby are present. It's a plain, pristine, white space.

"We should look for them," I say to no one in particular, watching the storm.

Enid stands beside me, shaking her head as she gazes out the glass doors. "We have no idea how long that storm will last, and we can't send anyone into it. They could get lost."

I turn my attention to Sho. "He could. He has Psychic Navigation."

"That doesn't mean he could survive the storm," Enid says. She places a gentle hand on my arm and turns me to face her. "You can't save everyone."

But I have to. I'm responsible for them. They accepted that when they chose me to lead, as did I.

Bianca waves her wrist at the elevators, but nothing happens. Leo is bent in front of one of the elevator door panels, probably trying to use his Atomic Vision to figure out why it doesn't work.

"We all need rest anyway," I say. "We can wait out the storm for a few hours."

I make the announcement to everyone, and many of the test subjects either let out a sound of relief or their shoulders sag as they slump down and close their eyes.

"You need rest, too," Enid says.

I shake my head. "Go sleep for a while." I couldn't sleep now if I wanted to.

Enid doesn't appear pleased, but she moves to the side of the room and lays on her side with her head on her arm, watching me until she falls asleep. But I continue watching the storm, praying for more to come through.

Exhaustion pulls me down, and I move to the reception desk, sitting on the cool tiled floor with my back to the counter, watching. Despite my best efforts to remain vigilant, I drift off to sleep.

A voice startles me awake. Celeste's voice.

"All the stars will fall," Celeste whispers, but the emptiness of the lobby makes her words echo. She gazes up at the ceiling of the lobby again.

A few of the others are awake, waiting for us to move on, looking for a way to exit. I scan outside, but no one has come, and the storm hasn't let up. We will have to move on, leaving about thirty people behind. It fills me with anger and a sense of failure.

I move beside Celeste, staring up to see what she sees. But the only thing above us is a ceiling with lights covered by semi-transparent images of the sky, creating the surreal effect of standing outside.

Like stars.

A sudden sickness twists my gut.

One of the Electromancers working with Leo on the panel screams, then collapses on the floor, seizing. The sound stirs everyone to their feet, alert.

"Rosie!" I point toward the boy, but she's already moving toward him.

Bianca kneels beside the boy, tipping his head back to open the airway as much as she can. Saliva froths and bubbles from his lips, then he stops moving.

"It's too late," Bianca says, meeting my gaze with tears in her eyes.

A rattling behind me makes me spin around, searching for the source, hoping others are trying to get in.

Miller is at the door, pushing, pulling, throwing his shoulder and hip against it. But he doesn't need to say anything to confirm what we already know. It's locked. There is no escape, which also means there's no way for anyone else to get in even if they do materialize out of the storm.

Rosie kneels beside the boy, putting her hands on his chest, over his heart.

"Rosie, don't waste your energy," I say, walking toward them. Another life I failed to save.

The boy sucks in a deep breath as if breaking the surface of water. Rosie wilts at his side. What just happened? He was dead. A small crowd has gathered around Rosie and the boy, and everyone stares with wide eyes. Resurrection? Did she just… but that's not possible.

The elevators all ding at once. Four of them open.

"That can't be good," Enid says, staring at the open door beside her.

Four. Enough for all of us to go up if we really pack in tight.

"Sho, have you found the exit?" I ask, holding an arm out to stop a few of the subjects who moved toward the open doors. "Wait."

Sho heaves a sigh. "Up. That's all I know."

"Do we have any telepaths in the group?" I ask, turning to the other subjects.

Everyone shuffles, moving toward the open doors, eager to go up now that Sho said it's the way out. I can't hold them all back.

A girl—about twenty by my best guess—steps forward and brushes her matted, dirty, dark hair away from her face. "I'm a telepath. Not very good, though."

"Doesn't matter," I say. "You go with Sho." I look at my companions. "Everyone split into even groups of four. Celeste and Miller are with me."

"I'm coming with you, too," Enid says.

"No. I need you and Boyd to lead another group. Bianca, Rosie, and Mo, another. Sho and Leo can lead the last to work on the exit and open it. Anyone with Manipulation Powers or Enhanced Sight should go with them to help."

Everyone eagerly files into the elevators in groups. Bianca looks at me, waiting for her group to load.

"What's going through that head of yours?" she asks.

"I want you to check the other floors to make sure there aren't any test subjects left behind," I say. "Take your group to each floor, together, and sweep them. I don't think the exit will be on any of them. Too easy." Bianca nods at that as if she expected it, too. "I'm going to check Dr. Cass's office."

"What about the other two groups?" she asks, glancing at Enid, who is watching and listening from her own elevator door.

"Enid, go to our floor and check for any stray subjects. Telepath… Girl…" I snap my fingers at the girl with Leo.

"Madison," she says.

"Madison, your job is to make sure each of us knows where to go once the exit is found. That's your only job. Can you handle it?"

Madison nods, but she looks uncertain. I can't do much about it.

She has a booster, and she's our only hope.

I kneel beside the Electromancer who had collapsed before. "You good to try again?"

"You serious?" he asked, rubbing his chest.

"I'm afraid there isn't much choice," I say. "We are getting out of here, but your group needs you to operate the elevator in case something else takes over. Go in Rosie's group, in case you need medical attention."

He is clearly displeased but nods and turns to Rosie's elevator.

"I want one Electromancer with each group," I say.

"We don't have enough," Bianca says.

"I have Miller," I say. There's no way I'm letting him lead another group. He's staying close to my side, and I know he has electric capabilities, so hopefully, that will be enough. "Let's go. We're wasting time. Look for other test subjects, then report to the exit. No pit stops."

I head toward my elevator, but Bianca pulls me in for a hug and whispers in my ear. "Be careful." When she steps back, the sadness in her eyes makes me afraid I won't see her again. No time to think like that.

"Ugene." Enid rushes over to my elevator, rubbing her hands nervously together. She bites her lip, then kisses my cheek. Where did that come from? "I'll see you later."

I nod, heat rising to my cheeks as Miller smirks at me and the doors slide shut in my face.

The elevator lurches into motion.

42

THE ELEVATOR IS PACKED AS TIGHT AS IT BEGINS TO rise, but somehow everyone has given Celeste her own personal bubble of space. All of them appear anxious or afraid of what awaits us on the other side of the elevator doors. Except for Celeste. Her expression is just as curious and innocent as always. Like she doesn't realize we are in peril. Maybe she doesn't.

"I didn't select a floor," Miller says, pulling my attention away from my thoughts.

Yet we are already moving up.

"We need to get to Joyce's office, at the top of the tower," I say. "Can you find out where it's taking us? Change it?"

Miller shifts, raising his hand to the access panel. His brows pull tighter as all his Power focuses on the task at hand. It only takes a few seconds, then his eyes snap to me.

"It's taking us all the way to the top."

"Well, there's that." I offer a smirk, but it's half-hearted. They already wanted us at the top. Why?

Silence falls over the elevator as we climb. No one even moves. All is still as if frozen in time. I'm thankful this doesn't make just me terrified. My knees are weak, my stomach in endlessly tugging and shifting knots. I cross my arms over my chest, hugging tight to keep them from shaking. This is way out of my league. I have no Powers. I can't fight for these people. I can't do anything.

Why am I even here?

The elevator lurches to a stop at floor 200. I take a moment to focus on calming my frayed nerves, eyes closed. The door dings and slides open. I step out, careful not to trip over my own feet.

Even in the simulation, this floor is immaculate and impressive. Tall ceilings. Glass panel walls. Polished white tile floors. Brilliant light making everything seem to sparkle. Miller lets out an impressed whistle.

"This what it really looks like up here?" he asks, moving out of the way so everyone else can file out.

"Yes," I say, moving toward the glass doors to Joyce's office. "Except not vacant. Hold the elevator doors."

"Right." Miller moves toward the elevator. "What are we looking for?"

"I'm not really sure," I admit. "Signs of an exit. Anything that might give us more clues about what's really going on." It's a stretch, but it's all I have to go on.

Last time I stood here, Bianca was in the office, and I was afraid of what Dr. Cass was saying to her, what she might do to her. What am I hoping to find here? Answers? Dr. Cass wouldn't leave them in a simulation for me to notice unless she wanted me to see it.

Summoning all the courage I can muster, I push open the glass door and enter the office. It clicks shut behind me. I'm not sure what I'm looking for, but I begin circling the room, fingertips sliding along the walls. The desk is gone. The chairs, too. Nothing but four walls and that one door.

Sho found the exit on Floor 189. Room 6B. Madison's Telepathic voice startles me, and I jump, spinning around before remembering who it is. I breathe out a sigh of relief and try to tell her we will be down shortly, unsure if it worked. It's no surprise that the exit is on 189. I assumed it would be either there or here.

"Is he safe?" The sudden appearance of another guy—maybe in his early 20's—in the room with me makes my heart jump into my throat.

He stands at the window, staring out at nothing. Or something. It's hard to say. There's nothing but wasteland beyond the windows. All I can see of the guy is messy red hair, slumped shoulders, his arms hugging his chest.

"Who?" I ask, approaching slowly.

This guy isn't part of our group. I have no idea where he came from. Another floor, maybe, like Bianca said? That means there are others in here, which doesn't bode well for us.

"Promise me," he says, oblivious to my question. "I need to know he's safe before I agree."

Agree to what? Somehow, I'm only hearing part of the conversation. Did this happen? Was this conversation real?

The door rattles behind me, then the muffled thump of fists against the soundproof glass. I glance over my shoulder. Miller pounds against the door, throwing his weight and his Powers against it, desperation creasing his face. He's shouting, but I can't hear anything he's saying. Everyone else has pressed away from him, against the far wall. I'm locked in here alone.

The guy turns from the window, squaring off against me so suddenly I stumble backward. "Do it. I dare you. Do it, and I'll bring this whole place down on your head." Pure hate burns in his sunken green eyes and sallow face. "I'll kill you all!" His scream is so wild, so purely feral. Spittle flies from his mouth. Tears roll down his cheeks. Despite his weak form, his clenched fists and animalistic hate fill me with absolute dread.

"I…I don't…" I back up as he lurches toward me until my back presses against the wall.

Miller continues his attack on the door across the room.

The guy stops inches from me, sneering, snarling like a predator ready to rip apart its prey. Something unseen twists his arms back, pulling him away. He resists, fights, kicks, and tugs desperately to break free from the invisible grasp, all the while screaming the same words over and over.

"I'll kill you! I'll kill you!"

Then just as suddenly as he appeared, he's gone. He wasn't real, wasn't really here. I'm on the floor, back pressed to the wall, hands over my ears, shaking. Real or not, he meant it. Death lived in his eyes.

The door clicks, and I lower my hands. Celeste casually holds the door open, watching Miller curiously. Everyone else in the hallway stands with their backs to the far wall, faces pale.

Miller kneels in front of the open door, sobbing like something inside him shattered. I watch for a moment, then look at the vacant spot where the guy disappeared.

Not just any guy. Murphy. Nothing else could explain Miller's reaction. The absolute devastation.

Still shaking, I push off the floor and walk over. All my hate for Miller melts away, replaced by pity. I don't forgive him for what he did. I can't. But there's no doubt why he did it. I kneel beside him, wrap my arms around him. Miller leans against me, sagging, all his energy and motivation extinguished like a dead flame.

"I'm sorry," I say, trying to offer some sort of reassurance. "It wasn't him. You know that, right? It wasn't really him there. Paragon is playing with your head, trying to break you."

But to what end? What do they have to gain by showing us that? Did that really happen at some point in time or was it just another hologram, a simulation created by Paragon to mess with our heads?

No one dares to move or speak, offering Miller a chance to grieve. Miller, who is always so tough, who stands up to everyone and everything. Miller, who never seems to care about anything or anyone else. I think seeing him in such a state reminds all of us that this testing needs to stop, that we all need out. The others in our group inch toward the open elevator doors.

Decisively, Miller pulls away, gripping my head between his trembling hands tighter than I would like, our faces inches apart. "Get me out of here," he growls. "I'll kill them all." He grits his teeth, then yells the words again, so much like Murphy had.

"Okay." I nod, leaning my forehead against his. For the first time since discovering what Miller did, I believe he wants the same thing as me. To escape this place. "Let's get out of here."

Despite the abrupt resolve to destroy Paragon, Miller still needs help standing, shaking as we make our way back to the elevator. It's only eleven floors down, but in this state, I don't think Miller will want to take the stairs.

43

THE ELEVATOR RIDE IS SILENT. MILLER USES HIS manipulation Power to select floor 189 and hold on to it to prevent us from being taken somewhere else. Everyone else gives him and Celeste space, staring at their feet, pressing against the back walls of the elevator—not that there's a lot of space to spare. At one point, the carriage lurches, stops, and starts taking us back up. Miller tries his Power on the panel, but it does no good. His hands ball into fists, and he lets out a roar as he throws his fist into it again and again until the panel loosens. Quite a terrifying sight.

Everyone presses even further away from him as he rips the panel out of the wall and grabs the wires inside directly. Something sparks, smoke billows out of the access space. I wave it away, coughing. For a moment, I fear he may start a fire, but the elevator stops its ascent and resumes the journey to floor 189.

"That's one way to do it," I say, hoping to lighten the mood. No one laughs.

The stink of body odor is quite foul in this confined space. I hold my breath to try and avoid breathing the air, counting down the floors.

The exit's a trap! Madison's message screams in my head, and I reflexively reach up to cover my ears, as does everyone except Celeste.

But it's too late. The elevator dings and the doors slide open on floor 189 before we can react.

"Shut it," a guy against the back wall calls out. "Let's get out of here!"

"No!" I dart through the open door before anyone else can stop me. I won't leave the others in trouble.

"Let him stay," another guy says in the elevator. "We can still go."

"The doors won't close," Miller says, though part of me wonders if he's lying to them.

The thought disappears the moment I see the hallway ahead, and I freeze in place, waving Miller and the others back into the elevator before they step out.

All three of the other groups line the walls on their knees, eyes downcast. Each group has half a dozen security guards standing over them, holding guns to their heads. Some of the subjects are prone on the floor, either convulsing or completely still. A quick count of eight in total. Likely the first to put up a fight. Judging by the blood or angry welts on some of the guards, the match wasn't completely one-sided. One guard's body is dragged through an open door down the hall, broken glass and concrete shards crunch under the guards' boots as they pull their comrade along.

Twenty feet down the hall, Bianca tilts her head slightly in my direction and meets my gaze. Blood trickles from her temple and the corner of her mouth as she kneels beside Rosie. The blood is a clear indication that Bianca put up a fight, along with the cracks and dents into the concrete walls around her.

Joyce steps out of a doorway at the far end of the hall, and the space between us seems to stretch. "Ugene. We've been waiting for you."

"Let them go," I say, doing my best to sound braver than I feel.

"If you cooperate, no one else has to get hurt," Dr. Cass says. "Though your friends in the elevator need to join the group."

I ball my hands into fists, the image of Murphy's pure hate filling me. For a moment, I understand that feeling.

"I'm afraid I must insist," Dr. Cass says.

Commotion arises behind me. I spin around, watching as additional security guards yank subjects out of the elevator. Miller sends a bolt of electricity straight through one guard, punching another in the face and taking his gun. He charges at another guard and bounces backward as he hits an invisible barrier. A Telekinetic bubble. Everything seems to slow as I watch a third guard throw one of the girls in our group to the ground by her hair and raise his gun at Miller's back.

"Miller stop!" I scream, rushing over and putting myself between them before the guard can fire.

Miller's chest heaves with mad breaths as he slowly turns in a circle, holding the gun out at each of the guards—whose full attention is on him. His grip on the firearm tightens, finger wrapped around the trigger.

"Drop it," I hiss. "We're outpowered. You'll get everyone in trouble."

"I don't care," he growls.

"I do," I say, raising a hand and carefully placing it over the gun's barrel, lowering it. "Please. Not like this."

The muscles in his jaw twitch with rage, but he drops the gun on the ground and raises his hands. In seconds, three guards are on him, binding his wrists behind his back.

"He's dead," one of the guards said, toeing the guard Miller shocked. The emptiness in the dead guard's eyes is enough to tell us all that. Miller killed him. Without hesitation.

"Line them up," Dr. Cass says impatiently from down the hall, waving along the wall with the other subjects. "Ugene, this way please."

The walk along the hallway feels long. Longer than the journey through the valley or across the arid plains. The world seems to stretch as I make my way toward the room into which Dr. Cass disappeared.

Chunks of concrete—remnants of the fight between the subjects and the guards—press into the sole of my worn loafers. Cracked tiles create strange patterns on the floor, reminding me of the cracks in the ground outside. Bullet holes puncture the walls in places, but not a lot. The fight clearly ended quickly.

Most of the subjects don't move or make a sound. A few struggle to keep control of their crying. Both the silence and the tears rip at my heart. I knew this was a trap, and still I walked every last one of them right into it. Right into Paragon's open arms. My steps fall heavy as I pass one of the prone subjects in a small pool of blood. Not just a subject. Mo.

Tears blur my vision, and I blink them back furiously, meeting Sho's eyes near the end of the hall. His meaningful gaze turns from me to the wall opposite him. I don't quite understand until I turn to enter the room where Dr. Cass awaits. The plaque on the wall beside the door reads *6B*.

The exit.

Taking a deep breath, I square my shoulders and step through, uncertain of what to expect on the other side.

44

DR. CASS SITS IN A SWIVELING HIGH-BACK DESK CHAIR, the black leather a stark contrast to her pale blue pencil skirt and matching suit jacket, and the white walls of the room. Her manicured hands are folded in her lap.

Hilde stands at one side, sweat on her brow, face paler than I remember. At the other side, Forrest examines his tablet, oblivious to anything else going on in the room. Behind them, a window looks out at the ruined world beyond—a clear indication we are still in the simulation.

"This experiment has been something else, Ugene," Dr. Cass announces as if we are just having a casual conversation in her office and my friends aren't waiting at gunpoint. "Your abilities have really taken me by surprise."

Abilities… "But I…I thought…"

"Leadership abilities, intelligence," she clarifies. "Sorry if that was misleading. I'm afraid we have not found even the slightest trace of any sort of Power in you."

The words are a blow to the gut. I gasp, wince, look to Forrest for something, anything, that says she's wrong. He just frowns and shakes his head. It's a perfect mirror of the disappointment I've seen in my dad so many times.

"But your skills haven't been without reward," Dr. Cass continues as if I care. "You've brought out readings from our other test subjects like we've never seen before—natural boosts to Powers and chemical reactions in their brains and bodies that people with their rank shouldn't be capable of. If we can find a way to reproduce the results in a more controlled and peaceful way, it could help society flourish; it could stop regression. And, I suppose, some thanks are owed to Forrest and his brilliant idea to initiate Protocol 10-98."

Brilliant. Right. Torture us. Starve us. Fight us. Shoot us. Best idea I've ever heard.

"But now that we have the data we needed, I'm afraid I'll have to insist that this charade end," Dr. Cass says.

"What charade?" I ask, noticing Hilde's sweat isn't beading anymore, but dripping down her temples. What is she doing?

"The pitiful attempt at escape, of course." Dr. Cass leans forward, resting her forearms on her knees. "You can't escape, Ugene. This is a simulation. It isn't real."

"Tell that to Mo or any of the other subjects you shot in that hallway." My words have far more venom than I intend. My gaze flicks around the room, and I can't help but wonder if this ever really was an exit. Maybe the whole point was to make us think we could escape.

On the far side of the room, just out of my initial line of vision, my dad stands between several guards. "Dad!"

I rush toward him, but bright, explosive pain blindsides me, turning my vision to floating specs of darkness momentarily. I crumble to my hands and knees.

"Ugene," Dad calls to me, stepping forward. Several guards restrain him. His frame is smaller than I remember, frail. It doesn't appear as if the treatments have worked. He's degenerating anyway.

Derrek yanks me to my feet, shoving me away from Dad. Where did he come from? Derrek reeks of sweat but otherwise appears to have fared better in this simulation than the rest of us. His gaze on me is vigilant, but something about him is off.

Making a feeble attempt at maintaining my dignity, I stand upright, taking a couple steps back, and brush my hands over my clothes in mock indignation. Pretending to ignore Derrek and the throbbing pain in my skull from his blindside punch, I turn my attention to Dr. Cass.

"If anyone learns the truth about what you are doing here, you're finished," I say, doing my best to sound as threatening as possible.

"Sweet, innocent boy." Dr. Cass clicks her tongue, then stands and closes the gap between us, like a lioness stalking her prey. "So sheltered by your world, insulated from the truth. What makes you think anyone will care once they know what we have to offer them? An end to the inequality. An opportunity for anyone to enhance their station in life. The end of regression! You've heard of the Purge, when Powerless humans tried to make our advanced species extinct. They killed us, tortured us, experimented on us."

"You aren't any better!"

"Hold your tongue." Dr. Cass's expression darkens momentarily before adopting its usual calm composure, still stalking toward me, picking her way carefully. "That devastation out there." She waves toward the window behind us. "That's their fault. They drove Atmos to the edge. And now, the only reason we are able to survive is because of our Powers. If we lose them, that's it. The bubble protecting our way of life will break. Crops will fail to thrive in the ruined ground. People will starve. Wells will run dry. The world is not ready for Powerless humans to survive! But imagine if we had the Power to expand, to grow and flourish and fix this broken world. And Paragon will offer that to everyone. Who cares how we came about it?"

Everything she says is so matter-of-fact and authoritative that anyone who didn't know better might actually believe her, that we can actually fix what is broken. That any sacrifice is worth the price to offer salvation. But Paragon can't pull blinders over my eyes anymore.

"Leave him alone, Joyce," Dad says with that tone of dangerous authority that always made my skin crawl and made me jump to action. And he sounds so familiar with her.

Dr. Cass, however, is unfazed by his outburst. "Our Powers are weakening," Dr. Cass says, stopping in front of me and placing her hands on my shoulders. "And you are living proof that we face complete regression. I can't allow that to happen."

My shoulders tense at her touch. Trina. Dave. Michael. Jade. Vicki.

Mo. The seven other subjects lying in the hallway. The forty-six lost in the fight against the guards on the plains or in the sandstorm. Enough is enough.

"Being Powerless is not a weakness," I say, not flinching under her gaze. "Being afraid of losing your Power is."

Dr. Cass recoils like touching me will give her a disease. "I leave this up to you, Ugene. Let go of this ridiculous fantasy of escape and save your friends, your father, your city, or continue this pointless fight and General Powers will never receive his treatments. He will die."

General Powers?

"I'm already dying," Dad says, sagging ever so slightly. "Don't do it."

But looking at him, at the frail state he's in and the once powerful muscles sagging or gone, it's hard to agree.

General Powers. I knew he was part of the military, but I had no idea his rank. I guess I never cared. In his condition, that rank wouldn't last long.

"You haven't been treating him," I breathe the words out.

Dr. Cass clicks her tongue again.

"After everything I did for you." My spine stiffens with indignation. "All the torture and near death I've endured, all the excruciating tests and samples and all the friends I've watched your goons cart away, you didn't keep your one promise." Anger boils in my gut and spreads through my body like wildfire. I want to fight, but they all have Powers, and I have none. It would be a quick end. "And now you dare to dangle him over my head like this is a whole new incentive to be an obedient dog? Why would I ever trust that you would keep your word? I don't. I won't!"

"Don't be childish," Dr. Cass says. "If we have no Powers, we can't grow what we need to survive or clean the water. But we need you. We've always needed you, but your father has foolishly sheltered you on some preposterous notion of protection."

I don't know what she means about my dad, but I do know that she's wrong about one thing. "We don't need Powers to survive. We need cooperation. Intelligence. What I've managed here should be proof enough of that!'"

A thunderous explosion erupts in the hallway, shaking the building and raining dust from the ceiling. Blinding light makes me shield my eyes, stumbling to hold my balance. The hairs on my arm stand straight up.

"That doesn't sound like cooperation to me," Dr. Cass says.

Feet pound against the floor. I raise my head and blink to refresh my vision. The situation has dissolved into chaos. Test subjects fight PSECT in the hallway. Gunshots sound.

I ignore it all and rush toward Dad, but Derrek grabs the collar of my shirt in a fist and lifts me off the ground, then slams my back into the floor so hard my ears ring and the floor cracks beneath me. For a moment, my vision goes dark. This isn't the same Derrek. He was strong before, but now...

Derrek's fist connects with my cheekbone, and I can hear it crack. Tears prick my slowly returning vision. The weight of his body presses against my chest. I try to move or kick to get him off, but my body resists moving.

A blurred form crashes into Derrek's side, throwing him off me. Broken tiles scrape the floor. I roll over, tasting copper, and spit a mass of red on the floor.

It takes a moment to regain my surroundings. Dr. Cass calmly steps through the window and disappears, followed immediately by Forrest and Hilde. The window doesn't crash or break. They don't fall to their deaths. They're simply...gone.

Derrek and two other security guards are fighting Bianca and Dad. I try to stand, but my limbs resist, and I slip, hitting my stomach and chin against the floor, causing pain to lance through my head.

The window is the exit from the simulation.

"Run, Ugene!" Dad yells. Somehow, his weak muscles have strengthened, and some part of me knows that what he's doing is dangerous, deadly.

"No. Dad, stop!" I push off the ground, and a set of hands grab me and haul me to my feet.

Enid supports my weight. "We need to go now," she says.

"Everyone, go through the exit," Sho is calling out to the other test subjects. "Before it closes!" He and Leo are at the window, ushering test subjects through. They filter through the hallway door and rush toward the window, plunging into the unknown.

"Dad!" I try to push Enid off, but Derrek did a number on my head, and everything swims with each movement. I can't stand without her help. A concussion, most likely.

"Get him out of here!" Bianca yells at Enid, kicking one of the PSECT guards in the knee to bring him down, then punching his head so hard he rebounds off the wall behind him. His body collapses to the ground.

Dad's strength wanes and Derrek slams him against the wall. The blow makes me flinch. Dad's head sags, then his muscles twitch and grow again. He's pumping everything into his muscles.

"Dad!" I scream, pushing against Enid to escape her serpentine, coiling grip on my body. She doesn't relent. Tears burn in the wounds on my face. "He's killing himself! Stop him!"

Dad punches Derrek so hard it sends the boy sailing across the room into the wall where he sticks, head slumped forward and limbs limp. Dad sags against the wall and slides down to the floor.

"The exit's closing," Miller calls from the window. "I can't hold it open much longer. Let's go!"

But the words barely register. I finally push Enid away and skitter and slip across the broken floor to Dad's side.

"What are you doing?" The voice that comes out isn't my own. It's thicker, desperate, filled with grief.

"What I should have done from the start," Dad says. His hand lifts, shaking like a feeble old man, but his grip on my neck is solid as he pulls me closer. "I'm sorry. I should have protected you from this."

I shake my head, clinging to him like he's the edge of the world and letting go will make me fall off. Maybe it will.

"Dad…" But no other words will come out. Everything chokes

in my throat.

His eyes droop, and I shake him until he blinks lazily at me.

"Ugene, we have to go now," Bianca says, crouching beside me. "Miller is losing his grip on the exit."

"Go," Dad says. "You're stronger than I ever was. Go." He pushes me away, and it feels akin to having my heart ripped from my chest. The pain is intense and blinding. "I'm proud of you, Ugene."

Multiple sets of hands grab my arms and waist, dragging me away from Dad as his hands go slack and his head droops against his sunken, unmoving chest. The Muscular Degeneration has taken him. I scream and cry and kick, knowing that this is it. I'll never see him again. But even in my grief-induced hysteria, I'm not strong enough to resist the hands pulling me through the window.

And just like that, Dad disappears from my life forever.

45

EVERYONE ELSE MOVES AROUND THE ROOM BUSY WITH something, but I can't bring myself to care. I curl up on the ground where they deposited me on the other side of the exit and let the grief sink in. The reality of what happened to Dad left a gaping hole in my chest. All of this, being here at Paragon, I did for him, and none of it mattered. His illness still took him in the end.

Or maybe it didn't. Was he even really there? Could Paragon do that—just put a realistic projection of him in there to mess with me? They did it with Murphy, but it's too slim a chance to hope on.

Distantly, someone in the room calls my name.

I'm proud of you, Ugene.

Dad's final words echo in my head, and I squeeze my eyes shut to try and stem the flow of tears, but it's too late. They still leak out down my cheek, across my nose, then fall away as tears on the other side of my face roll back into my ear. I lace my hands behind my head and pull my knees tight against my chest, trying to squeeze out the pain. But it doesn't work.

Cold hands touch my arm, but I don't look up. Dad's gone, and it's my fault. We had our differences, fought a lot, but I still loved him. Pins and needles prick my skin, pulling it tight. The bone in my cheek heals. The pain in my back and head disappear. But the healing does nothing for the aching pain in my chest. No Divinic Power can fix this pain.

Except…

Sniffling, I shift, sitting up to see Rosie kneeling in front of me.

Her face is pale and exhausted. I clutch her, desperation in my grip. Tears roll unchecked down my face.

"You… you can bring him back…" Even as I say the words, the look of sorrow on Rosie's face crushes my hopes. My hands crawl up to her shoulders as I move to a kneeling position in front of her. "You did it to that Electromancer. You brought him back. Please. I can't…Rosie…"

Rosie pulls me into an intense, tight hug. "I'm sorry. The window is closed. He's gone, Ugene." She strokes the back of my head.

And then I hug her tight, clinging to her as my body shakes with sobs. Rosie doesn't pull away. She hugs me close and doesn't let go, soothing my grief with soft words. At some point, Rosie pulls away, and someone else takes her place, stroking away my sorrow. I sniffle and catch a whiff of citrusy sweat.

"Ugene, I…" Bianca's voice is filled with anguish. "Your dad was always so kind to me, so welcoming."

I pull back and gaze into Bianca's coppery eyes. Her lower lip quivers, dimpling her chin, and tears roll down her cheeks. Her hand brushes my cheek, wiping away my tears.

"I loved him, too," she says, the words so soft I barely hear them. "He gave his life to save ours."

The two of us just sit like this as something elsewhere in the room booms and cracks. Bianca's lips part to say something, but nothing comes out. Then she kisses me. Under any other circumstances, I would relish this moment, but it doesn't feel right.

I lean away. "What—?"

"Sorry, I just…" Bianca pulls away.

"Hey kid, we need your genius!" Miller calls out. "We aren't out of this yet!"

Test subjects all huddle on one side of the room, their backs to me. The walls around us are slate gray, and I don't need Powers to know they are protected against the use of Powers.

I do my best to pull myself together. So many lost, and these few who remain are looking to me for guidance. It's impossible to just brush aside the aching pit in my chest, and grief has seized my throat, making it hard to speak at all. I swallow to try and break it free.

The walls are unfamiliar, unlike the clean, institutional walls on our floor. Which can only mean one thing. "This isn't our floor." I suck the words in, testing them to see if they're real. It's more of a revelation than a hope of affirmation from anyone else.

Bianca shakes her head. "Best I can tell, we are in one of the PSECT installation rooms on the ninety-ninth floor." At my confused glance, Bianca stands, helping me to my feet as she explains. "These rooms are designated as entry points into simulations with test subjects. Each is reinforced with extra protections from Powers and extra security measures in case…"

"In case someone escapes," I say, brushing the grimy tears off my cheeks before they can fully dry. "Which means this was a possibility all along."

Bianca nods. Did she already know that?

"Genius!" Miller calls out again.

I glance once more at the wall that was once the window into the simulation. Pain seizes me again, but I push it down. Miller is right. We aren't out. I will grieve later. I can't do it now.

About two dozen subjects count down from three, then the wall booms and shakes, and electricity crackles across the surface, but it has no other effect.

"Save your energy," I say once the sound fades away. "It won't work."

Celeste reaches into her backpack and pulls out a caramel, offering it to me. "Eat this. It will help you feel better."

I want to resist and tell her there's no way a piece of candy will help fill the void inside, but the absolute innocence of her expression sways me. I huff out a sigh and take the candy, unwrapping it and popping it into my mouth.

The flavor instantly explodes, and despite the tension and the pain inside, it really does help. Slowly, everything relaxes as I nudge through the crowd to the door and run my fingers along it.

I debate asking if someone else tried to see through the wall or find out how it's locked but realize the question is pointless. No Power can penetrate the wall. So how do we get through?

Paragon had to have put an emergency trigger in the room somewhere for security to use. But Bianca would know something about that, and if it existed, she already would have said so. Having someone sitting and watching a camera all day on these rooms seems pointless. Plus, I don't see any cameras. Sure, Paragon used them in our rooms to see everything, but the ceiling in this room is different, as are the walls. If what Bianca said is true, the walls, floor, and ceiling will be made of reinforced carbon polymers that you can't just put cameras in. Which means one of two things.

Either the doors are on timers—which is unlikely since Dr. Cass and everyone else escaped this way—or they have some sort of sensory detection with manual overrides.

We don't need Powers to get through the door. We just need to trick the door into thinking we aren't here.

"Ugene…" Miller cocks his head, arms crossed over his chest. "You there?"

Boyd waves a hand in front of my face. The hand blurs as it moves up and down, leaving a streak behind, like the residue from his hand. I blink slowly, stepping back and reaching out to touch it.

"Didn't you heal him?" Enid asks.

"Yes," Rosie says indignantly. "He's fine."

Suddenly Celeste's rhyme starts to make sense. A ray of hope—us finding the exit. A final breath—Dad's last words. A chance to cope—my moments of grief.

"Earth to Ugene!" Miller says.

That just leaves… A kiss of death. Bianca kissed me, but neither of us is dead. And all the stars shall fall. I thought I knew what the stars were, but it didn't happen.

"Hey!" Miller claps his hands in my face.

I flinch. "Hmm?"

"Jeez—" Miller throws his hands up. "What the hell did you give him?" he asks Celeste.

"Just a piece of candy." Celeste shrugs and pulls one out, offering it to Miller.

I can't help but grin at the idea of more candy, reaching out for it. Miller slaps my hand away.

Leo leans toward the candy, then turns to Miller. "It's a drug. He's drugged."

"It's an illusion," I say, taking Leo's hand. "Power. We need Power."

"Any Divinic Cleansers here who can get this crap out of his system?" Miller asks the room at large.

The room shifts. Or I do. Who knows? Then a guy with a crooked nose steps out of the sea of heads and puts his hands on my chest.

"Frisky," I tease.

The world bursts with light, and I can't keep from shaking. Am I laughing?

"He'll need rest," the boy says, voice growing distant.

"We can't afford it," Miller sighs.

Their voices stretch away from me. Sleep. Wonderous, blissful, glorious sleep. And I heartily succumb.

46

A SHOCK JOLTS ME AWAKE SCREAMING. MILLER CROUCHES over me, his hands poised over my chest. Everyone else is huddled in clumps around the room.

"Have a nice rest?" Miller asks.

"Did you just use your Power on me?" I ask.

"We don't have time to rest," Miller says. "We have to move before Dr. Cass can mount a full offensive against us."

I glance back at the wall we walked through before, thinking about my dad.

"It hasn't opened again," Enid says, staring at the wall as well.

"I didn't figure it would," I grumble. "Paragon has us pinned in here."

"Do us a favor," Leo says, "don't eat any more of that candy. I don't know where that girl got it from, but it's laced with some sort of drug. A barbiturate at my best guess, but I haven't really studied their atomic structure."

Barbiturate? Why would Celeste have caramel barbiturates? I close my eyes and sigh. Right. If she's really as strong as Miller says, then those candies would lessen her Powers, weaken her.

Enid motions Celeste forward, and Celeste cautiously inches past them, offering her bag to me. I'm tempted to resist, but something tells me they decided this during my drug-induced state. I slip the strap over my shoulder.

"Forget that for now," Miller interrupts. "We need to stay on track here. How do we get that door open and get out of here?"

I look at Bianca, who is leaning against the door with her arms crossed. "You've used one of these installation rooms before. So how do the doors open?"

Bianca licks her lips and glances at the door, then shrugs. "I don't know. It just opens when I leave the simulation. I'm not really sure how it works. All I can tell you is that it's heavily reinforced."

Something occurred to me earlier, and I struggle to pull it back. Something about how the door operates.

"Leo," I say. "Do you see any traces of surveillance?"

Silence settles as Leo looks around the room, then shakes his head. "But that doesn't mean—"

"Yes, it does," I continue. "Because to be able to see us or hear us, you, at least, would have to be able to catch some trace of it, even if you can't see it."

"I don't see it either," Sho adds.

Good to know.

"Which means somehow there is a trigger that knows we are in here," I say. "A while back I read an article about the potential applications of technology allowing people to lock and unlock their homes using nanotech."

"Dork," Enid teases, but her expression is affectionate.

"Yeah, well, this dork may know what's going on," I say, no humor in me to return her teasing. Bianca rolls her eyes, and I clear my throat, getting back to the problem. "We were injected with nanomonitors when we came to Paragon, which means that door knows we are all in here. To get out, we have to trick it into thinking we aren't."

"And how, exactly, do we do that?" Boyd asks, giving the door an uneasy glance.

I bite my lip before saying, "But killing the nanomonitors."

We don't have much time to debate. It's a bold move, asking everyone to let Miller shock us all to kill the nanomonitors, and the only way the plan works is if everyone participates. "We either let him do it, or we all will end up in Paragon's control again for certain," I tell everyone.

No one is thrilled about this, but we all want the same thing, so no one protests.

"I can't do this alone," Miller says, staring at the floor. "I've been using my Powers for days and haven't rested enough."

"A simple touch is a simple solution," Celeste says, cocking her head and gazing intently at Miller.

He shakes his head. "A touch. What…?"

"You said it yourself," I say.

Miller's eyes are wide as he meets my gaze. "No."

"You can't do this alone," I say. "She is powerful. She can amplify your Powers, sort of like a conduit. Yes?" I look to Celeste for confirmation, and she nods.

Miller has no trust for the girl. But I do. He opens his mouth to protest but snaps his jaw so sharply I can hear his teeth clack.

After a few more minutes, we've managed to gather a few more Naturalist volunteers to act as conductors to help the Power move through the whole group carefully and safely.

It *is* a dangerous plan. Now, as everyone collects together in a tight clump and Bianca positions herself by the door, Miller moves away from Celeste like he's ready to resist again.

"This is stupid," he says, glancing at Celeste from the edge of his vision. "Someone could die."

"If we don't get out of here, we die anyway," I say. "Besides, if we want to escape Paragon for good, we have to kill these nanomonitors, or they will track us down and throw us right back into those rooms."

Miller's jaw twitches, but he nods stiffly.

A few people behind me whimper. I notice the girl at my side ducking her head away, as if not looking will make it any easier.

Celeste steps up beside Miller, and he flinches away when she reaches for his temples. She makes a soothing sound. His shoulders tense and his hands clasp into fists. The contact makes his body convulse, then his gray eyes brighten, fingers extended toward the tight group. More whimpers, a few cries of alarm, protests. A mix of anxiety and fear overcomes the cluster.

The energy flows slowly from Miller's fingers, electric blue lines of Power headed toward the Naturalists conductors. The air in the room charges. Hair stands up. My heartbeat quickens. Everything burns brightly.

Then the Power hits me like someone punched me in the back of the head. A shock shoots down my body, through every limb, every nerve, then every muscle locks up. It doesn't burn, surprisingly, but it does knock the air from my lungs, making me feel like I'm drowning.

My head starts buzzing and the room—what I can see of it— tilts. I feel like I'm floating, no longer in control of my own body. Distantly, I'm aware of the gasps for breath and momentary cries cut off by the shock as others experience the same jolt.

When it ends, instead of feeling tired or near death like I expected, an unanticipated rush of adrenaline flows through me. I've never felt so alive.

"It worked." Bianca's proclamation sounds more like alarm than relief like she doubted me.

I suppose I can't blame her. I doubted myself but seeing that door cracked open emits a whoop of success from me—from all of us.

"Remember," I say to everyone, inching toward the door. "PSECT is waiting for us. Throw your Power out without moving the door if you can. If you can't, stay back. The second it's done, we go left, straight to the elevators. Same groups as before. Electromancers in each group. All the way to the ground floor."

Heads bob in agreement, and those ready to attack the hallway shuffle toward the door as Somatics and Divinics move toward the back of the group. I join them.

47

THE ASSAULT IN THE HALLWAY BEGINS. SHATTERING glass. The floor rumbles. Lights flicker, and Power electrifies the air. I huddle near the back of the group between Rosie and Celeste, listening to the horrific sounds of battle. Squelching screams. Guns firing at nothing. Fog filling the hallway, drifting past the doorway like a slithering snake. For so many people with so little Power, they certainly make a mighty force together.

And almost as quickly as it started, it ends. Silence settles in the hallway. Bianca thrusts the door open, and everyone makes a tunnel for the Somatics to rush through and clear the way of any lurking Paragon employees.

"Clear!" Bianca calls at the end of the hall as she and the other Somatics activate all the lifts.

Everyone bolts down the hallway, slipping on broken glass and blood, hurdling fallen bodies. So much death, and yet I feel so alive. Whatever Miller did to us, the effects still linger. I feel like I could run down all ninety-nine flights of stairs and out the door. Does everyone else feel like this?

Despite the adrenaline, I find it hard to ignore what we've done here. The dead Paragon employees—dozens of them. They would have done the same to us, would have used any means necessary to keep us from escaping. I shouldn't feel bad for these people. They made their choice. Yet, I do.

The elevator doors slide open and the groups file in. I count the heads of our group as Miller fiddles with the panel, breaks it out of the wall, and forces it to take us all the way down by using the wires directly like he did in the simulation. No taking chances this time.

"You realize we have no idea what time of day it is," Miller says as the elevator lurches into motion. "We could be running out into mid-day traffic, and we don't exactly look inconspicuous."

I glance over my shoulder at the other subjects with us. He's right. All of us are covered in dirt and blood. Our clothes are tattered and filthy, hair is stringy with sweat or clumped in mats. It's evident none of us have focused on personal hygiene in days. We look like a bunch of escaped mental patients. Maybe we are.

"Not much we can do about it at this point," I say. This could be our only chance at escape. If we hesitate now, we may never get another opportunity.

Miller tightens his grip on the wires, concentrating on the task at hand. "Something is trying to take control of the elevator."

"Not something." The implication is clear enough. We both know it's Dr. Cass. I look up, watching the numbers tick downward. "Let's just hope everyone makes it."

The effort to maintain control of the elevator is clearly taxing. Miller breathes through his teeth. Sweat beads on his forehead.

"Back in the simulation, I noticed something," I say, remembering as I watch the sweat roll down Miller's temple. "Hilde was there with Dr. Cass, and she was focusing really hard on something. I don't know what. But she was sweating. What do you suppose it could have been?"

"Does it matter?" Miller asks through gritted teeth.

"Maybe." I watch the numbers again.

Nothing apparent happened in the simulation, but it was apparent enough that Hilde was using her Power. I haven't really thought much about her Power because there were more pressing issues at hand.

"Not all books open so easily," Celeste says, standing at my shoulder. "Some books require finesse, gentle coaxing to bring forth the words."

"Mumbo-jumbo," Miller grunts.

But, in her own way, Celeste is right. Terry couldn't read me. He beat at my brain trying to get into my thoughts, like an assault with a scalpel trying to dig out the information. Mom never had to do that. Most of the time I didn't know she was doing it at all. Her telepathic touch has a finesse Terry's wholly lacked.

When Dr. Cass came to my house on Career Day, Mom said she couldn't read Dr. Cass, like there was a wall around her mind. I found it odd at the time since Dr. Cass is a Naturalist. Bianca said Dr. Cass already knew what was going on, too. It makes perfect sense.

Hilde built the mental block. She's a telepath. She probably tried to read me that day in the office and ran into the same issue Terry had. I don't understand why I'm so hard to read, but something naturally blocks them. And if Hilde tried to read me, she already knew about what Bianca told Dr. Cass—and what Miller confessed.

I watch Miller fight for control of the elevator, finding it harder to be upset with him for what he did. They played him right from the start. They set him up to fall out of faith with me in a lame attempt at bringing this whole plan down.

The elevator dings and the doors slide open to the massive Paragon Tower lobby. Unlike in the simulation, the furniture and décor are present in the real world. Whites and reds and blacks on the furniture, walls, floor. Everywhere.

"Look." Miller steps up beside me and points toward the doors.

Outside, there is only darkness broken by streetlights and the occasional light inside another building across the street. Very little traffic moves along the road.

"It has to be past midnight," he says.

Another elevator opens, and Enid rushes out toward me. "Thank god. We had a heck of a time with the elevator. It took us to the tenth floor, and we thought we were gonna have to get out and take the stairs the rest of the way. I was afraid your elevator wouldn't make it."

"The stairs…" My face scrunches up as I look toward the closed doorway leading to the stairs, just at the end of the elevator bay. "That's what Paragon wanted. At this time of night, the stairs offer a perfect trap."

"Someone would have been waiting," Miller grumbles. I notice he's doing the same thing as me, counting heads in Enid's group.

Nineteen.

"Enid, I want you and Boyd to start moving everyone toward the doors," I say. "As soon as the other two groups get here, you lead them out to the Metro. I'll have Madison let you know where we are headed from there."

"I'm not leaving this building until you do," Enid says, her back stiffening.

A shrieking of metal on metal echoes through the lobby from one of the elevator shafts. I cover my ears. Screams and suppressed shouting come from somewhere within the elevator. The scraping stops. Heated arguments are muffled by the walls.

"Do something," I bark at Miller and the Electromancer in Enid's group.

But the two of them are already running to the panel, trying to work together to gain control of the lift.

Metal shrieks again, grinding against my nerves. Then a thunderous boom shakes the floor and debris kicks out from behind the closed doors, now slightly buckled. I hold my breath as Miller and the Electromancer—who I regrettably don't know the name of—try to get the doors to open.

Inside the elevator is silence, and I fear the worst, that the drop killed them all. Would Paragon really go to such lengths to stop us?

A couple of Strongarms try to pry the doors open as Miller and the other boy work on the panel.

I can't breathe, focused on the sounds from inside the elevator. *Please don't be dead. Please.*

Shuffling. Whimpers and quiet words. I can't quite make it out, but I know that at least someone survived.

Without realizing it, I had moved closer to the elevator and now stand just out of the way of the Strongarms trying to force the doors open. Which elevator did Bianca get into? Was it this one? Why didn't I pay closer attention? God please, let her be alive.

Protesting loud enough to wake the dead, the doors inch their way open. Little by little. Sho is the first to slip out. A gash on his head pours out blood as he stumbles forward.

"They took control," he mumbles, his words near jumbled.

Leo is next out, and he slides his arm under Sho's for support. A deep cut bleeds on his cheek, but nothing more. "Concussion, I think," he says, nodding slightly toward Sho. "We lost control, and it started to take us back up. When our guy fought for control, the elevator just started to freefall. The brakes kicked in, but it only slowed us down. Didn't stop until we neared the bottom. We were arguing about what to do next when the Electromancer collapsed, and the elevator fell."

Seven others stumbled out, clearly dazed and bleeding. Madison leans heavily against a muscular guy who is carrying most of her weight. I shift to see inside, but Leo leans his head toward me, blocking my view.

"Don't," he says.

Strange, the impact just one word can have on you. Tears sting my eyes, but I swallow and nod. Eleven. Barely half his group survived. So few.

I pause and clear my throat to get control of the surge of emotions rolling through me. "Help Boyd get everyone to the door. As soon as the last group shows up, start leading them to Metro Station Nine-Five. If we get separated, take the train east to Station Four-Two. We'll meet there."

"But Ugene—"

I shake my head. "Please. We need to get the remaining people away from here before we lose more. But I…I can't leave without Bianca."

Leo nods, swallowing down his protests, or maybe his fear. Who knows?

Miller sags beside me. "Thanks."

"For what?"

"You know," he says, glancing at me as we wait. Where is the last elevator?

"We aren't out yet. You're free to go with them, you know. You don't have to wait here. I know you want to find Murphy." It's the best I can offer as a dismissal. He made it perfectly clear what his objective is, and here is his chance to leave.

"I do." Miller stands a little straighter but is clearly exhausted. "But if I left you here and did find him, Murphy would box my ears for being an idiot."

"You may not get another chance."

He glances at me, and the expression on his face says it all. There's no moving an immovable mountain. "I'm not going anywhere just yet."

"Neither am I," Enid says, stepping up to my other side and taking my hand. "I came this far with you. We either finish it together or not at all."

A stupid sentiment, but still appreciated. I give her hand a squeeze.

The hum of the elevator approaching pulls my attention back to the doors as two guys—both Strongarm subjects I barely recognize—join our meager line, waiting.

48

THE NUMBERS ABOVE THE ELEVATOR DOOR SLOWLY
tick down.

Ten.

Why is Bianca's elevator so late? What took them so long?

Nine.

A sickening feeling twists my gut. Something about this isn't right.

Eight.

Why didn't I send Madison with Bianca? Would it make a
difference?

Seven.

"I don't like this," Miller grumbles. I'm not sure if he meant for
us to hear him or not.

Six.

"It's fine," I say much more confidently than I feel.

Five.

Another sound draws our attention away from the elevator doors.
The thunderous hammering of stampeding feet from the nearby
stairwell.

Four.

The stairwell door bursts open and Bianca doesn't break stride,
running from the stairwell toward us.

"What—?"

"Get away from the elevators!" she yells.

Three.

As if of one mind, our line breaks and rushes for the group now emerging from the stairs.

Two.

Bianca shifts her feet and runs straight for the elevator door. Enid ushers Rosie and the other thirteen test subjects with her to the main doors.

The elevator dings.

Miller forms a ball of lightning between his fingers as the doors slide open. His hands tremble.

Three of the other unused elevators open with the one that just reached our floor. I hold my breath, not sure what to expect from these four elevators.

Miller launches his ball of lightning into one of the lifts the moment the door opens. Screams. Gunshots. The Strongman subject beside me falls back. Miller forms another ball, but it's smaller, and he's shaking, his face pale. Too much Power in one day. Too much of this. We need to get out now. But I'm frozen by fear, unsure what to do amidst so much Power.

Enid pivots, creating a wall of fog between us and the main doors, giving the other subjects time to escape. It's dense and quickly begins to dissipate.

"Ugene, let's go," she calls, flicking her gaze from the elevators and the security trying to pour out, to me, and to the disappearing fog.

But I can't leave. I can't abandon my friends. There has to be something I can do.

Everyone is in the thick of battle. Security guards try to fire. Some of their weapons are knocked away by the two Strongarms—one oozing blood from his side. Celeste stands in the center of the lobby, hands folded toward the ground. Despite the chaos, she is untouched, unperturbed. Bianca is tangled in battle with Derrek. Anger burns in my veins. He could have come with us, could have escaped. Instead, he is helping Paragon. Was he a plant? Bianca is strong, but Derrek seems an equal match. She needs help.

Breaking out of my stupor as everyone else fights off the guards, I rush to the reception desk and begin rummaging through the draws.

Gum with foil wrappers, a letter-opener, salt packets, and a lighter. Under the counter, a fire extinguisher. I grab it.

Security guards continue fighting their way into the lobby. I unlock the extinguisher and spray in their direction. It's not much, but it causes enough of a diversion and confusion that the others have a chance to pull back. Except for Bianca, still locked in combat with Derrek.

"Celeste, get out of here!" I call over my shoulder.

Gripping the extinguisher in one hand, I run toward Bianca but after two or three steps skid to a stop as a voice calls out my name from above.

"Ugene!" Forrest stands on the next level at the glass-panel rail, watching the chaos in the lobby. "Stand down. Come with us, and they can go."

Me. Just me. It's a tempting offer. My life for theirs.

Dr. Cass steps beside him, and I envision Dad's frail body all over again. They won't keep their promises. I can't trust them.

"Ugene," Dr. Cass says my name so casually as if there is no other chaos happening around us. "You are the key. I told you that the day you came here. Elpis is dying. Those with low-ranking Powers threaten our very way of life. But with your help, we can stop them. We can halt the needless resistance, cure regression, and offer peace to the people of Elpis. We just need you."

Miller groans, on his knees, holding his hands out as endless streams of lightning fly from his fingers toward the guards. He can't hold out much longer.

Celeste remains cemented in place, her lips moving but her words silent amid the chaos.

Derrek twists Bianca's arm behind her back, holding a gun to her chin. His eyes are blank like they were in the simulation. Some of the files I read before, on Forrest's tablet, spring to the front of my mind. The advertisement for IVD. The remarks about using one of the formulas as a potential controlling agent. I didn't understand before. None of it made sense. But looking at Derrek's obedient face, everything falls into place.

"You've learned how to control us," I breathe, now more thankful than ever that we killed the nanomonitors. "You aren't helping anyone. You aren't offering a cure. You're trying to take control!" Is that how Dr. Cass got the council to vote in favor of her proposition?

"Control of what?" Dr. Cass' sarcastic laugh echoes around the lobby. "There's so much about this world you don't understand. Your parents sheltered you for too long. There are people in this city threatening our very way of life, and if they succeed, everything will fall apart. Their agenda will bring on anarchy and bring an end to the safety and security of Elpis that everyone—including people like you—have enjoyed all their lives."

People fighting back, just like Mo mentioned that first day they met me in the halls. I step back, glaring up at her and Forrest, so safe up there.

"Don't you see?" Dr. Cass waves a hand around the chaos. "It's about liberation. I'm freeing humanity."

Enid gasps beside me, staring up at the lines of security guards all around each level above, guns pointed at us. Miller stops fighting—sweat making his shirt stick to his chest—and staggers to his feet, stumbling back beside me, along with the two Strongarm subjects.

Bianca slams her head back into Derrek's face, and he drops the gun, but his grip on her arm doesn't relent even as she rushes away. Something cracks. Bianca cries out as her arm breaks, and Derrek's fist connects with her stomach. She skids across the floor on her back, one arm at an unnatural angle.

Derrek stalks toward her, picking up his gun from the floor and cocking it. In seconds, he will be in point-blank range to kill her. The muscles in his arms tense and twitch.

Seconds. I can't stand by and do nothing.

"Stand down and come with us," Forrest says again. "And your friends can go."

"Don't do it," Enid says softly, glaring so much hate at Forrest I wonder if it will burn him alive.

"That's your sister." I yell the words at Forrest, utterly disgusted that he would allow her to go through this.

Derrek stops over Bianca, holding his position. We are outnumbered and overpowered. There's no way we are getting out of here. What choice do I have?

"I never said this was easy," Forrest says. "But sometimes, it's necessary to push to the limits of what we, as people, are capable of to achieve the greater good. No one can stand in the way of that."

The words are so cold a chill rolls down my spine.

Bianca turns her head, meeting my gaze. Tears roll down her temple, and she shakes her head. Even from more than twenty feet away I can see her tensing her muscles, preparing for another strike.

"Take him down," Dr. Cass says. "We will deal with the rest later."

Guns click above us.

"RUUUN!!!" Bianca screams the word as she kicks out, sweeping Derrek's feet from under him.

A shot fires.

49

MILLER JUMPS IN FRONT OF ME, AND THE FORCE OF the gunshot kicks him back against me moments before his body falls to the ground in a heap. The force knocks the extinguisher out of my hand.

Another shot. Bianca's scream turns into a gurgle.

Enid grabs my arm, yanking me back. Blood seeps out of a wound in Miller's shoulder, and his body begins convulsing. Above, security guards cock their weapons to fire.

Celeste shrieks, raising her arms in the air.

"Celeste, I said go!" I'm torn between my desire to rush to Bianca's side and my need to help Celeste.

Light bursts out of Celeste's body. A massive ray of pure cosmic energy shoots out in all directions. Enid tackles me to the floor where we huddle together as the beam continues to rocket over our heads. The floor begins to quiver. The building groans in protest. Something steel snaps, but it's hard to tell where it comes from.

I turn on my stomach, army-crawling toward Miller with one arm protecting my head, careful not to lift my body too high as the cosmic ray seems to go on without end. I have no doubt it will completely obliterate anything it touches.

Miller convulses on the floor, electric energy sparking and zapping all around his body. I can't get close enough to check his vitals, and the endless roll of thunder from the cosmic ray makes his screams almost impossible to hear. But his mouth is open, straining, and there's no doubt he's screaming.

Another groan from the building. If Celeste doesn't stop, she'll bring the whole tower down on us all. Something crashes nearby.

The assault from Celeste's ray stops. Debris, massive chunks of concrete, fall from the ceiling of the lobby five stories up.

And all the stars shall fall.

Security is gone. Whether Celeste destroyed them all or they escaped, I know, and I don't care. It's time to get out of here.

I scramble to my feet, turning to take in the wreckage as the smell of burned flesh fills the air. I gag on the aroma.

Where is Celeste? I spin in a circle, seeking her out, but there isn't a trace. She can't have just disappeared from the center of the lobby. Part of me fears that debris crashed down on her, but I can't hold that thought for long.

Derrek is gone, as well. The only remaining traces are his ankles and feet.

Bianca lies on the ground nearby in a pool of blood, hands pressed to her gut. I rush over to her side, leaving a seizing Miller on the floor—there's nothing I can do for him right now—and drop to my knees at Bianca's side.

The wound is bad. So bad. Her hands are covered in blood, which continues to pour out between her fingers. Bianca reaches a shaking hand up, grabbing my shirt and pulling me closer. I press my hands to the wound. I don't even care about the blood.

"It's okay. We'll get you to Rosie, and you'll be fine," I say, choking back the tears. "You'll be fine."

Bianca shakes her head, face contorted in agony. "I can't…"

"Yes, you can." I can't accept it, even if she's right. I can't lose her and my dad on the same day. "Bianca…"

"Go." The word is so small. Bianca pulls me closer, kisses me, then lets go of my shirt.

I shake my head, but nothing comes out of my mouth except a croak.

The building groans and glass shatters, raining down from somewhere above, striking the ground like thunder and chimes. Blood gurgles from Bianca's lips as her back arches.

"Ugene," Enid stands at my shoulder. "The building isn't stable. We have to move."

I nudge Enid away and scoop Bianca up in my arms. My body shakes, resists, completely exhausted, but I won't leave without her. Not like I did to Dad. I can't.

"Rosie can save her." It's all I can manage to say, and the words repeat like a broken record with each labored step toward the exit. It's so far away. Across the massive lobby riddled with debris.

One of the Strongarms remains, holding Miller over his shoulder like a flour sack. The two of them are already at the door.

I glance around one more time for Celeste, but there's no sign of her. Did she already leave? I can only hope.

Bianca's body has gone limp in my arms, and it makes her weight even more cumbersome. The exit is still more than halfway across the lobby. A chunk of concrete falls, blocking our path. I stumble and lose my balance, falling and dropping Bianca on the ground. Enid is right there, pulling me to my feet again. Her hands slip on the blood coating mine, but she doesn't let go until I do. I reach for Bianca, my hands quivering like never before. Her chest isn't moving. What have I done?

"We can't bring her with us," Enid says in the gentlest voice I've ever heard her use. "She's gone, Ugene, and we won't make it to the exit with her."

Too stunned to speak, numbness spreading through my chest, I gaze at the exit, frozen. It's still so far away. Fifty feet at least. More concrete falls across the room. And more nearby. Enid is right. But can I leave Bianca?

"Go," I tell Enid, nudging her toward the door, staring at Bianca's body. So much blood.

Enid grabs my hand in one of hers—it's so cold—and uses the other hand to turn my face to her. "Not without you. I'm so sorry, Ugene, but there's nothing you can do for her. But you can for us. Please. I'm not leaving without you. I…I can't. Please. Let's go."

Enid doesn't let go, and she tugs me toward the exit with her as more of the ceiling rains down. My steps, my limbs, my chest—everything is numb. Bianca's body remains where I left it... left her. I watch until we reach the doors and slip into the fresh night air.

"A kiss of death. And all the stars shall fall," I mumble, again repeating Celeste's portentous verse to myself, following Enid into the street. Our feet crunch on broken glass. Enid guides me along, and I let her, unable to think any longer.

50

PARAGON TOWER CONTINUES TO GROAN AS WE ESCAPE along the street, but somehow the building remains standing. Most of the lower floors are nearly hollow, just steel frames and remnants of debris beneath 195 stories of the untouched tower.

The late-night streets are empty, and the familiar smells of the city—fried foods and flowers—provide no comfort as we slip along the edge of buildings away from the groaning tower. Once, these compressed buildings reminded me of the bright potential of the future. Now the compressed structures offer no escape between cafes, restaurants, and specialty stores.

We pass a closed flower shop, and the storefront feels familiar. It's the same one I spotted after Career Day. The flowers are colorful and beautiful, creating a stark contrast to the feelings welling inside of me. The colors are insulting instead of breathtaking. The scent of roses, orchids, and lilies turn my stomach. How can something so beautiful dare to exist in this dark world?

Few people are out in the streets so late at night. Elpis is dangerous in the middle of the night. More than one ally catches my attention, the occupants trying to hide behind dumpsters in their grubby clothes. How have I never noticed the homeless before? How can they still exist in a city that thrives on everyone working together? No one pays us too much attention, either because they live in their own worlds or they are afraid of us. Our appearance makes that a real possibility.

Enid and I sneak down the steps to the metro. We are the last to arrive on the platform. Neither of us speaks. I check for Celeste, but she hasn't joined the group. Did I leave her behind, too? Is she dead?

One of the gates that allow passengers on the metro is open. Someone probably did something to permit everyone through. I don't really care. I follow Enid through.

Other test subjects sit on the floor or benches, leaning against columns or walls. Everyone appears an inch from death. I wish for that final inch to disappear and for death to just take me. Only a handful of people are in the metro station with us, and they all crowd on the other side of the platform away from us. The bright lights and dingy walls of the metro were once an exciting sign of independence, but now they remind me of how broken this world is.

Boyd rushes over as we reach join the group, and I manage only a few steps before he pulls me into a hug. "We were so wo-worried when they sh-showed up carrying M-Miller. They said y-you were coming, but then you di-didn't and—"

He pulls back, looking at the blood on my hands and shirt. Bianca's blood.

Enid leans toward Boyd and whispers something in his ear. Boyd's expression falls. There's no doubt what Enid told him, and I step around them to wait at the edge of the platform for the metro before he attempts showering me with condolences. I don't want to hear it. I don't think I can handle hearing it.

The metro arrives—thankfully with only two other passengers because it's so late at night—and everyone boards. The people waiting at the other end of the platform don't get on. Maybe the sight of us is too much. Maybe they're afraid of what we will do.

Wheels grind against rails and the carriage rocks ever so slightly, rhythmically, as it carries us away. The motion lulls some of the other subjects to sleep.

I begin counting heads. Sixty-five. A little less than half of us made it out of that tower. Half couldn't be saved.

Rosie kneels beside Miller, her hand on his forehead. His chest rises and falls in slow breaths of sleep. I sit on the bench beside his head, not making eye contact with anyone else. I lean my head against the window as the tunnel whizzes by, flashing red lights at regular intervals on the tunnel wall as we pass. The clink-clink of the wheels on the tracks dominates the sullen silence that's settled over us.

"I'm sorry about Bianca," Rosie says, her hand sliding off Miller's slumbering body. She pulls her feet under her and sits on the floor.

I don't respond. The pain of losing so much has been replaced by an impenetrable numbness.

Sho, Leo, Enid, and Boyd sit nearby, and I can feel their eyes on me, but I refuse to engage. I don't need their pity.

We've escaped Paragon, but at what cost? After everything we went through and how hard we fought, we're left with nothing but death and tenuous freedom. And for what purpose?

No one else speaks as we bumble along the rail line. Paragon will probably hunt us down. Hunt me down. My presence will only cause these people more trouble. They need a safe place to hide—away from me.

I glance down at a slumbering Miller. The wound in his shoulder is healed, but I can't cast off the image of him screaming and seizing on the floor after they shot him. It reminds me of the videos.

"What is it?" Rosie asks, gazing up at me.

"Nothing. Everything. Who knows?"

"His Powers are gone," Rosie says. "I don't know how. I can't do anything about it, though. Sorry."

I nod. "I know."

Miller took that bullet for me. Paragon weaponized a serum that strips people of their Powers and used it to fire at all of us. Miller lost his Power because of me. I owe him so much. But there's only one thing I know that Miller wants—to find Murphy. And I will... somehow. We don't know where Murphy is, or if he's alive, but maybe that drive might tell us something.

We may have lost half our number, but at least we escaped with the evidence. That copy drive is my lightning rod, and I will use it to stop Paragon from hurting anyone else.

A half an hour passes in silence. Just the rumble of the metro rolling along the tracks and coughs or snores of the others in the carriage with us. The holocasts are quiet at this time of night, with so few people still awake to see them, so when the news chime sounds in the carriage, everyone jumps and turns their attention to the holocast as it appears against a flat white metal panel every ten feet on the wall.

An urgent news report begins, and Elpida Theus—famous newscaster—reveals her smooth, sand-colored face and perfectly styled golden hair. And behind her, the looming remains of Paragon Tower, still standing. She reports an unexpected explosion resulting from one of their controlled experiments that quickly cascaded into devastation on the lower five floors of the building. "Though the building has been stabilized, Paragon urges all non-essential personnel to stay away until the debris has been cleared. The dangerous explosion claimed only a handful of lives, valiant security guards who managed to usher volunteers to safety."

Everyone on the metro is watching now, sneering or chortling at the news. Valiant security. Is that what Paragon, what Forrest, will tell Bianca's parents? It fills my stomach with fury as Elpida is joined by Dr. Cass, with Forrest and Hilde standing in the background. All three survived Celeste's cosmic ray. There is no such thing as divine justice.

"This tragic accident has displaced dozens of our generous volunteers," Dr. Cass says. I can't help but notice she has changed and looks fresh. That was fast. "Until this accident has been cleaned up and repairs are completed, these volunteers are free to return home and will be shown every courtesy by Paragon employees. We encourage the public to support these volunteers during this terrible transition."

The report continues, talking about how the accident happened and how long repairs are expected to take. Paragon has spun the situation to their advantage, and despite some of the apparent lies, everyone on the train begins talking excitedly at once.

We ride away from Paragon with permission to return home without retribution. We're publicly declared free.

"Where are we headed?" Leo asks.

"Salas borough," Sho says, nodding to the map on the wall.

Boyd whistles. "Nice p-place. What's there?"

"Home," I say, drawing looks from most of those around me. I don't meet their gazes, but I see one of the ads on the metro's boards. Red, bold letters practically popping off the surface, calling for attention.

IVD Veritax: Why be ordinary when you can be extraordinary?

It's already begun.

51

NOTHING EVER OFFERED SO MUCH COMFORT WHILE feeling so alien as walking down my own street. Familiar scents of sarsaparilla and milkweed fill the air. Streetlights cast long shadows as I walk past the line of trees and see Bianca's house—wholly dark and as devoid of life as she now is. She died a hero. That's what Paragon will tell her parents, and they aren't wrong. But it also doesn't shield us from the truth.

She died.

The other test subjects—former test subjects—wait for me at the park five blocks up. The same park that set me on this path. Returning home is risky, but I have to check in on Mom. Enid wanted to come along, and she tried so hard to convince me, but this is something I need to do alone.

Across the street from Bianca's house, the living room light and front porch light are on in my own. Mom is awake even in the middle of the night. Is she waiting for Dad to come home? I don't have the heart to tell her what happened. Though a part of me hopes that when I walk through the doors he will be there, and his death was just a trick of the simulation.

Unfamiliar vehicles are parked on the street, and despite Dr. Cass' announcement that we are free to return home, I can't help but feel a little paranoid. Instead of walking through the front door, I slip through the trees lining the street and use shrubs as cover while I make my way to the backyard.

The kitchen light is off. I use the darkness in the backyard to tiptoe up the stairs and try the door. Surprisingly, it's unlocked. I sneak through, giving one more glance to make sure the coast is clear.

The pristine, modern kitchen is illuminated only by the light filtering through the open doorway from the living room. Mom appears from that door, her face cloaked in darkness.

"Ugene." In seconds, Mom's arms wrap around me, careful not to touch the blood on my clothes. "I was so worried," she says. "I shouldn't have been. You've always been my tough guy."

I hug her back carefully, not wanting to get blood on her. For the first time in months, I feel like I'm home. But I can't help peering over her shoulder, hoping to see Dad walk into the room.

Mom pulls back, brushing hands down the sides of my head and smiling despite the tears in her eyes. "He said he would get you out of there."

I can't meet her gaze. He was really there. Grief threatens to knock back the numbness, but I force it down.

She kisses my forehead. "It's okay. We both knew what it meant for him to go. He tried so hard to protect you from Paragon. Your dad spent years dodging their requests. Took even longer to find his way in once you left."

"It's my fault."

"Hush." Mom lets go of my face and glances over her shoulder. "We should have told you sooner that Joyce was after you for this research. And when we wouldn't give you up to her, she found other ways to get around us. But she was right about one thing."

I follow her gaze to the table where one of Dad's military bags is packed and waiting.

"What's that?" I ask, knowing that bag is for me, and my homecoming won't last long. And although I didn't expect it to, disappointment still weighs heavy on my chest.

"You have the potential to save us all." Mom nods toward the duffle bag on the table. "I've packed a few supplies in there for you, and some fresh clothes and shoes." As if sensing my hesitation, she places a reassuring hand on my shoulder. "She won't stop, Ugene.

Joyce will come for you here. You can't stay. But you can stop her."

How? I slide the bag off the table and slouch against the weight of it as I strap it over my shoulders, crushing Celeste's small bag under it.

"Go to this address," she says, handing me a slip of paper. "You will find help. But right now, you need to run, Ugene."

A fist pounds on the front door, making me jump out of my skin.

"Run!" Mom hisses, turning me toward the back door. "And I will find you. I promise."

Another pound. I tiptoe to the back door and look back, watching Mom stand straighter and fix her shirt and hair. "I'm coming!" she calls.

As quietly as possible, I slip out the back door. And I run, clutching the address.

Before I left the group at the park, Enid reassured me that I saved everyone. I shake my head, headed back to the park along the alley.

Saved. What an ugly word used to mask the truth. We started with one hundred thirty-nine people. Half that made it out of Paragon. Now, barely forty of us remained. Thirty percent. Which means along the way I lost sixty percent of the people who trusted me to lead them to safety.

I didn't save anything. I started a fight. One we can't win.

Paragon will come after us. The copy drive will protect us. It will right the wrongs, even if it doesn't bring back those we lost today.

Andromeda's chains are broken. Cassiopeia will fall. Celeste's words ring in my head, and I glance at Miller's unconscious form in the corner. How did I miss it before? Cass. Cassiopeia. It's a bit on the nose.

Yes. Dr. Cass, and her vain sense of superiority, will fall.

Acknowledgements

I'LL BE THE first to admit that I had no idea what I was going to do with this story when I started it. All that I knew was that Ugene had to be special, and no matter what happened, Paragon could never discover a Power and give it to him. It was important that Ugene remain Powerless. Four different versions of this book exist just to get Ugene to this destination.

Everyone who enjoys Ugene's story should join me in giving a huge thanks to my husband, Tazz, and my stepson, Brynden. One night, we sat around talking about "what if" stories, and we built a short story by saying: What if there was a boy named Eugene who lived in a world where everyone has a superpower except for him, and the only job he could get was delivering flowers on a bicycle? Obviously, the story has evolved quite a bit from that early rendition, but without that conversation, this story never would have come to life.

Despite snarky comments and cantankerous attitudes, I owe all my fellow writers of SPWG a huge debt of gratitude. Tim and Kyle for welcoming me into your exclusive group of writers. Mike I., Mike P., and Dennis for letting me know what a guy would really think of these situations. Gail and Jennifer for sharing your female perspectives—and for telling the guys when they were flat out wrong. You've all helped me see the weaknesses and strength in this book throughout the grueling process. You pushed me forward with your encouragement, and by calling me a loser (jokingly) when I failed to keep up with my writing.

To my parents, Mary and Eldon Zipse, I owe you more than I could ever give. You believed in me even when I didn't believe in myself, and your support helped me push through the hardest days. To Tonia and Micah Vanlandingham, my sister and her husband, you supported my project and encouraged me to reach out into the world to get it published. And of course, to all my friends and family who have supported me when I became a hermit and encouraged me through every step of the process. A writer cannot succeed without support.

Just like it takes a village to raise a child, it takes a tribe to create a book. I would be lost without my fantastic tribe and the communities of writers who have already walked in my shoes. To my editor, Maddy, your kind words and guidance gave me the courage and encouragement to move forward with this project. Thanks to all of you.

To my readers: I absolutely love hearing from my readers. It's the highlight of my day! Share your thoughts by leaving a review. You can even email me directly!

READ THE POWERS SERIES

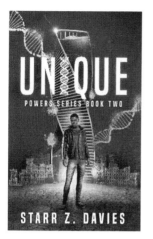

Unique (Powers Book 2)

Ugene and the other test subjects escaped Paragon. They thought they were finally safe. But the battle for freedom is far from over.

KEEP READING FOR AN EXCERPT

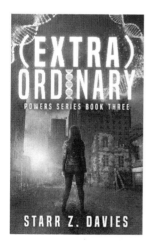

(extra)Ordinary (Powers Book 3)

She had no idea what was coming her way ... until she encountered Ugene.

Read all about Bianca's extraodrinary journey.

UNIQUE

1

THIS ISN'T WHAT I WANTED. I WANTED TO DO THE right thing, to help people, but now I can't help but question just what the right thing is.

I've lied.

I've broken promises.

I've failed more people than I would like to count—though I could, and the number would be too many.

And for what?

This isn't freedom.

2

THE CLEAN, CRISP SCENT OF EARTH AND STONE FILLS the small room I've been living in for what I can only assume to be days. I haven't felt the warmth of the sun or watched the stars for so long and I yearn for their comfort. Occasionally, I catch a whiff of rotten eggs, but the smell is so fleeting and rare I'm not certain if it's real.

Where am I? This is a prison. Did we even escape Paragon? Maybe this is all part of the same simulation, giving us hope then isolating us to see how we react.

Since waking up here, I've only spoken to two people. A woman who told me through the door in a very reassuring tone that I would be released soon. They simply had to make sure that everyone was safe, and with so many people it could take a while. I asked her a million other questions, but she didn't answer any of them. Instead, she offered the same assurances that all would be revealed soon.

The second person is the guy who delivers the meals. But he doesn't say any more than, "It won't be much longer." Sometimes, I swear I can hear the sympathy in his voice. Am I imagining it?

The last thing I remember is that we escaped Paragon and I followed the address Mom gave me to Lettuce Eat, where for nearly two days Harvey gave us food and a place to rest while he arranged our escort to safety. Those of us who remained—forty-two of us out of more than one hundred—climbed into the back of a cold transport truck on the second day. Harvey reassured us that we were being taken to a safer location and that my mom would meet with me soon.

But then I woke up here, in this cell. Alone.

Did he sell us out to Paragon?

Or maybe none of it actually happened.

I lay on my single bed, atop worn flannel sheets, and run my fingers along the smooth gray stone walls of the cell, carved out with Powered hands. The bed and a toilet are the only furnishings. The door is made of reinforced steel with a small window revealing a brightly lit stone hallway and a panel in the center of the door where the food comes in. More than once, I've tried forcing it open by pushing on it, or digging at the cracks until my fingers ache. It never budges.

Projecting in a small square on the wall, the Elpis News is the only station—a station Bianca's dad operates. The famous newscaster, Elpida Theus's, smooth, sand-colored face and perfectly styled golden hair is my primary source of contact with any form of life. Paragon has already rebuilt the destroyed lower levels of the tower to operational status, and they have called the "released" subjects to return. Not that anyone will. We are either locked in this place or too scared to risk returning.

"Daily operations are returning to normal," Elpida reports from the lobby of the building, which is still under construction.

Other reports, released by Directorate Chief Seaduss, remind the citizens that regression is a looming threat and that the eastern boroughs, particularly Pax, have seen a significant spike in crime and terrorist activity. Are the reports real? Can I trust that any of this is real?

It's exhausting, and these questions often put me to sleep.

When I sleep, I have nightmares about Dad, Bianca, and Celeste dying all over again. The other test subjects who once counted on me to get them to safety now crowd around me en masse, calling me a failure, a fraud, a worthless traitor. Of all the wounds I've sustained since arriving at Paragon, I have learned that words are the most cutting of all—and they take so much longer to heal.

My waking hours are plagued with worry about those who escaped with me and made it to Harvey's place. Where is everyone? Where am

I? So many questions tumble through my head that I try making a list, but as the days blend together that list begins to muddle, and I have nothing on which to write my thoughts. I can't decide what's real anymore.

Why did my mom send me here? Where is here?

Not for the first time, I try to reach out with my mind and see if Madison is out there somewhere. Not that I can use Telepathy, but my hope is that, if she can sense me reaching out, she will find a way to connect.

And not for the first time, nothing comes back. All my life, I'd been isolated in a crowd of people and I couldn't imagine anything worse.

Now I can.

Did you enjoy this book?
Don't forget to leave a review on Amazon and
Goodreads! It's like street cred for authors.

ABOUT STARR Z. DAVIES

STARR is a Midwesterner at heart. While pursuing her Creative Writing degree, Starr gained a reputation as the "Character Assassin" because she had a habit of utterly destroying her characters emotionally and physically -- a habit she steadfastly maintains. From a young age, she has been obsessed with superheroes like Batman and Spiderman, which continues to inspire her work. ORDINARY is her debut novel.

Follow Starr:
Web: www.starrzdavies.com
Facebook: @SZDavies
Twitter: @SZDavies
Instagram: @S.Z.Davies

Get Dr. Joyce Cass's prequel short story FREE!
Visit: subscribepage.com/starrzdavies_webform